THE HONOR
DUE
A KING

Also by N. Gemini Sasson:

The Bruce Trilogy
The Crown in the Heather (Book I)
Worth Dying For (Book II)
The Honor Due a King (Book III)

The Isabella Books
Isabeau: A Novel of Queen Isabella and Sir Roger Mortimer
The King Must Die: A Novel of Edward III

Standalones
Uneasy Lies the Crown: A Novel of Owain Glyndwr
In the Time of Kings (14th century Time Travel Adventure)

The Faderville Novels
Say No More
Say That Again

Sam McNamee Mysteries
Memories and Matchsticks

THE HONOR
DUE
A KING

THE BRUCE TRILOGY:
BOOK III

N. GEMINI SASSON

cader idris
press

For Jacques de Spoelberch,
who was the first to believe
and whose faith helped a dream endure.

May 'Our Bruce' live on in the hearts of many.

PROLOGUE

<u>James Douglas – Spain, 1330</u>

I BELIEVE, AS SURE as I have bled for such belief, that crowns were made for men like Robert the Bruce.

Two years gone since he died. Two years I have wandered aimless as a leper from one day to the following. So much I have aged in that short, hollow span.

When the storm clouds gather now, my right forearm aches where Neville's axe grazed my bone. Each morn, when I lift my head from my pillow and stretch my fingers toward the sunlight of yet another day, I feel a brittle stiffness in my hands—too many years clenching the hilt of my sword; a pinching at the base of my spine—bent from a hundred falls; and every cramped muscle, resisting wakefulness, longing to rest yet one more blissful hour.

Seventy battles I have seen, but I have wearied of fighting—the taste for blood soured on my tongue like over-ripe fruit gone rank. And yet without it, I have aged twenty years in just these two.

Did I think I would stay young forever? Peace, so long in coming, has made me not refreshed, but restless, a traveler without a map, no reason for being.

I should savor these years as Robert did at Cardross, even as his health gradually fled from him: hawking, hunting and sailing on the Firth of Clyde. Robert's son is a fine lad now. My own boys are but infants. Yet I have walked from them with only a fluttering kiss because of a promise made to my king on his deathbed and a purpose which has bound me ever since Longshanks' siege on Berwick when I was ten.

For so long, I have been a soldier—a soldier who serves his king above all else. Pray I am afforded enough years to prove myself as good a husband and father as I have been a knight.

Lanterns sway from the rafters. Their flames flicker and dim, then spring to life again. Every plank and beam from stern to prow moans against the strain of a tempestuous sea. The storms have been many. The crests of the waves as high as the sails themselves. The boat lurches as it battles another wave and I clutch the silver casket beneath my fingers as it slides sideways.

My promise was to carry my king's heart to the Holy Land. So I left my beloved Scotland, sailing first to Sluys in Flanders on a single-masted cog to seek out worthy knights to join us. King Alfonso of Spain has asked for our help to dislodge the Moors from his borders and so before going further east we are headed there.

Another knight, Alan Cathcart, sits across from me, smiles in greeting and offers a hunk of salted pork. The smell of fat turns my stomach inside out and I turn my head aside, declining the offer.

Above deck, the sailors call out to one another, but their tongue is strange to me. I pray we make anchor at Seville before the sea swallows us. In time, the storm subsides and the shouts from above cease.

From Seville, I will hire a rowing galley, hug the ports and arrive whole, if not better rested. Robert was the sailor, never I. Journeying by sea still robs me of my appetite. I shall be in the Holy Land before the heat of summer bears down on my thinning scalp and home by Christmas. Then, gracious Rosalind—oh, dare I dream of loving you longer and learning to know you after all those years I deemed myself unworthy? I beg forgiveness for going from you, dearest Rosalind, but this is one duty I cannot forego. It is an honor far exceeding any earldom.

As the waves thrash against the sides of this ship, its prow rising and dipping in its crooked course from flat, gray Flanders toward sun-bright Spain, there is much to look back on . . . and so little to look ahead to. Forty-four years I have walked this earth. Hardly old, but I have lived hard enough for ten men.

Never has Scotland known a greater king than Robert the Bruce, but where my purpose found me, he made his own. When Robert was born, none ever knew he would one day wear a crown, but the dream that first belonged to Robert's grandfather became his own and never escaped his heart.

A shadow looms and I look up to see young Sir William Sinclair. His beard is sparse and silken. The flesh around his eyes and mouth as smooth as a bairn's. Already several years older than I was when I joined Robert, why is it that he seems much too young to suit himself up in armor and pursue Moors?

It is warmer now. A long finger of sunlight pries through the cracks of the door to aboveboard.

"Port, Sir James," Sinclair says. "The King of Castile sends a messenger. A galley awaits on which we can travel upriver and join him. Osmyn has fortified Teba. The siege is on."

I raise my tankard of bitter ale and take a small swallow, forcing it down. My stomach disagrees. I wait a moment for the nausea to pass. "A dalliance, Sinclair. Granada's infidels first. Jerusalem shall wait . . . as it has for centuries."

Between calloused hands, I cup the silver casket. With great care, I lift the chain affixed to it and slip it over my head.

"Not quite sixteen years since Bannockburn, Robert," I say to him, for I know he hears my every word. In life, he knew my thoughts even. "But I am attempting penance. Give a good word to Our Lord for me, if you will."

1

<u>Edward II – Berwick, 1314</u>

A HARSH WIND RACED over the sea and whipped at my face in scorn. Hugh Despenser the Younger dabbed a bunched strip of linen into a bowl of water and wiped the grime from my forehead. Too spent to resist, I did not turn my face away or take the cloth from him, letting him rub soothingly at my temples. But in time, the pressure of his fingertips became an annoyance—claws digging into my skull—and I finally slapped his hands away.

Hugh pushed a hunk of bread into my palm and begged me to eat. I flung it at his feet, shoved him aside and rushed to the gunwale, where I clung weakly, and puked up nothing. The riggings slapped against the sails and the waves heaved as our ship veered shoreward in its course.

"You'll feel improved, my king," he encouraged as he placed a gentle hand on my quivering shoulder, "when there is dry land under your feet."

"If it's anywhere in Scotland, I'd rather you set me adrift at sea on a flaming pyre."

"Berwick straight ahead, sire. When we left, it was yet an English possession."

"When we left, Stirling was ours. All we had to do was get there."

I snarled and crumpled down cross-legged onto the decking.

Sinking to his haunches, Hugh touched my knee. "It was but one battle, sire. Brood not over the slain. You were preserved to fulfill some purpose. That I know."

Oh, kindest Hugh. You know as well as I, that is not what they are saying now. Not the Scots, not my commanders, not my soldiers. Not in my beloved England or on the continent.

They are saying that Edward II, King of England, is a coward, a fool and a failure. He marched to Stirling a hundred thousand strong and on the road at Bannockburn the Scots, a fraction in number, laid him low. His sire toppled the crown from Balliol's head and kept it for himself. His son . . . Edward of Caernarvon, lost it. Lost it to a traitor and a host of half-naked hill-men.

Hugh's hand slid over mine. His second finger bore the calluses of a scribe and his palms were smooth, as though he had never in his life wielded a weapon. Although his gesture solved nothing, it gave me comfort, if only for a moment. A sailor's rumbling shout signaled an approaching dinghy. Hugh rose and peered over the side of the ship, one slender hand shading his pale brow.

"Who else, besides Gilbert," I murmured, "was among our fallen, Hugh?"

Before the battle ever began, that blood-craving Judas, Robert the Bruce, slew my nephew and childhood companion Gilbert de Clare, Earl of Gloucester.

He took a breath, held it, and sank back down beside me, close. "I have not reviewed the lists yet. With the broken retreat, it will be hard to say for some while, who is dead and who is not, but I know of your steward, Sir Edmund . . . and Lord John of Badenoch . . ."

"Son of the Red Comyn?"

"Yes, I believe so. Sir Robert Clifford, as well."

"Clifford?" I stared at my hands, blistered raw from gripping the reins of my horse all the way from Stirling to Dunbar. Bruises ran the length of the inside of my thighs from clutching my mount's ribs.

Fire raged in my joints. "Thousands, wasn't it? Thousands."

So many dead. God's soul, so many.

He rose to his feet and reached down to me. "They're waiting, sire."

I placed my hand in his and felt the strength of his grip as he pulled me up.

THREE DAYS LATER, HUGH came to my chambers at Berwick Castle bearing yet more ill news.

I shifted the neckline of my ill-fitting borrowed tunic, having lost my entire wardrobe in the flight from Bannockburn, and trailed my fingertips across a sweat-dampened collarbone. There had been no wind since we made land and if not for the castle's prominent position on a high hill, the fetid air from the town might have suffocated me.

I poured Hugh a goblet of wine. He took one sip and set it down on the table. So unlike my beloved Piers, who would have downed the entire contents in greedy gulps and then boldly asked for more.

Ever since my sire died seven years ago and I took the throne, I had been betrayed so many times that I guarded my trust behind an iron door, as though it were my kingdom's greatest treasure. Hugh, in his subtle devotion, was the first to breach that barrier after my companion Piers Gaveston was murdered by my cousin Lancaster's crows. I had loved Piers beyond belief. I had even been willing to give up my crown for him, but Piers would not have it so.

"Everything. All at once," I told Hugh, as I reclined in my cushioned chair to receive the blow. "Better from your gentle lips than from the snout of one of those chiding barons."

"The Scots did not pursue us with more men to Dunbar," he began, "because their forces were engaged elsewhere. Your baggage train, in its entirety, was taken by the Scots. Among the items they claim to have are your Royal Shield and the Great Seal. Sir Philip Mowbray handed Robert the Bruce the keys to Stirling the very day he turned you away from there."

"Did he swear himself?"

"To Bruce? He did." Hugh sighed, echoing my own disdain for the fickle traitor Mowbray. "Edward Bruce was dispatched to Bothwell where the constable there, FitzGilbert, was harboring a number of your knights and barons. Upon hearing that the Scots had triumphed, FitzGilbert handed over to the younger Bruce: the Earl of Hereford, Sir Ingram d'Umfraville, the Earl of Angus and some fifty other of your loyals. A number of notable persons were taken captive at Bannockburn, including Ralph de Monthermer."

The number of those killed or taken prisoner was appalling. Bannockburn should not have been my undoing. It should have been my greatest triumph. *Should* have . . .

"Pembroke?" *Surely he is dead, too?*

"Headed toward Carlisle, much of his Welsh levy still intact."

Fortunate bastard.

"They'll want my kingdom for Hereford's ransom alone," I said.

"Fortunately not." Far cleverer than he let on, Hugh gave a wan smile. He picked up the goblet, swirled it vigorously, pulled a deep draft, and set it down again.

"Why do you say that?"

"The Marcher lord, Sir Roger Mortimer, is at the castle gate. He brings terms from the Bruce—and the body of your nephew, Gilbert de Clare."

Pain stabbed through my chest. Gasping, I turned my face up.

In the far corner of the ceiling, where the angle of sunlight could not fully reach, the silken threads of a cobweb glistened. There, an insect, entangled in the fibers, writhed. In moments, a large black spider had grasped the tiny creature by long, nimble legs and was wrapping it in a shroud of death.

"Gilbert's body?" My mouth went dry. The words were hard to

utter. "What will he want for it?"

On learning that Gilbert had fallen before the Bruce's axe at the battle's outset, it felt as though my heart had been torn from my chest, wrung dry of blood, and thrown to the dusty ground.

Confident, calm, Hugh planted his knuckles on the table and leaned his face toward mine.

"What Bruce wants," he said, "are his women. Give him them—and he returns Hereford, the Great Seal and the Royal Shield. 'Tis all in your favor, my lord. If you wish, toss back the languishing Bishop Wishart and a handful of worthless low-blooded rebels for added measure. Easy."

"Have Mortimer brought to the Great Hall . . . in an hour." A frayed thread hung from the corner of the tattered cushion on which I sat. I pinched it between my fingers and pulled, watching the cloth split open to reveal the crushed down within. "Stand beside me, Hugh. I shall have need of you."

SIR ROGER MORTIMER'S HALF-HANDED companion, John Maltravers, bore the stiff corpse of my beloved Gilbert on his shoulder and laid it at my feet. My heart sank ever lower.

Mortimer relayed the terms just as Hugh had stated them. Stripped of my pride, I agreed to them.

In the days that followed, with the remnants of my smote army, I slunk homeward to face the ruin of my hopes. My cousin Thomas, the Earl of Lancaster—who had refused my summons to join us at Bannockburn—jeered at me from the ramparts of Pontefract and later brought parliament down upon my hammered head, stirring my barons into a frenzy of condemnation. Then, to sully his own affairs, he wed the twelve-year old heiress of Lincoln and Salisbury in order to augment his already-overflowing money chests.

While Scotland entreated for peace, even as they plundered the north of England, the grim hand of famine struck. Rain poured from the skies in such a deluge that many of the crops could not be planted in springtime. Those that were sown rotted for lack of sunlight. Cattle and sheep fell to sickness. Pestilence and starvation ravaged the land.

The clerics, who had always despised me, preached that it was God's wrath visited upon us for what we had done to Scotland. The populace went so far as to cry that it was the corruption in my own court that brought this blight upon my people, while the merchants bemoaned their resultant poverty.

I closed my ears to them. Why would God punish *us* while Bruce and his blood-hungry heathens burned and pillaged and beat on their chests?

If the Bruce thought he was going to get everything he ever wanted, he was sorely mistaken. First, I would deal with that insolent kinsman of mine, Lancaster. When that was done and circumstances were more in my favor, heaven help the false King of Scots.

2

Robert the Bruce – Melrose Abbey, 1314

THE WIDE FRONT DOORS of Melrose Abbey hung crookedly on their hinges, splintered where the main bar had once held them shut. The stained glass of the windows stood in jagged shards like lions' teeth. The graveyard where we stood had been desecrated—all the sad result of vengeful English soldiers as they fled from Bannockburn.

"You've a face as long as your leg." James Douglas hopped over a broken gravestone and faced the stabbing rain to survey the abbey.

He had been with me since before my crowning at Scone eight years ago and I swear he had not aged a day. Why were the years not so kind to me? Slight of build and soft-spoken, he was unimpressive at first glance; yet time and again I had seen him cut down foes far bigger than him in a single blow. His father, Sir William Douglas, had once held Berwick against the first Edward, Longshanks. The siege, however, turned into a massacre and the elder Douglas gave up the town to spare its remaining citizens. Ultimately, however, he forfeited his own life.

I pulled my cloak tight across my breast, even though I had been soaked since leaving Edinburgh in a cold, black October rain days ago.

James patted my shoulder with a gloved hand. "Faith. They'll come."

"How do you know?" I asked softly. Behind him, above the roof of the abbey, the three bald peaks of the Eildon Hills swam in the darkness of roiling storm clouds. "*How* do you know? I've heard men say you have an extra sense that tells you when the enemy is near. Do you truly? Can you tell the same for loved ones?"

He gave that faint, familiar grin of his to impart his steady confidence. "Because you sent Gil and Randolph to take care of it. That's how I know. On their lives, they would never fail you."

Nor would you, good James. I should know better than to doubt any of you, but it is the uncertainty of fate that troubles me now—things we mere men have no guidance over.

Months of haggling with England's king, Edward of Caernarvon, had left me a pessimist. The wretch was still in denial, refusing to relinquish his alleged rights to Scotland, despite the pummeling he had taken. For now though, more than I wanted his blessing, I wanted Elizabeth—my wife, my queen—to come home to me.

The Earl of Hereford, captured at Bannockburn, was my pawn. To hand him back, I had demanded a hefty ransom that would rob his heirs for eternity. Then, to quell King Edward's protests over the amount, I promised to give back the Great Seal and Royal Shield at no further recompense, but for the return of my womenfolk and Bishop Wishart.

So it was here at Melrose that we waited on the appointed day to receive them, whilst my nephew, Thomas Randolph, and my commander and old companion, Gil de la Haye, went to meet an English envoy at Jedburgh where the exchange was to occur. At border's edge, Jedburgh was deemed too dangerous for me to go there. But staying behind, waiting . . . ah now, that was more torturous than the threat of a fight.

My men—their weapons rattling as they shivered against the cold—huddled beneath the naked branches of a massive yew at the far end of the graveyard. Days of rain leaching into the earth had stirred up the faintly sweet, sickening smell of decomposing flesh. As the wind drove the rain in staggering walls, Neil Campbell leaned wearily against his horse, uttering prayers for the soul of Mary—his wife, my sister—who would not be among those to come home. When she and the others were dragged from sanctuary at St. Duthac's shrine by the Earl of Ross in 1306 and handed over to Longshanks, who was king before his namesake Edward II, she was dangled from the walls of Roxburgh Castle in a wooden cage—left there to suffer through winter cold and heavy rain. Four long years later, they removed her and tucked her away in a Carmelite nunnery. But she never recovered from a sickness that settled in her lungs. When the negotiations with King Edward began, only then did we learn she had died over a year earlier. Neil, who for a short time had been radiant with hope, was now drowning in grief.

For hours we waited there, growing colder and hungrier, but no one would go inside the ruined buildings because I would not leave. So very cold I became in my drenched, padded leather and chain mail that my muscles cramped and the feeling drained from my fingers and toes.

They should have arrived by noon. It was now nearly sunset—or would be, if the sun could be seen at all. "Why are they not here yet?"

James paced over the soggy ground. "The Teviot is running deep. They may have had to travel further upstream to find a place to ford it."

Likely they had, but that did little to quiet my mind. As I stood in the pouring rain, with the engorged River Tweed sloshing and gurgling at my back and the desecrated abbey before me, I knew I should have been full of blissful anticipation at the occasion, no matter the misery of the weather, but instead I felt only the oppressive gloom of the clouds.

"You'll watch after my Marjorie? Make certain no harm comes to her? No dishonor? Swear it."

"On my life, Robert. You know that." James blew a cloud of steaming breath into the chilly air. "We should go inside and build a fire; dry off while we wait."

"Eight years is long enough to wait," I mumbled.

"So it is," he said, "but it would be a great shame to have them come home to find you drowned in your boots. Come inside, Robert.

The abbot is still in a terror over this shambles, but I warrant he'll make the best of it to lodge his king."

Without so much as a word from me, James put a hand on my back and guided me across the squelching earth, sidestepping the toppled stones, and up the broad steps of sandstone into Melrose Abbey.

A belligerent wind hammered its way through gaps and cracks, pushing gusts of rain across the floor. Although damp throughout, it was drier toward the chancel. As I drifted warily toward the altar, white-robed Cistercian monks scattered from the shadows of either transept and disappeared behind lofty columns. Rusted hinges groaned hauntingly.

"Fine welcome," I murmured. With cramped hands, I wrung the tail of my cloak, then unfastened the golden clasp inlaid with an emerald at my shoulder—courtesy of King Edward—and snapped the water from it.

James glanced around. "They're men of peace. They don't like soldiers: English or Scottish. It's not so much us they hate, but that we might invite battle to their doorstep just by being here."

"I worry about that myself wherever I go. Bring Walter to me and go fetch the abbot. Invited or not, we're staying here."

Reluctantly, James ventured back out into the deluge. Alone, I stood in the middle of the nave, nothing but shadows surrounding me and the distant hushed footsteps of monks in other parts of the church, tending to their devotions and duties. I took four steps more toward the altar. Hushed echoes seemed to question my worthiness of being there.

Fitful drafts of wind blew out a torch on a column nearest to me. I pressed forward, step by step, in defiance of my tepid greeting, until I reached the altar. There, I dropped my cloak, went to my knees on the cold, wet stones and folded my hands in prayer. A *pater noster* tumbled from my lips in thoughtless fashion, but before saying my 'Amen', I gazed over my knuckles to the crucifix dangling askance above the altar.

"I ask not for great riches or further glory, My Lord. Only to see those whom I love come home." I closed my eyes.

A simple request, and yet . . . How could I dare to ask for what God might not deem fit to give me? Here, I was no king, but a man of many sins.

The rain on the roof pounded louder and louder until it sounded like an army marching above my head. I must have stayed like that for some time: my hands clenched together, the blood gone from my lower legs. A gentle hand touched my back, startling me; I reached for the knife at my belt in a soldier's reflexes.

"You're blanched, my lord. Shivering terribly."

Old Ralph de Monthermer, the Englishman, stood at my shoulder. His hand trembled with palsy. How is it that he had survived Bannockburn so infirm? His skin showed the mottled spots of age, his reflexes were slow, he slept overmuch, and yet he never spoke of being old. In his heart, he was the same vigorous warrior who had fought beside my grandfather. A retainer of King Edward II's now, we had taken him captive at Bannockburn. Recalling how he had saved my life many years ago at Windsor when Red Comyn betrayed me, I had deigned to spare him the usual dreadful prisoner's existence.

I rose slowly to my feet, every joint and limb protesting. Remembering my cloak on the floor, I leaned over to pick it up. The backs of my legs tautened so fiercely I thought something might snap. A groan escaped my throat.

Forty now, my muscles had become stiffer. My sword arm wearied more quickly. The chill of winter and the heat of summer both gave me discomfort, when once I would have run shirtless through the winter snow or been mindless of the sweat pouring down my chest as I practiced at swords with my brother Edward.

But where vigor fades like fallen leaves, wisdom takes root and grows, courage is replaced by caution, and hope yields to doubt.

The day was nearly gone—and still they were not with me. Whatever made me believe that today would be any different than yesterday, or the many years before that?

"You could have gone on with Randolph, Ralph," I said, my voice raspy with fatigue. "Been on your way home by now."

He scratched beneath the neck of his mail coif so that it shifted and sat lopsided on his head. "But my lord, I have rather enjoyed being in your company. Do you treat all your prisoners so well?"

"Only my friends. I have never forgotten what you did for me. Longshanks would have staked my head on London Bridge had you not warned me in time." My chin sank to my chest. Being in this place, it was as if the weight of all my wrongs were about to smother me. "I am so . . . so sorry about . . ."

Shifting on his feet, Ralph nodded. "Gilbert was a fine soldier. As good a son as any stepson ever was. I wish you could have known him better. You would have liked him well. You were on different sides, that is all. Men die in battle. He was one of them. I hold no grudge on you, Robert. You're a good man. A good king."

"You're the first Englishman to call me that."

"'King' . . . or 'good'?"

"Either. Stay as long as you like, Ralph. Forever, if you care to. I'll see to it that you're comfortable and cared for. I do imagine it has already been a thorn under King Edward's saddle that you've been in Scotland so long, since I put no ransom on your head. You're a free man. Stay or go, as you please."

A gust of wind blew in as the front doors swung fully open and men began to come in.

Ralph readjusted the bothersome edge of his mail coif again. "I'd like to dry out by a fire for now, m'lord. I do want to stay, share stories in your hall some more, but with Gilbert gone there will be business to attend to in Gloucester. He has children and a wife that need looking after." He sniffed. His lips were blue and every vein on his face stood out starkly. Ralph was two decades my senior and still he had gone to battle at the bidding of his king. If I felt old myself, one look at him and

I ceased my complaining.

"A fire first, though," I said. "And a decent night's rest. I'll give you an escort to Berwick on the morrow." I looked toward the door, where the clop of hooves caught my ears. "Ah, Walter, here!"

Walter Stewart led my gray pony toward me, casting glances left and right as he did so.

James strode beside them and shook his head in disbelief. "If it's a blessing you want for the beast, my lord, I'm guessing the abbot would prefer to meet you outside for this occasion."

"Hear?" I put an ear to the great beast's ribs. "There's a rattle in his chest. He needs to be dried off. Then I want the warmest place for Coll you can find."

"Coll?" James gave me a quizzical look. The pony, whose head had been hanging low until then, perked his ears at the name and lifted his muzzle. "Wasn't that the name of your dog?"

"A name befitting the bravest of creatures, mind you." Seven years ago, while we had been lying in wait above the road to Cumnock for an approaching column of English led by the Earl of Pembroke, the Lord of Lorne's forces threatened to entrap us. I divided my men and soon found myself being trailed by my own dog, Coll. To silence the hound, I had been forced to put an arrow through his heart. In doing so, I had demanded the ultimate sacrifice of my loyal companion: his life. There had been no alternative. The pony turned his head to gaze at me through a black fringe of eyelashes. I reached out and stroked his nose. "This one carried me through Bannockburn. I'll not lose him to neglect."

"The stables are down closer to the river," Walter said, "by the pastures there."

"Too far. He'll stay here until the rain passes."

James and Walter exchanged glances. Walter shrugged.

"Find some blankets." James nodded toward the door that led to the cloister. "Madness comes with greatness, so they say."

I raised my eyebrows at him.

"I would think," James said, "you'd care to see to your men first."

"It would be a slow journey back to Edinburgh on foot, wouldn't it?"

Before he could return the gibe, a little man burst from a doorway and ran limping toward us, frantically waving his arms. The chains dangling from his neck clanked with each hobble. To avoid tripping, he eventually dropped his hands and plucked up the hem of his robes. When he landed in front of us, it was with an angry stomp of both feet in unison.

"You have no right to bring that unclean creature in here!" He recoiled as Coll blew steaming breath at him. "Take him to the stables. As for you and your hobelars, my lord, the byres are spacious enough."

"Byres?" I laughed at the suggestion. "Would you put your king to bed with a heifer, Father?"

At once, the little man's jaw unhinged. His gray eyes widened as he took in the ornaments of my clothing: the emerald brooch pinned upon the cloak slung over my arm, my surcoat and its lion emblem, the small coronet upon my helmet. He bobbed in an apologetic bow. "Sire, I did not know it was you. No word of your arrival was sent in advance."

"For good reason, Father—"

"William Peebles, my lord. I am the abbot here."

"William Peebles, you say? Bishop Lamberton speaks highly of you." Lamberton had mentioned the abbot many times and had encouraged me to trust and call on him, should I ever need to. That is why I had chosen this place. "He pushed to have you in this position, you know? Didn't like that Henry of Dunkeld that York was pressing for. Entirely too English, no matter what he called himself. Court politics have nothing over that of the Church, I tell you. But if Lamberton admires you, so do I. Anyway, as I said, it was for good reason we didn't announce our coming. I trust you have not been visited by any English of late?"

"No, no, sire. Not since they passed through after the battle. The damage they inflicted was small, thanks be to Our Lord. It cost us heavily, though, to set them on their way again. As you can see, our relics, our silver—all gone. We had to empty the reliquary to appease them. The cross on the altar came to us from a passing Scottish knight on his way back to Galloway. Said he took it from an English priest attending King Edward's soldiers in exchange for safe passage through these lands."

Abbot William blinked repeatedly and then suddenly flew back toward the door through which he had come. He beckoned to the monks hanging there in trepidation and in a fluster began to direct them to attend to my company. When that was done to his satisfaction, he rushed back to us. "My house is at your disposal, my lord. Not luxurious quarters, but—"

"Better than the byres, I trust?"

"It is my opinion they are, although our byres and flock are the best this side of the Tweed. You did not say what brings you here. Will you be in residence long?"

"We won't put you out, Abbot William, for longer than is convenient. And you'll be duly compensated for your losses, I swear to you. As for our purpose, I pray it will become evident soon enough. Until then, I'll say naught. Fate is a fickle mistress and I prefer not to command her, lest she take offense."

The abbot chuckled as he winked at me, and then scurried off to arrange our quarters.

Neither the remainder of that day nor that night brought us the evidence of the cause for our visit. My horse improved rapidly and was moved to the best stable the abbey had to offer, much to the abbot's relief.

After a bland but filling meal in the refectory in the scrutinizing company of mistrustful monks, we were all allotted sleeping arrangements. Most of my men were given space in the nave itself and as there were not enough blankets to be had, so many fires were struck up on the church floor to warm the men and dry out their clothing that the place soon reeked of smoke, rotting leather and damp wool.

In a room of the abbot's house reserved for passing visitors, I shed my armor, trusting that no English would have ridden through these storms after us, and laid my garments over a chair to dry by the brazier. Although the room was more than comfortable—austere though it was, with its mattress of stuffed straw and meager peat brazier in place of a real hearth—sleep eluded me, even though I was dry and fed and beyond exhausted. Worry had a way of gnawing at my soul.

As I lay in bed, my eyes flicked from the dusty ceiling, to the knotty door, to the small altar that doubled as a table. The candles in the room had burnt themselves to pools of runny wax. I did not notice that their flames had gone out until I glanced at the single, small window along the crumbling east wall and saw a faint, pale crescent of sunlight on the horizon.

With a cold hand, I smoothed the creases from my pillow, imaging that tomorrow would find Elizabeth's head there next to mine.

JAMES ROUSED ME JUST as the bells rang terce.

My fingers pinching the edge of my blanket, I glared at him. "It had best be good news, James Douglas. Tell me it is."

He grinned faintly. "They're coming. Over the hills, along the southern road."

I drew a hand over my eyes and inhaled the smell of my palm: rusted metal, earth, moldy straw and damp stones. The lingering traces of a soldier's life. Soon, I would trade all that for a more settled existence—with Elizabeth beside me. I shoved my blanket aside and leapt to my feet, only to be reminded by aching bones that the years spent living out in the open, always battle-ready, had taken their toll and I could not move quite so quickly anymore.

"Eight years, my good James." I straightened and clapped a hand on James' arm so fiercely he reeled sideways. "Eight. Long. Years!"

In minutes, I had donned my musty clothes and followed him from the abbot's house, through the transept door and back into the nave. A flood of light rushed in from the main door, reflecting dully off the tiled floor to obscure the figures who now made their way toward the altar where we stood waiting. They were nearly to us before I recognized my nephew, Thomas Randolph, his fair hair darkened by rain and his heavy wool cloak hanging lank and sodden from his shoulders.

"Make way. Make way!" Randolph pushed the palms of his hands wide to clear a pathway down the middle of the nave. Groggy soldiers yawned and rolled aside. Those closest to the middle staggered to their feet and scampered back to avoid being stepped on.

"We made it as far as Dryburgh yesterday," Randolph said as he approached, the dark crescents beneath his pale blue eyes making him look more tired than any of the rest of us, "but we could go no further. I begged her to let me send for you, but she would not waste the time waiting." He sighed, his shoulders sagging, and moved aside. "I fear the queen is gravely ill."

Behind him, Gil de la Haye carried my Elizabeth in his arms. The joy that should have been in my heart fled when I saw her like that—her limbs as limp as wet cloth, all color gone from her face, her eyes lackluster and barely open. I took her from Gil's arms and clutched her to my breast as I sank to the floor.

"Elizabeth," I whispered into her cold ear. "My love, is it really you? What ails you? Oh, please, for love of life, say something so I may hear your voice again and know it is you I am holding and not your ghost."

She stirred, weak as a fledgling fallen from its nest. Her eyelids fluttered as she turned her head toward me, but when she parted her lips to speak and drew a shallow breath, a fierce cough wracked her chest. I stroked the wisps of hair from her feverish face until it subsided.

"Robert?" she whispered.

"Aye, my love. 'Tis me. Dear, sweet Elizabeth, you really are home." I pressed my whiskered chin to the top of her head and swallowed back bittersweet tears. Her heartbeat was weak. Every breath came as a struggle. She coughed again and curled tighter in my arms. I glanced at Walter. "Broth, please. A blanket. Something."

Walter backed away, but his eyes were set on someone. I looked beyond Randolph to see the rest of the party. A young woman, slight and fair-haired and beautiful smiled at me with an aching familiarity. She came to me, knelt and placed a cool hand on my tear-moistened cheek.

"Father? I have so missed you."

"Marjorie?"

She nodded. I turned my head and kissed her palm. Marjorie embraced me lightly, touching her head to my shoulder. There was so much I wanted to say to my daughter, so grown and comely now I found it hard to believe she was the curious little girl I had last seen at Dalry, believing I had sent her on to safety, only to have her whisked away by my enemies when the Earl of Ross took them all at St. Duthac's and handed them over to the English. Then, another voice from years past greeted my ears.

"Robert?"

I laid bleary eyes on my sister, Christina. She appeared older, worn from her ascetic and secluded life, but alive and well.

"By the time we reached Richmond," Christina began, "she had begun with a cold in her chest. It worsened quickly. The fever comes and goes, but she weakens daily from the cough. She has barely eaten the past four days, but for some boiled cabbage and beans. When we woke at cockcrow, she insisted on riding with your man Gil. She wanted to see you. Gil had to hold her all the way."

Christina, once the striking beauty that had drawn many a man's eyes, had her dark hair hidden beneath a stiff, white widow's wimple that covered her chin. Her kirtle was the gloom of slate and she wore no other adornment than a silver crucifix on a coarse, tarnished chain about her neck. The nuns at Sixhills, where she had spent her captivity in England, had imprinted her deeply. On her left arm, leaned the old, nearly blind Bishop Wishart. He tilted his head and squinted, as if trying to make out faces close by or recognize voices. His hands trembled and every hair was gone from his head, except for a few white strands at the back of his mottled skull.

Christina cast a look over her shoulder toward the door where a young man hid in the shadows. In the middle of the nave, my brother-in-law Neil Campbell started forward, tentative. Finally, Christina inclined her head toward the young man. "Colin was released from the custody of Sir Henry Beaumont and permitted to come home with us. He's been eager to greet his father."

Neil walked across the nave toward Colin, who hung back timidly. Neil touched his son's cheek. "You have your mother's eyes, lad."

"I . . . I . . . don't . . ." Colin stammered and tugged at his own fingers. "I don't remember much of you. I'm sorry."

"There's time enough now." Neil put his arms around his son, a young man now and nearly as tall as his father. Stiff at first, Colin relaxed and then returned the embrace. Neil had taken the news of his wife's death hard and if not for his son coming home to him, he would still have been grieving.

As much as my sister Mary's loss pained me, it also made Elizabeth's homecoming that much sweeter. I bent my head and pressed my cheek to Elizabeth's as she moaned in discomfort. She was home . . . *home*. And I was holding her in my arms. But oh, so ill, so weak . . . her life so tenuous.

The abbot shooed away those who were crowding around and, stooping, offered a small, wooden bowl half-full of warm beef broth. I raised Elizabeth's shoulders up and encouraged her to take some. When the abbot pressed the bowl to her lips, she sipped a small amount, then closed her mouth and turned her face from me as a cough ripped from her chest.

With bone-thin fingers, the abbot touched her forehead. "A warm bed is the best place for her. Fortunately, she will sleep through most of this."

"Will she be well soon?" I asked, both needing and not wanting to know the answer.

His brow wrinkled. "There's no knowing about that. It may pass within a few days. It may linger. We can only say our prayers and leave it to God's will."

But holy men are ill liars. I could see it in his face and hear it in his words that he feared for her. As did I.

"A Mass every day until she's well again, Abbot William. If you can win His grace in this, then I'll see to it that this abbey and every one in Scotland knows favor as long as I live."

The abbot nodded. "I doubt any abbey will turn away a king's generosity, my lord. But if it's thanks to God you wish to give, He prefers souls over coins."

Near the main doorway, Neil Campbell was still crushing his Colin with such ferocity that my heart pained me.

Somewhere in Carrick, I had a son, too. A son Elizabeth knew nothing of . . .

FOR A FORTNIGHT, ELIZABETH rolled in and out of a burning fever while she lay in the abbot's own bed swaddled beneath deep piles of blankets. Her fever subsided several times, only to fire up again and snatch the fight from her. Her countenance paled to the color of ashes. Her breath was but a whispered reminder that her heart yet beat. The woman that they had brought to me—my beloved wife and queen— faded before my eyes like the very sunset that signaled the end of each passing day. And as winter encroached upon the earth, those days were growing shorter and so, it seemed, was her life.

Even though she seldom woke and spoke not at all, I set aside all thoughts and preoccupations of state and warfare to be by her side. But too often I was herded away and told to let her rest by her hovering lady servant, Gruoch.

On those too rare occasions when I could snatch time alone with my wife, I spoke of our days at Lochmaben riding at morning dew, of Christmases at Turnberry where we played games and danced giddy with laughter until our stomachs hurt, and of summers spent at Kildrummy roaming the paths above the Don by the old stone quarry where the wild roses bloomed, her hand fitted perfectly in mine. Those times had been few, for so often I had been abroad on Longshanks' business, but they were golden times. Times that I had lived for. Times that I did not know if I would ever see again.

When not by Elizabeth's side, I was in the barley fields beyond the abbey, one eye straining to focus on the broken barrel that served as my butt, the taut string of my bow cutting into my fingers and the fledging of an arrow tickling my cheek before I let it sing across the distance. But my arrows too often missed their mark, their points plowing into soft dirt. James attempted to join me one morning, retrieving the arrows scattered about the fallow field from the previous evening, but he soon sensed I was not in need of company and left me alone with my silence.

Cold whispered against my neck and I looked around to see the first snowflakes of the season falling. I tucked the last arrow back in my belt and dragged the corner of my cloak across a runny nose. All around, the world blended in shades of gray, transmuted between the faint light of a cloud-choked day and the heaviness of descending night. The faint silhouette of the abbey's narrow belfry against a silver sky beckoned and I started back. At once, I stepped upon a frozen puddle, too lazy or lacking in care to go around it. The ice cracked and broke under my weight. Mud splattered over my leggings and frigid water seeped into my boots. Toes numb, I trudged across the snowy ground, up mossy stone steps and down the narrow corridor that led to Elizabeth's room.

It was well past vespers when I nudged open the door. Instantly, I was assaulted with the caustic scent of lye mingled with a faint fumitory of pennyroyal. I put a hand over my nose until my senses grew accustomed to the odors. On a long, narrow table near the door sat an empty laver, a ewer full of water and a stack of folded, clean cloths. Wisps of smoke curled from the small piercings in the bell lid of a bronze incense brazier which was topped with a small, leaning cross, tingeing the air with the sweetness of rosemary and cloves.

On the far side of the room, a small hearth contained the flames of a well-fed fire. The stones around it bore little trace of soot, indicating that the abbot must not have used it often, probably thinking the luxury too much of an indulgence when wood could be used to cook food or warm the sick.

The abbot had afforded himself one comfort and that was a large four-postered bed, its mattress plump with feathers and encased in undyed canvas. Cocooned beneath layers of linen sheets and woolen blankets lay my Elizabeth, her head propped against a dark blue bolster.

If not for Gruoch's snoring, I might not have seen her lying in the shadows on her pallet between the door and the bed. I crept toward Elizabeth's sleeping form and stood at the side of her bed. Barely, slowly, her chest rose and fell. A ragged tendril of hair, damp with sweat, lay crookedly from her hairline to the corner of her mouth. I pushed it away, the backs of my fingers lingering at her jawline.

Dear God in Heaven, don't . . . please don't take her from me. Not after bringing her back. Not after so long without her.

I wanted to kneel beside her and lay my hand over hers, but instead I turned back toward the door. An indrawn breath, ragged but deep, stalled me.

"Will you go . . ." came a hoarse voice, "without a kiss?"

When I first turned to look, her eyes were closed. Surely I had dreamed the words? But then her lashes fluttered and parted.

"Turnberry," she said meekly, curling her fingers over the edge of her blanket. "Will you take me there?"

I returned to her and sought her hand. "Aye. In time."

Elizabeth turned her face away, but when she looked back at me, I could see the heartache of eight long years behind those once vibrant green eyes. "When?"

"Soon, my love. Soon." The coolness of her cheek as I kissed it reassured me that the fever had at last left her. "The sea air is brisk this time of year, but perhaps it will refresh you."

"It has been so long, Robert. *So* long." Her mouth trembled. "I hardly know what to make of everything that has happened. What to say . . . Where to begin, even."

Begin? Why not now, today . . . this very moment?

In truth, though, I knew it would not be so easy. We were strangers, she and I, in ways as yet unknown to us both. God knows I had changed—and not so certainly for the better.

I knelt at her bedside and cupped her hands between mine. "We have many years still ahead of us, sweet Elizabeth. Many, *many* years."

3

James Douglas – Melrose Abbey, 1314

G RUNTING FROM DEEP IN his belly like a rutting boar, Robert Boyd heaved the wooden post into a half-frozen mud puddle at my feet. Muck splattered over my shins. Behind me, sheep bleated at the disturbance and ran to the far side of the pen where a small sheep cote had already been erected. Wary of going inside, they crowded at the opening, shoulder to shoulder.

I rested my axe against the gate. "What was that for, Boyd?"

"You asked me to bring you another."

"You could've just laid it on that pile there with the rest."

His broad shoulders lifted in an insolent shrug. "Perhaps, James Douglas, I don't like being ordered about by some coddled underling half my age."

"That old now, are you?" I thumped Boyd hard in the middle of his broad chest with my fist. "The king says we're to make ourselves useful while we're loitering about here. The orders come from him, not me."

We had spent the day working in a stretch of pasture to the east of Melrose Abbey where pens were being repaired. The English soldiers, on their way through after Bannockburn, had scattered what sheep they had not stolen. The abbey's flock numbered in the thousands and it had been no small task for its shepherds to comb the hills and return them to the lowland winter pastures. The abbot took great pride in standing only his best rams to his ewes and so after every harvest the ewes were gathered up for breeding. But this year the monks and lay brothers had been too busy rebuilding. Lambing next spring would be later than usual.

The stone fences normally in use had been knocked over in many places and while the lay brothers were carefully setting the stones one by one, Robert had tasked his soldiers to repair the winter holding pens—as much to keep us from mischief as to lodge us in the abbot's favor.

While it was not my place as one of the king's commanders to ply my trade at menial tasks, there was only so much a man could do whilst confined at an abbey. So I took up tools beside my muttering men and the toiling lay brothers and did my share. It only seemed a fair exchange for all the times I had looted the stores of many a holy place to keep my men fed and alive.

It soon became evident that I was not born with a shepherd's crook in my hand. More than once that day, a frantic ewe had knocked me off my feet. One, spooked when I tossed a stone aside, bolted in fright, nostrils wide in panic, and slammed her head into a stone wall. She fell over, legs twitching, her neck flopped oddly backward. I slit her throat to relieve her of her misery. Tomorrow we would fill our bellies on a pot of mutton stew.

A weak winter sun peeked between scudding clouds of iron gray. I rubbed my hands together to warm them. Motioning for Boyd to join me, I grabbed the axe and hoisted it onto my shoulder as I strode past him. "Come along. We've done enough for today."

He hesitated, then caught up with me in three thunderous strides. We walked up the well-beaten sheep path toward the eastern gate of the precinct wall, through which one could see the great eastern window of the abbey. The church had been built a hundred and fifty years ago in the time of King David. The sandstone blocks of which it was constructed were quarried from the slopes of the Eildon Hills. A magnificent structure, two transepts stretched north and south like the arms of a crucifix. Westward ran the long nave, braced by airy buttresses on the outside and lined inside with an arcade of stout columns. On the north side were the monks' cloisters.

We passed through the eastern gate, its recent repairs evidenced by freshly hewn timbers. A cemetery with mossy stones so old and weathered their carvings could no longer be read filled the open ground on the southern side of the abbey. Many of the grave markers had been toppled by the retreating English. It was there, beneath the twisted limbs of an ancient yew tree, two women stood in the growing darkness, their mirthful laughter a stark contrast to the solemnity of their surroundings.

"When the queen is well enough," Boyd asked, "we'll move on, aye?"

"Why so eager? Need to get back to Lanark to your new woman?"

"Aye, that. My woman has a rump as round as a sow's. Good for clinging to at the right moment . . . But you wouldn't understand such things. Chaste as a monk, you are. My daughter would make a fitting mate for you."

"You've made the offer before. I said 'no', as I recall."

"Not that one. She's already wed. Her growing belly was . . . ah, getting a little hard to hide. Seems the Boyd women are tantalizing to any man with a heartbeat. This is a different daughter. Younger. Sturdier. More comely, even. And only fifteen. Tucked away in a nunnery, for now—although I fear some passing merchant or nearby crofter's son will sniff her out all too soon. You'd have to marry her, of course. Won't have any bastard grandchildren, not even by the likes of you . . ."—he gave me a sidelong glance—"pretty as you are."

"You flatter me with your jealous remarks, Boyd."

He snorted and punched me in the arm so hard I staggered sideways.

The old goat liked to nettle me. Not that he was as old as he said. He just liked to complain. And drink. And talk about his 'woman', although sometimes I doubted her existence.

As we neared the graveyard, I could tell by the golden veil of curls that one of the women was undoubtedly the king's daughter, Marjorie Bruce. She never wore a coif or wimple and dressed in the least ornate of gowns. Even from this distance and in the gloaming, I perceived a smile gracing her lips. But that was wee Marjorie as I remembered her in my heart from her girlhood days: as gay as a wren on the first day of spring. The spirit was still the same, but in beauty she had blossomed, just as the bud unfurls to reveal the glory that had always been there.

Supper would not be for another hour at least and I didn't relish Boyd's irritating company for that length of time. Besides, the king's daughter, I reasoned, should not be wandering about out of doors unguarded. "Go ahead, Boyd. I'll join you in the refectory for supper."

"You won't." His singular shaggy eyebrow waggled above a crooked nose. "At least if you've any notion, you won't."

I mustered a stern look, curling both sets of fingers around the axe haft to readjust its weight on my shoulder. "Watch your tongue or lose it, Boyd. It's the king's daughter of which you speak."

"Aye, and the king's daughter is a woman . . . a *beautiful* woman." Smirking, he tugged at his beard. "Or haven't you noticed?"

The only reason I resisted shoving him to the frozen ground, pummeling his face and breaking what was left of his teeth was because I was keenly aware that Marjorie and her companion were watching us. I hopped off the path, leaving Boyd to chortle to himself, and threaded my way between lichen-flecked, broken gravestones, up the short rise toward the women standing beneath the sprawling crown of the yew tree.

I did not look up until I heard her voice.

"We've been watching you all afternoon, Sir James." She held out a delicate hand, wiggling her fingers when I hesitated. "At least ever since you cursed loud enough to get our attention all the way up here."

Gently, I lowered my axe to rest its head on the ground and took Marjorie's hand by the fingertips. No sooner had I grazed her knuckles with a kiss than she yanked her hand back.

"An attempted escape, my lady. The ewe thought the grass would be better on the other side of the fence. I convinced her otherwise." The ewe, in fact, had jabbed me in the thigh with one of her curved horns, even as I freed her head from the woven branches of the pen. The bruise was deep and throbbed with every stride, but it was noting in comparison to a battle wound. When the tip of her horn snagged my leggings, I had bellowed more in anger than pain, but still, the women did not know that. I should have held my tongue.

"Sheep are such clever creatures." She winked in jest.

Her companion, only a few years older and as plain of feature as Marjorie was perfect, giggled behind her upheld sleeve. Soon Marjorie, too, bubbled with amusement.

Heat flushed the rims of my ears. I drummed my fingers on the end of the axe handle, then rested it in a fissure of the tree trunk. "May I escort you inside?"

Marjorie flapped a hand over her breast, gulping air until her laughter subsided. "Why? Was I going there?"

Her friend clutched her elbow. "It *is* cold, my lady."

"Cold? Invigorating, I say. Go on then, Sibylla. I'll be along . . ." —a warm smile lit her face as she glanced my way—"eventually."

Sybilla tossed me a shy glance, kissed Marjorie's cheek and rushed off, skirts bunched in her hands to keep from trailing the hem over the soggy ground.

"A distant cousin by marriage to Walter Stewart, I'm told." Marjorie turned to walk back in the direction from which I'd just come. With eyes the deep blue of a bottomless loch, she threw a look over her shoulder, beckoning me to follow. By then Boyd was nowhere in sight and Sybilla was almost to the door of the church. A light wind tossed a long golden ringlet across her face, momentarily covering her eyes. She tucked her hair behind her ears and scrunched her small nose. "Father insists I sit next to Walter at the supper table. He's polite enough, or tries to be when he can get the words out, but a complete bore and dreadfully awkward. Oh,"—she covered her mouth, as if to recapture the words—"*please* don't tell him I said that."

When I shook my head, she sighed, smiled and went on as we descended the short hill and joined the path back toward the sheep pen. "Anyway, Father sent Sibylla along with Lord Randolph when they came to fetch us from the English at Jedburgh. I remembered her from Rothesay, but she was a few years older and seemed so grown up to me. We didn't talk much then, but it's much different now. *We're* different, older. I'd go insane here without her. I feel so . . . *confined*. Just like those sheep there."

A cloud of black faces lifted to appraise us, ears twitching. By then we were standing not far from the sheep pen.

"I remember your brothers, too," she said. "Did you ever find them again?"

"Aye, they fought with me at Bannockburn. Hugh—he was born to fight. There's not much else he can do." Hugh was my full brother. His birthing had been so long and difficult that the effort had robbed my mother of her life. When the midwife cut her belly open to pull Hugh out and clean the blood from him, his skin was a deep, purplish shade of blue. That was the first sign of many that he was not right in the head. He was late to take his first steps, slow in speech, shy as a fallow deer—but I looked after him as best I could, even though it frustrated me beyond measure at times. As boys we practiced with our spears in the hills beyond Douglas Castle and he grew big and strong. While his hands were so large that he fumbled to nock an arrow, his arms were stout like the branches of an old oak and he could heave an axe with deadly force. At Bannockburn, he fought bravely, perhaps because he was simple and had no ken of death.

Between lashes as black and thick as strokes of ink, Marjorie's eyes narrowed. "There is another, much younger?"

"Archibald. My father had hopes that he would enter the clergy, but I do not think it was meant to be." In truth, he had a weakness for women, much as my father had. In the same year that my mother died, my father, Sir William Douglas, caused himself untold troubles when he abducted a young widow, Eleanor Ferrers, from Fa'side Castle. Longshanks, the first Edward of England, ordered my father's arrest for the incident, but by then they were already wed. It was not the last time my father incurred Longshanks' wrath. When Longshanks came north to besiege Berwick, Archibald was barely weaned and he wailed whenever another stone from the trebuchet thundered against the castle walls, smashing holes in its thick curtain of stone.

In time, the walls toppled and eight thousand people were butchered in the streets. Eight *thousand*. I witnessed it all from the castle's parapets.

"Archibald was still very young when I left Scotland to study in Paris. I didn't see him again until two days before Bannockburn."

"I'm told it was the greatest battle ever fought. Someday you shall have to tell me about it—" Her shoulders hunched up as a shiver rippled through her body.

"Here, my lady . . ."—I unclasped my cloak and placed it over her short mantle—"Marjorie," I added. We had once been as close as brother and sister and even though many years had gone by, the more we spoke, the more the familiarity returned. "It smells of damp wool and mud, but—"

"Before we were parted at Dalry," she interrupted, "you used to loan me your cloak. Sometimes just to lie on, when the ground was hard or wet. Do you remember, James?"

I nodded and, bashful as a mountain hare, averted my gaze. Eight years ago. She was only a girl then—and I barely a man. Our forces nearly destroyed at Methven by the Earl of Pembroke, we had gone into hiding, moving ever southward through the Highlands, intent on reaching the western coast and going on to Ireland. But at the Pass of Dalry, we were attacked by John of Lorne and his fierce Argyll warriors. In a moment of desperation, Robert sent the womenfolk back north with his brother Nigel. Robert saved my life that day when I fell from my horse.

"I never forgot how kind you were to me," she said, curling her arm inside mine and leaning her head upon my shoulder. The cadence of my heart quickened. "I wish there was some way I could repay that kindness. Some way I could let you know how much your company meant to me."

A lone blackbird cawed from the treetops in the encroaching darkness. Startled, Marjorie gripped my arm harder, her fingernails pinching my flesh through the cloth of my sleeve. As the bird flapped overhead and flew away, she exhaled, relaxing her hold.

"They could have been such bleak days," she said lowly. "I was so often hungry and tired. I remember that keenly. But I was never afraid. Never. Not with you beside me."

Her hand slipped downward, until she held mine. I closed my fingers around hers, sensing her gaze on me.

"I thought of you every day, James." She drew in a breath, held it long. "*Every* day. Sometimes, the hope that I would see you again was the only thing that kept me going."

I looked at her then . . . and saw her differently. Not as the laughing girl with golden curls who had shared my saddle over the many miles of Highland deer paths. Not as Robert's beloved daughter and heir, to be protected or taught as the occasion demanded. Not as a former captive of England's king, to be pitied for her years of undeserved solitude. No, I saw her just as Boyd did: as a woman, vulnerable and bewitching all at once and all too temptingly near.

And it filled me with guilt to think of her that way, just as it filled me with an undeniable madness to take her in my arms.

I slipped my fingers from hers and stepped back. "It's nearly dark."

She clutched at my forearm, full lips pouting. "Did you not think of me, too, James? Did you ever think of . . ." — she tilted her head — "of us?"

She had been a young girl then, like a sister to me. Until now, I had always thought of her as such. No, she had merely mistaken my concern for affection. My duty was, and always had been, to watch over her, to protect her. Robert had sworn me to it.

"I prayed often for your safe return," I mumbled, but even that, I feared, was saying too much. I jerked an arm toward the path leading back to the abbey. "Come, please. If your seat goes empty at supper, your father will come looking for you." *And flay my hide for letting you rove about.*

I expected a protest—some sulking at the very least. Instead, she raised her heart-shaped chin, blue eyes bright, and issued a challenge: "Race me, James Douglas. Twenty counts head start."

She snatched up the front of her gown, shins bare above slippered feet, and ran back up the path to the abbey steps, never looking back, the wake of her laughter rolling across the expanse.

IN THE DAYS THAT followed, I had strict orders from King Robert that Lady Marjorie was not to be allowed beyond the abbey's walls without an escort. True to her capricious nature, she proved incompliant, shirking her guards and slipping away at every opportunity. Sometimes I found her with Sibylla at the river's bank, watching the ducks skim over the water while the sun languished in the western sky; sometimes in the infirmary before prime, conversing with the sick and maimed as she dabbed salve on their wounds and gave them tincture of willow bark to ease their pains; sometimes in the orchard alone, footprints in snow betraying her.

By far, she had been less difficult in her youth. But I began to suspect her reason for elusiveness was something more than willful disobedience.

When I saw her that December morning, her cheek pressed to the smooth stone column in the south aisle of the church, humming a tune from many years ago that I had taught her, there was only that moment, only the sight of her. Nothing else.

4

<u>Robert the Bruce – Melrose Abbey, 1314</u>

E ARLY ARISEN, I KNELT before the humble altar in the little chapel of the abbot's house to give thanks to God and St. Waltheof for returning Elizabeth to me. Already her appetite had returned, but it would still be many days before we could depart from Melrose for someplace with more domestic comforts than a ruined abbey. Last night, she had been well enough to sit at the supper table in the abbot's house. Although she ate heartily, the exertion of having walked even so short a distance had exhausted her. More than once I placed my hand over hers, just to feel the warmth of her flesh beneath my own.

But I could not, should not hope for too much. She was home. She was well, or nearly so. That *should* have been enough. Still . . . an old oath dogged me. An oath I had yet to fulfill.

"My lord?" My nephew Thomas Randolph stood at the chapel doorway. He raked fair locks from his eyes, nodding a bow. Aside from the monks, I ventured to guess that he was the only one who woke as early as I did each day. Captured by the English at Methven many years ago, he had sworn his loyalty to Longshanks to spare his skin. When he later led a contingent over the border, James Douglas had slain his company, captured him and brought him to me as a prisoner. Randolph had been reluctant to renounce his loyalty to the English crown, but in time he did and had proven himself steadfast a hundred times over. He hitched a thumb behind him. "I took some fresh bread and cheese to your room. When I didn't find you there, I thought to come here."

Stooping over the candles, I cupped a hand behind the wicks and blew them out one by one. "I thank you, Thomas. But the food will keep awhile. Find Walter Stewart. Tell him I wish to meet him in the cloister at once. We can talk there privately, at least until Abbott William discovers us and runs us off."

"As you wish, my lord. Is there anything else?"

"Nothing, no. We can speak of repairs later. There's sparse little left to do and I fear we are a grave imposition. The Cistercian brothers are not keen to welcome the outside world. We distract them from their devotions and invite iniquity—or so the abbot often informs me."

I followed Randolph outside and we parted ways. With a new, brightly dyed, red wool cloak clasped at my right shoulder, I strolled the perimeter of the grounds, beholding the hallowed beauty of the abbey in the hush of early morning. Bold rays of morning sun cast their warming glow upon its walls, the great eastern window capturing the virgin light within the blush of its traceried rose. While spires strained heavenward, rows of winged buttresses anchored the massive structure to terra firma. Melting snow spouted from the mouths of gargoyles affixed at the roof's edge: clawed demons with pointed ears, winged angels plucking their lutes and dancing ladies with arms held aloft.

The abbey grounds were just now beginning to stir with activity after the morning's devotions. A cart piled high with hay and driven by two lay brothers rumbled past on the road leading away from the abbey. The lay brethren, while not initiated members of the clergy, gave their labor in service to God. Orphans and younger sons of the poorer classes, most could not read, but their efforts in farming and shepherding in particular provided the abbeys with their primary source of income. I continued on past the north transept and the outer door to the cellar, then through a gate between two dormitories and on into the arcaded cloister.

There, Walter Stewart stood before me at the edge of the tile covered walkway, one hand slack against the base of a stone column as if to steady himself, the other palm-flat against his abdomen.

"Walter, come, come." I motioned him to me, since his feet seemed moored in place on the cobble walkway.

He swept back the hood of his cloak, dipped his head in a slight bow and approached almost hesitantly.

"I came as quickly as I could, my lord." He rubbed at his chin nervously. Although he hadn't shaven since we arrived at Melrose, his whiskers were still so sparse they cast no shadow. "Is there, perhaps, some mission you wish to send me on? An errand you require?"

"No, Walter. Nothing so urgent. Much more important, though." The boy was eagerly obedient, if nothing else. "Your father was a good man, Walter. Wise, honest . . . loyal to Scotland, to my family. Willing to gamble his holdings, his life even, on what he believed in."

He sniffed and rubbed two fingers beneath his nose. Pale of face, his nose and eyes were perpetually red, as if he had a cold he could never rid himself of. "He was, my lord. I am honored to be his son."

"Would you be as honored to be mine?"

He blinked several times. "I'm sorry, my lord. I don't understand."

"Are you aware, Walter, that your father and I had an agreement?"

Biting his lip, he gazed down at his feet. "I am n-n-not . . . not certain, my lord."

"Once, long ago, when you were but a small boy, I came to visit at Rothesay. Your father and I made a pact. In my time of direst need, he aided me. Kept his word. Provided galleys so I could escape my pursuers, men to fight for me, and supplies to keep us armed and alive. I believe in keeping *my* word, as well. Even to a man who no longer lives."

Walter jerked at the sound of footsteps. Behind him, a young monk with soot-smeared cheeks appeared at the narrow passageway separating church and chapter house. Shifting the bundle of kindling on his shoulder, the monk nodded at us and shuffled across the open area of the cloister toward the warming house.

"Our agreement," I went on, "was that if he assisted me in my fight to free Scotland of Longshanks' rule and win the crown, that I . . ." —I grasped his thin shoulders, waiting until he raised his eyes to meet mine—"would give my daughter Marjorie to you."

Again, he blinked. His jaw unhinged. Slowly, the corners of his mouth curved into a smile so large it threatened to split his face. "*Your* daughter? Lady Marjorie?"

"She's the only daughter I have."

The smile drooped. He pulled his chin back and squinted at me questioningly. "To be . . . *my* wife?"

"Was I not clear? What else would I give her to you for? You will agree to it—to have her as your wife? I won't force her upon you if—"

"No, no . . . I mean aye. Nothing would please me more, my lord."

"Good. It's settled then. Say nothing of it yet to anyone else, though. I must impart the news to her first. She's not been home long, but she assures me she thinks most highly of you. Tells me you have impeccable manners and are exceedingly kind. You're a good man, Walter. Every bit your father's son. And a fitting husband for my dear daughter." I gave him my hand to seal the bargain. He clasped it so fiercely I feared he would break the bones. When he finally let go, I flexed my fingers until the blood returned. "Now, I need to find Marjorie. Have you seen her this morning?"

"Indeed, I have. Although I don't think she saw me. Not long ago. Entering on the other side at the door to the south transept."

I bid the smiling Walter a good day and left him.

Sidestepping puddles of slush, I climbed the stone steps into the north aisle of the nave and went through the door. I glanced toward the choir and far transept, but saw no one there. My steps echoed emptily in the expanse as I moved toward the center nave. It, too, was empty.

I nearly turned to go, thinking Marjorie must have merely passed through, when the bubbling murmur of voices in song—one airy and animated, the other softly lyrical, but resonating and deep—reached my ears. I paused behind the bulky support column that divided transept from nave, then took one silent step further. Half hidden by one of the lofty columns, Marjorie and James stood just within a bay of the south aisle, facing one another.

"I've been in England eight years, James." Marjorie braced her hands upon her small waist, her head cocked to one side. "Shut up in the nunnery at Watton, forced to utter vespers twenty times a day, sweep the floors and pull turnips until my hands were purple. Only hymns were permitted. I would have been punished for even a verse of such secular frivolity. You'll have to teach it to me all over again, I'm afraid. Word by word."

"Very well. The refrain, again is *'Ja m'amour ne te lerai'.*" He held up one finger, punctuating each syllable with a jab. "Once more: *Ja m'amour—*"

"And it means what, precisely?"

James heaved a sigh. "It means 'Never my love shall I give you'."

"And I am to say this? Wait. You learned this as a boy in Paris? Did you truly go to school there or did you frequent taverns instead? I'd think you were making it all up, if it weren't so absurd. This 'Fauvel' . . . is a horse?"

"That is my part, aye. And you are Dame Fortune. Now, you asked to learn a French romance. That is what I am trying to teach you."

"*Mon cuer vous doins sanz retraire.*"

He rolled his eyes in exasperation. "That is my part. It means—"

"I know what it means. It means: 'My heart I give to you without restraint'."

Silence stretched between them. Moments in which they drifted closer. I crept forward, piqued with a father's protective curiosity.

Marjorie forced a teasing frown. "How can I possibly concentrate when I'm so distracted?"

He tossed back his head, breaking the trance, a rumble of nervous laughter escaping his throat. "By what?"

"Have I been too coy?" Marjorie plucked at a loose thread on his tunic. "I thought it was obvious."

She gazed up at him then. But it was not with that same fluttering, girlish admiration she bore for him in her youth. And the look he returned to her now had a longing in it, something of desire. Not a look I was accustomed to seeing in the laconic, guileful soldier who was more comfortable slipping his knife between the ribs of Englishmen than wooing vulnerable maidens. For certain, it was not an innocent invitation that she extended to him as she slipped her arms about his neck.

James touched his forehead to hers. With light fingertips, he traced one of her ears, then cupped her chin as he brought his mouth to hers.

The church bells tolled prime, each clang reverberating from tiled floor to domed ceiling.

"James?" I stepped fully into the open, my fists clenched in barely contained rage.

With a gasp, Marjorie pulled back and clutched her hands to her breast. "Father, you frightened me. You should have made yourself known sooner."

"Should I? I think it is well I found you, before—"

"Before what?" Her voice was sharp with indignation.

James stepped further back from her, but did not, *would* not look my way. I wondered how far it might have gone had I not intervened. Or what more had gone on while I was tending to my sick wife, trusting in James, the one man I thought I could always rely on to keep my daughter safe. Marjorie was young, an innocent, impressionable. Again, I had failed to protect her. I gazed upon her, her lip quivering, chin held aloft.

Abbot William shuffled around the corner and flapped his hands at his sides. I nodded in understanding and he ambled away, muttering to himself. I closed my eyes a moment. Inhaled.

No, James would never betray me. Never. What I saw—it was nothing more. It can go no further. Give them time apart to be reminded of virtue. Myself time to cool my wrath. They will soon learn and understand: Marjorie is to be betrothed to Walter. I gave my word.

Remembering why I had sought my daughter in the first place, I turned her by the shoulders to impart a stern look. "I need to speak to you. Alone."

James shifted on his feet, cleared his throat. "M-m-my lord, I—"

"Find my brother Edward," I interrupted, not being of a mind to entertain feeble excuses. "Tell him he is to leave with you on the morrow for the north of England. I want reprisal for the damage done here. Until then, you are to keep from my daughter, understood?"

Although he nodded his assent, it was Marjorie's stomping foot that drew my attention.

"And are we to avoid so much as speaking to each other until then," she demanded, "penned up here like sheep to keep us from the wolves? One can go the whole day in this place and not hear a word, unless it's a verse of Latin scripture. The silence is enough to madden an ordinary man. What do you mean by interrupting a simple conversation and insinuating that—" She broke off, eyes narrowing acutely. Her tiny chin jutted forward. "I may be your daughter, but I am not some senseless child who needs your protection!"

"Please, Marjorie, let it be." James shushed her with his hands upheld. "I'll go, find Lord Edward. We can discuss this later." He bowed his head, a thick mess of curls hiding his eyes. "With your leave, my lord."

"Go," I said, stifling a growl, my lip twitching. As his steps quickened away, I called after him, "But we will indeed speak of this later!"

James gave no indication that he heard me, only hurried away faster, letting the outer door slam shut behind him in answer.

Marjorie's eyes widened. "Where are you sending him? Tell me! Where?"

A line of monks, hands folded in prayer, floated past. I waited until they were at the far end of the nave and had filed into the choir. More monks entered through the main door and northern transept. I lowered my voice to a whisper. "James Douglas is in my service. He goes where he is commanded."

I had not armed my heart for the hurt in my daughter's eyes. "And would you command *me* never to speak to him again? We were . . . are friends—*dear* friends."

I took her hand and held it, even though she resisted. The solemn chanting of monks flowed over me, easing my anger. "For months after I lost you, I went to sleep wondering where you were, if you were well . . . or even alive. Forgive me if I watch over you too closely. Shouldn't a father be given time to reacquaint himself with the daughter who has just returned home?"

A weak smile flitted across her mouth. "You said you wanted to tell me something."

I nodded. "As soon as Elizabeth can travel, I want you to come back with us to Turnberry for Christmas, then on to Edinburgh. Walter Stewart will be coming and staying with us. I have agreed that you and he are to be betrothed."

Her brow furrowed. "Walter?" As if I had struck her, she spun away. "*You* agreed?"

"Aye. He's a good man, Marjorie, from good stock. The betrothal will be long enough to give you both time to—"

"Why Walter?"

"I made a promise to his father long ago, when you and Walter were children."

"Children," she echoed hollowly. "So it is to be?"

"It was not an oath lightly sworn, Marjorie. Besides, there are other . . . matters that play into this. Elizabeth is of an age at which it is difficult for a woman to bear children sometimes, especially their first. From what Christina tells me, she has also been ill often these past years. There is yet hope, should God so bless us, but you must understand: you are my daughter. If you wed, and bear a son, if I never have one of my own, then your son shall be my heir. Scotland must be strong from within. I knew I would never give you away to some foreign prince, because I could not bear to have you gone from me, not after all that has passed."

She wrapped her arms about herself.

"The people," I continued, "must have conviction in their king and his heirs or else we will be shattered again and again into factions that cannot stand against forces from outside. I know this, because for eight years I have toiled to make Scotland as one. The Stewarts are as noble and loyal a family as this kingdom has ever seen."

Slowly, she turned and, with a cool edge to her voice, said, "So a Douglas is not good enough to share my bed, but his cousin is? I don't quite follow."

"Share your—?" I clamped a hand on her upper arm. "You speak of things I pray you know nothing of."

She glared at me defiantly. "And you know nothing of me."

The abbot scurried around the corner and darted up to us, wringing the sides of his robes. "I beg you to take your quarrels elsewhere."

He had no sooner said the words than Marjorie whirled about and fled through the nearest doorway.

"Marjorie," I called. Then, more forcefully, "Marjorie!"

Balling his fists, the abbot huffed at me. "I beg you, my lord, not to disturb the sanctity of God's house. We are men of peace, devoted to the service of Our Lord. This is not some squalid inn where—"

The rest of his words fell on unhearing ears. I walked from him, down the long aisle, the carved figures of angels surveying my every step and the carriage of my shoulders, while gaunt-faced saints weighed the probity of my soul . . . and the forgiveness in my heart.

In bringing my loved ones home, God had given me new battles to wage. And these were ones I knew not how to fight.

5

James Douglas – Kirkwold, 1315

TINY KIRKWOLD HUGGED THE River Eden in sleepy innocence. Curls of smoke meandered low over thatched roofs that glistened with the hoarfrost of a January dawn. The village stirred groggily to life. A flock of chickens wandered the streets, a dog barked in frenzy, sending them scattering in a dozen directions, and a small boy clutching a tattered blanket popped out of a doorway to scold the mongrel.

Come afternoon, the place would be one more heap of sputtering ashes to mark our trail through Westmorland and Cumberland.

Edward Bruce pulled a dinged and scuffed steel cap over his mail coif. His breath hung in lingering clouds about his dark-stubbled face. Snot was freezing on his upper lip. The two of us stood at the edge of a wood half a mile from the village. Behind us were sixty men, lightly armed and mounted on swift ponies. We had ridden deep into the north of England—as far as Richmond—and on our way home were making good use of the journey by gathering up whatever spoils we came across.

"One more," Edward said. "Then we're home, aye?"

"Home?"

"Edinburgh for the time being."

"No, not Edinburgh. Not for me."

Over the low crest of a hill, where a road cut across an open meadow, a horse and cart appeared. Edward eased his weapon out of its scabbard. Some of the men who were still on foot lurched forward. I waved them back into the wood, begging patience. The wobbling cart turned out to be nothing more than a hay cart driven by an old woman and so we let it pass.

Edward was still clutching the hilt of his weapon. "Where will you go then?"

"Selkirk or thereabouts. Wherever I'm needed. They'll want retribution for this, Edward. You know."

"You've months before the English will come north in full force again." He grinned wickedly and slid his other hand through the straps of his targe. "For now, there are spoils for the taking."

"I wager every man in town is armed."

"Likely. If they've any sense, though, they'll have sent their daughters elsewhere." He glanced at me sideways. "And if *you've* any sense, Douglas, you'll abandon thoughts of her. Aye, I know who's caught your eye. I wasn't in Melrose a day and it was as bloody obvious to me as the tail on a rat. And don't think anyone else was blind to it. Robert is no more a saint than the rest of us, but you're damned if you alter any of his plans and you, man, have stepped in the middle of one."

"Plans?"

"Aye. Heard him talking to that nursling Walter Stewart the night before we left. Seems the bastard is to wed Marjorie before the year's out. That would put a fat stretch of land in the royal holdings from Bute all the way to Lothian. Robert's wise that way."

I never knew if I should believe anything Edward Bruce said. But the news, whether true or not, left me momentarily numb. When we were gathered in anticipation of Bannockburn, I had heard Walter speak in passing of some agreement tendered between his father and Robert. But men say senseless things when they are staring at death. I thought nothing more of it than a lad's wishful ramblings, for he had grown up with Marjorie on Bute and doubtless harbored some lingering affections for her.

But if, *if* it were true . . . how long had Marjorie known of it?

As the weeks at Melrose had gone by, I found myself watching her, even as she passed at a distance on the other side of the courtyard, and wanting to be with her if it meant only standing next to her at Mass in a room full of people. The years had put a bloom on her and I was achingly aware of the curve where her neck met her shoulders and the easy smile that danced across her lips every time our eyes met.

None of it had gone unreturned. When we passed in the corridors, she had returned my glances, sometimes veering closer just to brush my elbow. At meals, her hand had lingered on mine when she passed me a cup of wine. One morning, I found her in the orchard, watching a pair of doves that were nestled wing to wing on the branch of an apple tree. We talked for hours that day. What began as a renewal of friendship had, in a very short time, blossomed into something more. Something undeniable. If Robert had not intervened . . .

An infatuation. She worships you as a hero in her youthful innocence and you, good James, are intrigued by the change in her. Find yourself a wife more suitable than Robert's daughter and fill your house up to the rafters with bairns. Forget her.

Somehow though, I could not convince myself I could do that.

Edward Bruce took a few steps back, grabbed at his mount's saddle and leapt up. He leaned over and said lowly so that only I could hear, "Word of advice from one who knows of such matters: When it comes to women you can't have, if you want to get under their skirts, wait until after they're married. It's that much more exciting and if anything . . ."—he winked subtly—"*anything* unexpected comes of it, no one's the wiser."

God knows, Edward Bruce would never earn my confidence, but the man had peeled back a layer of my skin and left something of my soul exposed. I would go back to Edinburgh. I *had* to now.

Sim Leadhouse eased his pony close behind Edward and me. He cleared his throat and spat. "Day's getting on."

"It is, Sim." Edward stared at me unnervingly.

Sword drawn, I climbed onto my saddle and gave the signal.

Edinburgh, 1315

WHEN EDWARD AND I rode through the gates and into the courtyard at Holyrood Palace on the east end of Edinburgh, the whole place was abuzz. Barrels of ale and casks of wine were arriving from the port in carts to fill the cellar. Menservants, prodded along by a squawking seamstress, hoisted bolts of linen onto their shoulders. Highborn lords and ladies meandered, pausing to mingle with their equals and tipping their noses up at any churls who dared come too close.

We dismounted and I passed my reins to an eager stable groom.

Edward scraped mud from the heels of his boots on the cobbles and surveyed the goings-on. "I'd like to say this is all in celebration of our homecoming, but somehow I doubt so. God's rotten teeth, this place is overflowing and smelling of armpits and manure. Is that . . .?" Suddenly he ducked behind me, lowering his voice to a mumble. "Mother Mary, it *is* him. I should have veered off to Galloway when we passed by. Excuse me, but I need to disappear. I just saw someone who might still be a wee bit cross with me for a meaningless little dalliance I had with his sister."

I looked about, but it was impossible to tell who among the crowd he was referring to. "When do you have time, Edward?"

"My good man, I *make* time for pleasures. And I recommend you do the same. Life is meant for living. Now, shouldn't you go find her?"

We had not spoken any more of Marjorie since that morning several weeks ago outside Kirkwold. In fact, I had managed to ignore

Edward quite well since then. He dashed behind a pair of sweating men, who were lugging slabs of salted meat on their backs, and disappeared just as he had promised.

I wove through the bustle of bodies and went up the steps into the hall. Being an unusually warm day for mid-February, the opportunity to air the hall of its sooty odor had been seized and the doors thrust wide. The floors had been scrubbed with copious buckets of vinegar water and the smell stung at my eyes. Already, they were bringing in fresh rushes and dried herbs to lay down.

"James!" Randolph called through the crowd, thrusting a hand above his head.

I made my way to him and we clasped hands heartily. There was something different about him . . . Ah, his appearance. Gone were the sensible clothes and armored trappings of a soldier; they had been replaced by a statesman's attire: a slate-colored tunic that hung to just above his ankles, its tight-fitting sleeves lined with buttons from wrist to elbow, and over it a dagged edge quintise of light blue.

I pointed to his tapering shoes. "Those look entirely impractical."

"My wife," he said, his lip curling ever so slightly, "has become quite enamored of court life and thinks I should look the part. The enthusiasm is not mutual, I assure you. This morning I tripped twice. Ah, but tell me, James. Did it go well? You're unscathed, I hope." He snapped his fingers at a passing cook and peeled off a list of items to be checked. Indignant, the cook gave answer that everything was in good order and strutted off.

"Sorry," Randolph said, turning his attention back to me. "There is so much to do and people pouring in every minute, begging for lodgings. I recall, at no time, any of this ever being written among my duties. The queen attempted to oversee it all at first, but she hadn't the stamina for it."

"What's this all for?"

"You haven't heard? A betrothal. Walter Stewart and Marjorie

Bruce, no less." His smile brightened, while mine slipped away.

So it was true, what Edward said. I had wanted to believe it was only talk, that nothing would come of it. Or maybe that Edward was merely tormenting me for sport.

Randolph grasped my shoulder as if to steady me. "Are you all right, James? You look a bit down in the mouth."

I rubbed at my back, feigning an ache. "Just in need of a bed, is all. I say you've too much energy."

"Too many responsibilities, more like. I should learn to delegate. Perhaps you'd like to organize the menu? Then again, maybe not. You'd be content with watered ale, stale bannocks, and a pot of venison stew without so much as a pinch of pepper." Randolph cuffed me on the side of the head hard enough to make my ears rings. "You'll tell me about the campaign when you're rested?"

"Aye, I will."

"Good, I'd much rather hear how you sent the English running in fright than spend one more hour"—he waved a hand in the air—"overseeing *this*. Between the two of us, I'll be happy when it's over."

I, however, could not say the same.

THE FEAST CELEBRATING THE betrothal of Walter and Marjorie was a grand affair. In all my life, I had not seen the likes of it. Indeed, Scotland likely had not witnessed such extravagance since the times of King Alexander. It left one to wonder how much of a spectacle the wedding would be.

Trumpets blared as another course was laid upon the tables. Boyd conducted a *virelay* in mangled French. Tumblers stood upon each other's shoulders and flipped themselves into the air to gasps of amazement, followed by rounds of applause.

The only time Robert and I had spoken since my return was at a meeting earlier that day, when I reported about the raid into northern

England. Edward Bruce was there as well, but he was noticeably irritable and sporting a black eye. The whole time he said nothing, staring at Robert in an uncommon, brooding silence, with his feet tossed up on the table of the council chamber and his arms crossed tightly. After giving my report, I withdrew to lighter company, sharing my exploits with Randolph as promised.

As the guests ate themselves into a state of indigestion, the night wore bitterly on. When Robert raised his glass to the newly betrothed couple, I could not help but notice that Marjorie failed to smile or look at Walter when he snatched up her hand and kissed it. She was dutiful, if not indifferent, while Walter was suffused with cheerfulness, dashing about the hall to receive compliments and congratulations.

Beside Robert, Elizabeth sat uninvolved, looking spent and frail, with barely a blush to her cheeks. Edward, imbued with the confidence found at the bottom of his cup, went from sullen to argumentative. Christina diplomatically buffered the exchanges that had begun to fly between Edward and Randolph, who unlike me, had never learned to shirk the younger Bruce's malicious comments as simple arrogance.

"Oh, come," Randolph began, as he flicked a ringed finger at the base of his goblet, "we would put ourselves in senseless peril by straying there and to what end? We're threadbare in the middle as it is. We should tend to our own for now. Conquest is for the greedy."

"But when you're the object of that greed, nephew," Edward Bruce said loudly, "you have to slam your aggressors at the back of the knees. Bring them down when and where they don't expect it. In this case: Ireland. It's been a base of English supply lines for far too bloody long. And once we have a foothold there . . ."—he grinned to himself, nodding smugly—"it will be the beginning of the end to English rule *everywhere*."

For a moment, Randolph was utterly speechless. He leveled an incredulous gaze squarely on Edward. "You're mad."

Edward pushed his chair back, his fists clenched before him. "Am

I, then? Mad, you say, for thinking the Irish would have anything to do with us? Mad for thinking we could gain any future advantage from the venture? Is that what you say?" He slammed his fists on the table, rattling cups and bowls so that their contents splashed over their rims. "Is *that* what you say?!"

Christina, eyes closed, pressed herself against the back of her chair as her brother raged above her.

Serenely, Randolph held his uncle's gaze. "I do."

With a gloating smirk, Edward eased down into his chair. "Then perhaps you should share that sentiment with your king. The idea was his."

Even though the musicians played on, the talk in the great hall of Holyrood had diminished to whispers. Edward snagged a passing servant and stole a flask of wine. After pouring his cup to overflowing, he did the same for his sister, who promptly departed from the table rubbing at a wine stain.

All eyes turned to Robert.

"We'll speak of this tomorrow, Thomas . . . Edward." Robert held the flat of his palm upward to indicate to the musicians to change to a livelier tune. Then with the same hand he gestured for the tumblers to clear the floor. Robert gave Randolph a fleeting look that cautioned him to silence. "This is a joyful night, not to be sullied with prattle of politics or warfare."

The soul-stirring drone of the pipes drifted on the air, notes rising, then undulating. The drummer thumped a languorous beat, the rhythm building to a brisk cadence. Robert rose from his seat and led Marjorie by the hand onto the floor. A peaked Elizabeth observed wistfully as more couples rushed forward to join in the ring dance. Soon, the fiddler's bow danced over the strings to strike up a lively *rotundellus*. As Robert whirled his daughter about the floor, Marjorie glanced at me, her eyes swimming in sorrow.

I would rather have been jilted and seen her happy, than to think it even possible that she regretted this happening as much as I did.

NIGH ON EVENING THE next day, Randolph and I were walking slowly through one of the palace's corridors. An hour ago in the great hall over cups of mulled wine, I had been sharing tales of my raids into northern England, but the talk had soon turned to Robert's plans to send Edward on campaign to Ireland. Aware that we could too easily be overheard, we left the hall.

"Do you think," I said, "that he is carrying this out merely to pacify Edward in some way?"

Hands clasped behind his back, Randolph paused beside a wavering torchlight and gazed at me sincerely in the half-darkness. "I've heard Edward say Scotland is not big enough for both him and Robert. And Robert would just as well prefer his contentious brother go elsewhere. We all would for that matter. But what is Robert to do with him? The plan is far-fetched, I agree. It gambles valuable resources and men that are needed here, particularly at our borders."

Hearing footsteps around the corner, I lowered my voice. "Should this come to pass, where will it leave either of us?"

Randolph shook his head. "A hundred times I'd have given my life on Scottish soil, but I deign not to die in Ireland, God willing. Curse my loyal head, though, I'll go where Robert sends me. But think not for a moment that I'll go without protest." He sighed and rubbed at blood-shot eyes. "Ah, I'm weary of thinking. Good even, James."

Shoulders slumped, he left. Shadows passed him ahead in the corridor. As the forms shifted into the light, I made out Christina's serene face and beside her . . . Marjorie. Her eyes widened in surprise. Immediately, I looked at the floor. As they brushed past, I muttered a greeting. Their footsteps faded away, but just as I braved a look back at them, Marjorie pressed a hand on Christina's arm.

"Go on," she said to Christina. "I forgot to light a candle for my father's brothers."

Christina kissed her on the cheek and went. Marjorie waited until she was out of sight before approaching me.

A halo of light shone from behind her as she stepped closer. "Would you escort me to the chapel?"

"I . . . w-w-would not consider it proper," I replied, stuttering to my embarrassment.

"Please." She tilted her head at me and looked at me with such depth and tenderness, that I could not have denied her any request.

I gave her my arm, but kept my eyes forward as we went to the chapel. The corridor was so narrow that her skirt brushed my leg. We turned a corner and went down a short flight of stairs. There, the door of the little chapel stood before us, iron studs arranged in the shape of a cross.

She turned to me and opened her mouth to speak, but stopped when snatches of conversation and broken laughter drifted through the tunnel of the corridors. After the voices ceased, she said to me, "Edward wishes I had never come back. Least of all does he wish for me to be married and having children."

I wanted to ask her if that was what she wished for, to marry and have Walter's children, but I was too angry. Angry at things being the way they were. Angry at myself for not having said more to her or to Robert. But . . . what if I had been wrong? What if she cared nothing for me at all beyond friendship?

"He's convinced Robert to let him conquer Ireland and claim it as his own. But he won't be content with that. Do not cross him, James. And if you can't support him, stay out of his way."

Voices struck up again somewhere. They were far away and not coming any nearer, but at once she pulled me into the chapel and closed the door. Candlelight danced across her features, painting every line and surface around us in molten gold. A small altar, draped with a cloth of red silk embroidered in silver thread, stood at the far end of the tiny room, but I felt no calling to go toward it and commune with the Holy Spirit. I could only stand there and gaze at her—flesh and blood within my reach—wanting to ask her a thousand questions. In the end, I could only dare one:

"Why have you confided this to me?"

The narrow space between her eyebrows creased in bewilderment. She drew back and spun toward the altar. "Is it not plain? Oh, James, how can you be so . . . so *daft?*"

I moved to stand behind her, close enough that I could have put my arms around her. Over her slight shoulder, I said, "I could guess a hundred things, but it would save time if you would say it outright."

She kneaded at her skirts, chin lowered toward her breast. "Because it is *you* I love."

How I wanted to lay my hands on her, turn her by the waist and pull her into my arms. Before Dalry, she had ridden mile after mile on the back of my saddle, her arms wrapped about me and her head resting on my back. I had known her touch well then, but differently. I was her protector, her guide and escort. She had returned a lady of marriageable age, in full womanly bloom, and that small seed of affection that we had nurtured for one another had somehow in a drastically short time sprouted and taken root. I had imagined nothing after all. But still . . . it was maddening. I began to mull over Edward's advice: *'Wait till after she's married.'*

She went to the altar and leaned against it. Wringing her hands, she brought them to her lips, as though she were about to pray.

"Haven't you anything to say? Anything at all?" Marjorie paused a few seconds before turning back to me. "How can you just stand there, looking at me like that?"

I shook my head, sorting through a flood of thoughts, feelings and urges. "I don't know what to say or—"

"Say that you love me. Or say that you hate me. Say that I am nothing but a confused little girl with her head in the clouds who ought to do what her father tells her." She wrapped herself in her own arms, as if to contain her troubles. "Walter is like a brother to me. I would not hurt him for the world, but I don't love him. I want to be with you. I always have. The very first time I saw you, when you came to look for my father at Lochmaben, I knew there was something about you, something that drew me to you. And I swear unto God that I have no wish to marry Walter and yet . . . yet I am told this is what I *must* do—for Scotland. Even though I care not one whit for thrones or who sits upon them. All because of some pact made long ago with Walter's father. If my choice is to be taken from me then I wish my father had never become king. I wish . . . I wish that you and I needn't care about what anyone else thought or said—that we could just run from here, together, and be alone for once."

The light from flickering wicks glowed behind her, outlining each subtle curve. The tight tendrils of her hair crowned an angelic face with trembling lips.

"We're alone," I said, "now."

Her hands fell to her sides. "Then say *something*."

I went to her and took her hands in mine. Gently, I pulled her to me. "Why say anything at all?"

And I kissed her.

THE TOUCH OF HER lips sent a wave of passion pulsing through every limb of my being. I kissed her harder. Her hands fluttered over my upper arms, up around my neck, tickling the hairs there. Light fingers wound deep in the tangle of my hair.

I explored her mouth, my tongue flicking in and out in a yearning rhythm. Caressing her back, my hands slipped gradually lower. In response, her body molded against mine so that I felt every curve and hollow, every angle and the suppleness of her. I drew her more firmly against me. She stiffened slightly, feeling that part of me which desired her most. But as our kiss lengthened, I felt her soften, then yield, then wanting more. There was still much of the little girl in her—untouched and pure and bursting with the joy of life—and I would take nothing from her that was not given freely.

Between breaths that I fought to control, I drew back slightly to lean my forehead against hers. "Or would you rather I simply told you that I loved you?"

"Say no more, James, my love. Only hold me. Kiss me."

I pressed my mouth down upon hers. Low in her throat, she moaned. I kissed her cheeks and chin, trailing my way wetly down her neck and onto the white slope of her shoulders. Gently, I slipped my fingers beneath the collar of her garment and shifted it aside, so that her one shoulder lay entirely bare. Her head lolled invitingly as I kissed her more, from shoulder to neck, to the base of her throat, damp with perspiration, to the ridge of her collarbone.

"Then I will tell you that I love you, whenever I am near." I slipped my hand beneath the collar of her gown and brushed fingers over the peak of her breast, my palm curving beneath the tight cloth to cup its fullness. "And if I cannot say it with words, only look at me . . . and know. Somehow, we—"

Light knuckles rapped upon the chapel door. Marjorie spun from my hold and bumped into the altar. The candles struggled to keep their light, then fed by a draft of air as the door creaked slowly open, they sprang to life again. Hurriedly, she straightened the neckline of her gown.

"Who is there?" came an old, frail voice. Gnarled fingers wrapped around the edge of the door and nudged it open. Bishop Wishart stood in the doorway, one gnarled hand on the door for support and the other clutching a walking staff. He squinted and turned his head from side to side, more to keen his ears than anything, for he could no longer see except for faint light. "Please, who is there?"

Marjorie motioned me toward the wall, then readjusted her

garment so that it hung properly. She swallowed and said, "Marjorie, your grace."

Wishart smiled and hobbled forward, leaning on his stick with each footfall. He tottered momentarily, then steadied himself and put out a hand. Marjorie took it and led him to the altar, looking back nervously at the doorway. I crept to it, then shook my head to let her know there was no one else there.

Wheezing, the bishop leaned against her. "I thought I heard voices. When I lost my sight altogether I felt no loss, because at the time I could still hear quite well. But now even my ears begin to fail me. I cannot hear what is said to me and I hear what is not there."

"I was saying prayers for my father's lost brothers."

"Fine lads. Thomas had gifts that would have made a fine knight of him. And Alexander—ah, what brightness he shed upon the world. A genius and yet ever so humble and gracious. Nigel spoke to me once of joining the church. It would have been good to have one of Robert's brothers take my place one day."

Robert's three younger brothers had each died as a consequence of Scotland's war with England. Nigel had been captured at Kildrummy Castle and was later hanged and beheaded at Berwick. Thomas and Alexander, ambushed in Galloway, met a similar fate at Carlisle.

"Let me close the door, your grace," Marjorie said. "Perhaps you can say a prayer on my behalf? These are complicated times and I have need of guidance."

"Of course, of course. If you would but place my hand upon the wall or some furnishing, to keep me upright?"

Carefully, she led him to the wall across from where I had stood and put his hand upon the stones.

"There. A moment."

I waited for her at the doorway, then left her with a fleeting kiss. Stepping out into the dim corridor, the door groaned shut behind me.

6

James Douglas – Selkirk Forest, 1315

I FINGERED THE GOOSE-FLEDGED arrow at my belt and slid it free.
Snow crunched underfoot as I shifted my weight. I grimaced. The
stag raised his head, flicked his ears and looked about. Clouds of steam
billowed from his black nostrils. I stood as rigid as the tree against
which I leaned, my bow stave gripped in my left hand. A long minute
later, he lowered his great, pronged crown and wandered forward a few
steps. With a black hoof, he dug at the ground and began to nibble.

Recently, Robert had stirred with fever for a hunt. The winter had
been both too long and too trying, and so we were all as eager as he was
to escape the city. On the first of March, we rode southward—the king,
his brother Edward, Walter and I—only to arrive in Selkirk Forest and
be reminded that winter was not yet over with. For two days we huddled in an abandoned woodsman's hut, tending a meager fire while
snow fell thick and fast. The third morning, we rose to the steady drip
of snow melting through the decaying thatch of the roof.

After a bland meal of beans and salted pork eaten in silence, we set
out together on the one discernible trail we could find. We stumbled
across deer tracks not a mile out, but there was more than one set and
so Robert and Edward went one way and Walter and I another. Walter

had long since bored of the hunt and I of him. I abandoned him on a fallen log as he whined about sore feet and frozen toes. Following the tracks alone to a thick stand of woods midway down a gentle slope, I had found the noble beast.

Slowly, I pulled back on my string and brought the bow up, leaning out from the tree to eye my prize. But the stag was directly on the other side of a thick beech tree. I had a clear mark on his brownish-gray rump, but a shaft to the heart would bring him down quicker. I had no desire to chase after him through the forests of Selkirk, following a thinning trail of blood. My fingers stung with cold as I waited for him to move, but he was content where he was, tearing at the stems of winter dead grass. Finally, he twitched and shook his head, then moved forward a step. I held my breath, pulled long until the string cut into my cheek and—

Hissss. Thud!

I whipped my head sideways to see an arrow deep in the trunk of the tree next to me. The feathered end hummed. Before I could look back to the stag, he was already bounding away. The tuft of his tail flicked tauntingly from side to side with each ground-swallowing stride. Vainly, I loosed my arrow. The arc was not high enough and it dipped too soon and skidded over snow-dusted earth.

Angered, I tossed my bow to the ground and looked behind me. Walter stumbled from the woods just up the ridgeline from me, his face long with shock. For a few moments, he stood there with his bow dangling from one hand.

I dug my heels in and raced uphill toward him, slipping on the muddy ground. I threw a hand out and caught myself on a sapling, then lunged forward again. As I bore down on Walter, he began to scramble backward, then run. The bow dropped from his grasp. I snatched it up and flailed it against a tree with a loud crack. As he faltered, I snagged the hem of his short riding cloak and swung him to the ground.

I stamped a foot on his chest, pinning him down. "You're either a damn poor shot . . . or a damn good one."

He quaked. "I swear, James . . . I swear, I only misjudged. I didn't know you were about to shoot. I didn't want to lose him. God in Heaven, I swear! Now let me go."

I lifted my foot from his chest.

Instantly swept with relief, he began to breathe more deeply. "I thank—"

"You saw me there and you let go anyway?" I roared, slamming my boot against the side of his face. He flailed like a fish thrown up on shore.

"What is this?" Robert called from somewhere further up.

Close on his heels, Edward Bruce wove through the tangle of trees until the two brothers were sliding side by side toward us. I held Walter beneath my weight, pressing so hard against his jaw that he cried out.

Edward slammed to a halt and scraped the bottoms of his boots on a stone. He clucked his tongue. "A tussle over lost quarry, lads? Did someone sneeze at the wrong moment?"

"Let him go, James," Robert implored. Breathing hard, he stepped closer.

I looked at Robert, then down at Walter, squirming beneath my foot, clawing his nails in the muck. When I glanced at Edward, a devilish smirk tilting his mouth, I suspected that Walter's mistimed shot was not an accident—that Edward had said something to Walter. But what could I say with Robert present? Or Walter, for that matter? To trust that Edward Bruce would keep a secret was like asking the wolf to stand guard over the sheep flock.

I lifted my foot from Walter's face and reached toward him. Walter stared suspiciously at my outstretched hand as he worked his jaw back forth and wiped black mud from his cheek.

"No foul meant," I said wryly. "No harm done, aye?"

Up on his elbows now, Walter nodded and took my hand tentatively. I helped him to his feet.

Robert gazed off into the trees, but there was no sign now of the big stag and certainly, pumped with fear, it would be miles away in a very short time. "Lost it then?"

"Long gone," I said.

"What happened?"

Walter glanced down uneasily. A damning act, however slight.

"Nothing much." I picked up Walter's splintered bow and gave it to him. "The shot was mine. He took it and missed."

"Well," Edward teased, "you shall have to set Walter here to the butts at once and improve his aim if he is to be so brazenly inconsiderate. At least we could have sat to table and been served up with fresh venison. Instead, we'll go without. But then we so seldom get we want anyway. Is that not so, James?"

Mischievous bastard.

I turned my back on him and went to retrieve my bow.

In solitude, I hunted the rest of the day, bringing down nothing but a sickly, old gray goose, from which I retrieved my shaft and left its carcass for the foxes. Nothing in my belly, I kept my eyes and ears keened for any who might follow and mark me again. But I reckoned it was not likely anyone would. Walter Stewart had merely delivered a warning to me. He would not try anything again. It was Edward Bruce who had stoked the fires of jealousy—I had not doubt of that. He reveled in a good row, whether his or another's.

I worried less for myself, however, than I did for Robert. Edward Bruce was a piece of dry tinder awaiting a spark. And Robert, wearing the crown and in Edward's eyes wielding all the power, held the flint.

We returned to Edinburgh in a warm rain that washed away the last scattered patches of snow. While Robert concerned himself with diplomacy, when I was not called upon to sit at council with the king's various advisors I withdrew, fraught with troubles of my own—too secret, too overpowering.

My desire for Marjorie had become everything—both joy and tor-ment. I dreamt of her in the darkness of sleep—the delight of holding her, having her. At dawn, I awoke to the cruelty of daylight and cold sheets, even as I burned for her. I watched from afar as she and Walter sat beside one another in the great hall of Holyrood Palace, their union looming ever closer, day by day. When together, they were always surrounded by others, for to leave a young woman alone with her be-trothed was to invite temptation and thus put a stain on the blessed marriage to be.

Walter kept a watchful eye on both Marjorie and me. At first, it seemed to consume him, but as the days and weeks passed and no evidence of wrong came to bear, he relented. To Marjorie and me, this game of façades was tantalizing. We passed each other in the corridors with fleeting courtesies and altogether ignored each other in the great hall. And yet, it was my lips that met hers—not those of Walter, who she kept at arm's length—as we joined together in unlit, forgotten places in the gray before daybreak and the long hours after nightfall.

Although it pained me unspeakably, I came and went as bid by Robert with never a protest. But I delayed every going and hurried my every return.

At court, Edward openly inquired of Robert if his wife was yet pregnant. The nettling evolved into a public quarrel, wherein Robert told Edward that once he left for Ireland, he was not to return. As the queen regained her health, she kept from her husband and even, Robert had confided to me, refused him coming to her bed. The king was inwardly distraught and since he could not feign happiness with her, he preoccupied himself with affairs of state.

Forces were mustered and in May, thankfully, Edward Bruce sailed across the channel from Ayr to Larne in Ulster, where he began to hew his way over the length of Ireland. I felt as relieved as Robert did to see him go, but for reasons entirely different. Edward was belligerent and hungry for power. It was by Robert's eager grace that he was given any soldiers at all, for many of Robert's advisors counseled against the venture.

As matters between us eased, Walter and I renewed our friendship. It was not until I had begun to earn his trust again that he felt secure enough to leave for Rothesay to attend to family business. I was never so glad to see him gone.

With each hour that Marjorie and I were together, we treaded dangerously closer to something irretrievable. So it often was that we parted breathless, our souls tortured, my flesh burning wherever she had touched me and my heart wrenched with a desire so strong that leaving her left me both weak and mad.

One summer afternoon, I waited for her at a quiet farm tucked away in a low vale, miles east of the teeming masses and bustle of Edinburgh. I had not felt surrounded by such peace since our days spent hiding from the English in the forests and Highlands. Yellow-winged finches flitted from thistle to thistle, while a vole ventured from its tunnel beneath a tussock of grass, only to scurry back in fright when a stalking gray cat flicked its tail in anticipation of a feast. As I let my horse take water from the trough, she came.

Sibylla, red-faced and fanning away the flies, rode at her side. But when they saw me, Sibylla rode on to the door of the farmer's croft as Marjorie waited on the road for me. Sibylla had distant kin at the house there—folk who had never even been to Edinburgh and seen its castle and who knew little of the lords that came and went from there—so to the squinty-eyed, brown-skinned man who opened the door for Sibylla and let her in, the lord and lady riding away were but a passing curiosity, of little relation to his life.

I tethered the horses inside an old sheep croft, veiled by thorny bushes and clumps of faded yellow broom. The pungent scent of hay drifted lazily on the warm breeze from a nearby field. I took her hand and led her through the tall grass. We walked a long ways, slowly, as if to make each moment extend into forever. Too soon, she would have to return to Edinburgh and our time together would come to an end. We never knew, from day to day, when we could be together again. I stopped before a tiny, winding rill. The water was barely a trickle, but its cut into the earth was deep and broad.

Marjorie tugged at my hand. "James, follow me. Fast now. Come. They won't find us."

Then she ran, bounding through the tall grass like a spring fawn. I let her go a ways before I started in pursuit. She leapt down the embankment and landed in the stream with a small splash, laughing. I slipped down after her, then scrambled up the opposite side with her but a hand's reach from me.

She took off again, faster. Her arms pumped in rhythm. Her hair spread out shimmering behind her like the sun's morning rays. Somewhere a shoe flew from her foot. I stopped to pick it up, mindful of the explanation she would have to give if she returned without it.

Just as I straightened to stand, Marjorie embraced me from behind and slipped her hands around my stomach. She kicked her remaining shoe free and then took the other one from my grasp and tossed it to the ground.

"I leave for Selkirk in two days," I said.

"Hmm." She pulled me tighter so that I felt her breasts crushed against the hard muscles in my back. "When will you come back?"

"Does it matter if I do at all? You'll be wed come autumn. Walter's wife." I unclasped her hands from around me and turned to face her. "You never said anything to your father, did you?"

Heavy silence was her only answer.

"Why should I come back when you are in the arms of another man, lying in his bed, bearing his children? You begged me to stay silent, that it was best to come from you, and yet you have said nothing to your father. It is cruel what we are doing to each other, in a way. A game so treacherous that we are wrapped and suffocating in our own lies. How long can we keep on, Marjorie? Do your fear your own father so? Or is it that I shame you somehow?"

"James, *how* can I tell him? Do you not think I have struggled with that—tried to find a way? If I ask to sever the betrothal to Walter, he'll say no and when he wants to know why and I tell him, then he'll send you away and not for a short while, I'm afraid. He will hate me for having hurt Walter and he'll hate you, his dearest friend, for having deceived him under his very nose. How can I think only of our own happiness when it will bring so much sorrow? It is not so easy."

I stared at her, hating the power she had over me and consumed by it all the same. "And so you think he has no compassion? That he would prefer to see you unhappy for the rest of life, just so he can fulfill some lightly tendered promise from years ago? Or that my friendship and loyalty are worth nothing to him? Do you really think so, Marjorie? Because if you do . . ." I looked up at the sky, endlessly blue with not a cloud in it, "if you do, then let us end this now and accept what we have no way of changing."

Fear gripped my chest. The fear that she would agree to this feebly cloaked ultimatum I had tossed out.

She balled her fists at her sides. "You're a fool to take my love for you so lightly. You could no more live without me, James, than I without you."

"Then if you will not say it, let me go to Robert. I'll tell him everything. And I'll tell Walter—"

"No!" She hammered my chest with her childlike fists. I took the beating stoically as she screamed 'no' over and over again until her fists were red and her cheeks were wet with tears. Then I caught her wrists to still her. In futility, she tried to free herself from my hold, but I would not let her go until this overpowering thing between us was either laid to rest or given freedom to lead us. Again and again she jerked her whole body backward, fighting me.

"Why not?" I asked.

"Because Walter would harm you, James. He nearly did." Her shoulders heaved as she began to sob.

I pulled her hard against me and wrapped my arms around her, one hand stroking the back of her head.

"No, no," I said. "It was an accident. Walter is a gentle soul. He's my kinsman. My friend."

"You don't know . . . what he has said to me. You don't know, James. He suspects something already. I'm afraid he would do you harm. Even try to kill you."

"If Walter had wanted me dead, I would be. He's jealous, angry. He sees what we cannot hide, even as hard as we try. Even Robert has witnessed our affection. I fear we tread too dangerously, my love, as though we are holding our hands over the fire for warmth while the flames leap higher and higher. For now, though, the greatest danger is past: Edward Bruce has gone to Ireland, seeking immortality in a crown. Walter is not the threat. He never was. You know him as well as I do— better perhaps."

I cupped her quivering chin between my thumb and fingers and tilted her head up. "But is it Walter's idle threats that haunt you, or are you afraid of loving me completely? Ah Marjorie, there is another side to me, one you've never seen, but of which you have probably heard much. A darker side. That of the soldier who grants no mercy to his foes, who never yields to defeat, who takes what he wants and leaves ruin behind. Do you think I will do that to you, too?"

She shook her head slowly, the savage anger in her eyes softening. "I have no fear of loving you or what you are."

"Are you certain?" I bent my head and kissed her above her left breast. Holding her loosely now, I waited for her to run from me, to pull away, to tell me to stop before it was too late. I felt nothing but the quivering rise and deep fall of each breath in her chest. And then the sinking of her knees. Her hands pulling me down to the bed of grass beneath us.

She leaned back, crushing a pillow of red clover beneath her head so that its scent rose up and enveloped us. I knelt beside her, then laid the length of my body next to hers, caressing her everywhere, even as I told myself how perilous it was to do this—to touch the daughter of my liege this way. That at any moment, someone could come looking for us and whether or not we had committed any act, that we would be found out and all this scheming would be nothing compared to the hell we would pay for being discovered in our twisted maze of lies.

I took her head between my hands and brushed my lips softly against hers. She answered hungrily, her tongue parting my lips. Her hands slipped beneath the bottom of my tunic and crept up along the top of my hose, over the ridge of my hip. A fire erupted in the pit of my belly and spread throughout me. I raised myself up, braced both hands on either side of her, and gazed down into her eyes.

"I'll do nothing you do not want as much as me," I told her, not allowing myself to consider what I would do if she refused me just then . . . or if I could have even left her without doing that which I had longed to do for so long.

Her hands left the lower part of my abdomen and for a moment I felt as if the earth had been pulled out from under me. Then, as she pulled her kirtle upward, the cloth of her skirt began to bunch in folds up around her hips.

I ran my hand from inside her calf, up her leg and as I touched her where the inside of her thigh was full and rounded and began to curve inward again, she shuddered slightly.

The sun seared my back. A trickle of sweat traced its way down the hollow of my breastbone and pooled in my navel. The horses nickered from the nearby croft. A skylark fluted its song overhead, while a pair of sparrows argued over a beetle at the edge of the rill. I was acutely aware of everything. But most of all her, lying there, wanting to know me.

I took down my hose and laid gently over her, exploring her, tugging at her clothes and she at mine until we both lay naked upon the grass, dying to release our passion and cautious to keep it alive as long as possible.

When I at last entered her, she gasped, gripping my buttocks, holding me there, looking into my eyes with a love so great that I would have battled all of England alone to have her. I began to move, wanting to fill her more deeply, and she raised her hips up to meet me with each thrust.

When our passion broke, it was not in one high, final wave, but a thousand long and gentle pulses that carried us to a place of eternity.

Afterward, we stretched out upon the grass with the sun warming us, falling asleep in each others' arms and waking to do it all gloriously again, heedless of the hours and all our cares. Damn the consequences. We had begun something we could not end.

The next night her woman Sibylla passed me the key to Marjorie's chambers and long after supper, when others had retired, I went to her and stayed with her until nearly dawn.

To say that we lived dangerously was obvious. Walter would return soon from Rothesay, any day perhaps, and we lived every moment as if it might very well be our last.

I would never have said it aloud to her, but I began to understand that she and I would never belong wholly to one another. Our opportunity had been taken from us without ever being offered. She would become Walter's wife and one day perhaps bear a son who would sit upon the throne of Scotland. Those things were walls I could not move.

But Marjorie had given to me something that would never belong to Walter or any other man.

I loved her . . . and I always would, despite the pain.

I WENT TO SELKIRK AND RODE on into England to raid and came back again. I was barely off my horse in the courtyard at Holyrood Palace when Sibylla hurried toward me with an anguished face.

"The stables, m'lord." Wringing her hands, she tossed a glance over her shoulder. "She will meet you there."

I led my mount to the stables. By the time I reached the stall where I usually kept him and tethered him to the corner post, Marjorie appeared in the aisle. Her hands folded before her, she walked demurely past a busy groom mucking out a stall, turned and suggested he fetch some grain for my horse. As soon as the lad was gone she came to me with a face as gray as a pile of ashes.

"I am with child," she whispered.

A stone of dread plummeted through my gut. I undid the cinch and removed the saddle, then placed it in the aisle for cleaning later. "How . . . I mean, there's no possibility that you've miscounted the days?"

She looked down and flicked an errant hay stem from her kirtle. "None."

I could not hold her, dared not. Not here. I braved a fleeting touch upon her lower arm. "How far along?"

"Nearly two months." Tears pooled in her eyes. She grabbed my hand, desperate, troubled. "The wedding is in two weeks."

"Oh, Marjorie, Marjorie . . . " I slipped my hand from her hold and turned away, grabbing a post as I fought panic. "Could anything worse have befallen us?"

Stepping around to the other side of the post, she swiped the tears from her cheeks. "What do you mean?"

"When the child is born, Walter will know you were unfaithful. Your father will know I betrayed him. *Everyone* will know." There was no way out of it. No hiding it. Suspicions would be proven. Our lies laid bare. Even if Robert forgave me, I could not forgive myself. We had been selfish, careless. And now we would both pay the price. I staggered away and sank to my haunches at the base of a hay mound, clutching my head in my hands. "Dear Lord . . . it pains me to say this, but I have no choice: I must leave Scotland."

"You don't need to, James." She knelt beside me. Her words were unusually calm, given the disgrace that we had brought upon ourselves and those around us. With delicate fingers, she brushed a lock of hair from my forehead. "No one will ever know."

"Believe me, I would never choose to allow you to suffer this alone. Marjorie, I will die inside without you, but we both knew all along that one day we would be parted. I *must* go. To France. Ireland, perhaps. Or—"

"No, James. You can't. You don't need to." Her smile bittersweet, she touched my cheek. "As soon as I knew it to be true, that I was with child, I went to Walter. He . . . he took me to his bed."

"You *told* him? And he took advantage of you?" I shot to my feet, shame suddenly replaced by a rage so complete that everything around me was bathed in the color of blood. My ears buzzed. My arms and legs shook. I whipped my sword free of its scabbard. "I swear, I'll kill him for—"

"No, James." Rising, she laid a finger on the blade to push it downward. "It wasn't that way. He didn't force himself on me."

I sucked in several hot breaths. Afraid of what I might do, I sheathed my weapon. "You gave yourself to Walter?"

"Just once, James. He is my betrothed. We'll be married soon. How is it any different?"

"Do you love him then?" I backed away from her, reeling with fury.

"I love *you*. I did it out of love for you. To protect your honor. To spare both of us from shame. Can't you understand that?"

I couldn't. Not now. Not yet. The pain was too deep.

A pair of my men passed by the stable door, talking loudly to one another. I waited until they were gone.

"I will leave Edinburgh soon." I tried hard to control the quaver in my voice. "It's best for a while that we're not near each other."

She turned and ran from the stables.

Against every urge, I did not go after her. I left Edinburgh that same night after a brief meeting with Robert, trying my damnedest to act as if there were nothing wrong.

From a distance, I heard of Walter and Marjorie's wedding. And of Edward Bruce's conquests in Ireland and the famine there that thwarted his progress. And no word of the queen being pregnant.

Then came the proud news, barely more than a month later: the king's daughter was with child.

7

Edward II – Lincoln, 1316

S IR ROGER MORTIMER STOOD before me, bereft of his pride. Behind
him, rayless January light diffused through small windows thick
with frost. He collapsed to one knee on the mat of decaying rushes and
a cloud of dust enveloped him. Black hanks of hair tumbled over his
brow as he bowed his head between slumped shoulders, obscuring eyes
that were surely dark with shame.

Upon news of his unexpected arrival, we had hastily convened in
the meeting room of the Dean of Lincoln's house. I sat in a high-backed
chair at the center of a stout table. Ink from hundreds of documents
scratched in diplomacy stained its surface. At intervals, jagged pits from
knives slammed in discord gouged the wood. To my left and right were
seated some of the highest in the land: Lord Badlesmere, the earls of
Hereford, Arundel and Pembroke, the bishops of Norwich and Winchester, and Hugh Despenser the Elder. My cousin Thomas, the Earl of
Lancaster, had yet to present himself—he claimed due to troubles with
the Scots.

A dozen other lords and barons lining either wall cast questioning
glances at one another. A terrible silence choked the room. No one
dared speak. Certainly not Mortimer.

The last time he had appeared bedraggled before me had been at Berwick, when he delivered the mutilated corpse of my dear nephew Gilbert de Clare. I feared the cause was, again, due in some part to that murderous demon Robert the Bruce.

Snow drifted through a crack at the edge of a window pane and piled upon the sill, where it wafted over the edge, cascading to the floor in a thin, diaphanous veil. Cold nipped at my neck and wrists. Tugging the fur collar of my mantle up higher, I stiffened against a shiver, but soon had to clench my teeth to keep them from chattering.

That very morning I had awoken to find my consort, Isabella, standing at the foot of my bed, clutching her abdomen. Before I could rub the sleep from my eyes, she blurted out that she was with child again and quickly covered her mouth with her hand as she retched. Even then I knew the day would not end well. Good fortune was ever an inconstant in my life.

I cleared my throat and tapped a fingernail against the table's edge to fracture the suffocating stillness. "What news of Ireland, Sir Roger? I pray you've flayed and gutted that odious shit maggot, Edward Bruce, before burning him alive. Tell us it is so—and we'll crown you with laurels."

Scoffing, he shook his head. "It might have been so, had the de Laceys not abandoned me at the third hour of battle."

A waspish buzz erupted into rumbles of malice.

"Traitors!"

"Bloody whoresons!"

I slammed my palm down on the arm of my chair so hard the shock of it rattled my elbow. My intestines knotted into tight cords. As I fought for breath, I waited until the shouts died away to murmurs. "Tell us more. What battle do you speak of?"

"Kells, my lord," he mumbled, mouth downturned.

"You were defeated?"

With that, his head sank lower, his breathing so shallow that had he not still been upright I might have thought him dead.

"The fortunate among us escaped with our lives." He raised his eyes, disgrace evident in their gloomy depths. "Edward Bruce's numbers were recently augmented by some five hundred, brought over from Scotland by the Earl of Moray, Thomas Randolph. Together, they marched south from Carrickfergus, wreaking their destruction as they went—burning, looting, raping. Instead of waiting for them to lay waste to Meath, I rushed north to stop them. I victualled Kells to serve as our base and went to meet them. When my vassals Hugh and Walter de Lacey saw how many the Scots were, they argued against engaging them. That alone should have alerted me."

Bracing both hands upon his forward knee, Mortimer drew his shoulders back, his broad chest swelling. Dents from sword blows marked his plate armor. Blood flecked his surcoat. A long diagonal smear of soot ran from shoulder to hip, where he had dragged a soiled hand across his body. "The Scots fought fiercely, my lord, as savages do. Somehow, they gained entrance to the town—by treachery, I suspect—and set it ablaze. It was then that the de Laceys fled. The Scots closed in around us, trapping us between their forces and the burning town, no way out for us but through the flames."

"How many lost?"

"Hundreds, my lord," he growled, jaw muscles twitching.

My chair groaned as I pressed my weight against its back. I wrestled with a smirk of contempt. "The de Laceys will be brought to accounts for their betrayal. As for Edward Bruce, he is a fiend in human form . . . and even more arrogant than his unrighteous brother, who was lost to shame long ago."

Slowly, Mortimer stood. He leveled an entreating gaze on the council, before turning back to me. "I need supplies, arms, more men. Enough to batter those barbarous, grubbing Scots all the way back to Ulster and drown them in the frigid, northern sea."

Pembroke half-rose from his chair and leaned forward to peer down the length of the table at me. "How are we to tame Ireland, my lord, when Douglas is plundering the north?"

"What of the rebellion in Wales?" Hereford bellowed from the other end of the table. "Llewellyn Bren has taken Caerphilly and burned the town."

"We have greater concerns than Ireland and Wales," the Bishop of Norwich said. "People are going hungry in the very heart of England. On my way here, I myself saw a field with sheep lying dead from the scab. Others speak of cattle so gaunt their ribs can be counted. Last year's crops were not even enough to half fill the tithe barns. We cannot generate revenue from taxes to raise an army because everyone is hoarding what little they have. And we are to send soldiers to Ireland when our own people are dying for want of a loaf of bread?"

I worried at my lower lip with a forefinger. Since convening two weeks past, parliament had been sluggish and irresolute, owing to Lancaster's belligerent absence. Now this news, crashing down on our heads like a roof suddenly deprived of its pillars. If I yielded to Mortimer's request, the bloodthirsty beasts of Wales and Scotland would bear down on us and devour us whole. Discontent in England would burgeon—and I needed no more of that.

"Your request is denied, Sir Roger. Ireland is indeed troublesome, but I doubt its common herd will allow Edward Bruce a pleasant stroll all the merry way to Dublin. No, we must keep the fringes from fraying, keep the cloth that is England one and whole. Attend to our own first. There is too much of starvation and pestilence at home to warrant such an outlay. Let those quarrelsome Irish chieftains undo the Scots. You, Sir Roger, will go with the Earl of Hereford to defend the Welsh Marches and tame matters there. The townspeople of Bristol are proving difficult, as well. For now, you are needed more at home than elsewhere."

"But, sire," he hammered a fist against his chest, "why not let Hereford—"

"Denied!" I shoved my chair back and stood, pointing a finger at him. "I warn you—do not argue with me on this. Do as I have commanded and there may yet be reward for you. Since you are the only one who seems eager to trample that patch of nettles, I daresay it is yours for the asking." I leaned forward, my hands spread flat on the table for support. "But first, you need prove yourself worthy by ridding us of the rats nibbling at our fingers."

Hereford thrust his chest out, triumphant in the moment.

Tight-lipped, Mortimer bowed and swept a hand across his torso. "As you bid, my lord."

In the months following, Mortimer indeed proved himself more than loyal and beyond capable of quelling the Welsh. He not only subdued them, but delivered Llewellyn Bren straight into my hands in London. Then, he laid siege to riotous Bristol and broke the wills of the townsfolk. While Mortimer was putting down insurrection in the west, Lancaster quarreled openly with me at the following parliament. He abandoned the session and flew back north because, he said, the Scots were menacing his lands. My one true hope was that Lancaster would meet his cruel, mortal end on the blunt edge of a Scottish blade.

One man, Roger Mortimer of Wigmore, had salvaged half my kingdom. One man. I made him Lord Lieutenant of Ireland in reward—if it could be called a 'reward'. Any other man would have declared it a burden and a curse.

But Roger Mortimer was unlike other men. He was the king's man. Mine.

I would have traded every small victory he brought me, however, to hear of the death of Robert the Bruce. But if Fortune was to mock me, I would take my triumph wherever I could.

8

James Douglas – Lintalee, 1316

INTO THE NORTH COUNTIES of England, I rode and laid torch to thatch while women with suckling babes clutched to their breasts ran from their homes barefoot and shrieking. I passed with but a glance as wailing bairns stood in the road with their hands outstretched, begging for food. I gave them none.

Edward, King of England, still too twisted in his own troubles with the Earl of Lancaster, had left the northerners to fend for themselves and thus at my fickle mercy. From Lancaster to Hartlepool, I collected great sums of money from the lords and burghers, so that we might grant a reprieve to their people and their towns. This I did at the behest of my king and I reveled in it for both requital and diversion.

Even though I allowed myself little rest, I thought of Marjorie daily. I welcomed the pain, for it was better than being hollow. Not far from Jedburgh, I sought out a place in the deep of the forest at a place called Lintalee—hard to find, remote and utterly beautiful—and decided that there I would build myself a timber lodge to be my home. I wanted no castle walls stacked with stone, nor a court overfull with servants buzzing about like bees. The number of private chambers would be sparingly few and the kitchen and storerooms small, to discourage any visitors who desired comforts beyond a pallet in the hall and a bland meal.

My brothers, Hugh and Archibald, had been indispensable in clearing trees at a good rate. Both had accompanied me on numerous raids, the benefits of which meant nothing to a simpleton like Hugh, who desired naught beyond a full belly. He did what I told him to and little more. Archibald, on the other hand, needed guidance. He had shrived himself of his prior sins by sending money to the kirk back in Bute. His bastard son there died before he ever knew of him, but neither that mistake nor my constant scrutiny could prevent it from happening again. We were not long in Lintalee before a dark-haired lass not a day past sixteen, who gave her name as Jenny, appeared before me one chill evening, poorly clad and with a soot-smeared face, asking for Archibald as she stroked her swollen belly. He even spoke of marriage to her. A notion which I quickly vanquished by dispatching her to a nunnery in Caithness for the birthing, far from Archibald's pining heart, with a charitable pension to live on afterwards.

As I drew back my axe and readied to split another log, it was Archibald, still surly and sulking days after I had sent his bursting lover along, who came to me and laid his hand on my arm, pointing along the low trail to an approaching party.

The company consisted of a dozen men on horseback, most sufficiently armed to lend the arrival some air of importance. At their head was the Bishop of St. Andrews, William Lamberton, who had shed his vestments for more practical riding gear. With a bearing as saint-like as any pontiff of Rome, he rode into the clearing and came down from his horse. I laid down my axe, knelt in the slop within the circle of jagged stumps and kissed his ring.

Lamberton nodded in approval. "When I fetched you from that dusty school in Paris, it must have been God directing me." He turned his hand over and helped me to my feet, embracing me with the lightest touch, then thrusting me to arm's length. "You've served your king with devotion. You said you would. You also said you wanted your lands back from the English. Yet I find you here . . ." He surveyed the site thoughtfully, a narrow flat strip tucked deep in the hills, with its swaying pines and teeming wildlife. "Far from courtiers and clergy."

"Surely you've heard of my quick hand in battle, your grace?"

"Ah, yes, to think I tried to make you into a man of the Church. How wrong I was. But you are what you are, James Douglas, every bit your father's son."

I motioned to Archibald, who was hanging back shyly. "Your grace, this is my youngest brother Archibald and that one over there . . ." —I pointed Hugh out, as he slung his axe and cleaved a log in one brutish sweep—"that is the middle Douglas, Hugh. They both fought at Bannockburn with me, alongside King Robert." I made mention of it to boost Archibald's pride and at once he grew taller. "I'm curious, though, as to what brings you here?"

He cast a glance at the stout framing that was going up. "You couldn't have hidden it any better, especially with the mist that was about this morning." Lamberton smiled wanly. His squire came forth and offered him a drink from a flask. He wetted his lips, then handed it back. "Envoys from the pope are expected soon in Edinburgh. The king will want you there to hear them."

"What has any of that to do with me? I've a home to build. Tell Robert to call on Randolph. Between us, he is the diplomat, not I." The first buds were on the trees. Given a stretch, I could have the place habitable by fall. Jumping back and forth to Edinburgh would put that goal at a greater distance. Not to mention the little problem of whom I might run into there.

Lamberton arched a dove-gray eyebrow at me. "Have you taken to doling out orders to your liege, then? The Earl of Moray is with Edward Bruce in Ireland, as you know. I think you best come, James. Aside from the correspondence from the pope, there is another matter the king wishes to settle."

I plucked up my axe again, as if I had no intention of leaving and would return to my work. "That being?"

"The naming of a guardian for his forthcoming heir. With things in Ireland being as precarious as they are and Edward Bruce being gone— for now, perhaps for some time—King Robert wishes to establish an order."

Sweet Jesus, I hardly wanted to go back to Edinburgh just now. I had not gone a day without thinking of her. Going there at this moment, with her belly growing and Walter Stewart fawning at her arm . . .

How does a man walk in the field of lies that he has sown with his own doings and hold his head high?

"Well, James," the bishop prompted, "am I to return to Edinburgh alone? The king will not take kindly to you refusing him."

Gripping the axe handle, I turned, brought it up over my shoulder and swung downward with all my might, burying the head deep within the notch of a timber.

I had been bid by my king. And so, I had to go.

Edinburgh, 1316

A FEW MILES FROM Edinburgh, the bishop and I were met by messengers from King Robert. The distinguished envoys from Pope John had already arrived and been kept waiting by the king at Holyrood Abbey some three days now. Built two hundred years ago by King David, Holyrood Abbey was where the black rood of St. Margaret had been kept before Longshanks stole it. To the east of the abbey and its adjacent palace sprawled a wooded park. The king often rode and hunted there. Beyond the wood, the hills of east Lothian rose to greet each day's rising sun. And to the west stood Castle Rock, upon which the old stone walls of Edinburgh Castle lay broken and jumbled from Randolph's razing.

When we arrived at the abbey, Bishop Lamberton was escorted away to meet with the envoys briefly, while I was directed to a small meeting room within the chapter house. As I stood before the open door, my stomach churned as it never had before any battle. My sword hung coldly at my hip.

A figure moved slowly across the light that spilled from within. I entered to find Robert looking absently out the middle of three green-tinted windows. His hands were clasped firmly behind his back, his spine stiff as an iron rod. I pulled the door shut behind me and acknowledged those present: Gilbert de la Haye, Sir Robert Keith, Bishop David of Moray, Earl William of Ross, Walter Stewart, and the king, who barely glanced over his shoulder at me.

Robert's voice bore a strained edge. "Be seated, James."

Walter gave me a look as icy as hailstones, then returned his attention to the king.

I began to suspect that Bishop Lamberton's summons had been a trumped up premise—and instead of a reception for envoys from the pope and the naming of a guardian for Robert's heir, this was to be my inquisition.

Two rows of benches lined either side of the cramped, austere room. Rolls of parchment, sharpened quills and pots of ink lay atop a small side table, where the abbey's records were transcribed. I sought a seat on the same side as Walter, so that I would not have to meet his accusing eyes. Robert continued to gaze out the window into the distance as the others hung their heads sleepily. No one took any particular note of me. They had become accustomed to my comings and goings and Randolph, who might have greeted me most heartily, was suffering Edward's company somewhere in Ireland.

Next to me, Gil stifled a yawn and stretched his legs. "Where is it that you're building?" He sounded as bored with the gaping silence as I was uncomfortable with it.

"Lintalee." I laced my fingers together and tried not to fidget. If I could have conjured an excuse to leave just then, I would have. "Near Jedburgh."

Gil scratched at the fine, silvery stubble beneath his jaw. "Bit close to the English for me, but I imagine it suits you."

I shrugged. "It does. For now." Someone had to work at keeping the peace—shoving it down English throats, as it were.

Bishop Lamberton joined us. On his heels was a shrewd-looking man in robes far more ornate than what our Scottish bishops wore and a sallow-faced cleric with hunched shoulders, who wheezed through a pinched nose. Bishop Lamberton introduced them as Bishop Corbeil and the Archdeacon of Perpignan. The king settled in his chair at the head of the room, slouching over one arm as though wearied by troubles. Bishop Lamberton took the seat beside him.

King Robert flipped an open palm at the envoys. "Your business?"

Corbeil drew his jaw into his chest. He indicated a roll of parchment curled up in the archdeacon's tightly clenched hand. "A letter from His Eminence, sire."

"And to whom," the Bishop of Moray said, "is that letter addressed?"

At that Corbeil drew his thin lips into a smile and nodded to his companion.

The archdeacon flicked a tongue over dry lips and read the name penned on the outside: "To Robert Bruce . . . acting as King of Scots."

He looked up to find Robert staring at him intently. Like a mouse suddenly exposed when the straw under which he was hiding had been lifted by a pitchfork, the archdeacon shrank in consternation.

Robert drummed his fingers on the arm of his chair and squirmed like a young lad at Mass. "I crave your pardon, but would you kindly read that again?"

The archdeacon, twisting the roll in his hands, began to stutter incoherently.

At length, Corbeil spoke up for him. "It says: To Robert Bruce, acting as King of Scots."

"Aye, that's what I thought I heard." Robert propped his jaw against his fist, as if weighing a thought. "It would be highly rude of me, I believe, to receive a letter addressed as such. You see, your grace, there are several men in Scotland by that name alone. None of them, as far as I know, merely *acting* as King of Scots. If His Eminence wishes to correspond to me in particular, then he shall have to address his letter in a more specific manner."

Bishop Corbeil snatched the parchment from the wilting archdeacon and took two swift steps closer to the king, then halted as abruptly as if he had walked into a stone wall. "More specific manner? What exactly do you mean?"

Robert rose from his chair to loom at his full imposing height above Bishop Corbeil. "Robert Bruce, *King* of Scots," he said, placing particular emphasis on the word 'king'.

There was nothing of anger or threat in his words, just authority— and it rankled the priggish holy man.

Lips twitching, Bishop Corbeil's face reddened. "Sire, that is to be presumed on your part. His Eminence could not commit to such openly because—and please comprehend if you will—to do so would be to abandon his impartiality in the matter of your kingship. Edward of England still disputes it and a resolution is yet to be reached. The pope, also, does not at present wish to favor one side over another. I assure you this letter is in your best interest." Corbeil thrust the letter forward.

Robert crossed his arms resolutely. "His Eminence *has* chosen a side, your grace, by electing to ignore that which is plainly evident: that it is not Edward of Caernarvon balancing the Crown of Scotland on his head, but Robert the Bruce, to whom you are at this very moment speaking so discourteously. The resolution was found on the fields of Bannockburn. Outside of Berwick, there is nothing left north of the Tweed that Edward of England can say is his: not one stone, one scrap of land, or the loyalty of any man who calls this land his home. So when you return to the Holy See, relay to His Eminence that it would be in *his* best interest to properly acknowledge my rights by both lineage and conquest and in his next correspondence to title it correctly. No less courtesy would I extend to him. Now,"—he clasped his hands behind his back again and strode toward the window as a shaft of weak sunlight was chased away by clouds—"I'll arrange an escort and passage for you. A good day to you . . . and a safe journey."

Indignant, Corbeil slapped the roll in the palm of his hand and stomped out with the archdeacon scurrying after him.

Bishop Lamberton's chair groaned as he leaned forward. "Do you think that was wise, Robert?"

Robert laughed dryly. "I don't know. But I'm bloody tired of Scotland being looked upon as some bastard spawn of almighty England. It was, though, precisely what I meant. Why do you think I kept them waiting for three days? Besides, have I anything to lose when dealing with the Church? I've already been excommunicated."

"Point taken, my lord. But the Scottish Church has already suffered for its estrangement from the Holy See. You'll in no way bring yourself closer to having that burden lifted from your shoulders by this act. There's still time, if—"

"Rubbish, William. Complete and total rubbish. They're a couple of boorish puppets who've had their pride slapped, strangled and tossed in the midden. They thought to stroll into Edinburgh and have a feast thrown in their godly honor—forgive me, William—thinking I'll accept some trifling epithet as I fall to my knees in thanks."

"It is a step, Robert," Lamberton urged. "A small step."

"It is the mention of a step, nothing more. So long as the pope ignores what the rest of the continent has already acclaimed, then he sides with England. And that will not make things any the better for the Church in Scotland, but more of the same and worse. Is it the duty of a pope to cast aside his religion and play at politics? I believe not."

"Robert, it is a much more complex matter than that and certainly not solved by rejecting a harmless gesture. Diplomacy is about making the other side believe that they have won a concession, however meaningless."

The king shook his head and knotted his hands in his hair. "I have so many, many times, your grace, taken your advice to heart, against my own leanings, and never regretted following it. But in this I stand firm. The Church has discarded me already. If they are to receive me back, it will be on the clear terms that they declare me as Scotland's king and that,"—he raised a finger—"*that* act will most definitely secure Scotland's right to freedom."

Lamberton rose from his chair and, bowing graciously to the king, took his leave. The rest of us were still sitting there, wondering why we had even been called upon.

Walter breached the silence. "You said, sire, there was another purpose to this gathering? An announcement of some sort?"

The proud determination on Robert's face at once faded, giving way to sullen gloom. He leaned against the window sill. "Indeed. A blessing it would be should I have a son or grandson and live to see another fifteen years on this earth so that he might come into his own to hold his ground against this Edward of England or the next. But what if I don't live so long? What if I never have a son, nor you, Walter? What then?"

"Then your brother Edward will inherit the throne," Walter admitted. "But Marjorie is near to her time. We will know soon. And she and I will have . . ." he broke off, realizing he had blown air into a festering wound for Robert. It was certain of Walter—he was not ill-mannered enough to speak of the queen just then or his fortune in having a fertile wife.

"Aye, time will tell. Perhaps I ponder upon what may never be, but I do believe it would be good to prepare. I've no desire to leave my country drowning in the same lake of troubles that I grew up in when King Alexander died. Scotland needs an heir to the throne and for now, today, that right belongs to Edward. I've convinced Marjorie to waive any claims that she might hold in—"

"My lord!" Keith broke in, bolting up. "Are you mad? Although it may not be customary for a woman to rule in Scotland, it has been established before that it can be done. Had King Alexander's grand-daughter not died on her voyage here from Norway—"

"Then perhaps," Robert said plainly, cocking an eyebrow at him, "I would not be king."

"What he's *trying* to say, my lord," the Earl of Ross intervened, "is that any of us here would prefer her enchanting grace and pleasantness to Edward and his irrational temper."

"I'm quite certain that's true, but hear me out, all of you. I wish Randolph were here to explain this more properly. His skill for arranging words far exceeds my bluntness in wielding them. But I needed him to make things go over well for Edward in Ireland. For as much as my brother has inconvenienced me, to put it most kindly, he would give his life keeping the English from our land. I acknowledge his loyalty and his love for Scotland, but I also know his ambition. Should an heir—my son or yours, Walter—come to the throne before he is of an age to rule independently, Edward would again be thrust back. Denied. Do any of you believe he will concede to that willingly? I doubt so, especially given that his appetite for power has now been whetted. I shall, in an official document, declare my nephew Thomas Randolph as regent for my heir, be it my son or grandson." He turned toward me and I, at once, cast my gaze to the patterned tiles beneath his feet. "After him, you, James, if you'll accept?"

I did not look up, even though I felt everyone's eyes on me.

"James?" Robert neared me, hands held wide, inviting an embrace. "Never has any man known a greater honor than the friendship I've found with you. It's much to ask of you. By now, maybe, you're dreaming of another life—something beyond battlefields and courts. But there is no one I trust half as much as you to guard and keep Scotland whole.

Accept, please."

This was ever my fate: to serve my king unquestioningly. My conscience warred with my love for him.

He laid his hands on my shoulders. "My good James, don't force me to beg. It's unbecoming of a king, aye?"

How could I deny my devotion to this man—he who had saved my life at Dalry, who had freely given his friendship, and marked me as a leader of men? I clasped his wrists and nodded. "Then I'll spare you and accept, my lord. Though I should have let you go on a bit until you were down on your knees. Fond memory that would make."

He dismissed the meeting. Along with Walter, who would not meet my eyes, we left the abbey grounds and began up the road on foot toward Castle Rock to peruse the markets. While Walter brooded, Robert and I talked—of matters in the north of England and the borders, of the home I was building at Lintalee, of Edward's triumphs in Ulster and the deceptive oaths tendered to him as Irish chieftain plotted against chieftain.

The street from the abbey to the old castle was alive with industry as the warmth of spring had stirred the town to life. Sacks of grain to be sown in the fields were stacked high in carts. A fatling pig was being bartered over. Fish, freshly arrived from the docks at Leith, were heaped up in baskets, bringing the rank smell of the sea inland. Mutton carcasses still draining their blood swung from hooks at the butcher's shop, while on the other side of the street bolts of cloth in hues of saffron, russet and sea blue were haggled over by highborn ladies and pennywise drapers.

Robert paused before an inn where the door had been propped open to let out the aroma of bacon dripping with fat, pastries sprung fresh from the ovens, and ale poured into sloshing mugs. "Walter, I've a fancy for a meat pie. Go inside and fetch us some, will you?"

Scowling, Walter ducked inside. Several passers-by had by now recognized the king and were pointing fingers and whispering behind their hands. Robert did not seem to expect any deference. He was, in that moment, merely Robert the Bruce of Carrick, browsing the shops of Edinburgh. I peered through the window at Walter, who was jingling the bag of coins at his waist to summon the owner.

"He feels smote, don't you think?" I asked.

"He'll recover. My daughter was treasure enough for him. He shouldn't ask more until he's proven himself—as you have. James, I owe you, more than I can ever repay. So much that there's nothing I would keep from you."

But he had. The one thing I dared not ask of him.

"All I want," I said, "is to fight in your name against the English. And a good piece of land to call my own. I have that. I need no more."

While we awaited Walter's return, a small crowd began to flock to Robert. A wonder they had all let him pass this far. Little children pressed in and reached out to touch the hem of his cloak. He laughed and ruffed the hair of a wee red-headed lass who could but stare up at him with her big, green eyes in amazement, the fingers of one hand stuck in her cherry mouth and her other arm clamped around a squirming pup.

While most of the people in the street that day were on foot, the presence of a lady not a hundred feet away riding on her chestnut palfrey caught my eye—at first it was only the sun rich in her flaxen hair that I noticed, for her head was turned away and I could not see her face. But then I saw Sibylla behind her on another palfrey and my heart leapt inside my chest. Sibylla said something to her lady and Marjorie turned at the waist to search above the throng, her middle near to bursting with the child she carried.

Robert was still enthralled in his host of small admirers. The gangly pup wriggled free of the red-haired lass's hold and bolted through a tangle of legs. The girl went squealing after the pup, which yapped with excitement.

Walter had just appeared from the shop, juggling an armload of steaming meat pies, when the high neigh of a horse distracted us. I saw nothing but a thrash of chestnut legs in the air, heard the thump and then stood in lost confusion as the crowd at once flowed away from Robert and toward the commotion.

Shouts arose. Faces rife with concern ogled from second-story windows. A smithy rushed from a nearby stall to steady the wide-eyed, startled horse. Robert wrinkled his brow, but it was I who rushed forward first, my belly taut with fear. I shoved bodies out of the way and when I got to where the little girl stood with her whining puppy in her arms, its leg broken, I saw there, lying limp on the cobbles . . . Marjorie.

Robert knelt beside her, touched her blanched face, spoke to her although she gave no response. Then he lifted her in his arms and called for a physician. Beside me, Walter dropped his pies in a heap and moaned inconsolably.

Marjorie was taken to the nearest house and laid in a small bed in a back room. The cut on the back of her head from where her skull had struck the cobbles leaked a river of blood onto the pillow until it was dark and wet and soaked through. Walter, shaking and crying, pressed rags to the cut, but the life kept on pouring from her.

The whole room smelled of warm blood. Sweet and final, as after any battle.

I stood with my back to the wall, wanting to stroke her hand as Walter did, but unable to do or say anything. Robert paced and kept watch on the front door. When the physician arrived with a leather bag full of potions and devices, he escorted him swiftly to his daughter and ordered the man to revive her. The demand brought a swift glare and a terse comment, thick with a Flemish accent about not having 'the powers of Heaven in my hands'.

The physician pressed an ear to Marjorie's small chest. A long moment later, he lifted her eyelids to look at her pupils. Then he rose and took the king aside in conference.

Robert's face drained of color. "I . . . I will tell him," he said in a hoarse whisper.

Walter, shaking his head forlornly, looked up at Robert.

The physician and I were sent to the front room. Robert closed the door behind us. I heard Walter cry out. At that moment, my heart plunged to a lightless place—an abyss of grief so deep and endless I felt it impossible that I might ever love again.

They took her back to Holyrood Palace in a litter piled with cushions. But by the time they placed her in her own bed, her heart had almost ceased beating. The loss of blood was immeasurable. By evening, a team of physicians had been called to her bedside and all agreed on what had to be done to save the life of the child within her. It was sometime deep in the night that Marjorie died.

You could no more live without me, James, than I without you.

Dear God, how true . . . I could barely draw breath to go on living.

They cut open her belly, just as they had my own mother's when Hugh was born, and took the babe from her. The bairn, a boy, was cleaned up and handed at once to a wet nurse, who suckled and rocked him. His lusty wails could be heard throughout the palace.

Marjorie would not open her eyes again to see the world around her. Or walk through the meadows in springtime to name the flowers at her feet. Or listen to the shorebirds as they crowded along the strand in their thousands strong. She would never hear the cooing of her own bairn or live to see his first wobbling steps. None of those things.

I heard the physicians speaking afterwards. They said he survived only because he was close to his natural time for being born; otherwise he would have been too small and weak to draw air on his own. In my head I counted the weeks over and over.

My son.

Red-eyed, Walter crouched into a tight ball, staring at the door where on the other side the babe cried. He took no notice of the people coming and going, not even Robert when he came into the corridor with the wee, squirming bairn swaddled in his arms. To others, it might have seemed a strange sight to see the fierce and noble King of Scots cradling such a fragile thing so tightly, but in the way he clutched the babe to his chest, in the solemn downward curve of his mouth and the shadows behind his pupils, I could see the sorrow there.

"Walter," Robert said above the babe's long wails, his tone thick with mourning. "You have a son. Whole and hale. A son who needs a father."

"And mother," Walter mumbled into his arm.

"Aye, we're all grieving for Marjorie. I no less than you. But she left us a child to remember her by. We must take some comfort in . . . " —his voice caught so abruptly that I thought for a moment his spirit might shatter into a thousand shards, but he drew his shoulders up and went on—"this small miracle."

Robert held the infant out, its tiny purple hands beating at the air. "Stand, Walter. Hold your son."

Slowly, Walter pushed himself up, supporting his weight on the wall behind him. For a long minute he stared at the child and then, as if afraid of it, he took him and held him loosely. But as the child writhed and kicked, threatening to shake himself loose from Walter's reluctant grasp, Walter drew the child in to his chest.

Minutes went by as we all let grief yield to wonderment. Walter's eyelids fluttered. He looked directly at me and said, "If she ever loved you, does it matter now?"

I hung my head and said the proper words, not the ones I wished to say: "You are blessed, Walter. The boy, too. I wish you both a long and happy life."

I placed a kiss upon my fingertips, brushed the bairn's cheek with them and left. Walter had had his say; I would never have mine. It was how it should be. Done. Forgotten. Given up for peace. Truth was sometimes best left buried and undisturbed.

They called the boy Robert. He was hale as any infant naturally born, but as time went on and he was encouraged to sit on his own, crawl and stand holding onto his nurse's skirts, the lad had a noticeable bend in his spine. Always he leaned to the left—the result, the physicians said, of his mother's spill—and although walking came a little late for him, it came and he was a bright and merry boy whom Walter loved incredibly.

Scotland now had the heir that all had hoped and prayed so long for.

And I alone knew the truth.

9

<u>Edward II – Lincoln, 1316</u>

I SPIT THE WORDS from my tongue like a lump of lye: "Edward Bruce, *King* of Ireland."

Hugh snapped his reins at a bothersome dung-fly loitering about his horse's ears. "Crowned at Dundalk barely a month past."

"A crown of brambles," I professed. "May his arrogant ambition be the death of him. What a tragedy Mortimer didn't do away with him while the louse was within his reach."

We rode on in silence, gold-winged butterflies flitting before us in a meadow forested with tall, lace-capped hemlock that swayed in the oppressively hot July breeze. At the top of a short but steep rise, I halted my horse and drank from my flask, the water warm and sickening on my stomach. A lazy but unrelenting sun lingered on the horizon. I swiped the back of my hand across a damp brow. Perspiration pooled in every crevice of my body.

To the south, the twin towers of Lincoln's cathedral pierced a cloudless sky. If I squinted hard enough, I could almost make out the iridescent rosette that was the stained glass of the Dean's Eye. There, in the traceried panes, the Last Judgment was depicted. Whenever Lancaster finally arrived at parliament, I doubted it would hold any meaning for him.

"Much further?" I asked. We had ridden out alone not half an hour ago, but the absence of guards, which Hugh had insisted on, made me nervous—not that I distrusted Hugh, but I did not trust others. Lancaster for one. My gaze swept across flowered fields, pausing where groves of trees stood in darkness, and continued around, back toward Lincoln's jumbled rooftops. Aside from a few peasants pulling weeds in their vegetable patches just outside the sprawling walls and the occasional traveler stirring up clouds of dust along the main road, there was nothing out of the ordinary. I heaved a sigh. "My patience for this mystery is wearing unbearably thin."

"A mile, slightly more." Shading his brow with a hand, he raised himself in his stirrups, the strong curve of his calves bulging beneath his hose. He pointed toward the edge of a wood on the far side of a shallow valley where a narrow, meandering stream coursed. "Over there, but you cannot see it from here."

"What will we find there, Hugh?" I plied in irritation. "You haven't told me a thing yet." I swept a beetle from the sleeve of my plain, gray tunic.

Over an hour past, when Hugh and I had left Somerton Castle in Navenby, he had given me the shirt and told me to put it on, imparting that we were on our way to a secret meeting, the importance of which would soon be revealed. Isabella and I often stayed at Somerton, eight miles south of Lincoln, the distance a welcome reprieve from the chaos and conflict of parliament. This time, however, she had not come north with me, for she was already at Eltham, awaiting the birth of our second child. Over the stiff shirt, which itched maddeningly, I wore a checkered leather jerkin so worn with age that it would have been useless against even a dull blade, and most definitely against the force of an arrow. Hugh, on the other hand, was dressed as fine as always.

A mischievous grin tugged at his lips. Evening's watery sunlight washed over his smoothly shaven face in a mosaic of amber and crimson. He stroked the black mane of his bay with a gentle hand. "Trust in me, Edward, will you? This day will put the Earl of Lancaster in his place. It will turn everything to your favor."

With that, he nudged his mount in the flanks. It lurched with a snort. He did not look back until he had gone fifty paces.

"Not one step more until you let on!" I shouted.

He jerked the reins, turning sharply, and halted in the dappled shade of an old elm tree. "Very well." Leaning back against the cantle of his saddle, he patted a hand against his shirt to blot the sweat away. "But I warn you—have patience."

I rode toward him, circled him, stopping close enough so that my knee brushed his. "Lancaster ignored my summons to do battle at Stirling *two years ago*. If you have mistaken my inaction for cowardice, rather than the patience it is, then I proclaim you know me not at all."

He cocked an indignant eyebrow at me. "Oh, I think I know things about you that even you do not."

"You are not the only one of that opinion, dear Hugh. Now out with it. I daresay you're not leading me alone into the forest to hunt mushrooms. Perhaps I should have asked 'who' we will find there?"

A red-breasted nuthatch peeped from a forked bough of the tree, its delicate claws gripping the bark fiercely as it hung upside down and perused us with irritated curiosity. I stared back, for a moment envious of the tiny creature's simplistic life.

"Her name," Hugh began, "is Lady Rosalind de Fiennes."

"Should that mean something to me?"

His eyes glinted with the hint of a furtive plan. "She is the widow of William de Fiennes, who once held Roxburgh Castle—until the Black Douglas took it."

"Ah. I'm paying attention now. Go on."

"She has relatives in Lancaster's household and has been taken in there."

"A connection that could prove exceedingly useful."

He patted a cloth sack slung from his saddle. "You have my guarantee it will." With a cluck of his tongue, he slapped his horse's flank. As he began to ride away, back toward the dark, ragged edge of the woods, he said over his shoulder, "One thing—she is not to know who you are. And say nothing, lest you betray yourself."

JUST INSIDE THE EDGE of the woods, a dilapidated cottage stood in a small clearing. The moldy, thatched roof had holes big enough for a child to fit through. A pair of horses was tethered to a broken down, wheel-less cart in front. The weathered door was shut tight, trampled weeds marking the path that led to it. A rambling vine smothered the walls and pried at the cracks around the closed shutters.

Broadly crowned trees cast deep shade, making it appear like nightfall. I scanned the surroundings, but it was clear the place had long been abandoned. A rusty axe embedded in the stump of a rotting tree trunk confirmed my suspicion. Still, as Hugh climbed down from his saddle and untied the sack, I hesitated.

The hooting of a tawny owl started me. A short cry escaped my throat and Hugh immediately jabbed a finger at me, warning me to silence.

My pulse raced. I loosed a foot from my stirrup and swung my leg over the saddle. A sharp stick hidden in a clump of bracken pierced the thin sole of my shoe. I bit back a yowl of pain, spat a curse and hobbled after Hugh. He tugged free the red rag that hung from the door's latch and tossed it aside. Boldly, he pushed the door open.

A chasm of blackness yawned within. He ducked beneath the low lintel and beckoned for me to enter. I waited, listened. Hugh disappeared into the shadows. There was an exchange of muffled voices, the shuffling of booted feet, the soft creak of leather. Dark shapes shifted, moved toward the door. A glimmer of metal blinked in a rare shaft of waning daylight and I scampered backward, nearly stumbling.

I groped for the hilt of my sword. Before I could close my fingers around it, two soldiers emerged, took one look at me and, without a second glance, went and untied the horses. Rather than mount, they led them further away, dropped the reins and both sank down on an old log to share a flask of ale.

Gulping back my heart, I entered. The faint, lingering scent of animal urine and manure stung inside my nose. A pair of doves burst upward from the rafters and flapped noisily away through the hole in the roof. Below, surrounded by a silvery haze of dust motes and seated on a stool—the only piece of furniture within the cramped one-room cottage—was the woman: Rosalind de Fiennes. I had hoped to be more impressed.

Straight, dark hair hung in tangles about her angular face. A thick, cracked layer of road dust dulled her youthful complexion, giving her the vague appearance of a haggard old field peasant whose skin had been leathered by harsh sun. Her kirtle was dark brown, although perhaps it had once been some paler shade of yellow or even white, with tears at the seams and strips hanging from the hem. Even my kitchen help was more cleanly attired than her. If there was beauty beneath the veil of dirt, it shone only in her haunting eyes: long-lashed, the color of loamy earth, deep set above high cheekbones. Her gaze was so severe, so unsettling, that I would have marked her for a witch if given the slightest cause.

Hugh, standing in the furthest corner, kicked an overturned bucket away and dropped the cloth sack at his feet. "Close the door, Ailred . . . unless you'd prefer to stay outside."

I almost looked behind me, then pushed the door shut, pinching a finger in the latch as it snapped into place. Moments passed before my eyes adjusted to the gloom. A single tin lantern sat on a window ledge next to Hugh. Bits of musty straw, feathers and mouse droppings littered the floor. A broken-handled broom was propped against the crumbling wall next to empty pegs.

Lady Rosalind clasped bare fingers together in her lap. She was more young than old, but her ragamuffin appearance contradicted her station. As Hugh paced behind her, her eyes shifted from side to side, following the sound of his movements. When he finally stopped an arm's reach behind her, she stiffened visibly.

"It is good you came willingly, Lady Rosalind."

Unflinching, she raised a grimy oval chin. "Had I any choice?"

Hugh went to the sack. From it, he pulled out a white square of cloth, cut from some larger piece, a child's gown perhaps, then let the sack fall. A twining leaf pattern embroidered in green thread edged one side of the cloth. Circling her, he dropped it into her lap. Her eyes widened.

"You are free to go this very moment," Hugh proposed menacingly, "if you so wish."

Her fingers crept over the cloth, tracing a ridge of thread. "This is my daughter's."

"No need for concern, m'lady. She is safely kept, happy, well fed . . . alive."

Although she could not see his face, she clearly sensed the underlying threat. A shudder gripped her shoulders, then faded as she wadded the cloth in her fingers.

Leaning over her from behind, he drew her back and locked an arm across her ribs so hard she struggled to draw breath. With the other hand, he pricked a fingernail into the flesh of her neck just above the vein.

"It would indeed be a pity," he whispered at her cheek as he trailed a red mark from the base of one ear to the other, "for you to lose a daughter yet so young. What is her name?"

She bit back a cry.

"*What* . . ." he spat between clenched teeth, "is her name?"

"Alice," she blurted, tears welling. Then more softly, "Alice."

"Yes, Alice, of course." He loosened his hold and she heaved a breath. "The sack, Ailred."

Far too intrigued by his guile to take offense from his tone, I bobbed my head in a nod and retrieved it from the corner. The sack, although seemingly full, was not heavy. I handed it to him.

He dropped it carelessly into her lap. "These you will take to the one they call Black Douglas. Letters from his stepmother. Dead now. A fever, they tell me, but she was nearly mad anyway. I believe you lived, for a time, in the same nunnery with her at Emmanuel?"

Her forehead furrowed above raven brows. "Why have you chosen *me* for this?"

"Why not you? You are of well-bred English stock. Loyal to your king, yes?" His eyes flicked toward me. A grin of complicity teased at his mouth.

"I came to Lincoln to beg the king to return the monies and lands that my father and brothers wrongly confiscated after my husband's death."

"Serve your king—and he may be inclined to do so."

She scoffed. "Many in the Lowlands will know who I am."

"Which is to our favor. Because they also know you've no riches to make you worth a ransom. Besides, Douglas had you and let you go once before, did he not? There is always a risk, but once you earn his trust, it will get easier with successive journeys."

She jerked around to glare at him. "Spy for you, you mean? Why would he ever trust *me*?"

"You are a clever woman, Lady Rosalind. It will come to you."

"You'll give me back my daughter, then?"

"For spying on the Scots? That alone would be too easy." He tugged the cloth square from beneath the sack and wrung it in his hands, twisting it from end to end until it resembled a short length of rope. "It is rumored that the Earl of Lancaster is secretly negotiating with the Bruce to spare his lands from raids. I have secured a position for you at Pontefract. The earl will think you are there to carry messages from him, to Scotland, and back again. You will, of course, also share this information with us. All of it. Quite simple, yes?" He knotted the twist of cloth and pressed it into one of her hands.

Lady Rosalind curled her fingers around it, knuckles whitening as she squeezed. "If I refuse?"

"You already know the answer to that, don't you?" He patted her shoulder as one would patronize an unruly child who has been cowed to obedience. "Come," he said, hooking a hand beneath her arm and guiding her to the door, "my men will escort you as far as Lanercrost. There you will receive new clothes, exchange escorts and be given further details about how to find Douglas. You need do nothing this time but deliver the letters and return to Pontefract. When I need you again, you will hear from me."

Hugh yanked the door open and the last light of day poured in. She turned and looked at me fully for the first time. Her lips parted, but before she could speak Hugh nudged her outside and called for the two soldiers who had brought her.

When they had ridden away, Hugh closed the door, leaned his back against it and sighed.

"You should have made her swear an oath, Hugh," I said.

Complacent, he smiled. "I need no oath. She thinks I have her daughter."

"*Thinks?*"

"Her daughter contracted the same fever that took Lady Eleanor Douglas. The child was barely ill when I had her retrieved from the nunnery. She died on the way to York. Little matter, since I had the girl's belongings." He pushed away from the door and came toward me, flourishing a hand in the air. "This ruse, you see, can play out indefinitely. By the time Lady Rosalind learns the truth, we will have all the information we need to undo both Lancaster *and* the Bruce."

I turned my head aside and laughed. Laughed until my stomach ached. "Ailred?" Gasping for air, I clasped his arms and pulled him close. "Ah, Hugh, Hugh . . . What can I ever do to repay you?"

"There is much within a king's power. Reward those who serve you; punish those who do not."

"Ah, but you more than serve, Hugh. Of all the men in my kingdom, you possess more genius than any. More than the entire, un-grateful lot put together. I will forever cherish you. *Forever.*" I cupped a palm against his cheek, meaning to pat his face in a gesture of affirma-tion, but my hand, so perfectly fitted to the contours of his face, froze there. Suddenly, I was aware of the warmth of his flesh beneath my fingertips, the pulse of the vein in his temple, the stirring of his breath upon my wrist.

He wrapped his hand around mine, lowered it, let go—his mouth downturned. Stepping back, he gazed up at the hole in the roof. "A waxing moon. We'll find our way back easily."

I meant to say something . . . something that would make him stay with me awhile. Away from prying eyes and ears. If only he—

He opened the lantern door and snuffed the candle flame between two fingers. Without another word, he brushed past me, striding out into the moonlight.

We skirted Lincoln at a brisk clip and rode back to Somerton in a silence so complete my soul ached.

10

<u>James Douglas – Berwick, 1316</u>

MARJORIE WAS BURIED ON a spring day that paled in beauty when compared to her. In those first promising few days of flushed warmth, the grass turned ten shades a deeper green and the birds trilled their mating songs, yet I saw and heard very little.

Dazed, I walked close behind Walter, who wept openly. Outwardly stoic, Robert supported a feeble and grieving Elizabeth on his arm. In all the words he did not say, the tears he did not shed, I sensed the void that Marjorie's death had inflicted on him, for I too felt the same nothingness. Because of the secrets I would guard until earth's blanket embraced my bones, I could not mourn outwardly, but for Robert her loss was different. He blamed himself, he later told me—not for her death, but for the wasting of her youth during all those years that she was held captive in England.

The funeral procession wound through bleak Edinburgh as the church bells struck discordantly. Mass was said for her soul, but what hollow ceremony.

Outside in the streets, a dirge of pipes keened sickly in mourning and a drum throbbed sluggishly. But I recalled those things only later. In the present, I was aware only of the memories in my mind, clear and real: Marjorie, half child, half woman, as we rode through the wooded mountains of Atholl, chattering gaily in bits of French with her on the back of my saddle and her small arms wrapped around my chest; Marjorie kneeling at the altar in Melrose, whispers of prayers on her lips, the glow of daylight filtered through rose-colored glass, the sight of her filling me with a holy reverence for the simple beauty of one woman; Marjorie lying in the grassy meadow, her flaxen strands strewn over a pillow of clover, hands reaching up to me . . .

If anyone had taken notice of my abysmal melancholy, they did not say. Walter and Robert, too absorbed in their own grief, paid me no heed.

I headed home toward Lintalee. *Home.* What a strange, unfamiliar word that was.

I had not been in residence a fortnight when trouble stirred from over the border. It was the season and to be expected. I called Archibald back to me from Rothesay and sent out word to others whom I trusted and wanted near.

"You should take a wife," I said to Archibald one night after supper. "You're more than old enough."

He flipped a bone across the floor and a pair of pups skirmished over it. The smaller of the two flashed her fangs and triumphed, then came slithering on her belly toward Archibald. He scratched her ears and grinned. "And how many years are you now, James?"

"Enough. And too busy."

He cast a glance around at the main hall of the lodge—empty but for the two of us and one old manservant clearing our table. "I see. Very busy, you are."

"I am. The others are coming in the next few days. We'll set out then."

"Who was she?"

"She?" I said, not sure if my tone sounded convincing enough.

"Aye, she. You've never been one to batter others with conversation, but now, it seems you don't even listen. That you're not here at all. And I've loved and lost enough women in my short years to shame the good Douglas name. I know how it makes a man sick in the heart. So tell. Someone who wouldn't have you? Belonged to someone else? Both maybe. Too young, too beneath you? Did you admire her from afar, or know her well? Would I know her name?"

Even though I ached to speak of her, I never would. Couldn't. We sat long in silence, our eyelids hanging heavy. Even the dogs were stretched out and yawning.

More than an awkward silence, it was a telling one. He could pry until the first of us died, I would not say and he knew as much. The only tactic available was a swift change of subject. "Will you take me to Eleanor," I said, "when this is over?"

He perked a moment at the sound of his mother's name, then cringed visibly. "If you like. But you're better off spending your time in prayer for her, James. She won't know you—if she'll see you at all. The abbess tells me she'll not set eyes upon a man or pass in one's presence, if she can help it. I have not been to see her in years myself. Sometimes I write letters to her, but then the abbess writes back on her behalf and asks if she can read them to her."

"Is it so bad? Has she lost her sight through some sickness?"

He shrugged. Deep melancholy washed over his young face, adding years. Archibald seemed sadly unable to keep women in his life and this one, his mother, was the sorest point of all. "She keeps tally of the abbey's stores, does that tell you not her sight is well enough? Och, there is something more to it. Some ugly scourge upon her heart that wills her to leave her past dead and buried deep behind her.

"After father died and you were gone to Paris, she was there alone at Douglas but for Hugh and me. She would not leave her home, even though she had offers from kin that would have kept her well and safe. There was an Englishman came by once. I was six, maybe seven then. He barged in, on king's orders, he said. Intruded into her chambers before she had risen for the day. Something happened. Something I did not understand until I was older. He barred the door behind him. I heard her scream . . ." Archibald met my eyes. "She was never the same afterwards. She later sent us off to Rothesay and left for the abbey at Emmanuel without ever saying why she was going or if she would ever come back. She didn't."

"This English knight," I probed, the knot in my abdomen pulling tighter, "do you know who he was?"

His eyebrows drew close. "I didn't then. Then one day someone said his name. She flew to her chambers and locked the door. Wept for a day. When she came out she was pale as a ghost, trembling."

"His name?"

"Neville."

Neville. I had not heard the name for a long time. Contemplative, brewing, I licked the cheese from my knife and set it down on the table. "He's seldom far over the border."

"Aye, sometimes in Berwick, I hear."

"Perhaps I should call on him?"

Archibald grinned. "Perhaps you should."

Jedburgh, 1316

WHEN WORD CAME OF English riding out from Berwick through Jedburgh, Archibald was the first to grab a sword. The wayward, surly youth had discovered in himself a need for being in the thick of the action. Robert Boyd joined us. He had a new wife, but she did not fight with him like the old one and so he soon bored of her. Gil came, too, more out of a yearning for the past than anything. Close to Roxburgh, Gil learned from a local the name of the English leader who was challenging me to come out and fight him: Sir Neville of Raby.

Like old, we rode hard by moonlight, kept to the woods by day.

"You'll kill us before we ever find him," Archibald complained, as he knelt to gather a handful of water and rinse road dust from his face.

We had stopped to water the horses at a stream that flowed down from the Lammermuir Hills. My youngest brother, not accustomed to such a pace, had grumbled from dawn until dusk.

"Lad's right," Boyd concurred. "Let the bastard come to us."

I cocked an eyebrow at Boyd and took a long drink myself before speaking. "Soft with age, are you, Boyd? You used to ride on through the night with me to fight at dawn."

Boyd dug through the pack hanging from his saddle for a hunk of stale bread and ripped at it with his broken teeth. Crumbs falling from his mouth, he muttered, "I can still cut you in half with one swipe."

I chose not to argue. His girth was only slightly larger now, but the road-hardened soldier had weakened in brawn with a year of rolling in bed with a young, docile wife. With us I had brought thirty men, most having been at Bannockburn, a few, like Archibald, younger and less experienced. They were all hopeful we would camp here for the night, but by then they all knew me well enough not to settle down too much.

Downstream, Gil rested on a rock, amused by fish leaping from the water. My eyes followed the stream as it coursed madly down the hillside, winding here and there before plunging into the Tweed further down in the valley. The light of day was fading, but something stirred amongst a stand of trees hugging the main road which followed the river below. I scooped up more water, splashed my face and sprang to my feet.

Boyd recognized my sharp gaze and at once peered in the same direction.

"Bloody about time," he remarked with a chuckle. "Fifty would you say?"

"About that."

"Neville, you think?" Archibald whispered, as if his words would sink all the way down into the valley and give us away.

I issued orders for all to move slowly. We were out in the open on a hilltop, no woods to conceal us, but if we could buy ourselves a minute or two before being spied, it was to our advantage. Someone among the English had keen eyes, though. They had been looking for us. Waiting, perhaps. They were ready before we had even started down the hill.

"There he is, Archibald. That feather stuck in his helmet is as good as a bull's eye painted on his chest. Bloody fool." I mounted my horse, took up shield and sword and the others followed suit without hesitation.

Archibald's dark eyes flashed like flints giving off sparks. "Now?"

"Aye, now." Sword upraised, I cried into the night, "Douglas! A Douglas!"

In the grim half-light, leaning back and clamping my knees to my horse's ribs, I yielded to trust and let him deliver me down the crumbling slope. A storm of hooves and whoops avalanched around me. As the ground leveled out, a shadowy mob of Englishmen broke from the trees at us.

The very moment I saw him, I knew the rakehell. I marked him and he me. Neville dipped his lance. My horse's long legs swallowed up the distance. I locked my sights on the lopsided sneer pulling at his mouth and thought of my stepmother Eleanor.

I watched his eyes, kept the tip of his lance in view, gripped the straps of my targe. A lance was most useful only in the first pass. I let my reins dangle over my mount's neck and guided him with my knees and spurs. If I could defend the initial blow, then rein my mount around and meet him swiftly again . . .

Neville kept his shaft steady, straight. Leaned into it. Raised ever so slightly in his stirrups and bobbed his armored torso to the left. I answered with my round shield, but the move exposed my left shoulder more plainly.

As I brought my sword up sharply to ward off the lance from

beneath, he swung it sideways, so that the whole of its length struck against the upper part of my chest. My body snapped backward. My horse flew out from under me. A moment suspended in the air. A moment no longer than a blink. The whoosh of my own breath as the air was knocked from my lungs. My body sprawled across the ground. A ringing in my head.

I looked up and saw above me—sky. The first stars swirling in a sea of blue-black. Took the first painful pull of air back into my lungs. Felt my heart hammering inside my ribs. The rumble of hooves to my left and right. Smelled the aroma of crushed grass. Heard hooves. Thundering. Banging. Oaths and curses. The grunt and clatter of close battle. Everywhere. And closing in upon me—the plod of boots upon a cushion of grass as Neville leapt from his saddle.

Through barely parted eyelids, I saw the black figure looming closer, closer, and in the outline of its silhouette a long, curving feather above the helmet's crest. I curled my fingers slowly. My sword was there. My shield . . . aye, still strapped tight. I slowed my breathing. Kept still.

He dropped his lance. Came closer, cautious, the weight of his mail resounding in every footfall. Only his cackle forewarned me as he lunged in triumph.

I swiped my blade low, digging into his ankle. He let loose a howl of pain. Stumbling backward, he spat at me, went down on one knee, then pushed himself back up, provoked by having so easy a victory snatched away.

I rolled away, rammed the point of my sword into the ground for leverage and gained my feet. We faced each other, each searching for a weakness. His mail covered his body from head to foot. Small plates and discs protected the vulnerable points that I normally would have struck for—the knees, the armpits. Only his face was bared. I could not see the scar I had imprinted on his face as a wrathful lad at Berwick— knew not if it was even there. I saw only the gleam of his teeth and the shine off his polished helmet. Snug against his right hip was an axe, meant for close work. He wore a long surcoat of scarlet, slit between the legs to allow movement.

Yet no armor was entirely impenetrable. Links can break at the pressure of a sword point. For all his false security, I was the more nimble and less encumbered. Man to man, he would be slower. He would tire long before me. Then he would falter, and stumble, and fail to keep his guard up. Surely, he must know that between us, his would be the losing cause.

But it was he who moved first. Barely in control of his balance, Neville blustered at me. I remained firm. As his sword parted the air, I met his ill-timed blow and heaved back. The jolt sent him reeling sideways.

I followed him and rained blow after blow. Hard, heavy. Throwing the brunt of my vengefulness into every move. Beating him backward with each quick strike as he could but defend himself and had not enough time to take the offensive. His flurry of energy expended, he melted step by step back toward his own ranks.

I paused to take breath. Looked around. The fighting between Scots and English had stopped but for a few struggling pairs on the fringes of the woods. Most had stepped aside to see how it would go between Neville and me. I saw clearly, not the flashing white of his smile, but the whites of his eyes and the masked fear behind them. In that instant, he felt and knew the inevitability of his own mortality. Sensing the moment, I plowed in and knocked his blade from his trembling hands as easily as plucking a twig from a child.

"I was a lad when first we met. Do you remember it? It was a long time ago. Let me help your memory, for it may be feeble now. Berwick, twenty years past. Longshanks stormed the walls. The town fell. The castle held a few days more. You and your men broke down the door of the room where my brothers and I, mere lads then, were with my step-mother, Lady Eleanor Douglas. You tried to rape her. Tried. I leapt at you and cut you. Your lord and king chastised you publicly. Perhaps that part you remember? You've grown old, Neville. I, in my prime now. You, past yours. Isn't this the moment when you beg for mercy?"

He scoffed and lifted the axe shakily from his belt. "You know full well I have no such mercy for you, bastard that you are. There'll be no prisoners this day. This fight's a long cry from being over with. I stand, and I'll still be standing when the ravens are bathing in the vile blood around your shredded body."

"Then if you won't go down on your knees and beg forgiveness for your acts, cast your eyes to Heaven and make your peace. There is but one end to this meeting. You raped her—and you will die for it today."

A thin laugh trickled from his crooked mouth. He lifted his helmet and mail hood and tossed them to the ground. In the moonlight, then, I saw the crescent scar on his face.

"Your mother begged me into her bed and made sport of the fight simply for show."

He was a sick man, beyond help or pity or understanding. I let my arms drift wide in invitation. "Is that how you remember it, Sir Neville?"

His axe wheeled through the air at the end of an unnaturally long arm. The bright colors of his surcoat flashed behind it in a collision of scarlet, azure and green. I thrust my sword arm to block the blow, as I had done a thousand times before, and moved to unarm my foe with a quick upward jerk.

But somehow I misjudged. Somehow . . . by a moment, a breath, a hair . . .

The bottom point of his taper axe snagged my forearm. I felt neither piercing nor cutting, only the pressure of metal against the resistance of my muscle as I tried to jerk my arm away.

I was on my knees then without knowing how I had been put there. The axe blade was buried in my arm, hooked on my bone it might have been . . . and yet I could not feel it. Nor could I feel my fingers or the sword hilt that slipped from them and fell to the earth.

Never before or since in the course of all my turbid, contemptuous years had I been without plan or action. But just then, a few brutal moments blurred past when an unfamiliar truth bared itself to me—that I might die, then and there, suddenly maybe, or cruelly slow. My head was as frozen cold as my right arm—unresponsive, numb, apart from the rest of me. I observed a weapon, tempered and lifeless, embedded in human flesh, life weeping in streams and splatters of carmine blood around. It was my flesh, my body . . . his blade buried there . . . and yet it could not be. *Could not.*

I fought, not with my head or my skill, but with a desperate strength that blinded me to my wounds. With my left arm, I plowed my round shield into his belly. The jolt sent him tottering backward, pulling me with him by the connection of his weapon buried in my arm. I wrenched away and in the same motion let loose my shield and then scooped up my sword with my left hand, its weight awkward there. A stranger in my grasp. But its purpose would speak more clearly. I found my feet beneath me, the earth like a platform holding me up.

I saw then the tear in my flesh—the skin flapping on my forearm like a rent piece of clothing and feeling no more a part of me than such. In that moment of realization, there was no time for needed breath or reckless prayer. Only time to strike out and defend, as I had so very long ago at Berwick in defense of Eleanor against this same man, as I had against Frederick the spoiled nobleman's son at the College of Cardinal Lemoine in Paris, as I had at Bannockburn against the vast might of England. Aye, those moments defined me, set me apart from other men, made me a creature of the devil's bowels—feared by honest men and forsaken by the gentler sex. If God indeed had a purpose for me, then he possessed a wicked streak and that was a trait I shared with him, cherished or not. I would avenge Eleanor, who had suffered by this man's evil touch.

My blade divided the air and drove into his neck, a scant finger's width below his ear. Blood rained as I pulled my sword back and struck three times more while he staggered, gurgling, his eyes fluttering heavenward. As I poised for one more blow of retribution, his head rolled onto his left shoulder like a shaken rag doll and he crumpled to the forest floor. His body jerked rigidly as he took his last gasp, then went limp.

I blinked away the blood stinging at my eyes. Neville's men kept their weapons at hand, regarding me warily. I snatched up the red, shimmering axe in my right hand, barely enough strength in my fingers to grasp the haft, and raised it to the height of my drooping shoulder. I shuddered with the rage of combat.

"Next!" I shouted at their blank English faces, all blanched like witnesses to some apparition of the infernal world. "Come now! My master won't be pleased with this trifling rot!"

They ran. Ran as though the devil himself were on their heels, fain for souls to devour whole, then spit out the bones to pick his teeth with. I would have pursued them each and all and dealt out the same unpleasant fate their vain and feckless lord had suffered. One fallen peacock. One slim, garish feather in my cap. I could stuff a featherbed with the lot of them. But my legs were leaden, my head as light as air.

An angel's voice beckoned, called out my name softly on the gentlest breeze. "James, follow me. Fast now. Come. They won't find us."

My lips shaped her name. "Marjorie."

Ah, Marjorie . . . let me hold you once more.

Melrose Abbey, 1316

I SLEPT IN A world adrift with alternating memories: some sweetly pleasant, some stark and frightening. A world of pleasures in sunlight and uplifting gladness. A world of clouds and darkness, of slow, seeping terror and sudden panic. I fought to stay . . . and to go.

I wandered in that world of half-dark, half-light, hearing Marjorie's voice—sometimes as a child spilling over with laughter, sometimes as a woman flushed with desire, calling to me—and yet, I could not find her there. Not in the meadows or woods, nor in the twisting alleys or winding corridors. Nowhere. Only her voice, at first loud above the chanting, and gradually, the longer I searched and searched, fading away to nothing.

At last, I came to a room . . . the chapel of Melrose. But there was no door through which I could leave. No window to look out upon the world. Only walls of stone, rough and damp to the touch, an altar draped with a cloth of red, and a crucifix hanging askance on the wall behind it. I had the vaguest recollection I had been here before . . .

A presence filled me, seized my heart and gave it strength. Yet, I felt no fatigue in my body, no weight to my limbs. I knelt, brought my palms together, touched my fingertips to my lips and closed my eyes. What else was I to do? I was put here to wait, I was certain, for some meeting, some judgment that would allow me either to ascend to heaven or hurtle me down to hell.

As a lad, I prayed when I was prodded, attended Mass when I was made to and doled out respect to the priests by way of blind obedience. When I returned from school in France, I honored Bishop Lamberton as my master without question. But I can never say that truly in my heart did I *believe*.

When I knelt at Mass, Latin utterances ringing above bowed heads, I tried, tried, *tried* to understand, to open my soul, to imagine the light cast by God's face or his hand instructing the affairs of men. But it never came to me. Never made any sense but to give the poor, hopeless peasantry some semblance of order to their aimless lives and that I thought was reason enough for churches and monks and bishops.

So how was it, after the life I had led, that God should allow me salvation?

"You fought well, James," came God's voice, thin and distant.

Odd. I could hear the chanting of monks in my dreams. I tried to open my eyes, to look upon Him. A shape, white and floating, appeared before me, but I could not make out the face.

Fool. Man is not meant to look upon God.

"You're fortunate to be alive," said the voice, this time closer, more clearly.

I blinked. I was lying down now . . . but how? "Alive? Alive?" I kept repeating it in confusion. I didn't want to be. I wanted to be with Marjorie.

A starpoint of white hovered above me. The face came near. Smiled quaintly. I blinked again. The point of light became a candle flame, but the face . . .

Another figure stooped over me. This voice was deeper, gruffer. Familiar.

"Aye. Those English must've thought you possessed by the devil. Ran like flaming hell to get away from you. Lost a lot of blood, you did. Nasty wound there. Turned fifteen shades of purple and green before Gil cleaned it up. Should I tell you how? Or would you rather not know? Let's just say it had to do with wee, slimy beasts. Och, look there. You won't be out of bed for a while, much less heave a sword."

Outlines sharpened. The light around the room brightened. Candles wavered—on a small table by the bed, in sconces by the door. With my returning sight, sensation began to return.

"Boyd?" I whispered. "Where are we?"

"Melrose." He chuckled, then handed Gil a piece of cloth. "But we'll have you back at Lintalee in no time."

"You must have thought to bury me, if you brought me here." I feigned a smile, but do not think I managed, so weak I was. I couldn't stay here. There were too many memories of her here.

Gil dipped the rag in water, then began to dab at the wound on my forearm. The water burned. White pain fanned upward, from my arm, to my shoulder, through my chest. I felt weak, as though I was slipping away again.

"Aye. We fetched the mason to cut you a headstone." Boyd guffawed. "Fools, all those folk who say you've a pact with the devil. Too damn stubborn to die, that's what you are. Any ordinary man would not have lasted a day in your condition."

Boyd, Gil . . . you should have let me die. I could have been with her again.

WHEN I WAS WELL enough to ride again, Gil and Boyd escorted Archibald and me back to Lintalee. Many times before I had been wounded, but never so grievously. The wound itself was not life-threatening, but the loss of blood had been great. If I could have chosen, I would not have returned to the world, but there was always something within my soul that would not succumb. My work, whatever it was anymore, was not done. No matter that I no longer cared to discover that calling. I only wanted back what I could not have: a chance to live over those few short months with Marjorie in which I had tread so errantly astray.

One dismal November day as my brother and I sat about the hall in Lintalee with our two favorite hounds sprawled under the tables, I was, as usual, deeply sunk in melancholy, pondering the same thoughts senselessly over and over. I had a sheaf of arrows arrayed on the table. One by one, I picked them up, inspecting the goose feathers for gaps or imperfections, eyeing the shafts for straightness, testing for weight and balance, lying them back down again, reaching for another.

When again would I be able to pull my bowstring? My arm was yet partly numb below the elbow and I had far from regained good use of it. Eating left-handed was something of an embarrassment, and so my waist had dwindled to spare my pride. I barely noticed when the bitch at my feet lifted her head, stood on her gangly, bristly legs and looked to the outer door.

"Have you heard anything I've said, James?" Archibald tapped his knife on the table. "King Robert asks, if you're well enough, if you'll be in Edinburgh for Christmas?"

The bitch hound twitched her ears and tilted her gray-streaked head. As I reached to stroke her neck, she trotted away toward the door, turned and looked expectantly at me.

"No hunt today, girl. Not for some time," I told her.

"You didn't answer me," Archibald whined.

"The Lindsays will be in Edinburgh, certainly. Have you answered them about their sister?"

His cheeks flushed crimson. He fidgeted in his chair. "Come with me, James. Tell me if you think Beatrice is fit to marry."

"Me? 'Tis you who'll have to share her bed, not me. I'm far from qualified in meting out advice in the department of marriage."

"Ah, but you used to prod me constantly on it. Told me I ought to marry. Even offered Douglas Castle to me. I'll say if I dare, but it frightens me to think of . . . of spending all my life with one woman. What if she's a shrew? Near thirty, she is, older than me, and never once married."

"There were offers. All fell through for sound reasons. I understand one of her betrotheds died in battle less than a month before they were to be wed."

He slid from his seat, paced uneasily. "Come, won't you?"

"You know the way as well as I."

He stopped abruptly, his back to me. Crossing his arms, he turned to gaze at me with the look of a child from whom the truth can no longer be hidden. "You said her name when you were down with the fever, did you know?"

Did he guess merely by observation, or had I, in my delirium, said too much? "Whose name did I say, then?"

"*Her* name. The reason you don't want to go back to Edinburgh and face Walter."

There was nothing malevolent in his manifestation and yet all the same it left me feeling helplessly exposed. As it had been since boyhood for me, words failed to form. Had I thought he harbored me any ill will, I might have struck him. That seemed to be the only way I knew. But circumstances had softened me. Made me look more inward than out for the things that caused me hurt.

"How do I give answer to that accusation?" I asked pointedly.

But he had no opportunity to respond or query further. The dogs scrabbled to their feet and pitched into a frenzy as the outer doors swung open. With his head bowed, my young horsegroom, Donald, held the door for a lady. As she swept past, Donald gazed at her beneath his dirty locks, then tugged the door shut and disappeared outside.

Archibald rose and managed a quick bow, but he looked blankly at the visitor, not knowing at all who she was. I knew, though, and was more than passing curious as to what had brought her here.

"Lady Rosalind de Fiennes?" Tentative, I went forward, took her cool hand and brushed my lips over it. "This is my brother, Archibald. What brings you? I would not have thought we'd meet again—less that you would ever seek me out."

She brushed back the hood of her damp mantle. It had been misting daylong and by her sodden outer garments, it was clear she had ridden many miles, days perhaps. Her chin drifted down to her chest. "I regret to tell you, my lords, that Lady Eleanor Douglas died this past spring of a rampant fever. She fought it fiercely. The nuns of Emmanuel even bathed her in the River Avon to cool the fever. But it was not meant that she should remain of this earth."

Archibald staggered to the table and leaned upon it, shaking his head slowly.

"Your mother, Sir Archibald, she befriended me. We talked often. She spoke of her sons incessantly with enormous pride."

"I wrote her. Wrote and wrote and in the last two years—and not one in return from her. I went to the nunnery to inquire of her. The abbess turned me away."

"Judge her not harshly, my lord. Your mother had taken the veil.

Almost daily she set out to attend to the poor and infirm and was not even at the nunnery. It was her own selflessness that exposed her to the pestilence in nearby Dalmeny. As for your letters, when we were sorting through her belongings, we found these." She drew from beneath the shelter of her mantle a leather bag and offered it to Archibald. "The pages were worn, some of the words blurred from her tears. She read them often. I pray they will grant you some comfort in your loss."

As Archibald stepped shakily forward and took the bag from her, I saw Rosalind's brave countenance deepen with the shadow of her own lamentations. She would not, however, allow her own sufferings or fear to deter her from her purpose. At Roxburgh, she had shown such fortitude. Even so, there was the slightest sinking of her mouth and her eyes were darkened beneath with private tears and lost sleep.

"Lady Rosalind, please," I said, "if you will stay a night or two . . . rest from your journey. You have family, surely, to return to?"

I was ill-prepared for the cutting glare she cast upon me, so quickly did her façade change.

"I have been widowed these two years, you may recall."

I glanced away to escape the inculpation in her words. But my eyes settled squarely on the row of arrows spread upon the table. No, no. She could not have known that it was my own hand that took her husband's life at Roxburgh. She could not.

"You have a daughter, I recall."

Again, a shadow passed over her face. "I do. She was with me at the Nunnery of Emmanuel—until recently."

I feared the worst, but asked anyway. "Where is she now?"

A muscle in her jaw twitched almost imperceptibly. "In England, with family. She is safer there."

"Then if you will not accept my hospitality, good lady," I said, "allow me to provide an escort. I shall ride with you myself back to Linlithgow. Or to the border, if you prefer."

Something of a laugh bubbled from her mouth. Just as sudden, her voice was steady and sure. "I see by my own eyes, Lord Douglas, you barely look fit to ride, let alone defend me, after your latest scuffle. Kindly, I decline. I hired a groom who has served me well enough. A fresh pair of mounts would do, however, if you can spare them for now."

"I'll have them brought out and saddled for you. But I beg, stay, eat with us, at least."

"I assure you, we are fine. We've a fair amount of day left to travel and shall leave anon for Berwick. My aunt there will take me in and so long as it's in English hands . . ." she paused noticeably in her speech, "I can reside safely there. Farewell, my lords."

I saw nothing but the swirl of her skirts and the flare of her mantle as she strode from the hall. At the table, Archibald was drawing the letters from the bag and opening them one by one. I left him alone with them.

Not an hour had passed before, while I sat in my study looking over household records, he came running in and slapped one of the letters down before me.

"James," he began, breathless from his sudden burst up the steep flight of stairs. "The Lady Rosalind . . ."

I leaned back on my creaking stool, waiting.

He brought his face close to mine. "Mother, in one of her letters . . . speaks of her. Lady Rosalind is the . . . was the daughter of . . ."

"Who?" She was English, but more than that I hadn't the slightest notion.

"The daughter of Sir Neville of Raby."

11

Robert the Bruce – Edinburgh, 1316

A N HEIR. A KINGDOM. Dreams turned to dust in my fingers as I
struggled to hold onto them.

Spring turned idly into summer. Summer faded to autumn, each
day's demise marked by sunsets of crimson. My memories of my daughter were as sharp as a newly whetted blade—which made them all the
more cutting to my soul. So many moments carved into my heart.
I prayed they would not fade with time—that I would never forget how
the sight of her filled me with such love and joy.

Just like her mother, Marjorie had brought a child into the world
and left before it could even gaze upon her face or know her touch.
While I should have found solace in her son's birth, it was hard . . . my
God, *so* hard to do, for now I had no legitimate children of my own.
None to watch grow, to teach the ways of the world, to one day take
my place.

Even before my grandson could sit himself upright, it was easy to
see the curve in his back. The way he strongly favored rolling to one
side. The crook in his neck. He would never be the soldier his forbears
had been. Robbie was bright and beyond loved, but I prayed that when
and if his time ever came to take the throne, there would be peace over

the land and that the rigorous tutoring I had planned out for him would prove of benefit.

Sadly, Marjorie and I had never completely reconciled after I happened upon her and James at Melrose Abbey as they exchanged fond gestures. There was bad blood between James and Walter now. A friendship past repair, the injury inflicted by my own obstinacy.

I often wondered if Walter would have taken any offense had I deemed to forego that long ago, hastily sworn oath to his father and allowed Marjorie to choose her heart. But oh, how meaningless to ponder on it. Marjorie's bones now lay beneath the earth and her soul, God willing, was far beyond the quarrels of a jilted suitor and her jealous husband.

Wedded bliss was far from being mine, as well. Eight years lost. Eight years longing for Elizabeth's return. Those first months alone, I had longed for my wife's gentle spirit, her lively talk, the fit of her small, supple back curled against my chest. Needed those simple things like I needed a soft place to lie down after a hard, body-bruising battle. But a life in the wilderness scrapping for existence has a way of eroding earthly desires and trifling sentimentalities. I had to learn to live day to day—without her.

Even though she had returned to me, I was more alone now than when she had been but a memory and a hope all those years. Why had she shunned me? Something had happened during our time apart. But what? Torture? She bore no scars. Besides, that was a tactic more akin to Longshanks than his feeble-willed offspring. Violated? Women do not speak of such things when they happen. It is a stain upon their virtue. A shame they bear inwardly. I seethed to think of it. If anyone had harmed her . . .

While I pondered it one day, I delayed all meetings and rode alone in the woods beyond Holyrood with a pair of my favorite hounds loping playfully behind. At the long fading rays of a late summer sunset, I returned to the palace and took dinner in my chambers, again alone.

Afterwards, I sent a message to Elizabeth that I wished to meet with her within the hour. How odd that I had to announce to my own wife that I was going to make the short journey down a single flight of stairs to speak with her.

I laid my hand upon the latch of her door, pressed on the blackened iron and was surprised to feel it give. When I opened the door, Elizabeth was sitting on a stool in the middle of the room, her spine as rigid as a spear haft, half a dozen maids scattered around her, laying out her nightclothes with ritualistic precision.

A younger, freckle-faced lass with nimble fingers untwisted the plaits of Elizabeth's shining auburn hair as it tumbled to her waist and lifted a bone comb to it. In form, my queen was still among the most beautiful in all Scotland, but the blitheness had long since vanished, making her more like some fragile trinket to be guarded from breaking than a woman of flesh and spirit to be desired and embraced.

Elizabeth raised her eyes briefly. "Good even, my lord."

Mortal enemies had delivered warmer welcomes.

"And to you," I returned. The women bowed as they went about their work, but they kept a watchful eye on me and yielded no ground as I drew closer. Patiently I waited, as the lass kneeling upon the floor deftly pulled the comb through Elizabeth's abundant tresses. Every lock glimmered radiantly and I imagined it smelling of sweet woodruff. I stayed the girl's hand with my own, took the comb from her and laid it aside. In my other hand I clutched a small, plain box hewn from a walnut tree with the letter 'E' carved on its lid. Leaning over, I whispered into Elizabeth's ear. "Tell them to go."

"I've need of them."

"And I a word with you. Tell them to go. You'll call on them later."

She turned her head in my direction, but did not look at me. "An hour then?"

I sighed. Glances passed between her women.

"Go. All of you," I told them myself. They hesitated, looked to my wife. She dropped her chin in abject compliance. I chased them away with a commanding glare, but the oldest, the woman named Gruoch, who had been there at Melrose nursing her back to health and who still accompanied my wife to chapel several times daily to pray, lingered, re-arranging the sleeves of Elizabeth's night robe where it lay draped across the bed.

Gruoch tossed back her gray head, leered at me sternly, and shuf-fled toward the door, pausing when she reached it. "Shall I wait without, my lady?"

"Go on, Gruoch," I urged. "All will be well until morning."

Elizabeth's breath caught with a sharpness that pricked my heart. Gruoch grasped the doorframe with gnarled fingers.

"Away, before I toss you out."

As Gruoch lumbered away, Elizabeth's lips twitched like a bitch guarding her pup from a stranger. "Must you be so unkind?"

I closed the door softly, leaned upon it. "You prefer her company to mine? Am I truly such an ogre, Elizabeth? If my nearness so fright-ens you, tell me why. If I don't know how it is that I've offended you, how can I ever remedy it?" I turned to her. With all the ungainliness of an adolescent courting his first maiden, I thrust my gift at her.

Her chin still down, she rose from her stool, came and took the box from me. Flipping the lid open, she gazed expressionless at the set of ornate silver hairpins lying on a pillow of red silk, then snapped it shut. An obligatory word of thanks passed her lips as she placed the box inside the chest at the foot of her bed. From it, she took out a hand mirror. Several cracks marred its shining surface. She gazed at herself blankly. A frown pulled at the corners of her mouth. "I was ill when I returned. It took all my strength. Have you forgotten?"

"No, Elizabeth. I remember. I was there, holding your hand for hours as the candles spent themselves, recalling every fond memory we shared out loud, offering you water when I saw the first crack between your eyelids. I was there more than you remember. But that was over a year ago. In the past few months, I have seen you riding your palfrey over the moors in the gloaming, rising at dawn and walking the gardens with your women clustered about you, laughing cheerfully. You are well enough now, Elizabeth. In body, at least. But something, some blight is upon your heart."

She shielded her breast with a hand. "You see what is not there."

"Then why keep from me? Why the lock on your door? The silence?" Vexed, I strode to the bed and sat on its edge, sweeping her robe to the floor in an angry gesture. "What harm have I ever done you? Day after day you thrust me away. Turn from me. Avoid speaking to me. Fourteen years your husband in the eyes of God and man and I am treated as a stranger? Such cold cruelty is deserving of an explanation, don't you think?" I held my hand out to her, beckoning. "Will you not come and sit with me? Speak from your heart and let me speak mine. My dear God, Elizabeth, I ached for years when you were gone from me. I ache even more now not to be able to touch you."

She stared at my outstretched hand as if in repulsion. "Touch me? Then take me to your bed? Is that what you wished for all those years? To lie with me. Make a child. Create your legacy? Perhaps your own army of princes to do your battles for you in your old age?"

"Elizabeth, for God's sake." I rose, braved those few steps between us as though I were leaping across a deep ravine, and lightly touched her arm. "I love you. And aye, I want those things, but not merely for the sake of an heir. I loved you long before that was ever a thing to be thought upon."

She clutched the mirror to her breast. "And now? Can you say you love me now? I am growing old, Robert—my hair thinning, the circles growing dark beneath my eyes. Look. See how the skin sags here?" She pinched a small pocket of flesh beneath her jaw.

"Come now. Self-pity is a sin in one whose beauty is known afar. You hardly look the part of Methuselah, I do swear. As for years slipping away—well, they have not escaped me, in case your eyes have not uncovered that blinding truth. And you, you were a flower in the bud when I met you. The bloom is yet there." My hand fell from her arm. I pulled at the roots of my hair as I circled the room.

Why in the name of Heaven must Our Maker fashion women to be so bloody complicated?

I halted in my tracks. "Very well, if this is to be a parley of truth, then hear. I loved who you were, once. I thought when you came back, you would be every bit the same. It didn't take but a day to understand that the years we have lived through have changed both of us. Both for better and for worse. And I believed somewhere, somehow, I would find a part of you I used to know. That one day or night, we would hold each other and rediscover it. A man and a woman, yearning to be close. Husband and wife, united by the Church and blessed to—"

"Blessed? No." Her eyes dampened. She placed the mirror on top of the chest feebly, went to stand before the hearth and stared into the amber flames. "Can you not see that we have been cursed from the very start, Robert? Cursed, plainly. My father refused you. King Edward denied you my hand for years. And then we were flung apart for an eternity while you battled . . . and I withered. Even in the happy times, we were never *blessed*, Robert. God did not see fit to give us children. Perhaps I was never meant to have any."

"Then if that is so," I said, joining her on the other side of the hearth with only its dwindling warmth between us, "we'll bear that sorrow together. But don't let it destroy the joy we once had. Let it live again. Let me be near to you, Elizabeth. Tell me all that troubles you. Everything." I splayed my fingers upon the warm stones of the hearth, wanting, waiting for her to place her hand over mine. Instead, she stood apart, swallowing back tears, as if I could offer her no comfort. Damn her for putting up these walls.

"Everything," I whispered, going to her. On my fingertip, I caught the first trickle spilling from her eye. "I'll not leave you alone until you tell me. By God, I have scaled higher walls than this."

The tiny chin quivered. "You truly want to know?" She closed her eyes to dam back the tears. "Remember . . . at Tyndrum, that morning?"

"Aye, you gave James a letter. It was from his brother. What a jealous fool I was to think it might have been something else. How swiftly everything changed in the span of a few hours, didn't it? I thought we would all make it safely to Ireland. All of us."

"I was going to tell you something."

"Ah, aye. What was it then?"

Her eyes opened. "That I was with child."

Sorrow choked my throat and I swallowed, hunting for words of solace. "My God . . . I'm sorry. So sorry. I didn't . . ." But there had never been a child. Conceived, but not carried. Our child. Mine. "What happened?"

"I lost it—the child. At St. Duthac's. That is why we never made it to the Orkneys. The Earl of Atholl sought refuge for us there because I could not go on. I was suffering great pains. Couldn't eat or sleep to gain strength, nor walk or ride to go on. He carried me up the steps of the chapel and laid me before the shrine. There I bled a pool from between my legs, gripped with a pain more cruel than any I have ever known. Finally, I expelled a contorted, monstrous clot. A misshapen lump of flesh. A boy. That much you could tell. But I lost him. Like all the others. Oh, I never told you of those, Robert. I spared you. Never wished to put the pain on you when you had so much else to bear. I lost them all. Only, that one made it longer. But not long enough. He was months and months away from his time."

Her eyes never left mine. But there was no hint of eased pain, only a void, a distance, a placid acceptance of something I could not yet fathom.

"You see, it was never meant to be, Robert. God gave you one dream, a great one: a kingdom. But he kept the simplest of things from you: a child. While other men, men like your brother Edward, litter the world with their get but refuse to marry, you have a barren wife . . . and that is your curse. Me.

"There was a time when I thought you could keep me safe from all harm. Then I discovered it wasn't true. I had no one to protect me, no one to care for. No one but myself. All alone with nothing but my thoughts and my prayers. You—at least you had your freedom."

She had never said anything about losing any babes before. Never mentioned it in all those blissful years we shared together. Never gave up her merriment to darken a single of my days with her.

"Ask me again," she continued, pushing away from the hearth, less piteously and more harshly, "to lie with you and conceive your child when you have known the sorrow of carrying a babe inside you, only to have it die and nearly lose your own life in the process. I beg of you, if indeed you love me as you say, touch me not. Accept how things are, Robert. Spare me the pain, now that I have made it yours."

Once, aye, once I had loved her more than anything. Given up my dreams to be with her, my pride even, until I uncovered a way to have it all. Now, I did not know whether I pitied or resented her. Pitied her for the sorrow she had chosen to bear alone. Or resented that she had taken it upon herself to serve as a vessel for my progeny at the expense of her own health and life and kept this secret from me all that time. If there was any blessing in this divine irony, it was that I should cherish my grandson even more. Yet even that did not ease the twisting in my groin, knowing that my own wife shirked my nearness, recoiled at my touch, and blamed me for the sorrow abiding in her soul.

"You could," she began, "annul our union. Take another wife. One who can give you sons. I'd not hold it against you, Robert. I decided that long ago, during the years in England. I wanted to come back, if only to let you know and yet . . . once here, I could not say it. I should have, before now. Let me go."

I could only shake my head. But I could not look at her.

"Then please yourself as you will. Have whatever woman you want. Don't even bother to think of me. I'm sure you forgot about me a time or two while I was gone."

Words more wounding than any sword blow ever struck. Because they were true.

Vaguely, I was aware of Elizabeth leaving me, the door standing open, the fire slowly dying . . . the rustle of someone standing in the doorway, the sound of my name.

"Robert? Uncle? Are you well?"

My eyes straining, I squinted into the half-light. "Thomas? What are you doing back here? Bloody far from Ireland, aren't you? I don't know whether to embrace you or shield my heart ere you speak."

Thomas Randolph stepped into the room, looking gauchely about, as if he did not belong there. "Your pardon, Uncle. Fresh from Ulster. With news."

I cleared my throat. "Go on. No one else here. My brother Edward?"

His hair was tousled from the wind, his cheeks striped with the sun. "Lives yet. Took Carrickfergus and is ready for you to join him with ample forces to take the rest of Ireland. And, as he so puts it, to accept with your aid what he has so long deserved: his own crown. Seems he believes you owe him for doing what the rest of us consider our duty."

"Arrogant bastard hasn't changed."

"Coming then?"

I plucked up Elizabeth's robe from the floor and tossed it on her bed. "Aye. Nothing here to hold me."

Carrick, 1316

WALTER AND JAMES WERE to serve as regents in my stead. The proper documents were secured naming young Robbie as my heir.

With several hundred fresh men and far better provisioned than we had ever been in those days of being hunted by the English, Randolph and I rode over the Lothian hills and across Carrick, passing near Loch Doon where my first love Aithne lived with her son Niall. I nearly called a short reprieve there before going on, but we were expected by Edward before the onset of winter. So on we rode, through the heart of wild Galloway to the shores of glittering Loch Ryan.

As we were boarding our galleys for the voyage, a messenger arrived. When he dismounted from his lathered horse, his steps lagged with sorrow. He bent his knee before me and bowed his head. Such an approach never bore out well.

"Sire, our beloved Robert Wishart, Bishop of Glasgow, left this earth peacefully in his sleep three days past at his home in Glasgow."

At my side, Randolph lowered his chin. "May the Lord bless and keep his soul."

"Scotland has lost a great champion . . ." I said, "and I an even greater friend. Without him, I would never even have taken the first step."

I thanked the messenger for his trouble and paid him handsomely in coin, for it is never an easy or welcome task to be the bearer of such news, even for the passing of an old man like Bishop Wishart, who late in life had endured two lengthy terms of imprisonment at English disfavor. Only his frock had spared him a traitor's fate upon the gallows. If I was glad for one thing, it was that he had come home to Scotland and died here, not in an English dungeon.

How hard it was to see Scotland's shoreline fade into the gray, spitting mist of the sea. Hard to receive the news of Bishop Wishart's death and know that one more friend was gone from me. Harder yet to leave my wife, who I had longed to be reunited with for so many wretched years, when in my heart I questioned where I had gone wrong and if all our troubles could be put right.

Always there was the ghost of the Elizabeth I had once loved body and soul, loved beyond life, loved her because she needed me, admired me, reveled in me and I in her. I left home, not so much because

Edward needed me, but because I did not know what to do or say or how to act around Elizabeth. When she had needed me to keep her safe, I had failed.

But there were no answers to be found in Carrickfergus. No lightning of revelation. Nothing but a troubled sea and gloomy sky and long-reaching swells of dun-colored earth and a thousand starving soldiers to pass the winter with.

Edward, as ever, was unbearable.

12

Robert the Bruce – Carrickfergus, Ireland, 1317

M Y BROTHER EDWARD: HIGH King of Ireland. A precarious and provocative title. As empty in meaning as it was within the hollow of its silver circle. But it pleased his head. Too well, I daresay.

Like the high-hearted fool I was, I offered to fight with him to establish his foothold there. Naturally, he took this as a submission on my part that I would be fighting *for* him. I held my tongue, if only to finish the task. Meanwhile, King Edward of England was embroiled in his own battles at home and could ill afford to follow us over the Irish Sea. The time, although never good, was never better.

Randolph and I arrived in Carrickfergus in Ulster late in the fall of that year. Edward was in good spirits, although he had sparing little to show for his endeavors thus far. He derived his sustenance from debauchery rather than food. While his men quarreled over a shoulder width's space at the campfire to warm their rag-wrapped fingers and were rationed out food that came intermittently by ship, since nearby farms had been stripped clean already, Edward reveled in his self-created glory. He drowned himself in it while looking for his true self at the bottom of a barrel of ale.

There was a time when he had lived as I did with the conviction that freedom was all—a time when he had bedded down on the bare ground with the very men who fought under his command and drank from streams cold with melted snow as he knelt beside battle-bruised soldiers and rallied them with words of encouragement. Now, I had arrived in this smoky, overcrowded hall which reeked of vomit, urine and unwashed bodies to witness him hurling insults at those who served him. Instead of brewing stratagem and weaving alliances, he rolled in drunkenness and bedded wenches young enough to have been his daughters.

The brother I once knew had been impetuous, grating, crude, but loyal and driven, however flawed. The Edward Bruce who received me at Carrickfergus barely raised his head to acknowledge me above his heaped trencher. He had become slovenly, irrational, and was clearly suffering from some strain of melancholy. Drink and hoarded food had increased his girth. Through the fog of ale that must have clouded his head, I believe it took him a few moments to recognize me. He raised a ragged eyebrow, scratched at a bristly chin, curled his lip in disgust and mumbled at me to join him.

Our relationship deteriorated further in the passing months as autumn gave over to winter. At my brother's beseeching, I had come well in advance of to plan out the campaign; instead, I spent my days with Randolph exploring ways of bypassing Edward's illogical stream of orders. If not for my nephew, I would have been driven to a fit of insanity and thrown myself from the sea cliffs.

I negotiated with Irish chieftains, mostly to no good end, and practiced tolerance while Edward's hotheaded barbs and reckless ways frayed at my wits. The only reprieve came when he slept from noon until midnight

Day after day, night after night, it rained. In my bed, I lay awake, tossing and turning, while raindrops lashed at the windows and hammered upon the roof. A trail of water flowed around the frame of the glazed window of my bedchamber, trickled down the lower portion of the plastered wall, and gathered in a pool in the nearest corner, slowly seeping between the planks to dampen the room below.

A chant arose in the great hall. Fists beat in unison on the tables. A primeval rhythm pulsed through the posts of my bed. The beating grew and grew until it collided in a great rumble. A roar. A crash. Wood splintering. Then, a big cheer and tumbles of laughter broken by guttural protests. Another evening of drunken oblivion. Another brawl.

I relinquished any illusions of sleep and got up from my bed, pulled on my leggings and boots and plucked up a wrinkled shirt. I tugged the shirt over my head as I went out my door, forgetting to duck the low lintel and nearly knocking myself senseless. I rubbed at my head as the pain faded to a dull throb, feeling a lump there, and descended the dark and narrow stairs until a yellow glow and the stink of smoke told me the hall was not far.

I trailed my hand along the corridor wall until I came to an all-too-familiar sight: Edward's companions scooping the battered loser off the floor and hauling him away to a bed somewhere to regain consciousness. A pair of grizzled hounds snarled at each other over a half-eaten chicken leg as I stepped around them. The smaller of the two went for the prize, only to find herself taken to the floor in a gnashing of white fangs. She yelped, then scurried off with her tail tucked up under her gaunt belly. The bigger dog nestled down with his paws on either side of the bone, growling as he devoured it with powerful jaws.

"And what was that one about?" I stumbled to the bench across from where Edward was draped over the table. Smoke stung at my eyes. "A woman? The last tankard of ale?"

"Fool knocked a chicken leg on the floor. Not his." Edward propped himself up on his elbows, spit over his shoulder. The drink had slurred his speech and reddened his eyes. "Was the damn Irishman that started it . . . and lost. Someone blurted the name of his kinsman, Murrough, and—"

"Brian O'Brien, then?"

"Aye, the only. He'll have a screaming headache, come morning. God, I love these Irish. Don't you?" After a long belch, he took another drink. "You know, you missed my coronation? Rudeness and envy, brother. I was there at yours." He sulked into his tankard. Then a smile flashed across his face, his eyes alight. "But what an occasion it was! We were all terribly drunk that night. Half a dozen fights—good ones. A broken jaw. Two cracked skulls. Found a tooth in the bottom of my goblet. Never did figure out whose. A roaring good time. A sea of drink. Women to drown yourself in. Music and dancing for three whole days. No bloody parliaments or documents to sign or —"

"Hasty and furtive is what I hear of your crowning. Your celebration—ribald and licentious. Women were handed around for sampling like wine. Whatever blood feuds had been mended in the past year were promptly renewed over thoughtless words those few days."

"Phhh . . ." He flapped a hand at me dismissively. "You never did learn to enjoy yourself properly. Try it once before you die. You might find life is not so miserable after all."

Perhaps I gambled that he was too drunk to engage in a fist fight, but I could not help saying what I thought. "Your beginning does not bode well for your future, Edward. If you insist on digging your own grave, then you can either lie down in it or climb out of it yourself. I'll not offer a hand. I intend to leave within the week, strike fast and hard toward Dublin. Come with me. If we win that, you'll have the upper hand."

He smacked his palm to his forehead. "Sweet Savior, but you're brilliant, Robert! A veritable genius. A god bumping elbows with mankind. If it would humor you—punish me not too harshly for my mortal flaws, if but to have one more churl to worship the clover crushed by your feet."

He snagged a passing servant girl with curling locks of gold down to the curve of her back, and yanked her into his lap. Grasping her just above the hips, he rocked her buttocks hard against his groin and whispered suggestively into her ear in garbled Gaelic. Cradling an extended belly, she grinned rompishly. Judging by the size of her, she was only a month or two from giving birth to yet another of Edward's bastards.

Edward chuckled, licked his lips and buried a hungry, wet kiss just above one of her breasts. He nestled his whiskered cheek against her bosom and in a little boy's voice pleaded, "Sorcha, my Sorcha. Tonight, again?"

She stroked her belly, looking down at it with concern, and shook her head.

"Pleeease?" His mouth sank in a boyish frown.

She melted at his plea, blushed crimson, nodded.

Then he gave her a swift smack on the rump and sent her for more ale. "I'd let you try her, Robert . . . Bloody Christ, she can do things to make your head top the clouds, but she's sworn herself to me." He flourished his hands in the air before him. "All along I've imagined rose petals strewn before me, casks of ale by the cartload and Irish princesses dancing half-naked around my bed. You've dampened my spirits. Is that why you came?"

My nephew Colin Campbell, whom I'd allowed along to appease my faithful brother-in-law Neil, stumbled across the floor, caught himself on a table edge, then slumped to the floor as he slurred a bawdy tavern song. Despite the fall, he managed to save most of the drink in his cup and finished it off when he came to a part of the song he couldn't remember. Colin was seventeen. Hardly able to hold his drink, let alone a sword.

"Sir Roger Mortimer and my own former brother-in-law, the Earl of Ulster, will give you a thrashing at the very first opportunity. I caution you, Edward. Your first mistake against the Irish may likely be your last."

"Is that your wish, or can you truly see into the future? Tell then, will that wife of yours, delicate as a broom moth, ever squeeze a puny, royal brat out of her tight cunt—or does she yet chase you from her bed? How many bars are on her door? Might as well have left her to rot in soggy, damn England. No secret I can get a woman willingly plowed in an hour and sown within a fortnight. That threw you into fits a dozen or more times, did it not? How often did you harangue me for that? I used to think you the world's biggest prude. Now I know it was mere jealousy that rankled you. Sorcha—you saw how proudly she waddles around here. Married twice before I came. I killed her second husband when he and a band of idiotic locals protested us taking our share of the harvest. Said she was glad I did it. He used to beat her when the goat had no milk or the hens didn't lay eggs. But I *please* her, she says. I can please any woman. Please them into blessed oblivion, I can."

He laughed raucously and the false confidence bestowed by ale made his voice grow louder with each passing sentence. "Why, I should send out letters to all the kings of Christendom and barter for the best offer. The King of Ireland seeks a bride—send your virgins to me! Send the one with the fattest dowry and the biggest army. I don't care if she looks like a cow and smells like a pig. I'll do her in the dark often enough to have her drop a litter of boys for me. Better yet . . . mayhap I should write to Aithne tomorrow and make an honest woman of her? Ah, God! Brilliant! Niall could be the first of many sons for me. He's old enough to fight. Old enough to take my place should the most unfortunate of all things happen: my demise. Then whose son would it be sitting upon the throne of dear Scotland? Whose, Robert? Would that make you flip over in your grave? Or would you simply not care what I did here on Earth once you are seated at the right hand of Christ Jesus Almighty at the Feast of Heaven?"

He was achieving nothing now but his own sick amusement. I doubted Aithne would have him in his current state. And I might have told him Niall's true patronage if not for the fact that Edward probably would have called me a liar and drawn a knife on me.

"Friday. We leave then, Edward." Wearied of his jabs, I rose to take my leave. "One thing, brother." I planted my fists and leaned across the table. "Should your men think for one moment that we are not in this together . . . well, then, why should any of them, Scots or Irish, join with us? Learn to bite your tongue and I'll keep mine. I came to help you. Let me. If we destroy the English hold on Ireland, it's one less front from which they can come at us."

He wagged his head from side to side and dipped his fingers into his cup, then sucked them clean. "Lovely advice. I'll take it to the core of my heart and live every day by it. Now off with you. To bed, lad. We're equals now as I see it. Reckon that."

I reckon it will be a miracle, Edward, should the Irish let you live out the year. Whatever there once was in you that might have been redeemable—you've none of it now. I could offer you advice from now until the Second Coming, but you would never take it because it came from me.

I would hate you if I did not pity you so much. I'm here to save you from yourself. But that may be beyond me. Far beyond.

Dublin, 1317

SNOW CLOGGED THE SKY as we set out from Carrickfergus. The cold and mud shot us through with misery, from our filthy boots to our wet heads and down to the very marrow of our bones.

On the march south our first day, Edward, riding in the vanguard, forged anxiously ahead. At the tail of our column were the womenfolk, some of them honest wives, others favored whores; all of them doubled as laundresses, cooks and menders of clothing. Nearly all of them went on foot, some with blackened feet covered in naught but rags. A few carried suckling infants at their hip. The stronger ones took turns dragging rickety carts with wobbling wheels through the mire and over rocky roads.

I saw Edward's Sorcha in the rabble, at first walking amidst the others, but as her feet swelled and her back pained her, they gave her a place on one of the few oxen-drawn carts piled up with pots and a few sacks of grain. She leaned back on the sacks, clutching her belly and gazing up at the baleful slate sky. Her time was drawing close. Eventually, a wife of one of my knights took pity on her and lent her a palfrey with a smoother ride.

The morning we left, Sorcha had screamed and clawed at Edward, even as he shoved her away and venomously ordered her to stay behind. He had found a new bedfellow, it seemed. One with eyes as green as jewels, hair the color of ripened grain, and a belly flat as a board. His new woman was more worldly, well born, and more of a challenge to him. When she denied him, he simply pursued her that much harder. Sorcha, sensing the distance between her and Edward, only fought to remain closer to him.

Whatever it was that made all ilk of women grow weak at the knees and swoon with devotion for my brother was a mystery to me. For certes, the world was full of desperate women.

A gap yawned between our divisions and I grew uneasy about the safety of the womenfolk. In an area where the enemy lurked at every bend, stragglers invited danger. Stands of woods closed in on either side of the road around us, blocking our view of the road beyond. I sent word ahead for Edward to await us at the next line of hills. There, he was to gather wood and build fires for the night.

Colin rode beside me, both excited and apprehensive in the questions he posed. There was a lull in our talk and my sights drifted away, watchful of the distance.

A light veil of snow was falling. Edward's division was long out of sight. It was but a few minutes later when I noticed the flicker of an archer's bow at the edge of a grove to the west.

I ordered my men into formation, but frenzy had already taken hold of a few impulsive fools. Colin, following them, broke loose and rode toward the enemy. I shouted at my men to hold their ground and took off after Colin.

As he caught sight of the first arrow cutting overhead, he halted. A wild aim, the arrow plunged into the snow-dusted grass thirty feet to his left. The second hail came in the next breath and pierced the heart of the man directly in front of Colin. The soldier flew backward and slammed into the snow in a bloody splatter. Colin wheeled around. I pummeled him hard in the shoulder as he lunged past.

Colin gave me a wide-eyed look of panic as he regained his seat.

"Fool! Back!" I shouted.

Randolph had ordered the men into tight circles. A horn-blast went up, alerting Edward to our predicament, but the distance that had lapsed between us was considerable, a mile or more. In minutes, Irish and English—eight to ten of them for every single Scot—were swarming over the white-cloaked hills and pouring from the edge of nearby woods on either side of us.

A moment of hopelessness filled me, like the absolute darkness that falls when the moon moves across the sun.

Curse Edward's haste. If I live to tell of this . . . If I live, aye. That bastard brother of mine will pay the price.

Wrath—and desperation—vanquished my fears. Colin and I returned to the others in the barest breadth of time. I placed myself at the front of our formation, raised my blade up in line with the prickling fringe of spears and roared my challenge to the Earl of Ulster, whose banner I could now make out.

"Red Earl! You partner with the English against your own kin? If spilling your own blood matters not, then have us. God will judge in the end. Come then. We await!"

The Earl of Ulster did not reply. Twenty years had gone since we laid his sister, my Isabella, in the ground. He had never liked me before that. Cared for me even less afterwards. Even though decades had passed and the distance between us now was so great I could not discern a face, I knew him. The short red mantle falling casually from his shoulders. The bright green cloth swathed across his chest. Most of all, by the English nobles at his side. Then by the thrust of his sword into the white sky.

They charged. Hooves churning. Weapons poised. A wet sheet of snow slickened the ground, hindering them. Men stumbled in the mire and were crushed by those from behind. Their horses, though, were sure-footed ponies like our own and they came straight on. I saw their Irish mouths open in screams of battle, their hair flying wild behind them, but I heard them not as I shouted words of encouragement and instructions to my own men.

Randolph's clear, steady voice rang above the roar. Beside me, Colin trembled, gripped his shield and closed his eyes. Snowflakes settled on his long red lashes and glistened like shed tears.

I nudged his leg with my boot. "When you see their eyes, you'll know who's marked you. With these odds, it will be more than one. Watch their eyes, lad. All you have to do is outlast them, aye, Colin? Then you can go home to your father and boast of it. When Edward gets here, we'll have the advantage."

He nodded feebly, staring at the oncoming horde through his own fog of breath. A trickle of spit froze on his beardless chin. Snot ran freely over his upper lip.

I had developed a gift for lying when it would give my men faith. Only, it wasn't lying, but rather telling them what they needed and wanted to hear. In this instance, I wasn't even sure Edward would get to us in time. Or when he did, if it would even prove to be enough.

Their first wave crashed against our tight lines in staggered buffets. Impatient to end us, they had not held together in their charge. Our spears stayed firm and repulsed their riders with a furious tumult of unhorsed knights. The chaos bought us precious time. Whenever one of our men was injured, another, fresher man took his place.

A small gap tore in our outer line and I redirected them to pull back and close up. The Irish and English had by then completely encircled us. I deflected a hurled spear with my shield, but the jolt stunned me. My left arm stung from wrist to collarbone. As I waited to regain feeling, I glanced between my shield and shoulder at the road south. There, in the blurry distance, Edward's column flew through the mud and snow.

My God, what took him so bloody long?

I lowered my shield a hair more to look around our wavering circle. There were more gaps. Men down. Row upon row of the enemy crushing inward. Terrible, loud, relentless. A chaos of Irish plaids and painted faces. By far, these were not Edward of England's best trained knights, but they were a fiercer sort—the kind that embraced death as glory, not nobles seeking to preserve themselves for titles and ransom, but men-wolves frenzied by the smell of blood.

We could not outlast them. Strong as we were, they were just too many.

Thwack!

A rock, hurled from a sling, struck my forehead just above my temple. The sudden blast of pain blinded me. I blinked and blinked, yet could see nothing but black. My horse heaved like a roiling sea beneath me. My sword fell. I gripped the edge of my saddle with what strength I could summon.

Blood pulsed, cold and oozing, from my wound. It seeped into the corner of my eye, stinging. Around me rang the sounds of metal on metal, men grunting with strain, the curdling cry of the wounded, horses stomping.

I held on, clamped my knees to my horse's ribs, reminded myself to breathe and wait for the blinding wave to pass. The black cloud began to lighten to gray. A spot of light appeared. Two fuzzy shapes wavered on the ground below me, uttered my name. Their outlines sharpened until I could see the hints of rust in the links of their mail shirts.

I heard my name again, more clearly. A hand touched my leg and then went around my arm. Randolph and Colin reached up, pulled me to the ground.

"Edward's come," Randolph said between grunts. "They're retreating."

"What?" I swooned and fought to keep my legs beneath me as the blood drained from my head. A loose circle of men held their ground around us, weapons gripped, but no longer warding off blows. I could still hear the ring of metal, oaths, curses, but fading away now.

Colin steadied my horse with a light hand upon its halter.

"Seems the Irish wouldn't follow the orders of the English noblemen," Randolph said. "The Earl of Ulster was wise enough to call them away before it all fell apart." He removed a glove and very methodically began to dab at my head wound with his cloak, taking care not to pull at the flap of skin that had been loosed by the sharp edge of the stone. "Another inch and you'd be less one eye. Does it hurt much?"

"Had worse," I lied between gritted teeth. More serious wounds, perhaps, but I could scarce remember a pain more intense. It hurt like flaming hell. The stone had slashed deeply, down to the bone. I pressed my fingers to the wound. "Where's Edward now?"

Randolph took a few steps away, said a word to another knight surveying the scene still from horseback, and returned. "Chasing them off. He'll be soaking up the glory over a fire tonight."

How like him. Never owning the blame. Always holding up the rare moments when he had made himself of use.

RANDOLPH GAVE ME ALE. I drank until I was numb from it. Just as I was about to take the last gulp, he snatched it away, made me lie back and told me to close my eyes. I had almost forgotten the pain when he doused the open wound with the fiery drink. I yelped. Then he called on two men to settle me and went to work with a needle and thread, stitching up my head. I winced at every jab.

"Make quick of it, Thomas. I've aged a few and—Ow! Bloody

Christ! Careful."

"Sorry, Uncle. Still now. Best if you don't talk anymore until I'm done."

I obliged as best I could, but a few cross words left my mouth as he fumbled with the needle. Finally, he inspected his work in the pale firelight and, satisfied it would close up well enough, handed off the needle and thread.

"Try not to touch it." Randolph pressed his fingers to the side of my face, tilted it back and looked more closely. "See that it's cleansed twice a day so no infection sets in."

I ignored his commands and let my fingertips wander along the ridges of the lumpy, fresh scar, cross-crossed with its blood-stiff threads. "How the hell am I supposed to get my helmet on?"

"Don't touch it, I said."

"No more than I need to. It hurts to talk, even. Where did you learn to do that?"

"Gil. I've watched him many times. He can hew an arm off the enemy in one swipe and yet with just a few gentle whips of the needle close up a murderous wound. He sewed me up a few. We could have used a good man like him today."

"Aye, and Boyd. Neil. James." I sighed, recalling old times when none of us would have abandoned the other. "Damn it. Where is Edward?"

"You've a foul mouth this evening."

"In a foul mood. Now where is the bastard?"

Randolph twisted his mouth up and pointed in one direction of our camp where the largest fire blazed and the talk was loud. I got to my feet, waited for the blood to return to my head and went to seek out Edward. He'd done everything to avoid me in the time between his return from pursuing the enemy and now. Naturally, he was in good spirits. Nary a care in the world or a sliver of penance in his heart.

I ambled into his circle of revelers. Colin, who had developed an unfortunate habit of imitating whoever caught his attention at the moment—in this case a sottish Edward—lowered his drink and ogled my wound.

"Five dead," I said. "Duncan Graham lost an arm clear up to his elbow. Another twenty wounded."

"That all?" Edward remarked with a lighthearted laugh. He poked a stick at the fire and stirred up sparks. "Fortunate it wasn't much more. Twenty to one before I got there. Lucky for you I didn't leave you to wallow in the mud. I could have been halfway to Dublin already."

I raised both hands out to the fire. "Shouldn't have been any dead, Edward. And you should never have gone on so far ahead."

"Then drive your men to keep a better pace. The longer it takes us to reach Dublin, the more warning they have."

"They already know we'll be there eventually. Only a matter of when. The women need protection and I'll not beat my men—"

"What? *Your* men?" he interjected.

I raised my voice, aware of my chastising tone. "Aye, my men. I'll not beat them on through this mud and squalor to sicken and go lame, or leave the womenfolk to the wolves for the sake of saving a day or two. Then again, why do I argue with you?"

The cauldron was boiling over. Edward rose from the sack of provisions he was using as a throne, came at me and delivered a restrained punch to my chest. "I knew when I asked you to come, brother, that you would forget whose kingdom this is. Well, I'll tell you. This is *my* land."

He punched me again, squarely in the breastbone. "*My* kingdom." Another punch, and another, thrusting me back with each blow. "*My* campaign. If you can't resign yourself to that then go the hell home. Better yet, just go *straight* to hell."

I held my ground at first, wanting badly to rain fists upon his muddled head, but our arguments had never been fruitful. Instead I took a few steps back, let him think a few moments, and calmly said, "Would you truly want that, Edward? Not half of these men are in your service. If I leave, if I say it, the rest go with me."

"Is that a threat?"

"I never threaten, Edward. That was a promise."

A sea of faces pressed in, watching, listening. Had we been any two other men, they would have been roused to hoots and insults by now, taking sides, wagering on a fight. Although curious, they were apprehensive, divided—more on my side than Edward's, I would have imagined. Randolph's flaxen hair caught my sight and I saw in his clear eyes words of warning. He wove his way through the throng and hooked a hand under my arm.

Randolph whispered into my ear, "Make peace, Uncle. I beg. He'd sooner wage war with you than bow to you now. Let's finish what we came to do and be done with him. Please."

Aye, pride is everything for Edward Bruce. To bloody hell and back with brotherly love.

But pushing down my own pride was like swallowing a shard of glass. I nodded and moved back toward my brother, my chin hung low in feigned abeyance. "I'll remain. And my men. If you'll accept my humble apology, Edward . . . and my service." Cautiously, I held my hand out in truce.

Edward stormed at me and slapped my hand away. His eyes glared with the heat of a branding iron. "Your apology stinks as much as the hand you wipe your ass with. Keep it to yourself. But you'll fight for me, by God, Robert . . . because you're good for that and you made a promise to do it."

Every fiber in me struggled to stay in control. "You're right—I did. I . . . I should not have threatened you. My temper is my master, at times." At that point, I thought I couldn't lower myself much further. To roll belly up before Edward was to risk being gutted alive. But anger and threats had gotten me nothing but more trouble from him.

Randolph was right. I should finish this. Go home. Edward was the stone and I a drowning man.

I bowed my head to Edward and marched away from the edge of camp. The stars cowered behind clouds of ice. Beyond the circle of the campfire glow, the world lay dark and dangerous. I walked further and further until the drunken laughter and bloated tales of battle shattered on the brittle air like icicles falling.

Although drawn to the stand of woods far beyond the camp, I stopped at the base of an ancient tree that stood alone on the plain, realizing the danger of venturing into the forest. I sank down there, clasped my knees and tried to think. But all I could do was fight with my own anger and curse my own poor judgment.

Footsteps landed softly upon the crisp, winter-dead grass. A shadow, a black figure floating in a field of gray, strode low and swift across the open ground. As I listened for the stranger's coming, gauged his position and distance, with smooth slowness I drew my blade from its scabbard. I slipped behind the tree and waited.

The figure stumbled forth, panting. I leapt out and rammed my sword point at a heaving chest, stopping just inches from plunging it through bone and lung.

"Mother of—!" I shouted. "Did you wish to die tonight, Thomas? What were you thinking, sneaking up on me like that?"

Randolph gulped, then pushed the blade away with his fingertips. "What was I thinking? I was wondering what *you* were doing. I certainly wasn't going to let you just wander off without a word and walk straight into Irish hands."

Relieved, I sheathed my sword and plopped down on the cold ground, exhausted in both body and spirit.

"I'm not sure that was the right thing to do, giving in to Edward like that," I lamented. "I've never done that before. Never thought I would. Don't even know why I did it just now. But I had to make peace to salvage this campaign. What I fear, worst of all, Thomas, is that he might take sides with the King of England the moment I will no longer do his bidding."

"I don't think you need to fear that, Uncle. He's too proud for that. Edward Bruce will stand stripped naked alone in the world before he fights alongside the English."

"Once that would have been true." I plowed my hands through my hair, grimacing as I pulled at the tight, sore skin around my wound. "But anymore, I don't know him. And I certainly don't trust him. I pushed him here to get him out of my sight. All I did was sever the one thin strand left between us. He no longer cares about Scotland. Only about Edward, King of Ireland."

"Robert, Uncle..."—Randolph knelt before me, touching my knee lightly—"you cannot save Edward, because Edward . . ." He lowered his eyes and turned his head away.

I put my hand over his and clenched it. "I know. Edward seeks to destroy himself."

From camp, I heard again the stories and songs of the after-battle, rolling in waves of elation. Remembered better times. Good times, crouching in the forest next to Edward in the thin night of summertime, no sleep to be had. Falling upon the enemy at dawn. Watching foe after foe fall before his blade.

Edward—strong, handsome, brave to a fault—as he used to be.

As I had risen, he had fallen. My greatest mistake had been in loving him and wanting for him what he himself did not care to grasp.

13

<u>Robert the Bruce – Dublin, 1317</u>

A THICK, CHOKING SMOKE hovered above Dublin. I stood beside Edward and Randolph, our collective forces spread out over the crest of a hill, watching the black plumes billow from thatched roofs. Rather than allow foreigners to ransack outlying dwellings, the towns-folk of Dublin had set fire to them first. Bridges had been sawed away, toppled and torched. Crofts reduced to ashes. Livestock driven off or slaughtered and left to rot. The very same things we had done to the English for years.

"Shit upon them." Edward poked his sword point at the ripped innards of a spoiled cow carcass lying across the road. "This one could have fed a family for weeks and now what? Wasted for spite. In the midst of a famine, even. Imbeciles."

"Is there no way across the Liffey?" Randolph asked.

"Not without drowning half our men," I said. Across the river, Irish waved their arms and jeered at us, while around them flames leapt from one house to another. I turned my face east toward the sea and drew in air, but all I could smell was putrefying animal flesh and acrid smoke. "What now, Edward?"

Shrugging, he scratched behind his ear. "We could lay siege . . . but as you know, brother, I've not the patience to sit on my hands and wait for those worm-brained idiots to starve."

"Aye," I began, "it could just as well be us eating our own horses before they give in. Food is sparse. But no doubt they've been hoarding grain in anticipation of our arrival. Where do we go now?"

Edward raised his chin. "West, maybe? Or south? Let us seek the advice of O'Brien. He knows his own people."

I said nothing to that. O'Brien may have been Irish and yesterday he may have known what another of them was thinking or had said, but today was altogether different.

O'Brien was retrieved from his clansmen and brought forward. He stood in front of us wearing a smirk and with his fists planted firmly on his sword belt. A young man, but bold and desperate to lead, he had won the loyalty, if only for now, of those of his kinsman adamantly opposed to the English and any of their adherents.

"Munster," he announced in a jaunty tone, as if eager to lay low old archrivals. "I have word they'll rise in your favor when you go there. It will be the beginning of the whole army of Ireland flocking to your cause."

At that, Randolph and I exchanged dubious glances. The army of Ireland had not been one for centuries. If ever the Scots had trouble agreeing amongst themselves, the Irish were tenfold worse.

At Edward's insistence, we marched at once toward Limerick and found ourselves faced across the Shannon by Brian O'Brien's own kinsman, Murrough. They were not going to allow us to pass without a gory fight. Once again, we turned back—this time toward Ulster.

The journey was arduous. Sleet pelted us daily. When it was not raining ice, the north wind peeled the skin from our faces. Spring came late and even then barely. The land had been stripped clean as a bone and run roughshod many times over. The locals we chanced upon bore the ghostly look of starvation. Fights erupted daily, not only between Scots and Irish, but also among my own men.

Along the way, many of the Irish crept away in the night. My greatest fear was that they would join with the opposition and fall upon the very men they had fought beside: us. But such fears never came to pass. More than likely, they just went on home.

We lost dozens to sickness. Miles that might have taken us only days to travel instead took weeks. Our horses went lame, even the best of them, and we were forced to relieve many of their misery.

One late March morning, a pale sun broke above the river of mist that hung over the boglands of Tipperary. On either side of the road, the bog spread far and flat. Only here, where one could see to the horizon, could we escape trouble. We had been harried recently by a contingent of local peasants and although we had managed to fend them off without loss of life, some of our remaining supplies had been stolen. We barely had the resources to go on and yet we could not stay. Edward rode the length of the road, roaring threats to prod the bedraggled column along.

As we gathered our scarce belongings to begin on the road north, a cry rent the air. I bolted in the direction of its source. Amongst a small group of women, Sorcha lay curled sideways on the ground, holding her knees up toward her chest. She stifled another scream, splayed her legs apart and forced her energies into her belly, bearing down hard.

An older woman with sharp cheekbones and gray hair gazed at Sorcha, then at me. "The bairn comes. The king's bairn."

A crowd gathered around Sorcha. Edward bellowed for the throng to part before him, as if he were Moses himself expecting the Red Sea to divide at his very presence. Still on the back of his bony mount, Edward rolled his eyes and flipped the embroidered hem of his cloak over his shoulders.

He spat at the ground, barely missing the old woman. "Leave her behind with some of the women. The brat will come when it's ready. We've miles to cover and no friend in this territory."

"Which is why we shouldn't leave her like this." I knelt and took

Sorcha's hand, clammy with sweat. Between her gripping pains she looked up at me, smiled faintly and drew a deep breath as she waited for the next wave to push the baby downward through her pelvis.

A cloud passed over Edward's countenance. "Women bear children all the time, brother. It could take all bloody day. And we haven't got all day."

"Women do not bear *your* children every day, Edward—although it seems nearly so." I looked at him pointedly, but he gave no admittance to the fact that this woman, who had worshipped him enough to follow him to battle through the dead of winter, starving and footsore, loved him and was about to give birth to his own flesh and blood. "You owe her your protection. You owe the child a chance to live."

He snorted. "*That* is in God's hands."

Two of Sorcha's companions flanked her, clamping her elbows as they helped her into a squatting position. Her loins were but inches from the soggy ground, which reeked of decay and stagnant water. It was no place for the son of a king to enter the world.

"Fetch my furs and blankets," I said to some of the other women, "so that she might have her child in warmth and on a dry place. Not like this."

The old hag shuffled off. Gritting my teeth, I strode toward Edward. "I am tired of fighting with you, Edward. For weeks now I have yielded to you, kept my mouth closed, so that we could march as one. But it is here I draw the line. Here that I stand. Move on if you will. You'll not make it more than two leagues down the road before those who loathe you will fall upon you and scour the flesh from your bones. And with only half an army, you'll expose your backside just as you did when we first left Carrickfergus. Sorcha will have her child under the safeguarding of my men and once that child comes I will grant her escort sufficient for her to return home when she is able. Only then will I move my feet from this very earth."

His expression did not change. To go on with a depleted force was absolute suicide. His lips twisted in a scowl.

Sorcha screamed loud enough to topple the nearest mountain. One of her companions gripped her arm, urged her to focus her strength on her belly and squeeze. Sorcha gulped, stifled another scream and bore down. Another woman shoved forward and yanked Sorcha's skirts up past her belly.

Enthralled by the vulgar miracle taking place before me there on the boggy plains, I did not notice Edward leaving. Sorcha pushed and cried and pushed some more until finally, a small, purple bundle slid from between her milky thighs. The old woman took the child and wiped him clean with my bedding, then held him up so all could see his sex.

Blood spilled bright and red in a puddle at Sorcha's small feet as the women pulled the afterbirth free. Then she collapsed backward into the pile of furs that had been brought for her. The boy was placed on her bloated belly. With tears bright in her eyes, Sorcha traced a finger over his tiny nose and chin. He looked, I mused, more like a wrinkled old man than a newborn. When he paused in his crying and began to turn his groping, naked gums toward her, she unlaced and pulled down her gown, showing without humility a brown jutting nipple. She clenched her hand around her breast, sliding the teat into the infant's greedy mouth. Carefully then, to shield her new bairn from the wind, she arranged a borrowed, woolen cloak over him as the child suckled. Sorcha, although spent, wore a look of pure ecstasy, just as she must have when the child was created.

Edward was nowhere to be seen. He had called off the march evidently though, as the soldiers had sunk back down to their quivering haunches and were grumbling miserably over the void in their bellies and how much better it would all be when they got back to Carrickfergus. Better yet when they returned to Scotland.

Too sore in the loins to ride, Sorcha was given space on one of our last remaining carts. She would not stay behind, insisting on going on the very next day with us. Prideful, she kept her bairn in plain view of all. The wee lad paid no heed to the cold, seldom crying, for he was too busy guzzling his mother's milk in between naps. Edward, she called him. How unfortunate for the lad to be so cursed. I had not known a worthwhile Edward in all my days, least of all my brother. Not once did he acknowledge Sorcha or the child.

By the time we crawled, famished and raw-footed, into Carrickfergus, Sorcha was down with a fever. She did not live out her son's first month. Too ashamed of her, Sorcha's family did not claim her body for a proper burial, nor the child.

April rains were falling gently when she was laid into the ground in a common grave on a hillside outside the fortress. The first wildflowers of spring sprouted blue and pink over her grave. I found a mother in the nearest village, one of the O'Neil clan, who had recently lost a child to the rampant sickness abounding over the island. She gladly took Edward's son to her breast as if he were her own child. I made certain that she and her husband knew whose child it was that they were fostering and told her that when he was weaned I would send for him and have him brought up in Scotland. Even as I said that I knew they would not part with the little dark-eyed babe so readily. He would be loved by these strangers more than his own father ever would.

In May, Randolph and I took ship back home. With every mile that fell behind us over the horizon, separating me from my last remaining brother, I felt a burden lifting.

I would no longer come to Edward's aid. I would no more ask for his. In truth, if I never saw him again I would not suffer for the loss. So very little had been gained by this venture onto Irish soil. So many men lost along the way. Our losses had been as numerous as our victories. We had neither fallen to the forces of the English in Ireland, nor wiped them from there.

<u>Carrick, 1317</u>

THE HILLS OF CARRICK were in their flush when I returned to the land of my boyhood. I sent my soldiers home and dispatched Randolph to Edinburgh with word that I would be delayed while looking over my holdings in the southwest. Ever mindful of my safety, my nephew balked at leaving me with so small a retinue, but I ordered him on, mostly because I could not bear the accusations behind his every look. He knew where I would go.

Aithne greeted me at Loch Doon Castle with arms wide, a smile warm and inviting on her mouth, and a willing ear.

Her husband, Gilbert, had once relinquished the castle to the English and fled south, but before he could find refuge he died. I had never known much of him, except that he had beaten Aithne for her inability to bear him a child, telling her that God had cursed her for her sins. Marriages are often made out of convenience, but some are so devoid of kindness as to be cruel. In this instance, fate had served the hand of justice and released Aithne of her domestic imprisonment. Sometime after Bannockburn, I returned Loch Doon to her, so that she would have a home and the means to raise her son.

With unmistakable pride, Aithne showed me about her shrewdly managed estate. The dense pines and grassy hills surrounding the loch stirred melancholy sighs in me that did not go unobserved by my gracious hostess and first love. For two days, we walked through her budding orchards at forest's edge and rode past fields thick with cattle while I talked of all that had befallen me in the decade since we last met. And talk we did—from the breaking of fast to the verge of midnight. I spoke frankly about Elizabeth, her guarded secret, her rejection of me. Aithne listened astutely, held my hand when all was said, lent me words of comfort.

Then I asked to see Niall. She beckoned him from the loch where he was straining to pull up a net onto shore with one of the local fishermen. They had picked out their scanty catch and were unraveling the knots in the webbing of the net. As the lad came walking up the road toward the house, pulling a sweat-soaked linen shirt on over brown shoulders, I said to her, "You make him do that? Go out in a boat and bring back his supper?"

"Make him? No, not at all. He fancies the fisher's daughter. I've no doubt they've had a tumble or two when he sneaks off before dawn. You were the same at that age, as I recall."

"At sixteen is there anything else?"

The lad who bowed before me was no more a boy. As he raised his eyes, I imparted a few words of well wishes and venerable wisdom, all of which brought only a blinking stare interrupted by swift glances over his shoulder. The object of his affections was lingering next to an old, crumbling wall draped with rambling ivy. Obviously, she was curious as to why the King of Scots would come calling upon a country woman and her orphaned son, but the lass was also anxious with separation, twirling her black braided hair about her fingers. So I bid Niall to return to his work, at which he dashed breathlessly away, grabbing up his lass's hand and yanking her along the road toward the wood.

"I must ask," I said to Aithne, as we began walking, "does he know he's my son?"

Her chin sank. "No, I could not tell him. Not without your consent. Do you want me to?"

"He should know, but perhaps . . . I don't know. There is Elizabeth to think of. I have no wish to hurt her."

"What happened between us, Robert, it was long ago. Before Elizabeth." She hooked her arm through mine. "What does your heart say when you look at him?"

"That he is happy as he is."

"Then listen," she said enigmatically. "Your heart always speaks the truth, doesn't it?"

The late morning sun glinted silver off the dark waters of the loch.

There was an indescribable void within me. I needed more. Children of my own that I could call as such.

But sometimes, what we wish cannot be had. Not for all the hope or all the prayers of a lifetime.

"Aithne, I want you to bring Niall to Edinburgh. I'll set you both up in the court. Give him a fine education. And you, everything you want or need."

She stopped where it was safe from prying ears, rose on her tiptoes and pecked me on the cheek in endearment. "As the mother of your bastard? Thank you, truly, Robert, but I decline. It's not my fashion to be dependent. All we want or need is here. And you may come back whenever you wish. My door is always open to you—any time, for any reason."

An invitation that was sweetly tempting, had I not the future of a kingdom on my shoulders. Indeed, though, this would be a fine retreat when burdens and woes were too much to bear. And Aithne, I would have liked to believe all my life that she had loved me alone, but I knew it not to be true. If she could make me feel that way for a time, though . . .

I took her hand, kissed it cordially. "I think I will. But breathe not a word of it to Edward, aye?"

"Not a single word." She winked above a frolicsome smile. "You've something else to say, Robert? I know the look of an unspoken thought."

I let her hand slip from mine. "I should like to say a thousand things, but even now God frowns upon me for thinking them. If ever you or the lad need anything, anything at all . . . just say."

"As I said, we're well enough. Truly. Besides, if I took what you offered, the gossip would fly like crows over a field of ripened grain."

So it would, Aithne. Oft times, gossip is spun from a thread of truth.

FIVE DAYS I LINGERED in Carrick and never once did I come close to Turnberry or Lochmaben, where I had told Randolph I was headed. Instead, I dallied at Loch Doon, teaching Niall the intricacies of sailing and relaxing in Aithne's pleasant company.

Sunset had long come and gone. When we both first yawned at the supper table and left for our own beds, we talked the length of the corridor and up the stairs and were still talking at her doorway when she moved inside. Without a thought I followed her.

"If you could only see him for yourself, Aithne." I sipped from my goblet, then drained the cup in the next swallow. "My God, what a wreck he is. And plans of procuring allies in Ireland—shattered, destroyed. All because he could not restrain himself."

Aithne filled my cup again. "What did you expect, Robert? Truly now. That Edward would, by some convenient miracle, become a better man without you there beside him? Aye, he fought you. But is it possible that he reveled in that? Somehow needed to do that?"

"Please. He lives to annoy me."

"Ah, then you've known all this time and yet you chose to play along? If he could never quite be 'you', he could at least ply at the one imperfection in you that he could grab onto."

I gazed at her soft-edged face through candlelight. We were sitting across from each other in her spacious chamber, her bed on the far side by the hearth, a few benches scattered about, and between us a small round table. Even through the fog of wine, she was making entirely too much sense. My brother had learned how to master revealing to the world my weaker side—that of anger and intolerance. "True as it may be, I am not responsible for who he is, now or then. He picked his final battleground . . . and he'll go out, not in a blaze of glory, but sputtering like a candle that's been spit upon."

She sighed and shook her head. "He could never be like you, even when he tried."

"He *never* tried. Never." I reached out, took her hand. "Did he ever say that to you, though? That he wished to be like me?"

Beneath long, thick lashes, she gazed at me with a cutting sincerity. "Men say many things when they're flushed from lovemaking, don't they? Some of it true, some a dream. It is, for some, the one time they open their hearts. For Edward, that was so. All those women in his life—they all knew a different side of him than he showed to you. He was like a little boy when he was with a woman—vulnerable, sensitive, needing. All you know is the Edward who makes a hell of your life."

I said nothing to that. She did pity the wretch. And I pitied that she had been so duped by him. I had thought her wiser.

"Once, no . . . twice, you said that you loved me, Robert. And I, you. Why did we never marry then? What kept it from being?"

"Love alone is not enough. I seem to recall my father thought your family beneath mine." But I wondered—had she spoken words of love to Edward? I had known them to be together and it had filled me with jealousy. Yet why did I keep coming back to her? What was it that I wanted from her or could not do without? I thought to pull my hand away, but she had by then laid her other hand over mine, holding me prisoner. "What if Edward had asked to marry you? By the way you speak of him, it seems you would have considered it."

"What Edward and I had . . . it was nothing."

"Nothing? He came back to you time and again."

"As have you." She rose then and, facing away from me, said, "I thought about what you asked—about Niall and me coming with you to Edinburgh. I might consider it, if . . . if . . ."

If I said that I loved you now? Could I have said it just then, or ever, that I more needed than loved her? That I often wanted her? That somehow, in this odd way, we were good for one another? I had not lain with Elizabeth, or any woman, in so long a time . . .

We gazed upon each other that evening, Aithne and I, for a long while, sharing no more words. The warm spring breeze wafted around us from an open window, candle flames fluttering, the wine flowing endlessly. In time, as the drink filled our veins, we saw each other as young again, with no cares or duties or guilt to stand us down. The small lines at the corners of her mouth had faded and her eyes twinkled with the joy of the moment. I pulled my chair closer to hers, touched her cheek and leaned to her, the wine on my breath swirling with the wine on hers. Our lips came together, lightly, then full and hard.

My head was light. My will gone. The allure beckoned of spending myself within her and then falling into a deep and dreamless sleep against the curve of her back.

My eyelids drifted downward. I forced them open. Sadness began to drown me. Too much wine. Too little sleep. Was I sad for Sorcha's lost innocence? For Edward's cruel indifference? Sad for the child, growing up poor in a hut in Ireland? Or sad for myself—the king who could not have the one thing he truly wanted? Damn popes and English princes and all the rest of the world. If I never had their approval I wouldn't care. I only wanted a child to carry on my name. A child to share with Elizabeth. Sitting back, I pulled a hand over my face, as though I could erase what I had just done.

Aithne looked searchingly into my eyes. "Robert, what is it? Have I done . . . I assumed that you . . . wanted me? Don't you?"

I went to sit on the edge of her bed. The feathery mattress sank miles beneath my weight. "Edward had a woman who loved him, gave him a child and died for it. How could he not care?"

"Do you envy Edward?" She joined me, laying a hand lightly upon my thigh.

"Strangely, aye. As much as I hate him, he has had, a dozen times over, what I wish for—children of his own. Yet they mean nothing to him, except as trophies of his own virility."

She rested her head against my arm. "You need to go home, Robert. Home to her." Then, in a distinctly pained voice, she added, "You don't belong here. Not with me."

In my heart, I knew it, too. I brushed calloused fingertips over the softness of her cheek.

"Aithne, if you only knew the hole in my soul that you fill. If only you knew . . ." I rose, kissed her lightly on the crown of her head, and left, never looking back.

Edinburgh, 1317

WORD OF MY RETURN had preceded me. People gathered along the road to greet me, slowing my progress even more. The days of racing lightly armed through the hills and heather were long gone. A man of middle years, scarred, stiff in the joints and dusted with gray at the temples, I did not travel so fleet of foot any more. But as that black dome of Edinburgh reared up against a lead-colored sky misted with rain, my pace quickened in rhythm with my heart.

I found her the first place I went to: the rose garden outside Holyrood Palace. The flowers were still clenching their first buds. Elizabeth sat alone on a stone bench beneath the drooping branches of a willow tree, its slender tips gilded with dangling catkins. She wore a green kirtle a shade darker than her eyes. I inhaled the fresh scent of rain and paused before setting my feet on the flagstone path that led to the bench where she was with her back turned to me. I did not have to call out her name or pound the stones with my feet. She knew my presence and turned to look over her shoulder. In that moment, she was up and gliding toward me.

I wrapped my arms around her and held her tight without apology or restraint. The wound between us, which had been clawed open and salted, had already begun to heal during my absence.

"I won't leave you for so long again, my love. My heart needs mending as is." I kissed her lightly between her neck and shoulder. As I placed both hands on either side of her head to tilt back her face, my fingers brushed over the teeth of the hairpin I had given her before my leaving. "You do like it then? You did not say."

Her mouth curved in a smile. I reached to the hem of my cloak and groped for the tiny hole I had torn there. Then I drew out the old, tarnished hairpin of hers, rusted at the tips, that I had discovered over ten years ago and showed it to her.

"This," I proclaimed, "has been with me every day and every mile that we were ever apart. I found it after we spent the winter on Rathlin and were making our way back to Scotland."

"So small a thing." She grazed its jagged point with her fingertips. "Oh, Robert, can you even imagine how my world fell apart when I rode away from Dalry? For months I wondered if you were alive or dead. They wouldn't tell me anything. Not of you or of the war. Finally, I realized that as long as they kept me alive that you were succeeding. Eluding them. Winning, even." Her chin dipped. Her eyes wandered to a row of rose bushes. "And I hated that. I wanted you to submit, so that I could leave and go home. So we could be together then—you as my lover, my protector. I wanted it to be like it was before . . . when you were Longshanks' man. We were happy then. Instead of missing you more with each passing day, I only grew angrier. Yet you kept faith, even when you lost so much. I am unworthy of you, Robert, and selfish for wishing your failure."

You unworthy, Elizabeth? If you knew my heart, my sins, you would not say so.

The smile had vanished. I thought she might weep, but her eyes were dry and sincere. It was I who wept. I had not kept my faith. I had fallen, many times over.

She kissed me then. *She* . . . kissed me. With lips as moist as morning dew. And skin smelling of roses.

"You should have told me, my love," I said, pressing her to my chest and stroking her hair, "about the child. I didn't know. My God, I am selfish myself to ask anymore sacrifice of you."

"That's what Mary said of you."

"What did my sister say? When was this?" I leaned back a little, so that I could look upon Elizabeth's face, so fair after all these years, so much less drawn than mine.

"After I lost the babe at St. Duthac's. I cursed your absence, because I needed you more than ever then and I couldn't understand why you sent us away from you. I thought that if you had been with us, or we with you, that you would have protected us, kept us safe from the English, that I would not have lost the child. And Mary said to me that your greatest strength and your greatest flaw was that whomever or whatever you loved, you gave to them everything within your heart.

"Once, that was me. In time though, it became Scotland. I have both loved and detested you for that. But if I am second in your life to anything or anyone, then I shall play mistress to your kingdom. Perhaps there is a purpose in it after all and I should give myself to that, instead of dominating your attention like some jealous cow-eyed lass of fifteen."

"Blame yourself for nothing, my love," I said. "Perhaps I should pray for a bigger heart, so I have more of myself to give you."

Fine creases etched the corners of her mouth. Her cheeks were more gaunt than in years past, her lips thinner. Somehow though, that only made me love her more.

Hand in hand, we walked slowly through the garden before going inside, even though my clothes were damp and my stomach a cavern of emptiness. Putting aside talk of diplomacy and war and parliaments, I spoke with Elizabeth of the roses, her favorite hounds, of little Robbie, of the early years when I was that arrant knight and she the maiden I could not have.

In the days that followed, I sought her out as she walked in the gardens in the glimmering dew of early morning, before even the sparrows had stirred. Together we rode through the woods and meadows, taking in the intoxicating scents of wildflowers and watching the finches flit amongst high branches. Sometimes, we rode out on the moors with our hawks resting on our outstretched arms, not to hunt, but merely to watch them float free on the breeze, regal and keen.

The passions of youth are so quickly quenched. But a love that endures all only grows deeper with time.

14

James Douglas – Berwick, 1318

"DARE YOU TRUST AN Englishwoman, James?" Walter whispered into my ear as he bent over me. "I think you hazard too much in one stroke."

"And if we take Berwick?" I crouched in the thicket, listening for any slight sound that might rise above the murmur of the stream before us. "We've crawled too many miles to fall one inch short. Aye, it's a risk we take and men, Scottish men, may fall. Fear is something we all carry in our hearts, Walter. I fear to trust this woman. I fear the next foe I meet may be stronger and swifter than me. But fear lasts only a short while. Victory lasts forever."

"So does death," he said morosely.

For hours we watched from the densely wooded bank, waited in the damp, clinging mist, until at last a mysterious lady approached like some courier of the hereafter on her ash-gray palfrey with a nervous, slant-shouldered escort riding at her side.

The stream we hovered beside fed into the Tweed two miles away. The riders had come from the direction of its source: Berwick. The place of this clandestine meeting was hidden to any who did not already know it. The hour: precisely midnight. Exactly as penned in her letter to me.

She sat on her horse, immobile in the argent light of a half moon, thin wisps of fog drifting and curling around her. The hood of her gray cloak was pulled far forward, concealing her face in deep shadows.

Walter tapped my shoulder. "The man with her—"

"Is Peter Spalding," Boyd confirmed, squinting.

"How can you be sure?" Randolph, ever skeptical, folded his arms.

Boyd sank down to his haunches with a grunt, opened his flask and rinsed his mouth out with ale. "Fourteen years ago I was at his wedding. Married a Scottish woman from Dunbar where he did business sometimes. Took her back to Berwick. I doubt the English have been overly kind to either him or his wife. The world knows if you marry a Scot you become one."

I glanced at Walter, his eyes straining to search in the darkness. Reflexively, I reached over my left shoulder, searching for the quiver of arrows that I no longer kept there. I had never quite regained full strength in my one arm after the fight with Neville and so had given up the bow that had been an extension of me for so many years. I forced my hand down to my hip, touched the hilt of my sword for reassurance.

"Aye, by God's eyes," Boyd muttered as he stood again, feet planted wide, "that *is* him. Plain enough. And they came alone. Brave fools." He took another swig, dropped his empty flask, and pulled out his sword with a dangerous, silent strength.

"Put it away, Boyd. They come unarmed." I motioned for him to follow me on foot.

We skidded down the embankment, grasping at tufts of grass to steady our descent, then waded through the rushes crowding the stream's edge.

The lady stayed her companion with a flip of her hand. He clenched his reins nervously, as if weighing whether to stay by her and see this through or bolt and be gone.

I hoisted myself up onto the far bank and helped Boyd ashore.

Then, heedless of the risk, I strode forward. "My lady?"

"Sir James." Lady Rosalind de Fiennes drew her hood back and extended her hand to me. "Always such peril and tragedy when we meet. I wish it were otherwise. I trust all was clear and you find this agreeable?"

Relieved, dazzled, anxious and suspicious all at once, I took her hand and kissed it. "True to your word. Everything is in order. But I fail, as yet, to understand, why it is you are doing this? And why, of all people, you requested for *me* to meet you here?"

"Because you allowed my husband and I to go free from Roxburgh when you could have done us harm. How can I forget such kindness?"

I gazed up at her, her back as straight as a birch tree, her shoulders held tall in strict formality, her clothing ordinary and unimpressive in its cut. She could have ridden there on a donkey and herself in sackcloth and still been a force worth reckoning with. I had judged as much in the few times we had met so far. "Governor William de Fiennes was gravely wounded. To ransom him would have been senseless. To retain you, under the circumstances, cruel."

"So you are indeed a merciful soul beneath that hugely fierce reputation? All the same, it was not required of you. Furthermore, I owe a debt to you, my lord."

I blinked at her. "I have done nothing on your behalf that I know of."

"Not directly so, perhaps." Blithely, she crossed her hands over the front of her saddle and tilted her chin. Even in the moonlight, her dark hair shone with each subtle turn of her head. "You know by now, do you not, that Sir Robert Neville of Raby was my father?"

The hairs on my neck prickled. I heard the leather of Boyd's jerkin crunch as he shifted his arms. "Archibald told me, after he read the letters. I didn't know before that, I swear. I should think . . . expect that you would despise me."

"No, I don't. The fight was fairly done, my lord. It could as well have been you who died that day, and nearly did, from what I hear. But let me inform you further. Your stepmother and I became very close while at Emmanuel. Do you think she was the first woman he ever laid hands on? Or that even his own daughter was beyond his craving? A simple world you live in, kind lord, if you have not witnessed some of the evil that lurks in it. After my husband died, I naively returned to my father's house. How ignorant of me to do exactly as a dutiful daughter should. Too soon I discovered my folly. I even feared for my own daughter, to tell you something of his affliction. Little girls or defenseless widows, it mattered not—he liked them all. That is why I took up residence with my daughter at Emmanuel—and the deeper in Scotland I was the safer I felt. No, my lord, I despise nothing about you. You've justly rid the world of a sinister man."

"Still, you risk your own life—for what?"

"Let us say I have a bone to pick. And enough sense to judge right from wrong. The funds that my late husband intended for my daughter and I were without warning seized by my father and promptly squandered by my brothers. King Edward dismissed my grievances without ever hearing them. So I have nothing. No home, no husband, no daughter— "

"But I thought that she—"

"She died before we even spoke last. The same sickness that took Lady Eleanor."

"My condolences, my lady. But why did you not say so then?"

She glanced down, as if to gather her thoughts. "Because I did not know you well enough to trust you, Sir James. And the irony is that now I'm asking you to trust me. Lord Hugh Despenser wanted me to believe that she was still alive—and that he had her. He wanted me to spy against you, your king and the Earl of Lancaster. But I knew all along it was a lie. And so now I have no one, no family, no home, no country, nor a penny to my name. Let all who hear me be my witness—I have no loyalty left for England's king. Therefore, I do this, because for now it's all the power and retribution I have."

I nodded, the complex web of her troubles slowly beginning to make sense.

"Peter here," she indicated, as he shrank inside his collar, "will take you to the place where the wall tonight is left unguarded. You may gain the town there, and quietly, so that you shall be well inside before the garrison is roused."

"And how can I be assured, Master Spalding, that I will find all as you say?"

He jerked in his saddle, as if pricked by a thorn. I realized then that this quivering mouse was no spy—the English would have chosen better had they some baleful plot set in action. No, Peter Spalding was no pawn, but the lady was not so plainly read.

Spalding pinched at his horse's reins with trembling fingers. "Watches are easily bought off. The watch at the east end, mine, stands empty. The next one north, as well. Stay low in the ditches. You'll have no trouble. The castle is another matter."

My task was but to take the town and allow way for Robert to wear at the castle when he arrived.

As I nodded to Boyd and readied to call on my men, Rosalind spoke, "I ask, m'lord, but one favor of you in exchange for this boon."

I shrugged. "If the town is won and it's within my power. What?"

"Refuge. Far from where the English will ever think to find me. I ask no more."

I stepped in close and grabbed her stirrup. "You ask much indeed. How can I be assured that you are not yet in the employment of King Edward as a spy? Or an assassin, even?"

She reached down and laid a gentle hand on my arm, precisely where that deep scar lay—as if somehow she knew that it spoke of my own vulnerability and she, in coming here, sought to share her own. "Assassins make quick work of their targets, my lord. I could have killed you when I brought your brother his letters. I could have led the

English there in the two years since to burn you out, couldn't I? And I would not have wasted my time with this drawn out talk we've just had. As for a spy . . . so far I've given you every bit of information and gained none. If I am a spy, I fail miserably, don't you think? Most certainly I would not be here with just one man," she lowered her voice, "this harmless man, at my side while you have dozens armed and mounted within a stone's throw. Go. Seize Berwick. Take back what was long ago taken from your father. Let *that* be your reassurance."

She both bewildered and intrigued me. The gamble was great, but the prize, if taken, was immeasurable—the last patch of Scottish soil still under England's foot. Either Rosalind would deliver me straight into the hands of the English king and thus be the death of me . . . or drop Berwick like a floating feather into my outstretched palms. I bowed and gave a sharp whistle for my men to come forward.

"If we take Berwick, my lady, seek me out. I'll put you in a place that even you yourself wouldn't think to look."

WHEN WE CAME WITHIN sight of Berwick, we halted in a grove of pines to study the ramparts for activity. The sentries on the castle wall were sparse. The town walls appeared even barer. An English guard walked the length of the wall between two towers of the castle slowly, almost sleepily. He disappeared behind a merlon.

My breath whistled in and out of my nose. Beside me Archibald shifted. The leather of his gauntlets creaked as he brought his hands up to stifle a sneeze. My stomach pulled tight. When he had quieted, I raised a hand in signal.

We scurried along a hedgerow and inched closer to the ditch. If my men had learned one thing, it was how to move fast without the slightest rustle. We snaked on our bellies in a shallow gully that drained spring floodwaters. I crawled over the frozen mud to where the gully broadened out and laid a hand on Peter Spalding's trembling arm.

"There?" I asked, pointing to a section of the wall that he had described earlier. A broad ditch ran along its length.

He nodded. "Aye, that's the place."

"Time," I said to Randolph, close behind me.

His smile flashed in the darkness. He got to his knees and gathered up one of the rope ladders over his shoulder.

I took a long spear from Boyd and motioned to the others to follow. Over the bank of the ditch I scuttled and slipped carefully in. Although grassy, the bottom of the ditch was clogged with oozing mud. I struggled to step forward, crouching so low my legs began to cramp. The fresh stench of human filth and urine stirred. I keened my ears for the flick of arrows. Midway out the muck began to suck back at my boots and so I jammed my spear pole into the bottom and pulled myself along. As I went I checked the depth and found a deep spot that would have left me sinking in my armor. I moved around it and gestured at those around me to avoid it. Walter stood up to his knees in muck, his teeth clicking together and the bulk of the ladder weighing him down.

"Half way there," I whispered.

I returned my sights to the opposite bank, a ragged line of black against a high gray wall, willing it closer. I tightened numb fingers around the long spear towering above my head and began to rise from the black, stinking ooze. I gained the bank and gasped for breath, fighting the urge to curse at the freezing clumps of mud that had turned my feet to stone. Carefully, I laid the pole down so it would not roll back in and slithered back down the bank as I grasped at slick clumps of grass that tore loose in my hands. Once on the far side, I helped pull several of my men to drier land.

We spread out along the thin edge of earth at the town wall's lip and began readying the ladders. The spear ends went through a hole in the top rung which had a hook of iron on one side to fit over the wall. Glancing back to the ditch, I saw that Archibald was the last to emerge. I lent him my hand, but his fingers, stiff from the cold, slipped. He fell with a thud. Back toward the bottom he tumbled, finally rolling into a tussock of grass. Unsteadily, he staggered to his feet, resting a moment with his hands on his knees. Then he scrambled back up the steep, slick sides of the ditch. He was almost to me when the sound of shuffling boots reached our ears. His dark eyes, reflecting the moonlight, darted to the wall.

"Hurry," I urged, thrusting out my hand again and leaning far forward. Boyd grabbed my other arm to steady me. Together we pulled Archibald to safety and dragged him back to where we hugged the wall.

The footsteps came closer, paused and passed by. I held my breath. Several minutes went by before I signaled for the first ladder to go up. As Boyd steadied the bottom of the long spear against the ground I worked it upward until it was standing straight and very, very carefully leaned it against the wall. My arms burned. A cramp knotted my shoulders. I bit my lip till the worst of it passed. Looking upward, I gave the shaft one good heave. The iron hook landed over the edge of the rampart with a sharp click. We let the spear down. Two other ladders went up and a third and a fourth.

Walter, in a rare burst of courage, was the first to scramble up. The ropes went taut with his weight. With my knife blade clenched between my teeth, I followed him. It was the knife my father had given me when I was ten on these very walls, just before Longshanks massacred thousands of Berwick's citizens. Archibald later returned it to me before Bannockburn and I had kept it at my side ever since.

Cautiously, Walter pulled his torso through the gap of the crenel and stole a glance left and right over the ramparts. Then he swung his legs over. On his cue, Scots poured over the unguarded walls of Berwick.

A cry rang out from a nearby tower of the castle. Shouts relayed our unwelcome arrival. My men dispersed in a dozen directions, descending from the walls by rope to the ground or onto nearby roofs. The town's watch stirred groggily. Shapes raced through the darkness.

Metal gleamed in scattered flashes in the blackness of nearby alleyways. Walter moved away from the wall to stand in the street, taking in the chaos erupting around us.

"Walter, don't—"

Whoosh.

He reeled backward. His head slammed against the wall. An arrow clattered to the ground beside him. He crumpled, his sword dropping from his grasp. His empty sword hand slid across his body to cover a gash in his mail, just above his other elbow.

"Walter?" I stooped beside him. "Are you hurt?"

He grimaced and kicked his legs in agony. Air hissed between his teeth. "Hurt? Near to dead, I'd say."

Blood oozed between his fingers. I hooked a hand beneath his armpit and helped him up. He would live—I hoped.

"Merciful . . . What is that ringing?" Walter rubbed at his temple with bloodied fingers. "Jesus, make it stop."

"Church bells. Town's awake now."

Our men were by now fully engaged. But the surprise had loaded them with a distinct advantage. The townsfolk had no time to rally. They were coming at us one by one and falling against a wall of Scotsmen. The fighting closest to the walls was thick and wicked. A flicker caught my eye and instinctively I yanked Walter down. Another arrow smacked against the wall behind us, ricocheted and dinged against Walter's helmet.

"They're aiming for us." I plucked up his sword and dropped it in his slick, wet hand.

Before I could lead him to a safer vantage point, he wrung my arm.

"James, I . . . I would have thought . . . Why do you risk your life for me?"

"We're on the same side, are we not?"

"Aye, but—"

"Shhh, hurry on. We've work to do." No gain in opening old

wounds. Not now.

Shoulder to shoulder, we shoved forward into the fray. The moment he entered the clang and thrust of hand-to-hand combat, Walter forgot the seeping gash in his arm. He bounded up onto the roof of a low shed and rained terrific blows upon vulnerable English heads.

By the time a blood-red sun rose above the midnight blue of the sea, the town was entirely ours; however, the garrison was by then well within the castle walls. Randolph and I barely held off a brave sally by the English, but when the red lion standard of Robert the Bruce broke over the horizon past Halidon Hill on the coastal road, they retreated fast before he rode into the town.

The siege on Berwick began. In a very short time, the castle surrendered and contrary to his past practices, Robert deigned to spare Berwick a razing.

I STOOD PROUDLY UPON the ramparts of Berwick Castle beside Robert as he talked of plans to fortify the fortress better than any castle in Scotland. Edward of Caernarvon would return, he said. Time was the only variable.

"We'll quarter as many archers and spearmen here as the town can support, James. I want every resource concentrated here. Berwick must hold. It must."

"It shall, Robert. It's in good hands now."

"How does Walter fare?"

"Mending well. You'll not regret installing him here."

"Not my business, perhaps, but for awhile, you made it a point to keep from him, didn't you? Whatever was that about?"

"Long done, if you don't mind."

Perhaps the rift between Walter and I had indeed healed. His thoughtless attempt to drive an arrow into my back had been a jealous impulse, breath blown into the embers by the vindictive Edward Bruce himself. No, that was all past. But the pain . . . my heart still burned for Marjorie. It always would.

I leaned over the edge of a crenel of the wall. Everything seemed to have diminished in size with my aging. The heath that spread out landward was but a quick ride and put behind to reach the next town, when in my childhood it seemed to stretch to the ends of the earth. The sea, however, was as dark and deep and far as ever.

To the north, a blustering April storm gathered strength. As the wind lifted my hair from my face and knotted it, I thought of a day over twenty years ago, when I had stood on that very same wall with my father, gazing down in awe and terror at the great, fire-belching beast that was Longshanks' army.

Robert laid a gentle hand on my shoulder. "You've a far off look, my good James."

"Do you ever tire of it? Of the fighting?"

His arm went about me in a half-embrace. "Aye, but if Edward of Caernarvon were not so obstinate, or I for that matter, it might not be the only means to the end we've set ourselves toward. I often thought we'd never finish what we set out to do before old age defeated us. But here we stubbornly stand, aye? Berwick to Skye. Galloway to Buchan. Every pebble and branch and blade of grass under Scottish rule. I've sent word on to Ireland, to let my brother Edward know. I wish I could say it was going as well for him there, but I know otherwise."

He took me by the shoulders and gazed at me with disquieting sincerity. "This life we've chosen, aye? Is it all truly peril and sacrifice, though? No, we've something to show for it. Something they all doubted possible when you were but a wet-eared squire startled by the sound of your own voice and I a free and easy blade with a flaming temper. We're hard in the head and mayhap it's that they said we couldn't, that we had to prove we could."

For the first time I could ever remember, I was not so entirely certain that I shared his perseverance. I had wearied of wielding my blade, wearied of seeing my friends shot through with arrows or leaking from a sword thrust. The thirst for vengeance that had propelled me through my youth had been quenched by my successes. I took up arms now because he—Robert, my king, my friend—called on me and I would have crawled to the end of the earth and plunged to the depths of hell to serve him.

Aye, I had even given up my life's greatest pleasure, Marjorie, to avoid displeasing him. Robert the Bruce had a way of making you believe that every discomfort, every pain, every abstinence would beckon forth a veritable paradise in times to come. That every man had his part to play in that dream—not his alone, but Scotland's.

He held his hand toward the tower door. "Come along then. I'll walk you around and show you what I've been planning to stave off the English. I mean to keep Berwick not only all in one piece, but to add a few stones here and there."

We entered the tower stairs, me a pace behind my king, and had not gone far when the rushed pounding of footsteps from below reached our ears.

"Sire!" Randolph called from the tower stairway. He burst around the turn below us and halted. Breathless, he thrust a roll of parchment at Robert. "A dispatch from your nephew Colin Campbell in Ireland."

Robert hesitated. That tidings had been sent by his nephew, rather than his own brother, boded ill. With a face set in stone, he received the letter and read it silently in full, although his countenance never betrayed the words thereon.

Finally, he rolled the parchment up and raised his chin. "Edward set out to attack Dundalk. His forward columns were annihilated. Despite advisement to wait for reinforcements that were but a day's march away, Edward stubbornly went forward. He fell that same day. His head . . ."—and there Robert faltered, jaw taut, eyes misting, for if he had no admiration for his brother's faults, he loved him still— "was preserved in . . . a box of salt and sent . . . sent as a trophy to the king in London."

Robert tapped the roll against his palm, swallowed hard and nodded. "So it is, at last."

Lintalee, 1318

I STOPPED IN MY tracks, thumbing my bowstring as I gazed down at the Lady Rosalind, who was crouching in the broad shade of a newly leafed oak tree and dipping her hands in a bucket of clear stream water.

Just the day before, I had returned to Lintalee from Berwick, then slept deep and hard in my own familiar bed. After breaking fast, I had wended my way out to this clearing where I used to practice at the butts with a sheaf full of arrows for entire days. It had been a long time since I had done that and I was in no mood for an audience to witness my first pathetic attempts.

I wondered how long she had been waiting, watching for my approach. "What brings you, my lady?"

She looked up. Her hair was tousled and her bare wrists and feet browned by road dust. A smile, faintly sweet, crept over her mouth. "A brusque greeting, my lord, for one who made Scotland whole again. I trust you found all as promised?"

I held my hand out to help her up and felt the cool drops of water in her palm as she laid her hand in mine. "The town fell easily. The castle garrison, however, put up more of a fight. Our king arrived in heavy force soon after. The governor there had no stomach for a long siege. He handed the castle over with hardly a drop of blood being shed. But that was over a month past. Where have you been? And where's your horse?"

"Then you did expect me? Good. I've need of a wash basin"—she held her arms straight out from her sides, showing the tatters and soiled spots of her clothing—"and better clothes. I must look a beggar to you. I had to cross over the border to seek shelter, being, well, English as I am. But even that was unwise of me. I've given myself so many new names, I'm no longer sure of who I am. Then on my way here, I was rudely robbed of my belongings, including my fine horse—Scots, judging by their speech. Stones, I have discovered, make great weapons when they're accurately thrown. All I have is what you see before you. So, I've come, shamelessly, to collect."

"Collect?"

"A place to stay, food, something to wear. I've walked for a week on foot and am weary to the bone. Surely you would not turn out a lady in need?" She cocked her head. "Now where is this secreted place you're going to put me away in? Or were you in doubt of me when you said that and there's no such place after all? If I'm discovered, I'm not long of this world, my lord. You can't recant on your word."

"I won't. Now, I'd advise you to move, my lady, because—"

"Rosalind."

"Because you're standing next to my mark there."

"Am I? Then aim well, James Douglas, and hit your mark. You've a brutal reputation, but striking down harmless women is not among your darker marks of distinction. No, I'm going nowhere this moment. It is your turn to repay a debt. I've been enormously patient, don't you think, while you set yourself up in Berwick to—"

"Set myself up?"

"As governor, surely."

"Do you always assume so much? No, that honor went to Walter Stewart."

"Ah, you see now, I have been quite out of touch. But how could your king insult you thusly? Your father was governor there and held it against Longshanks himself."

"As Lieutenant of Scotland, the scope of my duties lies far beyond Berwick's coveted walls. King Robert granted the governorship to Walter at my suggestion. I'd prefer to be on the outside and ready to fight, not holed up in that rock when the English return—and they will, mark me."

"Perhaps not as soon as you fear." She stepped around the tree, grinning slyly, and touched her fingers to the deeply pierced holes in the trunk. "Every day Lancaster grows more and more powerful in England and Edward less and less so. There is talk . . ."

"Of?"

"Civil war." Behind her smile lay a hint of something more. Casually, she leaned with her back against the tree and raised one teasing eyebrow at me. "I have a kinswoman, an old companion of my childhood, who is a handmaiden in the earl's court."

"There's a room," I conceded, "small but comfortable, that Archibald usually uses. He's gone to meet Beatrice Lindsay. I doubt he'll return soon. You may stay there a while."

"Here, you say? With you?"

"For the time, aye."

"Dangerous, don't you think, to keep an assassin so close?"

I gathered up my bag of arrows and unstrung bow. "And yet you've thrown away another opportunity to end my life. I haven't yet, however, dismissed the possibility of you being a spy."

"Hmm, a spy . . . but for whom?"

As I showed her the way across the meadow, yellow-eyed with buttercups, and along the meandering footpath that led through the woods and to my home, tucked deep and safe within Jedburgh Forest, I said in passing, "'Tis not forever, Lady Rosalind. My home is my own and not meant for the comfort of womenfolk, mind you."

She laughed. "Do you think, James Douglas, that I've been living the good life of late?"

One glance at her soiled feet and tattered skirt hem said 'no'. For a gentlewoman she lived a life most perilous.

Aye, I dared to trust an Englishwoman. This one, at least. I might even dare more—if the opportunity arose.

15

Edward II – Loughborough, 1318

THE BRIDGE THAT SPANNED the River Soar on the road between Leicester and Nottingham was as ramshackle as the premise which had brought me there.

The village of Loughborough embraced the bank further upstream. Its inhabitants, upon noting the royal standard, poured from the mess of crowded, leaning huts that lined the far end of Market Lane. Pikemen were dispatched to keep them away, for this was no royal parade where I would toss coins to beggars as little children tried to steal a strand of my horse's tail. Rather, it was a ploy for survival—an acquiescence for the sake of harmony.

Aside from the faithful few with me at Loughborough that day— Bishop Walter Stapledon of Exeter, my chancellor Robert de Baldock, and Aymer de Valence, the Earl of Pembroke—those who had not abandoned me in favor of my cousin's persuasions had stood mute, waiting to see in which direction the axed tree would fall. Lancaster's party was now cautiously approaching from the north. They halted a short distance from the bridge in a cloud of dust. The Earl of Lancaster moved forward alone, raising his hand in salutation.

My queen, Isabella, had prodded me to agree to this encounter.

Had I not wanted to gloat over various matters, and she not been bloated with my child and ready to burst, I would have sent her here in my stead.

I dabbed away the sweat pooling on my temples and said to Pembroke, seated on his dun-colored Spanish mare to my right, "Explain again, Aymer, if you will, the wisdom in this. Is that not a pig dressed up in cock's feathers on the other side of this bridge?"

Pembroke imparted a brief, quizzical look, then returned his gaze across the way. The sun reflecting off the water was so bright he squinted. The air was stagnant and sweltering. "Keep your enemies close, sire. They will betray themselves in time."

"And how much easier for them to slip the assassin's knife between your ribs, as well."

"Do you truly think he's clever enough to plot your murder without telling half the world ahead of time?"

"True enough, Aymer. Lancaster enjoys the sound of his own voice. But he also revels in a following and keeps in his circle a bevy of toadeaters. If he told them all his plans, I daresay, they would be sharpening the knife and handing it to him."

"Sire, you give him too much credit. For certes, he can stir the masses into upheaval, but his devices end with that. He does not seek to supplant so much as hold sway. Let him think as much."

Indignation fired in my veins. "The Lords Ordainers were his doing. My sire never had to bow to his inferiors. Why should I?"

"Your father not only kept the savage Scots firmly under his heel, but he also erected fortresses in Wales that kept *those* worm-eating devil-spawn in shackles. Without ever breaking his treasury. He was shrewd and meticulous to the point of obsession. Times change. Circumstances alter. And you are a different man from your father altogether. If any rise up against you, it is because they see those differences and take them as weaknesses."

Pembroke allowed a thoughtful pause, then continued. "Take what

I have to tell you, not as insult or criticism, but as concern. Your treasury has been strained for some length of time due to the ongoing wars in Scotland. That is a situation you inherited and which, I regret, has been exacerbated by your own generosity and the carelessness of those around you. Practice frugality and discretion . . . and you will have your peace."

"I would rather have Cousin Lancaster's coffin paraded down Cheap Street. But in lieu of that—and since I've no want for this eternal squabbling—I'll dance the part, my lord."

Stapledon's too small chin jutted forward as he spoke. "The time has come, my lord."

Aside to Pembroke, I said, "Our holy mouse has the gift of sniffing out the obvious. Let us not disappoint him then. Shall we?"

I pricked my spurs and made way to the bridge, Pembroke alone with me. The weight of our horses sent the bridge planks into a terrible groan, so that I feared it might collapse at any moment. From the other side, Lancaster began across, his horse skittering sideways until he calmed it. I could not discern the face of the man with him until we met halfway.

"Sir Andrew Harclay," I said, as Lancaster and his companion dismounted. Pembroke joined them, but I stayed aloft on my horse. Harclay bowed, but Lancaster did not. In that moment, I was certain he felt omnipotent. I ignored his glare and spoke again to Harclay. "How goes it in Carlisle?"

"Harsh in the countryside, my lord. When the crops don't fail, the Scots burn them. And now there are reports of scab in the sheep. But Carlisle stands unscathed. Too great a challenge, I wager."

I was secretly pleased with Lancaster's choice of companions. There were a dozen he could have picked to have at his side that would have made me very uneasy. Harclay and I were not close compatriots by any means, but there was nothing duplicitous about the man.

Lancaster inclined his head, a smirk tilting his jowls toward one side of his thickset neck. "Cousin," he addressed me in the familiar, rather than as his lord, "I thought for certain we would come all this way either to find you not here or to discover ourselves entrapped."

"I'm here. As for your other suspicions—this day's not done. For the moment, all you have is my word. Now, let us dispense with this unpleasant business. Let me begin—for I've a fair bit to say."

At last I dismounted to stand beside Pembroke. "You've displaced my officers Langton and Sandale, constricted the funds required to run my household, and had yourself appointed head of the council oversee-ing all my affairs. At every turn you criticize, reconfigure, delay and bully anyone who disagrees. And where, dear Thomas, has it gotten us? Oh," I went on, so fueled by my long swallowed pride that it would have tak-en a calamity of nature to halt me, "what is the latest I hear? Ah, yes. Your little child-bride, who brought to you the earldoms of Salisbury and Lincoln, has run away and hidden herself. The tale was that she, who had not yet lost her maidenhead, discovered you tupping one of her handmaidens, a childhood friend not two years her senior. Tsk, tsk. How sordid, Thomas."

Barely rankled, he tossed his head back and rolled his eyes. "Done?"

"Hardly. As if your own indiscretions were not poor behavior enough, you accused the Earl of Warenne in aiding her and then burned his home without evidence. Even if he did have anything to do with it, which he did not, you could have resolved the matter more civilly. If not for him, do you know, you and I would not have this oppor-tunity? I told him that in return for meeting you here and making peace, you would offer him compensation. Although your private little war has naught to do with me, I'll take it as an opportunity for a new beginning."

"And how do we do that, Edward?"

"We leave the past, the past. We start today, exactly as things are. Negotiate from here. Make decisions for the common good. Sound decisions. I'll work with your henchmen so long as they prove themselves capable of their duties."

He considered it, stuck his chest out like a cock about to crow and nodded.

"But I cannot live properly on the pittance you have ministered. I am forced to apologize on every occasion for which I have guests to entertain. My residences are in dire need of upkeep and my staff has been diminished out of necessity. Begin by alleviating these matters and we . . . shall we simply agree it is our first step?"

Lancaster folded his arms and chewed on his lip, trying to appear thoughtful. "Yes, then. Some allowances to your income could be made."

"Good. Now," I parted my arms to invite an embrace, "we exchange a gesture of peace—you and I."

His mouth twitched. He craned his bulky arms apart and stiffly embraced me. Our lips brushed tepidly over one another's cheeks.

As his arms dropped to his sides, eager to free himself, I held on. With my hands still firm upon his shoulders, I looked him squarely in the eye. "So we are beholden to each other in this simple oath, yes? I pray that was not the kiss of Judas."

His arms flew wide in an incredulous gesture, knocking my hands away. "Forfend! If you are not Christ resurrected, how could I possibly be Judas?"

Amused that I had so pricked him, I took my leave, mounted and left. As Pembroke and I rode away with the bishop, chancellor and my guards falling in behind, I said to the earl, "Was my performance convincing enough for you?"

"More so if you had not opened with an attack on his character. You're fortunate he did not return the berating."

"It would have hardly mattered. He does so publicly as often as he can. I must admit, I find this dance intriguing. Who leads, who follows? When does the music end?"

I made it to Woodstock shortly after the birth of my daughter, whom I named Eleanor, in remembrance of my dear mother.

A year of peace. Too brief. Too meaningless to have a lasting effect. I had shaken off one leech, only to have another attach itself. The ungrateful bitch, Rosalind de Fiennes, had betrayed me. Berwick fell to that scoundrel Bruce and the very barons who would not permit the funds to raise a proper army were then clamoring to take the city back by force of arms.

If I ever found Lady Rosalind again, she would die a most inglorious death.

16

<u>Edward II – Berwick, 1319</u>

"**S**IRE?" JANKIN SAID AS he parted the tent flap. A gale wind tore past him and toppled the goblet from the stool that served as a table next to my pallet. "What shall I fetch for you this morning?"

Barely dawn, I burrowed beneath my furs. My luxuries in this piss-pot hovel were crude and few. I might have thought them bearable, though, had it not been for the wretched clouds hovering over us for two weeks now, spitting moisture enough to dampen bowstrings and rot a quarter of our food supplies.

"A tuft of lamb's wool—to stuff in my ears." With chilled fingers, I peeled the coverings from my head. Jankin immediately looked down, as if afraid that I might be less than decent for his innocent eyes to behold.

"To eat, I meant." He collected the goblet and brushed the puddle of elderberry wine onto the ground. After blotting his fingers on his own garment, he tasked himself with setting out my clothes for the day: shirt, clean leggings, padded tunic, mail and plates of armor. "The cook received several bushels of pears yester morn, sire. Tinge green, but not bruised."

A knife of pain sliced across my cheekbones and into my temples. "Strained barley water with horehound. I have but to place one wretched foot north of York and I am stricken with a cold on every occasion. God's soul, but I did not sleep one wink last night betwixt my nose and that hammering wind. A miracle we haven't been blown into the sea."

The wind had roared for days on end—battering our tents until they were uprooted at the stakes, draining the life's energy from me, howling in my bloody ears until I nearly went mad. Rain came more than it went. Otherwise, I would have had my archers put a shower of flaming arrows into the very heart of Berwick and let it burn to the ground in an inferno of screams.

I rolled to the far side of my humble bed and blew my nose. Still, it felt as though wads of cloth had been packed inside my nostrils, making it impossible to breathe. My upper lip was chafed so raw it stung.

"Is there anything else you require, my lord?"

"A new head?" I flipped back over to peer at Jankin. Many were the days I resented my duties and would gladly have shriven myself of them. Kinghood was a burdensome yoke that dictated my presence in such frozen hellholes. I would have traded places with any common man—a woman, even—to be able to loll in bed, a real bed, one hour more.

"Do you know, Jankin, that as I ail here, Isabella is crafting her needlework at York? Was it only a year ago that she birthed our daughter Eleanor? My namesake, Edward, is a sober seven-year old now. How unfortunate for his little brother John that his favorite sport is playing at swords. John takes his thrashings admirably. And he never fails to return them with all the fanfare of that legendary Plantagenet temper. Young Edward has none of my gentler ways, cares nothing for music or fineries. He has, instead, my sire's fascination for games of war. One day, when he is old enough, I shall send him to this odious wasteland in my stead. Tomorrow would not be soon enough, though."

Jankin listened with polite intensity. I liked his quiet ways, his ready ear. He was rather like a greyhound past its hunting days—always at my feet, treading softly behind wherever I went.

"If you truly wish to relieve me, Jankin, make me into a woman. Then I would not be here. I would not be ill. And I would not have to endure the incorrigible company of my murdering cousin. Have Barnabas add a few drops of licorice to my tisane, will you? That would comfort me." I blew my nose again and then for lack of a kerchief wiped my hand on the outside of my coverings. Jankin nodded and backed out through the opening, this time being quick enough to permit less wind into my little cavern of sparse comfort.

I had left Hugh behind in London, wishing to avoid the animosity that had lately crept over the rest of the nobility toward him. Besides, better to have Hugh Despenser keeping watch over my exchequer than one of their ilk. Gentle Hugh was never the champion of tournaments that Piers had been, but he had a sharp mind for money and politics—devious, even.

This sham of a courting that Cousin Lancaster and I played at would wear thin soon enough. My lips had singed when I gave him the kiss of peace at Loughborough last year. I may have publicly forgiven the transgressors of my beloved Piers' death, but my soul had far from forgotten.

This business of war was going too slowly for my liking and I chafed with boredom. At the mouth of the Tweed, instead of the usual parade of ships pregnant with wares from abroad, there lay at anchor a fine fleet of English war vessels, their masts pointing skyward like spears on the water. My entire army encircled the city—far more armed men than the city had inhabitants.

Whenever there had been breaks in the weather, sappers worked by lamplight to tunnel through the earth whilst archers flicked Scotsmen from the walls like fading flies from a window ledge. Engineers winched back the siege engines, loaded them until the ropes and cogs strained and then lopped flaming faggots over the battlements.

I had no liking for warfare, but this was rather like cornering mice.

I found it amusing.

When the wind had abated and the dismal clouds that had hastened in the first chill of autumn parted to show slices of blue sky, we had launched our attack fully on Berwick. Arrows hissed incessantly. Ladders were thrown against the wall, but were quickly toppled by hooked poles, falling to earth in a shattering of wood and bones. Those that made it too far up the rungs were burned with boiling tar.

One of our cogs slipped upriver, a small catapult gracing its deck. But before it could get close enough to pummel the castle walls, an ebbing tide sucked at its bulky hull, grounding it on a sandbar. A single arrow trailed a tail of smoke through the heavens and pierced the billowing square sail of the cog, adorned with its Plantagenet lions. Great shreds of flaming cloth fell to the deck. Soldiers leapt into the river to either drown or die in a hail of arrows.

The sow, a sturdy roofed machine constructed to shield our sappers as they picked at the foundations, was wheeled forward with an enormous groan. Thrice the Scots hurled sizzling faggots from the castle, finally bursting the main beam of the sow and decimating it in an eruption of flaming pitch. Men ran screaming from underneath as burning clothing seared their flesh. Some stumbled into the moat where they drowned.

Hour upon hour wore on as Stewart's men filled their gaps and staved us off. As dusk settled, we pulled back, nursed our cuts and bruises, and sought rest before going at it again one week later. Twice we had taken the offensive and twice we were repelled.

Any moment one of the commanders would swagger in, seeking a place to lay blame for our failure thus far.

I sat up, coughing, and buried my face in my hands. I was accustomed to being the accused. If not for Pembroke on my side . . .

Jankin shuffled in with a small basket of pears, a pewter cup and a jug of barley water. Timidly, he peeled away my blankets and began to dress me. I sipped at the pasty tisane, listening to the tat-tat of flags snapping in the wind. Then, the rumble of hooves disrupted their rhythm, followed by shouts from the guards outside. Words of urgency were exchanged. Other shouts followed, one a voice that revived my headache in full.

I groaned. "See what it is about, Jankin, and if not a matter of life or death—tell them to scatter and come back when I am well enough to tolerate their shrieking."

He had not even turned to go when Lancaster stormed into my quarters.

"The queen has been flushed from York, sire," Lancaster announced. "The archbishop hurried her away to Nottingham before Douglas and Randolph could get to her. He went and met them near Milton where—"

"Met them?" I questioned through a fog, eyes watering and head pounding. "Diplomacy serves no rebel's purpose. What did the archbishop think to gain by that banal gesture?"

Lancaster grumbled at my interruption. "Not diplomacy, Cousin Edward. He marched on the Scottish hobelars with a rabble of townspeople and clergy. Pompous ass, robes or no. The Scots fired up stacks of hay and sent them into confusion. By day's end there were three hundred priests lying dead in that hayfield."

"Well, God will levy his judgment on the Scots for that. But the archbishop, as you so eloquently stated, is a fool. You say my queen is safely away then?"

"She is. But Randolph and Douglas did not stop at Milton. They are annihilating every town, manor and cattle byre in the countryside about York. I tell you, my lord, we need to put a halt to this destruction now, else they plunge as far south as London and scorch Westminster for sport."

"They'll do none such, Thomas. Calm yourself. You're working up a fearsome lather." I took a last gulp of the tisane and set my cup down, then stood and held my arms out to my sides so that Jankin could begin affixing my arm plates.

"We need to defend our lands. I am not the only one who—"

"A clever ploy by Bruce, don't you think? Just as Berwick begins to wane, he lures us away. Their ash trail would be cold by the time we found it. No, Thomas, the siege will go on. The Stewart can't hold out for much longer."

"And you," he fumed, blowing his red cheeks out, "can't take Berwick alone. On the morrow I shall leave—not to spite you, but to spare my holdings. The northern barons won't idle at your royal slippers as their homes go up in smoke."

I dropped my arms to my sides. "Come now, dear Thomas. That would be treasonous, wouldn't it, if part of my army left at your bidding?"

"Your army? How easily you forget your lessons, Cousin."

"How suddenly your loyalty vanishes when it inconveniences your ambition."

Lancaster gnashed his teeth together. "You covet one city while others perish. What if your councilors advise against staying?"

"Advice is merely that: advice."

It would have been more in vein with his character to rave on. Instead, he suppressed a smug grin as he sought his exit.

"So right," he said. "It is."

EARLY THAT EVENING, THE council convened in the main pavilion. I arrived to scowls and grumbles. Warenne was on his guard like a baited mastiff, but his resolve crumbled shortly after Lancaster and his party rallied against continuing with the siege. The northern barons wanted to go back to their lands and chase the Scots away. Hereford sided with them for no sound reason other than that he had allied himself with Lancaster from the start. This harassment of the north of England was nothing new I reminded them.

But no matter how hard I tried, I couldn't convince them.

The next day Lancaster and the other northern barons decamped and headed home. The number Lancaster robbed me of was substantial.

The rains persisted. Spirits dampened. Supply lines became unreliable. We had not enough men to launch a potent attack and assure the outcome. In the end, we were forced to abandon the siege on Berwick. No sooner was my army disbanded than Douglas returned to the north, ravaging Cumberland and Westmorland.

How queer it was that Lancashire was never set upon.

17

James Douglas – Cumberland, 1319

NOVEMBER WIND SCOURED MY cheeks. I wriggled my fingers free of my gloves and wiped the snot from my upper lip.

"What village is this?" I asked.

Boyd dangled his reins across his mount's sagging withers and braced one gloved fist on his hip. "Don't know." He sniffed, shrugged. "Does it matter?"

"Have we been here before?"

"Not that I recollect," Boyd said.

Carlisle was five leagues or less from where we were. In two weeks' time, we had laid waste to a good part of Cumberland. The two years prior to this, poor weather had stunted their crops. Famine was rife. This year, gentle spring rains and a mild summer had promised and delivered on a bountiful harvest. The surrounding fields had already been cleared of their sheaves and the grain threshed and doubtless some had been milled by now. The cattle were fed and fat. The sheep, however, were suffering from a scab that would prove their wool worthless.

We were about to head home when this temptation sprang up before us: a modest town tucked in a low valley somewhere between the Lyne and the Irthing rivers and with a tithe barn packed to the rafters.

Feeling a cramp in my neck as I raised my arm, I gave the signal to advance on the town, just as I had done before more times than I could remember. All in the name of Scotland and my king. For once, because of a lingering cold I had been nursing, I was more exhausted than exhilarated by the onset of this raid. So I sat back in my saddle and watched as Boyd and the other men rode down into the dale, across an open field and into the town.

We had been spotted ahead of time. A rabble of a dozen townsfolk, crudely armed, rushed out toward the edge of the town, brandishing their weapons with all the courage of ancient Rome's greatest gladiators. If only they understood that they had a choice: they could have paid us a tribute instead and gone on to know a long, peaceful life with their families. Not one of them was left standing after five minutes. But such was war. We took what we needed. We did only what had been done to us.

My men pounded on doors and tossed the inhabitants out into the snowy streets. Womenfolk dragged their children along by the wrists, crying, calling out to one another. Then, the first orange flames licked at thatch; soon, they were leaping from one rooftop to another.

I rode my pony down into the town to see that my men did not carry away more than they could manage and turned down a crooked street, where the buildings were not yet consumed by the inferno. In my path lay a child's rag doll and trampled clothing. A shoemaker's stall had been toppled and crushed, the dyed goatskin and wooden lasts scattered in disarray around it. Ahead, Cuthbert was holding onto the reins of three panicked horses before a stable. Sim Leadhouse came out and indicated it was empty, then took a torch from a passing soldier and set fire to the hay inside before emerging again. Cuthbert grinned at me.

"Take them and return to our cattle herd, Cuthbert." I gulped down smoke. "We're going home after this."

The corners of his mouth sank a little at that, but he nodded and began up the street toward where we had come from, yanking and coaxing his frightened prizes with sporadic success. Sim plowed past me, remounted and went to help him.

Without pausing, they bypassed the fallen bodies of the town's brave defenders. Others were still ransacking the houses and shops for valuables and upending whatever was left standing. On the slopes of the hills beyond, the last of the townsfolk were streaming toward some far off haven, running, straggling, falling, picking themselves up to go on, but not until they had looked back once more at what they had left behind. A veil of gray smoke drifted before me, drying out my throat and eyes.

Then, I heard the crying of a child. Soft, whimpering. *But from where?*

I removed my helmet, turned my head from side to side. There it was again. I held my breath to better hear. In the distance, Boyd's rocky voice called out orders to begin clearing from the town. I slipped down from my saddle, my gut tugging me toward the door of the smoking stables. From the doorway, I peered into the flickering darkness. I heard nothing and began to wonder if my imagination had begun playing tricks on me.

The posts and beams were beginning to burn. I took another step inside, peering up at a flowing river of flame in the rafters above me. As I did so, a frightened horse charged at me, toward the daylight behind me. I had the barest moment to jump aside and let it pass. The creature was an old, barely useful nag, and so Sim had left it behind. Satisfied that it had been the source of my curiosity, I turned to go. The structure around me groaned and cracked, weakening. But I had not yet set foot beyond it when the cry came again, calling me back.

I drew my cloak up across my mouth, turned back and went further inside. The heat pressed in on me. Embers dropped from the beams. Ahead, a small loft held a stack of hay, tinder for a growing fire. The flames ate away at the thick, rain-dampened thatch above. Smoke rolled downward and engulfed the barn.

Below the loft, in the corner of an area reserved for manure and between two stalls, a tiny form huddled. Above dirtied strips of rags, a pair of dark, glittering eyes studied me. The eyes of a child sizing up the enemy as he had retreated to a hiding place that was fast becoming his very own deathtrap. Then from between those rags a kitten mewled and wiggled its way loose. It clawed at his arm and struggled free, at first skidding to a halt at my feet and then scampering around me and outside as its striped little tail whipped back and forth.

Realizing I still had my weapons with me, although sheathed, I held my arms wide, then knelt and called out.

"Come, lad. I mean you no harm."

Behind the mound of manure, he sank down deeper into his tattered clothes, even as smoke rolled thick and stinking between us. A cinder drifted down from the hayloft. The spark struggled and glowed, feeding off the bits of dry hay around it.

I took a few steps closer, reached out my hand. "Please, I only mean to take you from here . . . away from the fire. Let me help you." I went closer until I was just on the other side of the manure from him.

He scrambled sideways. I stepped across the mound and sank deep in its slippery filth. I threw my hand out to catch myself on a post of the stable. As I did so, the post gave a little, the beams and planks above moaned. The weight of the blazing hay shifted. There was no time to waste in negotiations with a scared little boy who would not chance trust to save his own life. I lunged at him, but before I could grab him by the arms, he whipped a knife out and snagged my sleeve.

"No!" I yelled, my throat closing against the suffocating smoke, my eyes stinging. "We'll both die unless you come with me."

I snatched at his wrist, wrenched it hard even as he fought and kicked at me. Then I tore the knife from his grasp and tossed it into the encroaching fire. I yanked him to me and lifted him up and over my shoulder. He kicked furiously, flailed his small fists at my chest, but never said a word of protest or let loose a scream.

I turned around, looking for the doorway. Flames danced wildly all around. The hairs on my head were singeing, my face getting unbearably hot, the undershirt beneath my mail melting to my flesh. Darkness and brightness shifted and interchanged. The lad began to cough.

"Stop moving! Stop it!" I yelled at him. If I didn't get him out soon, he would succumb to the smoke before the fire ever reached us. I stumbled forward. A clump of burning thatch fell hissing in front of me. I stepped around it, struggling to hold onto the boy, moved a few more steps, looked for the door, for a sign of daylight that would lead me to safety.

But everywhere I looked there was only fire. Fire. Fire. Hotter. Closer. Brighter. Another blazing clump fell, this one across the back of my hand. I flicked it away, but it had burned me. The pain was intense.

I fought for air, but there was none. The smoke drew the breath from my lungs, crushed my chest. The lad, light as he was, was becoming a burden. Still, he squirmed and coughed and I, too, felt a cough rising in my chest.

Then, he bit me on the hand. I cried out in surprise. Holding him tight, I lowered him to the floor. My hand throbbed. I wanted to strike him senseless. I stared him hard in the eyes.

"I don't want *you* to die. *I* don't want to die." I squeezed both his arms, desperate for him to understand. In all my years of fighting, I had never come so close to death as this.

He held my gaze. "But you're a Scot."

"I'm a man. And you're a child. I'm trying to help you."

Something behind his small, coal-black eyes softened. Perhaps at last he figured that had I wanted him dead, he would have been so by now. Then he twisted to his left, inclining his head that way. I loosened my grip, let him pull me through the blinding wall of heat and choking cloud of smoke.

My lungs burned. Chest heavy. Hard to breathe. Coughing, gagging.

I blinked, wiped at my eyes, discovered I was no longer attached to the boy's sleeve. Found myself on my knees, on the dirt, daylight spilling over me.

A pair of burly hands hooked themselves in my armpits and hoisted me up. I coughed more. So hard I retched. Couldn't stop. Somehow pulled a few gulps of clean air into my lungs.

"What the bloody hell were you doing in there?" Boyd admonished. He yanked me further away, then propped me against a cart and brought my horse to me.

I shook my head, unable to answer him, tears welling in my stung eyes. Then I looked about for the wee lad who, in my attempt to save him, had saved me instead. The streets were empty of life. Flames and smoke consumed the town.

The lad was nowhere. Gone.

Lintalee, 1319

THE FIRE HAD SCRUBBED my lungs raw. It felt as though a set of irons was clamped around my chest, making it still hard to breathe. Gil, now serving as Constable of Scotland, had not been with us on that excursion. I longed to have him near, for surely he would have known of some magical drink or some herb that would ease the pain in my chest and return me to normal. But my healing was slow and I could not let my men know the extent of the damage done to me. If anything, I was only more silent than usual, foregoing the jokes that Boyd and I usually shared, and the picking of Cuthbert's brain for details with which to fill my reports to the king.

We headed home, northeastward. I released some of my men along the way so they could go on to their own homes, but many of the others would stop at Lintalee with me for a rest before going on. It was a week to Christmas and the snow had begun to fall. When we came to the dale of the Teviot, it was my men, not me, who quickened the pace. My cough had by then lessened, although my chest still ached and my throat was still constricted so that it was hard to swallow without a lump of pain.

My hobelars, by now adept at herding cattle, prodded their bewildered beasts along and kept them from wandering. The task became more difficult as we entered the forests around Jedburgh and so there we waylaid at a local manor and settled the herd, to be later divided and delivered. Then we set on the road again. By then we were only a few miles from my home. The men in the fore pressed their ponies to a canter. I hung back in the rear, gazing over the tops of naked trees at a pink sunset.

My horse pulled up suddenly as Boyd rode across my path and halted.

"Dragging a wee bit, are we?" Boyd said.

I had not noticed the snow falling until I saw it glistening in melted droplets on Boyd's bushy red beard. I guided my pony around him and continued on. "Haven't you a young wife to rush home to?"

"Wife, och. Fair to look at, but docile as a lamb. No fire in her belly—or below. Bored of her already. Must have been drunk the day I wed her."

"More likely she was drunk when she wed you. Otherwise, who'd have you?"

He grumbled a profanity under his breath, then burst out in a tide of laughter. "Last I saw of her she was getting fat with a bairn. Mine, I hope. Our third."

"Then you should go home. What does that make for you altogether now—eleven, twelve?"

"Thirteen."

"Aren't you a bit old to be raising bairns?"

"Why do you think I'm gone so much? No, I'll stay a while. Bring some life to that deadly quiet hall of yours. Besides, I trust you've a good store of ale for us? Just rewards for all we've brought back, I say."

"You'll help yourself whether I ask you to stay or tell you to go. I know, by now, how it is with you."

Jaded from yet another campaign and indolent from a long ride slowed by meandering cattle, I fell into a mundane state, not quite noticing how close I was to Lintalee. The road curved, narrowed, rose and fell as the trees crowded closer around us. My men had streamed on ahead of me, even Boyd, so that by the time I dismounted before my lodge there was not even a horsegroom at hand to take my pony. Too eager for food and drink, my men had abandoned their mounts without care, enticing them to remain by scattering grain and hay in the open yard before the lodge steps.

I stood there before my home, the pale glow of winter dusk etching every snowy tree limb in silver. Tired though I was, I finally led my own pony to the stables, removed his saddle and hung up his bridle, broke the ice in his bucket, and fed him well in reward. After putting down fresh straw and seeing that he was content, I went back toward the house.

A thick curl of smoke drifted from the chimney, indicating that the hearth was well-fired already. Waves of song spilled from within as I tugged at the door and opened it a crack. Had there been a way inside and up to my private chambers without wading through a sea of half-drunken Scottish soldiers, I would have taken it. Alas, I would have to suffer their jubilation for as long as it took me to cross the room. I plunged inside, heading straight for the stairway on the far side.

I kept my head down, nudged my way through, nodded to anyone who called out my name, but kept on, never speaking, never pausing. I had my foot on the first step when a slight body wedged past me and barred my path.

Rosalind had one hand braced on the wall and the other on the railing. "Could you have not sent word ahead that there would be so many?"

I glanced back over my shoulder, seeking some kind of retreat, some small corner of solitude, but the place was packed elbow to elbow. Defeated, I looked up at her, begging forgiveness. "Your pardon, Lady Rosalind. Come morning, send them on their way."

She held her ground, studying me as I leaned against the wall. Her eyelashes fluttered. Her voice softened. "It was only . . . unexpected. This is your home, my lord. How long these . . . these men stay your decision as well, not mine. You are not wanting for food or drink though, if that is your concern. In your absence, I took the liberty of arranging better provisions with your steward. Enough to last the winter. Perhaps I should not have imposed, but it was an old habit of mine to stock the pantry whenever it was running low and so I—"

I held up my hand to stop her babbling. "Please, you needn't apologize for for looking after me. Forgive my rudeness, but I need to rest."

Her chin dropped. She stepped aside to let me pass. When I was a few steps beyond, she asked, "May I bring you something to eat?"

"Aye, that would be good." In truth, although my body required sustenance, I was too weary to even think of eating. I went on up the stairs. In my room I found the candles already lit, a peat brazier glowing warmly, and a jug of spiced cider on the table. The floor was swept clean and the scent of mint, crushed and sprinkled over my bed sheets, echoed of a woman's touch. Too tired to maintain the premise of tidiness, I dropped my cloak upon the floor.

A sigh made me turn. Rosalind stood in the doorway, holding a wooden tray with an assortment of cheese and bread. She placed the tray on the table, poured a cup of cider and handed it to me. Then, she picked up my cloak and hung it on a peg by the door.

I had not noticed how cold I was until I felt the cider warming my palms. Greedily, I emptied the cup, then put it back on the table and sat down on the edge of the bed. I longed to sink back into the downy mattress, but I still had my shirt of mail on. As if reading my thoughts, Rosalind floated to me, lifted my hands above my head and freed me of the mail, then draped it over the back of a chair. She poured me another cup. As I put my left hand out to take it from her, she caught my hand, turned it over and inspected the back of it.

Her brows drew together. "You've been burned."

"'Tis nothing."

She fetched a bowl of rosewater from the table and a cloth. Kneeling before me, she began to cleanse my hands.

"You've been preparing for my return," I noted.

"At Roxburgh, it was my duty to see that everything was always ready for my husband's return. He gave me more responsibilities and freedoms than most men would permit their wives. I had my own seal, oversaw the reeve's records, worked diligently beside the steward, learned every duty and every servant's name . . ." Her voice trailed away in a whisper. She blinked away old memories and shook her head. "Five weeks to the day you've been gone."

"Has it? I never count the days. Only the battles. And the years now."

As she worked her way up from my wrists, she pushed up my sleeves and shuddered when she saw the long scar on my right forearm.

"This one?"

"Courtesy of Sir Robert Neville, your father," I said.

She glanced away a moment, then dabbed at my face with the damp cloth. With one gentle finger, she traced a short scar that lay hidden in the crease between the corner of my mouth and my nose. "This?"

"Dalry, I think. Robert saved my life that day."

"And the burn on your hand?"

"A child led me from a burning building. He thought, at first, that I had come to kill him." I closed my eyes. "A child. Why would I harm a child?"

She put the bowl aside and laid her hands over mine. "You aren't the man tales portray you as. I know."

"When I looked into the eyes of that little boy, I saw fear. I saw death. A hundred times over now, I should have died, Rosalind. I have eluded it. Cheated it. Run from it and fought it. And yet, it won't have me."

She tilted her head, accentuating an eyebrow raised in thought. "Perhaps that is for a reason?"

I scoffed at her. "Reason? I live only to fight."

"Why *do* you fight then? Why go?"

I would have preferred to yield to the mountain of down behind me and escape to sleep, than to explain my purpose to this probing woman. It was too hard a question to give an answer that would satisfy her, but I tried.

"Because I'm called upon. It's what I do. I do it well." Aye, well. Raid. Pillage. Strike terror. Carry home the spoils, then return again while the tales are yet fresh. But it was what made my heart beat more wildly than anything in life. When it came to the lure of battle, I was like the wolf that had scented blood and would stalk his prey until that hunger was satisfied. Like some primeval desire deeply seeded in me, some part of me I could not separate the rest from. A lust I could not live without.

"I doubt, James Douglas, that anyone would dare challenge that— Scots or English. But is it, perhaps, more than that? Revenge, maybe? For something that happened long ago?"

Berwick. Twenty-three years past. How is it that she knows me so well?

She slipped her hands from mine and sat back on the floor, drawing her knees toward her chest. "When I was but fourteen, my own father got me with child. My mother, when I told her of it, struck me across the face and called me a liar and a strumpet. She had me sent away to bear the child and then saw to it that the child did not live to see his first month out. Suffocated in his cradle by a hired criminal. It seems my parents had some difficulty in finding me a husband and when they finally did, it was a man forty years my senior. But a blessing that was: William was good to me. At first he was more of a father to

- 205 -

me than a husband, but he knew, somehow, that I needed that of him. I knew I could feel safe, so long as he was with me. One night I found William singing to our daughter, rocking her in his arms. But he looked so old, as fragile in his many years as she was in her few. I knew then that our time together would not last forever. One day, I would have to be strong without him."

By then, her chin was on her knees. "I'm sorry. I've talked too much of things that must not interest you at all. I only came here to give you comfort after your journey." She rose to her feet. "Do you need anything? If you want me to go, I—"

"Your daughter—what was her name?"

Her mouth was still hanging open, suspended in the middle of her last sentence. She blinked away a tear. Then the slightest smile passed over her lips. "Alice. My beautiful Alice, I called her. She truly was beautiful. I know all mothers say that, but it's true."

Beautiful. Like her mother.

I stood, ignored the aches in my muscles and fatigue in my bones, took her hand, felt the warm flush of her skin, leaned closer. "You still think of her often, don't you?"

She answered with a sullen look. "I used to think of her every day. But I . . . I had to let go. To live. It is hard . . . when you have no one to share your grief with."

Her words cleaved my heart deeply. In one, shattering moment, I glimpsed my own soul in the reflection in her eyes. A raven-black lock of hair tumbled across her cheek as she tilted her head at me, a question forming on her tongue.

"If you had wanted Douglas Castle back all those years," she said, "why then did you ruin it and leave it so many times?"

"Because it was our . . . Robert's way—to raze our strongholds so that the English could not use them against us."

"And each time you took it back," she said, peering at me with those dark, exploring eyes, "did that 'revenge' make the past disappear?

Did it cure your grief? Right wrongs done to you?"

Once, the entire purpose of my life had been about exacting revenge on Longshanks, of repossessing my family's lands and home. That obsession had translated into my fealty to Robert: answering his call without question, riding out and raiding with cruel ruthlessness, feeding off the danger, my soul thriving on it. Once.

"No," I said.

"So why do you bestow Douglas Castle upon Archibald? Why not make yourself a home there? Begin anew?"

"Because," I began, the first crack opening up in the wall of my heart that had shut out so much and so many all these years, "because *this* is my home now."

And because you're here, I yearned to say.

Something inside me more than stirred. It was like a light exploding. I wanted to run both toward it and from it at the same time. I longed to hold her, give her my heart and yet . . .

She gave me her other hand as lightly as if nothing out of the ordinary had just passed between us. "You should rest, then. Before I forget though, your fletcher, Ranulf is it, delivered several sheaves of arrows day before yester. Some white feathered, special."

"Swan."

Abruptly, her hands slipped coldly away and drifted down to her sides. "I thought archers preferred goose feathers?"

"Prefer? They're more readily come by, is all."

Without another word, she went, leaving me wondering why the fletching of arrows was of any interest at all to her. I pulled off my boots and burrowed beneath my blankets. Hours passed by before I slept, though. The candles burned themselves to stubs, the brazier went cold and the sounds of song and story died a slow, miserable death in the hall below.

18

Robert the Bruce – Edinburgh, 1320

THE MOMENT JAMES STEPPED down from his saddle at Holyrood, I crushed him in my embrace almost before he could steady himself.

I had just emerged from my newly constructed kennels, bits of straw still clinging to my shirtsleeves. As I thrust him back for a look, clouds of breath steamed from his smiling mouth and hung in the cold February air. Behind him, Archibald dismounted. Randolph joined in our reunion, clasping both men in turn.

"Hah!" I cried. "Randolph has been here for a fortnight—and where were you? Winter it is, but the weather has not been all so bad." I could barely hear myself for the elated yapping of the dogs, but as the kennel keepers tossed out their bread, the noise subsided. "The tributes you collected have already been received and distributed. The scales of wealth are tipping more and more in Scotland's favor every day. The more we scrape from England's treasury, the less men they can put in the field against us. What of the scab in the north?"

"Devastating," James said. "I'd not lay a hand on a sheep from Alnwick to Carlisle or beyond."

"A blessing Walter was able to hold Berwick. You were right he'd not relent. And more right that Lancaster would turn tail when you lured him away by going after the queen in York."

"That courtesy came from Lady Rosalind. It would seem she knows more than a bit of what Lancaster's leanings are, as well."

I yanked him in close. He'd been keeping this English lady at his side for a while now. "You've been spending far too much of your time in Lintalee lately. I trust, James, you'll plight your troth to her?"

His answer came emphatically. "Whatever you've heard, I assure you, I've neither mistress nor betrothed."

Behind him, Archibald bent down, scooped up a handful of powdery snow and watched it melt in his palm with childlike wonderment.

Randolph said, "He's a man of his word, Robert. The woman's a competent informant."

"'Spy' is the word, Randolph. Ah, James, I had hope. You'll die an old hermit gnawing on bones. But an ugly thought that is, so we'll leave it. Come along, all. Follow me to the stables. I've something to show you. Archibald," I said, turning to James' brother, "marriage agrees with you, I can tell. How fares Beatrice? Well?"

Archibald beamed as he handed the reins of his horse to a groom. The lad who had once gamboled about in the hay beneath milkmaids' skirts had in fact embraced domestic duty. Beatrice had more than satisfied Archibald; she had tamed him. He readjusted his belt and puffed up his chest. "Well indeed. James has given me leave to rebuild Douglas Castle. We'll raise our family there, God willing. She'll be along to join me here soon. Four days hence, five at the most. She cannot travel as fast, given her condition."

"'*Condition*', you say? You've wasted no time in the marriage bed." I winked at him. Then I gestured for them all to follow me toward the stables. At the far end of the stall row, wee Robbie sat astride a stable door, feeding radishes to one of the horses as he talked to it in a most convincing and mature tone.

"Robbie, down from there now," I called to my grandson. "You're to be in the study with your tutor, not out here making playmates of the animals. Along with you."

Robbie peered at me from beneath unruly waves of dark hair. His lower lip turned sharply downward in chagrin. "I don't want to. I want to go riding."

"In time, lad. But first you're to learn your letters and your Gaelic." I plucked him from the door's edge and held him in my arms.

"But I don't like garlic, Grandfather. I don't like turnips or cabbages, either—just like you." He pushed his fingertip at my nose and then began to pluck at the scattered gray hairs in my beard.

"Gae-lic," I enunciated. "It's how some Scottish folk talk. You want people to be able to understand you when you talk to them, Robbie, don't you?"

Robbie pulled at his lip and shrugged. "I'll be king one day. I can make them talk like me, can't I?"

I scowled as fiercely as I could manage. Then I set my grandson down and sent him on his way with a firm smack on the rump. "Straightaway to the study with you. And if I find you sleeping in the kennels again, there'll be no puddings for you. Instead you'll be eating bread scraps with the dogs for the next three days. Archibald, see him along. And be certain he does not wander."

Mortified, Robbie's eyes widened. Then he turned about slowly and, dragging his heels in the dust, treaded down the length of the aisle. Archibald had to prod the boy at the backbone twice before getting as far as the outer door—once when a kitten scampered across their path and the second time when Robbie paused to look back over his shoulder to give James a hard and curious stare before going on. James quickly averted his gaze.

"Och," I growled. "Spends too much of his time with the beasts when he ought to be playing with other boys." I then said quietly to James and Randolph, "There is something I wish to tell you both, before anyone else. It's been torture, keeping it to myself, but . . . well,

Elizabeth is with child. Near four months along. She's had trouble in the past, so she would not let me say it any sooner, but the time has come. For so many years, I wanted nothing more than to have this joy to share with the world and yet now . . ."

James touched my shoulder. "It will go well. As you've always said yourself, Robert—'faith', aye? Does the lad know?"

"No, I've not told Robbie yet about Elizabeth's baby. He's old enough to be aware that for now he is my heir. I don't know if that's seeded something of ambition in him or if that was inherent of his nature, but always he reaches further than his grasp. Ah, the lad has nothing of his father in him. Walter is dutiful, pliable. Robbie's intractable, prone to quarrel. As much as he nearly comes to blows with the boy, Walter loves him dearly and would want him at his side every day. But I can't risk the lad's life by letting him go to Berwick to be with his father. Walter is sorely needed there."

"You needn't fret over Robbie, Uncle," Randolph reassured. "There can only be one king, should you have a son. He'll weather it well enough and prove himself loyal. Besides, someone has to take *our* place someday. Turn the wheels, as it were. Defend the border and all."

"Indeed. Where ever would I be without the two of you? But I confess—there is something more to calling you both here. Edward of England sent a dispatch to Walter following his failed siege on Berwick. He asks a truce of two years to keep us from across the border. Given the scab, I'm of a mind to agree to it."

"But what of the tributes?" James protested.

"I know, I know. Believe me, I've considered that. You'll lose the monies you've grown accustomed to collecting from Cumbria and thereabouts, but we could use this peace to make repairs within Scotland."

Randolph stroked his chin. "A fair trade, perhaps. Short term loss for long term gain. But what else, Uncle? I reckon you have other plans."

"Oh, I do. Interestingly, even as King Edward seeks to give his northern barons a reprieve, his envoys are still at the Holy See reminding the pope of our iniquitous occupation of Berwick. Scratching the cat's ears while pulling its tail. I may rest my sword a bit, but it doesn't mean I'm going to lie down on it. Come March, you'll both be with me in Arbroath and there we'll put to parchment a declaration that will leave no question as to our intents or beliefs. It doesn't matter how many popes there are in my lifetime. I'll persevere with my message until reason visits upon one of them."

I clasped my hands behind my back and ambled closer to the other side of the aisle, admiring the horses there. "Have a look at these fine creatures. Our hobins would outlast them in the hills, but there are none better on the flat. Gifts from the O'Neills of Ulster—a gesture of thanks for Edward's doings. My brother may not have achieved much in the way of kingship in Ireland, but he did drive a wedge deep enough between the clans to shake loose England's hold there. Not the desired end, but it served us some good. Take your choosing of the beasts. I've a mission for the two of you."

Immediately, James was drawn to the black. The horse had not even a spot of white on him, but in the animal's quick, shining eyes was some untamable spirit that James must have felt kindred with. He reached over the stable door and held out his palm. At first the horse arched his neck, as if to say his loyalty had not yet been earned, but then he flicked his tail, stomped twice and stepped nearer. He did not look James in the eye yet as he allowed him to stroke his neck.

"Whatever you ask, Robert," Randolph said, admiring the collection of fine new horses, ten in all, "you know we're up for it. Idleness does not much agree with us."

"Good then. For some time before King Edward proposed this convenient truce of his, I have been receiving correspondences from Lancaster—through Lady Rosalind, as you may have suspected, James."

His head snapped around. "No, I didn't actually, but go on."

"Ah, well, he and Hereford are prepared to work peaceable terms. It's but a gossamer thread of a truce that Edward has tossed out to buy himself time to keep from civil war and it's in our definite interests to side with Lancaster. The earl is the one who shepherds the barons of England, not King Edward. Alas, I don't wholly trust a man who plays his natural enemy against his own king, but he has power. He requests that you and Randolph meet with him in person—in Lancashire."

James' jaw dropped. "Lancashire? Dare I ask how we are to get so far across the English border and back again—yet breathing and with our skins whole?"

"Lady Rosalind shall serve as your guide. Correspondences have been ongoing. Arrangements have already been made with Lancaster. The date is set."

I noticed something of shock in his countenance. "What, James? Something unsettles you."

"I beg of you not to place her in such peril."

"James, may we remind you," Randolph began, propping an elbow against one of the stalls, "she helped deliver Berwick into our hands? In the two years since then, how many times is it that she has gone back and forth across the border? This is not some fair, wilting maiden who needs a man to protect her. I say it is we who need her on this occasion."

I DID NOT STRAY beyond Edinburgh that summer. Elizabeth grew round with child. Scotland was abuzz with joy and as each day passed without misfortune, gradually I gave in more and more to joyful anticipation. That I would father a child again, after so long a time, and most happily of all, that Elizabeth was neither barren nor cursed—for those things, some small joy entered my life. Not as quickly as I had planned or hoped, but in its own pleasant time.

The sheep scab and prospects of a truce with Lancaster had kept our hobelars at home. Edward of England had too much to worry about to venture north. Finally, I could bear no more indolence and rode out one fine day to the hills of the royal park with three of my favorite hounds. They delighted in the exercise and soon took off after a hare. I watched them run across the grasslands, July sun hot on my head and sweat trickling down my breastbone. When I looked back toward the road leading out from the royal residence to the park and saw a servant riding fast toward me, I knew it was time.

While I waited, I paced a rut in the floorboards of my chambers. Afternoon rose to evening. Evening faded to night. I inquired if Elizabeth were having any trouble. The midwife shooed me away. Night passed.

By daybreak, I had fallen asleep in my chair. I was roused and summoned to my wife's bedside. At her breast lay a swaddled babe—pink and wailing. I approached the bed. The midwife unwrapped the babe to show me the sex and then pulled the blankets back around it and placed it on Elizabeth's still swollen stomach.

Her auburn hair lay in matted, stringy clumps around her head, sunk deep in a mountain of pillows. She gazed at me through weary eyes. "A girl, Robert. I prayed so hard, every day, for a boy for you."

I wiped away her tears and kissed her forehead. "Ah then, God must have listened to me, instead, for five times a day I prayed only for a healthy child and an easy birth for you."

"Margaret?" She bit her lip and then broke forth in a sleepy smile as the bairn wailed louder.

"Aye, the lass agrees. Margaret it is."

19

<u>James Douglas - Lancashire, 1320</u>

T HE DECLARATION DRAWN UP at the Abbey of Arbroath and sent by King Robert to Pope John in Avignon relayed the sufferings of our people as a result of the English invasions and stated that we would lay down our lives for our freedom. If His Holiness, it implored, could but persuade England to permit us our peace, Scotland would be free to answer to its duty in the Holy Land. Thus far justice had fallen on deaf ears, but persuasion had as much to do with persistence as it did truth.

Deep in awe at the wild beauty surrounding us, Randolph, Rosalind and I traversed the hills of Cheviot and drove across the moors of Cumbria. The gold and green of the mountaintop moors, or fells as they called them there, mingled with the blues of sky and the silver of wind-rippled tarns where swans swam, their little cygnets trailing behind them. The summer sun was high and strong, but always there was a breeze.

One evening, we stopped at sunset by one of the tarns. Randolph took our horses down to the water to drink. In the long, bronze light of a July sunset, Rosalind led me along the bank to where a small stone church sat nestled in a ring of trees, the shadows reaching tall across its stone-walled yard. She bid me to stand back a moment, knocked twice on the door, then gently nudged it open. After calling out and assuring herself that no one was within, she plucked up my hand and pulled me inside.

The place smelled of dampness and mold. Cobwebs cluttered the rafters. There were two windows, one on each side, both with their shutters half fallen off. The crooked gaps allowed just enough light into the tiny building to see by. The altar was neglected. The roof full of holes. The floor of dirt and crawling with insects.

"We can sleep here for the night," Rosalind announced.

I, who had slept a thousand nights beneath the stars on open ground, shuddered as I smashed a spider beneath my boot. In the peace that had lapsed since the previous autumn, I had grown too accustomed to the domestic comforts a woman provided. "How far to our meeting with Lancaster?"

"Not far," she said. "Half a day. We can rest here tonight. Tomorrow, we'll follow the trail along the lake, then turn east and go across the moor. Beyond that is a deep valley, wherein lies a farmhouse concealed in the trees. The Earl of Lancaster will be there." She went and peered out at Randolph, still tending to the horses, then tugged the door shut. "Once I've escorted you there I will be going on my way."

"Way? Where?"

"To Lancaster. There is a place in his household for me there."

I laughed lightly. "Ludicrous."

Her voice rose only slightly. "Why?"

"Rosalind, come now. You can't stay in England. It's dangerous for you to even cross the border. You've been an agent for the enemy. If Edward learns of it . . . if he even suspects . . ." I crossed from the furthest corner of the tiny church to the opposite where she now stood—a full four strides. "At best, he'd imprison you—and not in a nunnery, but a dungeon, dark and cramped and writhing with rats. At worst . . . need I tell you?"

She held her head stiff and straight. "I *am* English. I've no place among Scottish folk, least of all secluded in some wood and most often left by myself to prattle. It's quite lonely in Lintalee. Now if you please . . ." Angrily she brushed past me, making for the door.

Swiftly, I cut across her path and threw my arm up against the wall next to the door, blocking her exit.

"Let me go," she demanded.

"I can't." Words hard to say, hiding a truth harder still. All this time, she had been near to me and I had held her at arm's length, treating her like a favored old servant. I had lost Marjorie. I would not lose her, too. I reached out, took her face in my hands and kissed her. She neither pulled away nor yielded, and yet it was I who broke the kiss.

Disarmed by my own thoughts and feelings, I turned away and plunked down on one of two stools in the place. But one leg was woefully short and wobbled. I stood up again, went and leaned on my elbow against the near wall. Rosalind moved further away from me to face the altar.

Randolph strode in, looking invigorated and optimistic. "There's enough wood for a cooking fire and the fish are throwing themselves up on the bank for our supper." He smiled and sat down on the other stool, closest to the altar, as he began to sweep the dirt from his boots with a spit-dampened rag. "We're staying here, then? Looks like it would leak in a light rain, but the skies are fair, so we're in no danger there. We'll be on our way back to Scotland soon with a beneficial proposition from Lancaster, I pray. Should I bring our packs in?"

Rosalind kept her face averted from Randolph and folded her hands before her breast, pretending to face the rickety little altar as if she were posed for prayer. He looked from one to the other of us questioningly. I touched my forehead to the wall. "Leave us, please."

Mouth open, he blinked at me, glanced at Rosalind, then left.

Another few minutes must have passed while Rosalind and I floated in some kind of bewildered and angry silence.

Finally, I went to her, stopping an arm's reach away. Fading daylight softened the features of her face. I had gazed at her numerous times from a distance as she brushed the dried mud from my horses or cut up cabbages in the kitchen. Always I watched her when I knew she was too busy to notice me. She kept her night-dark hair loosely gathered at the back of her head, with a thousand wild strands tickling her neck and face. Yet she would never pause to push them away, too engrossed in caring for the menial details of my household even when I had never asked or required it. Despite this easy domesticity about her, she possessed a willingness to take command of her own life and a courage unlike any woman I had ever known. Time after time, she had ventured forth, laying her own person in great peril. She had outlived both husband and child, been stripped of her rightful possessions and chosen to aid a people not her own. I had killed her father in combat, but in that she'd found relief, not sorrow. I had also shot the arrow that took her husband's life. *That* she knew nothing of.

I did not deserve this woman and yet . . .

She moved closer and curled her hand inside mine. "Tell me to go and I will."

I searched deep within her eyes, wondering what it was I felt for her. Slowly, I leaned my head toward hers and placed another yearning kiss upon her now open lips. Her mouth trembled, then yielded, sweet and soft. I found her in my arms and as she pressed against me, a rush of memories—memories both dear and bitter—roiled inside my head, overpowered me with bodily desire for the woman I held, filled me with deep sadness for the memory of another woman who, until then, was the only one I had every truly loved and longed for.

'*Marjorie is gone. She's gone,*' I told myself over and over, even as I held Rosalind in the curve of my arms and covered her mouth with endless kisses. Eventually, breathless and dizzy, we both ceased and looked into each other's eyes. That she might discover too much of the truth still buried in my heart—that I yet mourned for a love long dead—frightened me more terribly than the bloodthirsty rush of any enemy line of spears.

It is Rosalind who is here with me . . . Rosalind who loves me for who I am . . .

I broke from her, afraid I might betray myself, and began to search about the room for any diversion to keep her eyes from mine. "There's a hole in the roof, there, big enough to let out smoke. No flame to give us away from outside."

On hushed feet, she walked up behind me and slipped her arms around me. I felt the impression of her cheek on my back, a light kiss, her fingers fluttering on my abdomen.

"I'm here, James Douglas. Here. With you. Now. This day. This moment."

I stilled her hands. "Rosalind, I could . . . I could never bring dishonor on you."

Lithe as a cat, she slipped around in front of me. Her brows were low, puzzled.

I cupped her chin. How certain I was that I did not deserve her. How desperate I was to hold on to her. "Be wife to me."

"Wife?" Tilting her head back, she stepped away. She brushed a hand over her neck, her eyes darting everywhere but to meet mine. Her breath came in gasps, as if she fought for air. "James, I . . . that is much to ask. I don't . . . I don't know. I need to think on it."

She rushed from the dilapidated church out into the twilight and on down to the shore of the glistening lake. I felt both the urge to race after her and the forced patience to let her go, hoping she would come back to me.

When he saw her emerge, Randolph secured his fishing line to a branch, gathered up our bundles from beside where he had tethered the horses to graze and trekked up the hill.

"What was that about?" he questioned. "She looked unhappy."

I took my bundle from him and unrolled my blanket close to the door. "I said either too much or not enough, Thomas. I should have joined the Church when Bishop Lamberton took me in. If this doesn't work out, I'm giving up on women."

AS STARS SCATTERED THEIR light through the lacework of the roof, we dined on fresh fish. I spent most of the meal picking the bones from my teeth and tasting none of what went in my gut. Rosalind and I intermittently glanced at each other and then away. Randolph tried his best to coax a word or two from either of us to little avail. That night I slept fitfully, if at all, my sword propped on the wall next to me and my back to the door. The next morning I was up before dawn with our horses ready.

The vagary that had leapt from me the night before had somehow invited a sort of peace to my mind. Every time I came home road-weary and battle-beaten, she was waiting for me, asking no more than I was ready to share. She mended my clothing wherever it was torn and I, in turn, found myself keener to the details that needed repair around the manor. When I was home longer and trying to strengthen my wounded arm by shooting at the butts, there was an ease of idle conversation between us as she watched me, for I welcomed her company. In time, she learned archery with great success. Whenever she departed Lintalee I feared for her safety, but never said as much. When she was due to return, I would ride out toward the roads that reached southward, watching for her, gnawed with concern if she was not there. In ways both subtle and entire, our lives had interwoven as fine as any silk, as strong as any castle.

With Marjorie and I, there had been no future, only the moment in which we lived, no matter how we tried to delude ourselves. With Rosalind, every tomorrow yielded a hundred possibilities and promises.

Through the morning, Rosalind led us along the trail she had spoken of, to the tranquil wooded valley where the little farmstead lay, concealed among the broad, emerald mountains. For a while we studied the place. By then, the shadows were reaching long across the land. A few horses, still saddled, were tethered by the barn beyond the house. We observed cautiously. As men who had often laid ambushes ourselves, we knew the signs—outliers posted for early warning, heavily trodden paths—and there were none. Rosalind pointed the way and Randolph, in the fore, began to ride down the sloping trail toward the farmhouse. I held back, waiting for her to take her place between us.

She paused at the cusp of the ridge. "This is your work, not mine. When the sun sets beyond the mountains, I will be here, waiting for you."

I nodded at her as I lifted my reins. "Best you are. You yet owe me an answer, Rosalind de Fiennes." With a slap to my mount's rump, I gave her a parting smile and descended toward the meeting place.

Pigs and chickens roamed around the house, erupting in an odd chorus as we approached.

"We've been announced by the English sentries, I'd say," Randolph mused.

Two soldiers, who had been idling atop a haystack, roused and called out, "Name yourselves."

"Messengers from the north," Randolph called back, in the smoothest English accent that ever passed over the lips of any Scot, "looking for a Thomas of Newlands. Is he within?" With a careless toss, he plopped two English pennies at their feet.

The two guards eyed each other. The slimmer, clean-jawed one sprang forward, snatched up the coins and jabbed a finger at the house. "There."

At Randolph's nod, we both dismounted. He then strode through the flock of chickens, which clucked and beat their wings until a cloud of feathers arose. At some distance from the door, he paused, studied the perimeter of the farmstead briefly, and indicated for me to stay. He knocked twice, waited and pushed the door open wide.

A voice, indiscernible to my ears, must have bade him to enter, for he answered lowly, then inclined his head for me to follow him inside. He ducked the low lintel and disappeared into the dimness. I kept my hand on my hilt as I followed.

The house was but one room with a loft overhead for sleeping. The smell of hay and animals permeated the air. Only the furthest window was open, so that the light that shone from behind the barrel-chested man seated at the table surrounded him in a dusty aura. To his left sat another man, bald except for a rim of auburn hair fringing the back of his head from ear to ear, just as stout, but smaller in stature, observant and yet agitated in demeanor. The house was otherwise empty. Whoever its ordinary keeper was had been dismissed for this clandestine occasion. Still, I kept my ears keened to the sounds outside and left the door well open in order to see.

The Earl of Lancaster guffawed and clapped his hands. "Ah! The fattest ransom Scotland has to offer. The Earl of Moray . . . and Sir James Douglas, is it? Now you I have a measure of respect for, though I bloody detest what you've done to some of my lands. Do you know, Sir James, that they call your place Castle Dangerous? Said whoever took it into their hands had sealed their own death warrant. After a time they couldn't get any but the most idiotic to govern it. Oh, but I have a grander scheme to spin than the securing of my own fortune. Sit, sit!"

He flapped his plump hand toward the two short benches on the opposite side of the table, then jabbed his elbow at the man beside him. "My lords—Humphrey de Bohun, the Earl of Hereford."

"Well met, my lords," Randolph greeted. "I've faith this will be to all our benefits."

Hereford nodded once. We bowed and took our seats.

Immediately, Lancaster abandoned his jovial nature, scooted his stool back and stretched forward over the table. He jabbed a finger bluntly on its surface. "Sirs, I've made myself fully known to your king, so I'll not bore you with details. England has a kitten for a king. He has no wish to restore his own kingdom, because he is intent only on defy-ing those of us who have crowed the loudest. My blood though he may be, he is unfit to govern without guidance. Therefore, I lead the way, and have been for some time. The truce you're enjoying now is my work—although I'm careful not to let the simpleton know it. I have a drove of barons at my back and, dare I utter, even the sympathy of his disconcerted, pretty French queen. For as many as I can keep to my cause, I ask that you and your king keep from certain territories. Simple?" His cheeks blotched scarlet from the fervor of his speech, Lancaster finally sat down again and drew several breaths before ending. "I can rob Edward of half his levies or more. He cannot again launch another successful invasion of Scotland, given that."

"Which is not to say," Randolph observed wryly, "that he would not try anyway."

Lancaster's fist rattled the table. "Did you not fully comprehend what I just said, man? So long as I breathe, he will not have the means to."

Unfazed, Randolph made to rise, sending the message that he wanted Lancaster to finish. "What then shall I tell King Robert when . . . *if* Edward marches on Scotland again?"

"That I will strike my own pact with Scotland. Every day the sorcerer Hugh Despenser controls Edward's every action and every day England's people grow more and more disillusioned with their fee-ble-willed sovereign." The last words he drawled, "He stands on infirm ground."

Randolph settled back down on the bench momentarily. "You say this by your own thought, or by fast knowledge, my lord?"

Confident, the earl glanced at Hereford. "What I have said here today, I say as absolute truth."

RANDOLPH AND I RODE from the hidden valley, scanning the trees around us, searching deepening shadows as the sun slid languidly behind the horizon. Beyond a ridge on the road, Rosalind was waiting for us.

For hours we rode, Rosalind leading the way, as Randolph explored every implication of Lancaster's proposal. With Randolph near, I dared not broach the question that floated so delicately between Rosalind and me.

The moonlight shone strong upon the open, undulating moorland, lighting our path northward. We had not seen a soul since departing from Lancaster's company, and likely would not at this witching hour. Clouds of white-wooled sheep stirred from their slumber and scattered from our path.

"It is all for Lancaster's own benefit," Randolph observed, "that he woos Scotland. Robert has pushed for this because he's desperate for peace and seeks the recognition of the pope, so I fear his mind is already made up. I don't think it's in his favor. *If* he refused Lancaster's offer,"—his bright blue eyes flashed with certainty in the silver-dark of night—"it might cost us in the short term, but—"

He reached across the space between us and touched my leg. "James? Have you heard a thing I've said? I'm trying to figure what is best for us in the long run. Where is your head today? You didn't say a word when we were with Lancaster and Hereford."

I shook myself. "I'm sorry, Thomas. 'Tis you who are skilled in diplomacy, not I. I thought it best to remain silent. I'm a Scots soldier. He's English. My thoughts were not on statecraft, I regret."

"Nor were they in the room, I say. But whatever it is," he said curtly, "Robert sent you on this mission for a reason. If you have other problems, you need to leave them behind before we reach Edinburgh." He peeled from the trail and went to claim his resting spot for the remainder of the night next to a few shoulder-high boulders on a low hillside.

I moved up swiftly beside Rosalind and caught the bridle of her horse. "Go back," I said. "Go to Lancaster. Make yourself a life there."

She recoiled. "What? You ask me to stay, to be your wife . . . and now you tell me to go? What *do* you want?"

Our horses were facing opposite directions. Our knees touched. I clutched the edge of her saddle, leaning close. "I told you what it is that I want. You ran from me and said not a word more. In the several hours we have been together since, you have barely acknowledged me and far from given an answer. Unless you tell me otherwise this moment, the reluctance of your reply is answer enough."

"That is a crude way of wooing, James Douglas."

"You love me or not, Rosalind. Which is it?"

She swung her head away. "Yes . . . I do." Sudden tears choked her, so that she could say no more.

"Then why, why is this so hard for you? You have been welcome in my house, have you not? No one there cares which side of the border you were born on. I vow King Robert will give his blessing. I want you with me, Rosalind. What do *you* want?"

"I don't know. I don't know." Her lips quivered. Moonlight shimmered upon the crystal tears that streaked her cheeks. "It's not as easy as saying 'yes' or 'no'."

"Why?"

"Because . . . I know." She looked at me through eyes as dark as the bottomless lakes by which we had ridden. "It was your arrow that killed my husband William."

My heart faltered. I let go of her saddle.

But I did not know you then, Rosalind. And if not for that grievous stroke of fortune, you and I would not have come to know each other. How could I ever say I am sorry for it . . . when I am not?

No words to heal her hurt or make right any of the past, I got down from my horse and began to untie my pack. I took it to where Randolph was straightening out his own blanket and threw my things down, then went back to my horse to tend it. Rosalind was still mounted, her shoulders slumped, the tears dripping from the clear line of her jaw as she cried silently.

"Come down," I said holding my hands out to her. "Get some rest tonight."

Her face lifted, but she did not look at me. Instead, she gazed out toward a ridgeline, a rolling silhouette against the steel gray of the sky. For a few moments, she did not move.

She snapped up her reins. "We're being watched."

I held my breath, strained my eyes and ears. Randolph by then was keen to something as well. His blade flashed. Bent low and on silent feet, he came to us, pulled Rosalind's horse toward the boulders where he had left his bedding. He coaxed her down and indicated for her to hide behind the rocks. As I joined them, I dug a loop-ended bowstring from its pouch, took my bow stave from where I had slung it on my saddle and in a matter of seconds had it ready. I had only a small cache of arrows stored in my bag. Several I tucked in my belt, the rest I stuck in the ground at my feet. The last I laid against the waxed bowstring.

"Why don't we take to our horses? We can outride them," Rosalind whispered. "Isn't that why the king gave them to you?"

"Outride them?" Randolph's brow lifted. "Aye, perhaps. But we've no way of knowing that there aren't more of them out there. If we ride out over these moors, with no cover, anyone could sight us. And we could be lured straight into a trap." He sank down, his face pressed against the rock. "Where did you go while we were meeting with Lancaster, Lady Rosalind?"

I pulled back on the bowstring and aimed the point of my shaft straight at Randolph's head. "I'm of a mind to let loose on you for even thinking that, let alone giving breath to it."

"What a grievous impulse that would be. Put your arrow to better use, James. There's someone coming at us now."

I stepped up on a low rock and peered above the bigger one. Scrambling over the dark hillside, a form skulked. Quietly, I jumped down, then crept alongside the boulder and leaned out from it. The boulder was to my right and so I had to expose more of myself than I wanted to.

Like a wolf on the attack, the man ran at me. His legs wheeled rapidly over the barely lit ground, sidestepping every stone and clump of grass with the nimbleness of a hill sheep. I gripped the belly of my stave, pulled tight, and waited. He let out a yip, as if signaling the rest of the pack to join in the kill. I honed in on the sound and released my arrow. The shaft ripped into his throat, drowning his cry in a gurgle of foaming blood. He staggered, fell forward, kicked in agony. Thrashing, he rolled down the hill. By the time he came to rest in the swale at the foot of the hill, he was no longer moving.

Behind me, Rosalind squealed and dropped to a crouch. A shadow leapt over the lower boulder at Randolph. He slashed wildly with his sword. Hand to hand, they struggled as the attacker tried to wrest the sword from Randolph's grip. I nocked another arrow, but it was too hard to see, they were too close. I dropped my bow, pulled loose my sword. But before I could engage our foe, Rosalind had picked up a fist-sized stone and smashed it down hard on his left foot. The howl he let out was pause enough for Randolph to slam the butt of his weapon into the man's jaw and send him reeling backward toward me. The wretch never saw the point of my blade coming as it gored his liver and exited his front side. Then I wrenched my blade free. The man fell dead at my feet, face down.

When I glanced at Rosalind, she was shaken, but not shocked.

Randolph gave a pert nod of thanks. "There are more."

"How many?" I said.

"One at least." Randolph nudged the dead man away with the toe of his boot. "Somewhere over near where the first one came from. If there were many more they'd have fallen on us all at once and taken us. Highwaymen, judging by their lack of device. Trained soldiers would have done a better job of it. Just the same, if they've any notion of who we are, or that we're Scots, there's a price on our heads worth their effort. So stay here, keep the lady safe. I'm going to ride the last one down."

I would have told him he was mad had I thought it would do any good. In a bound, Randolph was on his horse, slapping it hard on the rump and racing laterally along the crest of the ridge and then up and over it. The pounding of hooves ceased as blade struck blade.

I wiped the flat of my sword against my leggings, staining them. From the small sheath at my hip, I took my father's knife and handed it, handle first, to Rosalind. She grabbed at it without hesitation. Then, above the sounds of combat, came the rumble of feet over the heathery ground. I leapt on top of the low rock and saw, coming from opposite directions, two men, brandishing their weapons.

"More," I warned.

Rosalind wedged herself into the tightest corner she could find and squatted, the knife grasped white-knuckled in both hands. I jumped to the tallest boulder, luring them toward me with a taunt.

"Come on then! Two dead already. Where's the challenge?"

But only one came at me. The other went straight for Rosalind.

My assailant flew at me, his sword raised high. But I had the higher vantage point and when he levied his first swipe, I had but to step backward to avoid it. Agile and determined, he scurried up the slope. As he sought to gain balance, I ducked low and swung. My blade cut sideways and dug into his knee. The surprise sent him toppling backward in a flurry of waving arms. He hit the ground and I leapt on top of him. With a telling flick he started to swing his sword upward at my leg, but I crushed his wrist under my boot. With one shove, I drove my blade into the soft of his belly.

When I turned, Rosalind was being held tight against the chest of her attacker. White hair, shorn unevenly, stuck straight out from his head. He laughed cruelly and pressed the sharp edge of his sword against Rosalind's smooth neck. I made a step toward them, but he pressed it harder, making a clear indent across her flesh. She mouthed the word 'no' at me, then looked down. I followed her eyes and there, the blade tucked up against her forearm and the handle hidden in her palm, was the knife.

His lip lifted in a sneer. "The king will pay dearly for her."

I held my arms out wide. "Tell him she's not worth whatever it is he's promised you. Cost me my last shilling, she did, and even that was too much to pay for her ordinary favors. So I've no quarrel with you. Have her yourself. You'll toss her aside erelong."

He gave me a puzzled look at first and then changed to one of wicked triumph. I took a step back and as I turned to go, the knife in Rosalind's hand bit deep into his thigh. He roared in agony. Rosalind sank her teeth into his arm. His sword fell to the ground with a 'clank'. She tore from his hold and came to me. In her hand, she clutched the bloody knife.

"You should have tried stealing the horse instead," I told him. "I would have let you go then without a fight. The horse was worth fifty shillings. Idiot." Without further thought, I punched the tip of my blade through his padded jacket and into his gut. He died with a gasp, toppling to the earth, my arm following the blade still buried in his intestines.

I let go of the weapon and took Rosalind in my arms. Her heart beat wildly against my chest, leaping and pausing before taking up its erratic rhythm again. I slowed my breathing, listened, raised my head to the fading stars of the night sky.

"What is it?" she whispered.

"Nothing. I don't hear anything." We stood there together, holding each other, the three fallen bodies lying close by, another lifeless in the heather beyond. We listened, but we heard no sign of Randolph or the fight he had taken up. Carefully, I freed my sword. Then, holding Rosalind's hand, I peered out over the heather as the first sliver of dawn lit the eastern horizon.

There, over the ridge, hobbled Thomas Randolph. He limped toward us on foot, a scowl of disgust twisting his fine lips.

"Where's your horse?" I asked him.

"Two of the bastards." He snatched the flask tied to my saddle and sank down on his haunches next to the boulder. "One of them dragged me down while the other stole my good Irish horse. The thief between them was greedier than he was loyal. He was gone that fast. The other, though, was a fair opponent." He drank deep and long, then wiped his mouth on his sleeve. "I see you had hard work. Well, no time to waste. We can't take a chance on the one who got away leading others to us."

"Rosalind can ride behind me," I said. "You can have the other horse."

He looked from one to the other of us, then nodded. Rosalind bent down to look over his wounds.

"Can you ride?" She slid her fingers below a small cut on his forehead and wiped the thin trail of blood from it.

He scoffed, took another drink. "Certainly."

"King Edward sent them after us," I said. "But it's you and I, Randolph, who were marked for dead. They wanted Rosalind alive."

We rode north as fast as we could with no sleep to be found or food in our stomachs. My horse was slowed by the extra rider, being a horse meant for speeding over the open and not for carrying extra weight. It was near to three days before we reached Lintalee and there we rested well before readying to return to Edinburgh.

I paused on the steps above him, just outside the double doors to my hall. A fresh horse had been readied for him. "I'd go with you, but—"

"Stay, James. Rosalind needs a strong arm to guard her. I'd say she was as much hunted as we are."

A guard of ten men waited at his back, so that he could carry his message to the king in all safety. "Then you have no suspicions of her anymore?"

"I do, actually, but none of that matters. You don't, James, and you'd do everything in your power to defend her. I'm not sure what it is between you, exactly, but I'll give you time to figure it out." He lifted his hand in farewell and took to his mount. "I'll see you again when duty calls. Until then, take good care of her."

Randolph's riding party disappeared along the wooded trail. The song of birds filled the forest as they danced limb to limb in the dappled sunlight. When I turned to go back up the stairs, Rosalind was looking at me from the open doorway.

"A shilling?" Her mouth curved in a pleasant line. "I do hope you were jesting when you said I was only worth a shilling and your horse was worth fifty."

I went to her and lifted her chin with a finger. "I've no idea," I said, placing a light kiss on her lower lip. "Though you may prove me a liar, if ever you wish to. Now, you still owe me an answer."

"I'm here, aren't I? What more answer do you need, James Douglas?"

20

Edward II - Pontefract, 1322

LANCASTER AND HEREFORD. IN union with the Bruce. I had suspected it even before the aborted siege on Berwick. Now I knew.

Hugh Despenser and I rode at the head of a large contingent past Baghill and through the south gate of Pontefract. The morning had dawned in rare brilliance. Even the flies, it seemed, were too content to be a bother.

"I feel . . . omnipotent—like Zeus throwing lightning bolts to smite my enemies." I glanced at Hugh beside me. "Is that blasphemous of me to say?"

"It is." His mouth curved into a wicked smile. "But what a glorious feeling it must be. They defied you, Edward. They'll now receive their due: Lancaster, Mortimer—"

"Phhh, the queen insisted on sparing his life. Went to her knees. Tears, wailing like a—"

"Mortimer? Why?"

"Because he gave himself up willingly." Last year, the barons had forced the exile of Hugh and his father. In January, Sir Roger Mortimer, along with other Marcher Lords, rose up in rebellion. The same old argument had surfaced that they had used during Piers' time: that I had disregarded the Ordinances and allowed Hugh undue favors. Rumors were that Lancaster was treating with the Scots and had plotted to take part in the uprising, as well, but at the final hour, he had turned coward and stayed home, leaving Mortimer and his aged uncle to fend for themselves. Starving and with soldiers deserting them daily, the rebels surrendered at Shrewsbury. Had it not been for Isabella's pleas, Roger Mortimer, his eldest son and his aged uncle would have been hanged and quartered. Instead, they would live out their natural lives in the Tower—unless some untimely misfortune or malady befell them. Entirely possible. Meanwhile, I recalled Hugh to my side and set my hounds on Lancaster's trail. Sir Andrew Harclay engaged him at Boroughbridge. And won.

"Harclay will receive a vast reward. Only "—I ran a fingertip over my lower lip in thought—"it's such a shame Hereford didn't survive the battle, too. I would have liked to have seen him grovel for mercy alongside Lancaster."

"And the queen has not pled for his life?" Hugh asked with a delicately raised eyebrow.

"Her cousin he may be, but sometimes blood ties are not enough." I smiled at my triumph. Soon, all my troubles would be gone. Vanished like winter snows under an ardent spring sun. "After so long, everything is finally going in our favor."

"As it should, my lord. As it should."

In the barbican outside the porter's lodge, we dismounted. Hugh and I strolled into the castle yard and made our way to the round tower that stood at the western entrance.

Before we ascended the tower stairs, I waved our escort back, stepped through the door and pulled Hugh inside for a word.

"My dear Hugh,"—I touched him lightly on the cheek, drawing my fingertips down over the slight stubble on his face until they rested beneath his jaw—"Lancaster signed his death warrant when he forced me to banish you. Please, know that I was only biding my time, waiting for the proper moment to levy a punishment upon him. It will not happen again. You will not leave me—now or ever."

He lowered his eyes and in the same moment turned his face toward my hand so that his breath curled inside my palm. "You have him now."

"Yes, and as I live and breathe I swear he will not get away with one whit more." I moved my hand to his shoulder in a firm grip of reassurance. "His wickedness will end ere the sun sets this day."

"Will you . . . make an example of him?" His eyes sparkled with the glimmer of revenge. Whatever grudge he held on Lancaster for sowing envy in the ranks toward him, my grudge was a hundredfold that: for the undermining of my birthright, for the murder of Piers. I could not allow Lancaster to live if even the slightest possibility remained that he would one day do the same to Hugh.

"A very fine one. And he will not be the last. You will attend to hear the charges?"

He moved back toward the doorway. "I regret not. Confront him on your own, Edward. Let this be *your* moment."

"Call on me an hour before sundown. Lancaster's case will be heard and decided by then. Together we will revel in our triumph."

I SAT IN THE Earl of Lancaster's own chair in the great hall of Pontefract Castle. Six days past, Sir Andrew Harclay had met and defeated Lancaster and his co-conspirator the Earl of Hereford at Boroughbridge. Hereford died most ingloriously when a spear pierced him from below as he tried to flee over the bridge spanning the river.

A hobbling Thomas, Earl of Lancaster, was prodded at sword end the length of the hall. Before the dais, he fell to his knees. The gilded rays of a March sun stabbed down through high windows, warming the peers who had gathered at my bidding to witness the flaying of a traitor. Flanking the aisle, there stood a throng of nobles—among them my younger brother Edmund, in his fine furs and golden chains; Aymer de Valence, Earl of Pembroke, whose loyalty to the crown since my sire's time had earned him high offices; and the Earls of Surrey and Arundel, shaking their heads at the misfortunate fool before them.

My chief justice, Robert de Malmesthorp, began by informing Lancaster that he was not permitted to speak or enter a plea. His treason was a known fact. He had been present at and instrumental in the murder of Piers Gaveston at Blacklow Hill. Mocked me from these very walls as we retreated in defeat after Bannockburn.

Malmesthorp continued on. "—letter found on the person of Humphrey de Bohun, Earl of Hereford, bears evidence that there was both collusion and intent to form an alliance with one Robert the Bruce of Scotland. That said letter did contain a direct invitation to the Scottish rebel to cross over into England in force and bear arms against Edward, King of —"

The presumptuous bastard had put a leash around my neck and I would now hang him with his own device.

Those who reach for the sun burn when they grasp it, Cousin.

Tilting my crown so it sat more imposingly forward on my head, I gazed upon Lancaster. Felt no compassion for him. No pang of love, remote or real. Only a yearning to bring this chapter to its natural conclusion. To take the breath from him. To stop the blood from coursing through his body. To look upon his corpse and know that this was the day I could truly begin to live and rule as I desired. As God intended.

I ran my fingers over the threads of my brocaded robe. From the corner of my eye, I saw Lancaster's body jerk and stiffen as he took in the chief justice's final sentence:

"—shall show no mercy upon him. Our lord sovereign, in regard of Lord Thomas' noble descent, waives two of the punishments, that he shall not be hanged and quartered, but executed by beheading."

For the first time that day, I met Lancaster's eyes. His countenance was blanched, his eyes bloodshot. The lines that edged every fold in his guilty face were as deep and dark as chasms to the underworld.

"Edward!" He reached forward with both hands, palms up in a gesture of humility. "Mercy, I beg, as our Heavenly Father would wish you to—"

"Plead your case with Him, Cousin. I am the law of the land and the punishment for your crimes has been meted out. If you have sins to reconcile, you will meet Our Lord soon enough."

WHEN HUGH ARRIVED AT my chamber door, I beckoned him to the window.

"There," I said, standing aside so he could have the better view. "Do you see St. Thomas' Hill in the distance? The castle yard would have been more convenient and expedient. But I remembered the name of that hill. Couldn't resist the irony."

The execution party had just arrived at the hill's summit. The journey there had itself been a public trial for Lancaster. The verdict delivered in a hail of stones and pigs' rumen.

From a velvet-lined box of carved cherry wood, I gathered the long gilded chain from which dangled a lion pendant, its eyes afire with rubies, its paws clenching four milky pearls. Hugh looked from the window.

"A gift—for my most loyal." I held the trinket up for him to see, but he appeared more observant than impressed. "Given to me by the King of France on my wedding day."

"Ah." His brow lifted slightly. A smirk tilted his fine mouth. "Not a Plantagenet lion, then?"

"Oh, it *is*. One of many. But it is the most treasured one of all."

He clasped his hands behind his back, feet braced wide, and bowed his head. I slipped the chain over his head. The pendant fell to one side and I nudged it to the center of his chest with a single finger.

As I went to pour Hugh and myself goblets of fine French wine, he caressed the facets of the jewels with his thumb.

"You like it?" I asked.

He lowered his hand from the pendant, looking at me long before speaking. "It belonged to him, didn't it?"

"Piers, you mean?"

"Perhaps I should not—"

I scoffed. "What? You think there is some curse attached to it? I assure you not. The cause for Piers' death is soon to die himself. In all my life, I have only ever valued one soul worthy of it. Keep it. It is a measure of my . . ."—I could not say the word I meant to, even though it teetered on the tip of my tongue—"my *regard* of you."

The sluggish pulse of drums struck up. I returned my attention to the distant hill. Sipping my wine, I watched as Lancaster was led to the block, hands bound behind him. Kneeling, he gave his last confession to a black-robed priest. The priest guided his head down, turning it to the left so Lancaster could look north and see that Robert the Bruce had abandoned him at his darkest hour.

The crescent axe blade glinted in the scarlet rays of a setting sun. It swung downward. Went up again. Down. Lancaster's head, at last, rolled from his corpulent torso. Even from this distance, I could see the blood spurting from his neck, staining the block. I had requested the blade be dull so that he might know the same torment my fond Brother Perrot had endured.

Hugh moved away from the window and settled into a chair, taking several long drinks from his cup before speaking. "What next? Scotland? We've so much less in our way now."

I pulled up another chair and took his hand, twining my fingers in his. "For now, let us forget revenge and revel in this moment of triumph. Let us be but here, now. You and I. No armies. No parliaments. No world beyond this room. Indulge me that?"

His eyes twinkled with mirth. "Your sole company and a flagon of wine?" He tipped his goblet up and drained every last drop. "I oft dream of it."

"And what more, dear Hugh, does this dream entail? A lingering gaze? A touch?" I brushed my knuckles across his cheek, ran my fingertips around the warm rim of his ear and slowly down his neck, over the vein where his pulse throbbed. "Do you dream of sharing a kiss, Hugh?"

The goblet dropped from his grasp and clattered across the floor. He leaned toward me, eyelids fluttering, lips parted. With both hands, I held his head, tendrils of silken hair entangled in my fingers, and drew him closer. He slid from the chair to kneel before me.

Our lips grazed. His mouth trembled, yielded. Supple, craving. My breath became his breath. His heartbeat, mine.

"How long I have waited for this," I breathed. "For you, Hugh."

21

Robert the Bruce – Melrose Abbey, 1322

S MOKE WHIPPED ACROSS THE sky like a black ribbon being pulled by the wind. Behind me, horses chomped anxiously at their bits, nostrils flaring wide. Men drew their swords free and strapped on their shields. But these were only familiar reactions to the unmistakable smell of blood and death that floated on the air to them from the distance. A nauseating smell, like offal left to rot behind a butcher's shop. A terrifying, enraging excitement that fired a man's blood in his very veins.

No enemy lingered in the valley below. They had come and gone, leaving behind nothing but the remnants of their hatred, transforming a place of tranquil holiness into a litter of rubble and hewn bodies strewn over a field of scarlet.

Gil came abreast of me on his horse. We gazed at the ruins of Melrose Abbey in sickened stupor, witnesses to the aftermath of a massacre. Helpless in our knowledge that no measure of revenge could atone for this. Only the Almighty could make the transgressors of this abomination answer for their sins.

Gil de la Haye shaded his brow with a long-fingered hand. "Randolph and Douglas are here already."

"Too late as well." My mount lurched forward, his ears flicking back and forth. The grass beside the road was heavily trampled in a broad swath, the ruts of wagon wheels still deeply imprinted. King Edward's army had been here not long ago and in numbers enormous. Starvation had forced them on. If they could not win victories on the battlefield or plunder riches, then they had determined to make their mark and leave behind a spoiled land. As we came closer, the stench grew overpowering. Queasy, I swallowed back bile and looked toward the abbey. I prayed that lives were spared, but I was wholly unprepared for the profane sight that met my eyes.

Randolph, as grim of face as I had ever seen him, was there in the churchyard to hold my stirrup as I dismounted. Scottish soldiers were going to and fro, carrying away the bodies of dead monks for burial, clearing the rubble, lugging buckets of water to douse lingering sparks, searching for survivors beneath the smoldering timbers of the abbey buildings.

Randolph's forehead dripped with perspiration. Soot was streaked across his face and clothing. "The locals say they rode through two days ago, looted the place of every relic and hunk of bread, murdered every holy man they came across and set everything aflame before clearing out."

"Where is James?"

"There." He pointed toward the abbey steps. "But be fairly warned, Uncle. Your eyes will behold the outcome of acts beyond hideous. Arm our bodies against spears and arrows we may, but our hearts are another matter entirely."

With Gil behind me, I made way through the litter and milling soldiers toward the front steps of the church. I had not even set foot to the first course, when I froze there. The double doors of the abbey were still on their hinges. But between them, the body of William Peebles, the abbot, was strung up like Christ at the Crucifixion: arms outspread, hands and feet pierced through with rusty nails, his head flopped to one side. Arrows had been shot full through his chest to leave his vestments dyed dark with blood. Neil Campbell pried at the nail heads with his axe. James and Boyd were reaching up, holding the abbot's arms, waiting to free the gentle martyr from the evidence of his horrific death.

I sank down on one knee and made the sign of the cross. "Father in Heaven . . . is nothing sacred?"

For minutes I remained like that, sickened with disgust, one knee grinding against the stones, my fingers clenched bloodless in prayer. A hand came to rest lightly on my shoulder. I looked up to see Angus Og, Lord of Islay. His fingernails were blackened with the crescent moons of crusted blood. Sweat matted the red hair in dark clumps around his freckled face. Through all the grime he forced a smile, then gave his hand to raise me up.

"We got here only a few hours ago, my lord," he said, the corners of his mouth plunging beneath the fringe of a moustache that twitched when he spoke. "We wouldn't have taken so long to retrieve the abbot's body, but . . . survivors first."

"Did you find many?"

"A few. The only unscathed monks we came across had been down by the river, unaware until they saw the smoke rising. Of those that were here at the abbey—little good to tell. There were two badly burned still hiding in barrels in the kitchen, another trapped in a pile of stones when the second floor of the dormitory collapsed. He will live. The other two—they will have a hard time of it. They haven't much of their skins left. It would be merciful if God would spare them the suffering and let them go to their graves with their brothers."

I gazed at the desecration and shook my head, rife with shock. When the truce expired, Edward had wasted no time. His treatment of Lancaster had been swift and full of revenge for Piers de Gaveston's murder. He then lunged northward into Scotland by way of Durham. In answer, I had dispatched James and Randolph to burn everything in the path of the oncoming English and had sped with my own forces into Lancashire to lay waste there, hoping to lure Edward away from the heart of my kingdom. But my ploy had failed miserably. This was a different Edward—a man bitter with revenge and imbued with more than a drop of his father's wicked blood, not the irresolute commander who had hobbled home from Bannockburn.

Loath to look upon Abbot William though I was, I forced myself to ascend the steps. With great sorrow and pity, I gazed at the abbot's mutilated form as they laid him down. Gil began to extract the arrows from Abbot William's chest, but the barbs were hooked deep beneath his ribs, so in the end all Gil could do was snap some of them off as far down the shaft as he could. Then Neil placed the abbot's arms across his body and began to wipe the brown, dried blood from his face.

"How far north did King Edward get?" I asked.

"Edinburgh, before he turned back," James answered. "Burned the abbey at Holyrood nearly to the ground. Thanks are due to Angus Og and his galleys for blockading the coast and stealing away three English supply ships at Black Rock before the king's very eyes."

Angus grinned. "We're well fed now, thanks to the English king's generosity."

"While his galleys did their work," James continued, "we waited on the other side of the Forth at Culross, as you had ordered, reckoning it better to avoid pitched battle just then. It was only a short time before the English decided Edinburgh was too empty for them and abandoned it. As soon as we got word of their retreat, we swung around the Forth and joined up with Angus. We pressed hard on their trail, as fast we could. I'm sorry, Robert. If we could have—"

"No, James, even I would not have guessed this of him. Besides, you had not enough men to provoke blows with him. I thought to lure him away and thought wrong. The blame's on me, if anyone. He can't have gotten far. He's crawling along with a massive army, short on forage, plagued by illness and pestered by rain. He'll quit when he feels safe enough to rest, thinking we'll let him go as long as he's retired from our land. But we won't. We'll leave enough men here to properly take care of this mess and follow him. As far as London if we need to."

I myself turned the shovel that opened up the ground to receive the dead of Melrose Abbey: Cistercian monks with their white habits shredded into blood-soaked rags on their bodies, some maimed grotesquely, others burned beyond recognition. Men who had never sought any grace but God's blessing.

Peace in this life is a fleeting illusion: never eternal, never entire. Why then have I expended so much of my life pursuing it, even at the price of my own sweat and tears and blood?

Because, this is what it is to live. This is what it is to strive for something better. This is the price you pay for your children and grandchildren and on down through the ages, with but a thin hope that they will not have to suffer the same.

But the price, the price . . . how high?

Faith, Robert. Faith. Never relent. Never abandon hope. Say it and you'll believe it.

Byland Moor, 1322

VENGEANCE GAVE US WINGS. Our numbers swollen by a frenzied contingent of Highlanders under Neil Campbell, we forded the Solway, slipped past Carlisle and dipped down through the Eden Valley in pursuit of our quarry. Meanwhile, I had dispatched Angus back to sea to fly down the coast and be ready for King Edward there, should he make it so far. Every day the scent grew warmer and the trail fresher. Edward had slackened his pace, while we intensified ours. The English locals by then had learned to run clear of a Scots army and man their town gates against us, for whatever meek comfort it afforded them. But we passed them by without a glance, bent for retribution.

By the 13th of October, we had made it as far as Northallerton, a smoking ruin after we shook its inhabitants from the planks and rafters of the town and set spark to it. It was there in the north of Yorkshire that a scout informed us King Edward was taking respite at Rievaulx Abbey, a mere fifteen miles away. Striking distance.

I stroked my beard within the pliant, leather palm of my gauntlet. My commanders were clustered around me at the fore of my army: James, Walter, Neil, Boyd, Gil and Randolph. "If we quicken our pace, can we bring him within our grasp by morning?"

"We're short on hours," Boyd said, squinting into the dreary western sky where clouds of autumn occluded the sun, "and opportunities."

Randolph stepped forward. "I've not delved this far into England for years, but if memory serves, the quickest route is directly south toward Sutton Bank and then a swift turn eastward toward the abbey. Any other way east from here to ford the rivers that run southward from the Hampton Hills and we lose dear time. Half a day's warning and he's to York and safely beyond our reach."

Gil and Walter nodded their agreement. James remained stoic, willing to do whatever I bid. Boyd wore a devilish grin.

"You're up for it, Boyd?"

He cracked the flat of one palm against the other. "Never more, sire."

FORGING ON THROUGH A mist as thick as porridge, we marched night-long, resting but a few hours and then rising before daybreak to go on. As we crept southward, the mist began to break and lift with first light, lending a better view before us.

To the east ran a steep hill-line, faced at various points with cliffs as sheer as any castle wall. Beyond the cliffs, an ancient cairn, half-toppled, projected jaggedly against the pink morning sky. Past the cairn, the ridge ran further southward, dotted with clumps of trees and patches of farmland at its base. From this crowded and obscured scene, the fires of several encampments curled upward.

Damn. Edward of England may have been indolent enough to take respite before holing himself securely up at York, but he had not been remiss in covering his backside. His soldiers were weary and wasted, mine pulling at the lead like hounds on the hunt. Our task now was to weigh our odds. I dispatched scouts and waited with agonizing impatience for their report. The chief standard, they relayed, was that of John of Brittany, Earl of Richmond. I called Randolph, James and Walter to me.

"Sutton Bank is the summit there, I believe," Randolph said. He cleared away a patch of dirt with the toe of his boot, plucked up a nearby stick and began to trace the layout of the land, marking *X*'s to indicate the English bivouacs. "Roulston Scar here. Scawton Moor's beyond and a straight shot to Rievaulx . . . over here."

"Any way around? It's King Edward I want."

Randolph bit his lip in thought, studying the map. "Better than a day lost if we retrace our steps north. And south—impossible without being discovered. Richmond has himself firmly planted in the pass there."

"They'll find us out shortly anyway," Walter said. "Did we sight Harclay's standard?"

Walter was becoming keener about his adversaries, but his confidence was still hampered by a tinge of doubt.

Randolph shook his head. "No, he skulked off to Carlisle, if rumors are true. Some deep rift there. Surprising—Harclay was Edward's champion after Boroughbridge. But what doesn't surprise me is that Edward would argue with those wiser than him."

I viewed the rudimentary map from a different angle and still I came to the same conclusion. I drew my sword, pulled its point sharply through Randolph's etching and then stuck it deep into the spot that was Rievaulx. "No other way but through then. Let's signal our arrival, shall we?"

Soldiers quickly set to work building pyres along a long line west of the English and setting them alight. The wood was damp from a long season of rain and slow to start, but once the fires began to blaze, clouds of thick smoke drifted lazily and then sank low over the windless valley. As the smoke swirled and settled, James positioned the bulk of the army nearer to the steep pass which lay just south of Richmond's camp. Randolph was at his side, as ever.

They struck directly up the pass—steep and rocky and dangerously narrow. Schiltrons in the van, shields raised overhead to meet the scatter of arrows that pelted them from the heights. The outcroppings to either side provided cover from above. Countless English arrows shattered on boulders. Some flew wide. Some short.

The first wave of English cavalry, compressed elbow to elbow, crashed against the prickly wall of Scottish spears and broke. Shafts hissed and then struck like random hailstones. Men grunted and roared, fighting for one more foot. The rattle and clang of metal biting metal filled the narrow valley.

In time, a faintly warm autumn sun had parted the curtain of smoky clouds from the nearby fires and ascended to its zenith. We were not only holding our ground, but gaining. I sent Neil up and around with his sure-footed Highlanders to engage the English on their flanks.

Walter sat astride his mount, his mail mittens lying ready across his lap. He had been silent, waiting his turn, both eager and apprehensive. The remainder of our forces were well hidden in a steep-sided, wooded gully behind us.

"I do think . . ." I squinted against the glare. Once I was certain of what I saw, I took to my saddle and put my hand out to my squire for my helmet. "They've broken through, Walter. Your chance. Ride on to Rievaulx. Hurry! Take the king."

Walter tugged his helmet on, then carefully strapped it under his chin before nodding to me. "I'll give him a good scare, at the least."

"Do better, Walter. He won't learn anything from it otherwise. With the King of England as our prisoner, we can set everything right. We can end this war once and for all—today."

As if I had asked the impossible, he said as he was going away, "Let us pray it will all come as easy as that."

I watched him go, he and his men cutting their way deftly through the openings in the breaking lines of English. As the smoke of our quickly built fires rolled across the woodland on a rising breeze, I hailed Gil and gave the signal. With the rest of our footsoldiers and hobelars, we cut through the smoke-shrouded forest, up the slope to punch through the space between Roulston Scar and Sutton Bank, angling toward Richmond's camp. As we gained the ridge, I shouted at Gil, "Richmond's standard—there!"

Just as he raised his hand in acknowledgment, his horse shot up on its hind legs. Its muddied brown hooves flailed in the air, then twisted around. It tossed its head back. An arrow had pierced its brain, just below the forelock. Gil was not fast enough to free himself before the thrashing beast crumpled beneath its own weight. He disappeared in a sea of raised swords.

Before I could turn back to search for him, a blast of English trumpets sounded. James had Richmond backed helplessly against the cliffs of the corrie near the pass. By the time I turned again to look for Gil, he was already on a fresh horse, calling out orders and swinging his blade with clean precision.

With hardly a fight, the Earl of Richmond surrendered to James, rather than be butchered like a pig in a slaughtering pen.

Rievaulx Abbey, 1322

"ARGH!" BOYD BLEW HIS nose and wiped it with the backside of his hand. "Damn English weather."

Rievaulx Abbey stood defiantly against a gray sky. A heavy mist saturated the air. I shivered as the oncoming cold of night settled in my bones. "When the rain clears, Boyd, see that they torch it . . . just like Melrose. Have they found the abbot yet?"

Through the wretched rain, a parade of monks was prodded past. Beside me, Randolph scowled in reproach at Boyd for not keeping a tighter rein on his men.

"Careful there," Boyd said as one of his captains, who was taunting the monks with threats of castration, marched smartly by. "Mercy on Our Lord's, ah . . . pack of bloody, worm-eating, boy-swiving chanters . . . I'll take a look about, sire, and bring him to you . . . if he lived."

Boyd pounded up the steps to the church, paused to share a brief word with Gil, and then ducked inside. Gil came across the open green, his lean legs swallowing up the distance lightly, even after so long a day on the battlefield. He held out a silver plate, a barely touched meal of salmon and fruit piled upon it. He tipped the plate sideways and let the food rain onto the ground. "Appears the King of England left in a hurry. Two roasted swans untouched on the table, kegs of French wine, jeweled goblets. Everything stone cold by the time we arrived, but the men are cleaning it up well."

"Which road did they take?" Randolph asked.

Gil looked to the dimming east and raised a finger. "That one."

Toward the coast. Ah, very good. If Walter cannot run him down, then let Angus pursue him across the sea.

That night I slept not in the chill and damp of the open, but in the Abbot of Rievaulx's own down-filled bed, my belly stuffed full and the taste of Burgundian wine on my tongue.

We had stood against the English at Bannockburn and brought them down. Taken from them Stirling and Perth and Edinburgh and best of all—Berwick. Driven them from Scotland time and again. This time we had pursued them deep within their own borders and beaten them soundly.

Still, it was not enough. Never enough. I wanted Edward of England kneeling in deference before me, promising all.

Always, there was one more task to accomplish.

"KING OF BLOODY NOTHING is what you are. I'd sooner scrape my knees raw to pet a flea-infested mongrel than kneel to you." John of Brittany, the Earl of Richmond, sneered at me. "Now have these bindings removed. I am a nobleman, not some commoner."

In the center of the abbey's nave, Randolph and James flanked a mounting pile of valuable relics and royal treasures. Randolph picked through the items on his side, methodically separating them into piles, while James plucked up the tall, curve-topped crozier and tested its weight. Beside him, Abbot John of Rievaulx swayed and made the sign of the cross.

"There's no doubt of your identity," I said to the earl. "I'd know you by your Plantagenet tongue alone. That is why you were spared. That is also why you will be escorted back to Scotland, like it or not."

Rain had lasted through the night, drumming steadily at the roof. I stifled a yawn. Hoping for news of success from Walter, I had risen far too early and now, near noon, I was suffering the effect of too little sleep and too much drink. "You took a thorough thrashing yesterday. Again, you English underestimated us. Didn't think we would come this far, aye, let alone outwit you, did you?" I turned to Abbot John, who had been brought before me that morning, looking every moment like he was on the verge of spouting some protestation. Vaguely, he reminded me of Bishop Lamberton in demeanor—that noble, restrained countenance, the cool, thoughtful squint, the slightly pursed lips. The build, though, was altogether different. Lamberton was taller and square-shouldered. The Abbot of Rievaulx had sloping shoulders, a stunted neck, shorter limbs. I studied him a moment and was about to speak when Richmond started again with his complaints.

"You cannot keep me this way. Where's your chivalry? Name your price. Release me on my honor, Lord Robert, and you'll get your ransom as soon as can be arranged." He strained to slip a hand free of the ropes that kept his hands behind his back, but they were tightly done. It would, in fact, be quite a trick to cut them loose at all without doing some harm to his person. Gritting his teeth, he kept on trying. It was amusing to watch.

"Ransom?" I said. "I do not think I mentioned any ransom. I may, however, consider it, after I have had some time to weigh your worth. Then again, perhaps you're not worth anything. After all, your king abandoned you both. Sped off without his queen, as well, from what I understand. How much do you reckon she's worth?"

The abbot's jaw dropped. Richmond's cheeks blanched.

I played along. "And the king himself . . . even more, aye?"

The abbot drew himself up to his full height. "They're both long gone. There is no information to be gained from either of us, because we haven't any to give. You've come as far as you can and earned your success, my lord. The king and queen have fled to safety and unless you intend to march on London—"

"Hah!" I raised my forefinger in the air, laughed and then thrust both hands heavenward. "Randolph, James . . . did you hear that? We've been invited to London." I stomped at the abbot and put my face so close to his that I could smell the scented oils he had recently bathed in. "You want us gone from here, do you? To merely stroll back north, content in this one battle's victory? To clasp you to our breast in brotherhood, sharing well wishes and call the day done? Is it arrogance or delusion that guides you, your grace? After Melrose, how can you believe that we would not, for a moment, seek justice?"

Wide eyes bespoke his innocence. "Melrose, my lord? I know nothing recently of Melrose."

From the corner of my eye, I could see Richmond visibly cringing, retreating into his shirt collar like a badger backing into its burrow.

James thrust forth the crozier. "Let him swear upon this."

As the abbot reached for the curve of the crozier, I waved the gesture off. "No, no, I believe him." I laid my hand on the abbot's shoulder. "Let me tell you what your fellow Englishmen have done. I trust your king boasted of his occupation of Edinburgh? Did he tell you, as well, that he put torch to Holyrood Abbey? That on his way south, he did the same to Melrose? If it were naught but timbers burnt to the ground, we could easily do the same in reprisal. After all, what is an abbey, but a group of buildings, hewn of stone and cut from wood and erected through the sweat and muscle of men, aye? Ah, but Edward of England did not stop at that when he came to Melrose. He ordered the murder of every monk there. And they nailed old Abbot William to the doors of the nave and shot him full of arrows for sport."

I withdrew my hand and unsheathed the knife from my waist.

The abbot flinched, but he did not retreat. "Vengeance belongs to Our Lord."

"You and I agree on that." In one swift motion, I cut the cord from his waist. "Now remove your vestments, although you may keep your undergarments. The rest of the monks will be asked to do the same. I'll send you from here, lives and souls intact. But the next time you, in any manner, support the actions of your baseless king, think of Melrose, your grace. Meanwhile, we will be collecting our recompense from the abbey before we burn it to the ground. There are plenty of your brethren in Scotland who will appreciate these fine raiments."

"And what of me?" Richmond demanded.

"I said"—I turned toward him sharply, annoyed at his flippancy and curtness—"you will come back to Scotland as my prisoner. I'll set your ransom if and when I have need of more monies. For now, we're well provided for."

"You can't!" Richmond flailed his arms behind his back and stumbled forward, nearly falling on his face before catching his balance. "I am King Edward's cousin!"

"All the more reason to bloody stuff you down a hole and close it up. Your kind should never be allowed to procreate. And there is a solution to that." Having suffered enough of Richmond's company, I spun on my heel. "See that the abbot and his people leave their clothes behind and send them on their way, Randolph. And Douglas, keep the earl well under guard and out of my sight on our return. Once all the treasures here are uncovered and packed away, this place will be filled with smoke."

I made it down the outer steps and was halfway across the cloister when I heard the clatter of hooves on stone. Walter, mounted on his own horse, led a spirited gray charger by the reins. Behind him was a small contingent of about fifty men. He dismounted and pulled the gray toward me. Wild with anticipation, I hurried toward him.

The moment his features came sharply into view, my hopes tumbled.

Breathless, tired, he hung his head a moment, then looked up at me. "I'm sorry. We lost him on the road at nightfall. That was after we followed him as far as the coast and came within sight of him. Angus' galleys were there, just up from Bridlington. The only ships available to Edward were nothing but trading ships—they could not have outpaced Angus. So he turned back inland—that is when we lost him. By the time we found his tracks again, he was already well on his way to York. He did abandon this horse on the way, though. Not much compensation, but . . ." His head dipped again.

"You did well, Walter." I pounded him on the upper arm. Although gravely disappointed, I dared not show it. "Keep the animal for yourself. You've earned it this time."

"Queen Isabella?" he asked.

"Left from here in a nun's habit, we learned. I sent men out as far as I dared. Nothing." Together we walked across the open cloister. The first tang of smoke drifted on damp October air.

"We'll collect what tributes we safely and swiftly can," I said. "Then I want to go back home. You, as well?"

He heaved a sigh. "Aye. Home."

THE FOLLOWING YEAR, ANDREW Harclay, the Earl of Carlisle, weary of our renewed raids on the north of England and swimming in futility with his king, proposed to me in person at Lochmaben that a lengthy truce be drawn up between Scotland and England, so that both kingdoms could recover from what was proving to be a never-ending quarrel.

Upon hearing of this, King Edward of England flew into a rage. He had Harclay taken by treachery, tried and hanged as a traitor—the very man who had captured and delivered Thomas of Lancaster to him. Carlisle was now without a competent governor. Edward of England hurried to undo his error. He extended the offer of a truce between the kingdoms of England and Scotland—of thirteen years. A pity such a worthy opponent as Harclay had to give his life for our benefit.

I affixed my royal seal to the treaty as King of Scotland. Though smug in the acknowledgment, I was no more a fool than I was hopeful. Peace would prevail only for as long as there was no alternative for Edward of England. He had little loyalty among his liegemen. And I had one of his few faithful in my captivity: his kinsman, that surly Earl of Richmond. I had not yet named a price for his ransom and when I did, the amount would further bankrupt poor Edward.

There remained one further confirmation I sought that the crown I wore sat justly upon my head. I would dispatch Thomas Randolph to the pope in Avignon. My nephew was both delicate and adroit in his diplomacy. In return, I would tender a promise that one day I would do the work of God and lead an expedition to the Holy Land. Only then would my heart rest content.

For now, there was peace. Scotland belonged to the Scots.

And Elizabeth was with child again.

22

<u>Edward II – Tower of London, 1323</u>

A DOZEN BEESWAX CANDLES flickered on the supper table at staggered heights like stars suspended. They sputtered and waned with the cross-draft that swept from the open window behind me and stirred the hairs on my neck. With one breath, I thought, I could perish the lights of heaven.

The pressed ride back to London from Lancashire had only intensified my growing suspicions and sunk me in a mood so glum and surly nothing could have revealed the light of hope to me. Following the execution of Thomas, the earldom of Lancaster had become a matter of contention. His brother Henry, Earl of Leicester, had clamored for it, but I reminded him such matters were not so lightly handled. I hoped he would be less recalcitrant than his sibling had been, but recent events had indicated otherwise. I gazed down the length of the table at Isabella as she hunted through the cinnamon sauce drizzled over her capon. She speared a cherry with her knife and brought the red, glistening fruit to her lips.

Her hand froze in place as she looked up at me, gold-green eyes flashing like the flicker of lightning in faraway clouds. "You arranged matters in Lancaster quickly? He was agreeable?"

"Indeed, I did not. Henry is every bit as much of a boorish prig as his brother Thomas was. Worse, perhaps. Like a ram that butts without provocation."

"Then," she began, as she looked back down at her meal, searching for another cherry, "why did you return to London so soon if trouble remains?"

"Because, my dear, when one of my most dangerous enemies escapes from imprisonment here, don't you think I'd want to look into it?" I scoffed at her. The woman could be sly, but her feigned ignorance was nakedly absurd. "Roger Mortimer escaped not a fortnight ago from here. The rope he scrambled down was still dangling from the wall the next morning. He disappeared from London without a trace—time afforded to him by the sheer fact that nearly every man in this garrison, as well as the kitchen cooks, succumbed to a sleeping potion slipped in their ale as they celebrated the feast of St. Peter. Obviously, Mortimer did not manage this feat alone. But of course, my dearest wife, you already know that, don't you? I came back because I feared for your safety. We have spies, traitors, at work in our midst."

I paused there, studied her a moment. She looked away. So telling. "When I find them out, I will hang them by their necks from London Bridge. Already, I have dispatched agents into Wales and the Marches to hunt the foul bastard down. Anyone who aids him shall pay a dear, dear price. I've no tolerance for liars, none at all."

At one time, she had befriended Thomas, the Earl of Lancaster, in an effort to oust Hugh from my council, until she perceived it to be more to her advantage to abandon my cousin and nestle under my protective wing. Her jealousy over my intimate bond with Brother Perrot had been the sole cause for the wedge driven between us in the first years of our marriage. Now she sought to dislodge Hugh. When would the woman ever desist from creating such strife? Did she thrive on it out of amusement?

Isabella's voice was irregular, uneasy. "I pray you find the traitors, whoever they are . . . and that they are punished properly. But enough of unpleasantries. May we talk of our children? You see them so little." She forced a smile and tilted her head of pale, golden curls in an attempt to lighten the mood, but even so her shift in subjects was blatantly awkward. "Edward excels in his studies, his tutors say. His French, it is perfect. As if he had been born there."

"Commendable." I slid my chair back and turned it so that I faced the hearth, watching the sparks fly out and skip over the stones before the embers faded and died. Heat, as in a passion, lives but briefly before it goes forever cold. Such had it been between Isabella and me since fair Joanna had arrived in the world, four long years ago. Years without the Lords Ordainers. Years in which power had sifted through my fingers like quicksand when it should have grown.

Once upon a time, there had been some tenderness between us— Isabella and I. A need of sorts. True love? Never that. Dependency rather. I had required an heir. She had come to accept her purpose, where once she had resented it. Now she had her children to coddle and fawn over. And I had immortality. Young Edward was a boy just crossed over into manhood who sat tall and comfortable in his saddle, wielded a sword with surprising strength and captured glances from blushing court maidens with subtle aplomb. Isabella had dominated his early years, insisting upon overseeing his lessons and teaching him courtly manners herself in the casual French fashion. Although I had not the luxury of time for my children, Isabella's close involvement with them unsettled me—particularly in regards to my heir. A woman's influence was seldom beneficial.

I leaned forward, planting my elbows on my knees as the fire warmed my face. "Can our son thread a loom, too?" When she didn't return the barb, I looked again at her.

Isabella carved her meat into thin slices and nibbled delicately. "I do not know. Perhaps you could ask him? He spends much of his spare time with his friends now. "

"May that be his salvation," I said with an unintended growl. She did look at me then—so intensely that I could tell there was another announcement coming. One I would not like.

"He said he would gladly go to France in your stead. Pay homage for your holdings there as my brother has demanded. I have written to Charles, to ask if that is acceptable."

Her brother Charles had of late come to the throne of France, but only after three older brothers had died. Unlike his slovenly and stoic predecessor, his father King Philip IV, he was worldly and full of guile. My consort's proposition had stirred yet more suspicions within me. An itch I had to scratch. I got to my feet and approached her. "How dare you do so without first asking me."

She stiffened at my words. "I write to my brother frequently. It was a question, only. I do not speak for you. That is why I mentioned it."

"When? *When* did you write to him?"

She slammed the butt of her knife against the table. "I told you—I write to him often. I do not know when I asked. Charles has flaunted his demands since he took the crown. You cannot avoid him forever, unless Ponthieu and Aquitaine mean so little to you that you would give them away. Why is it important to know when I asked him that? Should it matter? And as your wife," —her eyelids thinned to slits—"am I to cease corresponding with my own brother unless I gain your permission first as to what I compose?"

Rather than consume the bait, I tossed it back at her. "I suppose, if I allowed young Edward to go, you would want to escort him, yes?"

"Of course." Isabella tucked her hands in her lap. Like a cat with its claws flexed and ready to pounce, she drew her shoulders up high. Then, a thought passed over her brow and she relaxed visibly, as if arranging her defenses. "Do you not think it wise, my lord? He is young, inexperienced, knows nothing of Charles as I do. With me at his side for guidance, young Edward would be spared the humiliation of a misspoken thought, an overeager gesture. Perhaps I could carry a letter for you? In your own words. A humble gesture to keep peace with France. Keep your lands there. Maintain the income from them . . . Yes, that would be good, do you not agree?"

I plucked up my wine goblet and returned to my chair, let it swallow me. How grand it would be to have the unfaithful bitch out of my sight. I hadn't enough evidence to lop off her head. Even if I did, I no more wanted war with France than I wanted the mother of my children sent to her grave prematurely. "Allow me to think on it. We could at least settle a treaty between England and France—parliament has been clamoring for it long enough. Just . . . not right away. Not yet."

I downed my drink in one long gulp. Without waiting for its effects to overtake me, I rose, poured myself more and drank again. My head was fogging up by the time Isabella finally spoke.

"Winter will come soon. A voyage across the channel would be safer now, would it not?"

"*Not yet*, I said. Sweet Jesus, you're as dogged as you are dense. Listen and listen well. There is no telling where Mortimer is lurking and I'll not have him exact his revenge by absconding with you." I wondered if she caught the sarcasm in that sentiment. "Write your damn letters. Mountains of them, if it so pleases you. Tell your tyrant of a sibling that I fear for the safety of my son, should he travel abroad. I must consider this long before giving my consent. Arrangements would have to be made. Measures taken. These are dangerous times, Isabella. My mind is heavily burdened lately."

It was growing late and the Tower of London, although quiet at such a time, was a foreboding place. How difficult to think of it as home, but the city of London was the core of the kingdom and being here was a necessary evil—just like this game Isabella and I were playing. Bits and parcels of information drawn out—as painfully as if we had dangled fish hooks down our throats and were attempting to pull out our own entrails. What secrets we kept tucked away. Little sordid sins never confessed.

Her skirts rustled as she rose and crossed the room. I gripped my knees. "Where are you going?"

"To bed, my lord. I am tired and have eaten enough."

"No, not yet. Sit."

"Ask me and be done with it. I wish to go."

"Very well. What do you know of Mortimer's escape?"

Oh, she had been waiting for that question all along. She pressed her fingertips together, batting her long fringe of eyelashes. "No more than you."

I rose from my chair, circled her, looked her up and down and then stopped squarely behind her. I leaned in close, touching my lips to her ear. "Good, because I would hate to learn that you had ever lied to me."

"You do not believe me?"

As I placed my hands on her shoulders and dug my fingers in, she flinched. "Oh, yes," I said, "I believe every word you say. That is why I asked. Merely for reassurance. You may go now. Sleep well, Isabella— my faithful queen."

She pried herself from my grasp and rushed to the door. As she placed her hand upon the latch and pulled the door open, she turned. "I would sleep better were Hugh Despenser not always whispering in your ear, commanding your every move."

As swift as she could, she was gone, not even bothering to close the door behind her. I moved out to the corridor and watched her swish angrily away in her abundant skirts. The smoking torches waved their goodbye as she passed. I shut the door firmly and drew the bar.

Leaning against the door, I began to laugh. A chuckle at first, but soon I was rolling in tides of laughter and clutching my belly. I gripped a narrow column close to me to keep from sliding to the floor. "Mother Mary, does the witch think none of this will follow her?"

Finally, I stumbled back to my chair and wiped away the tears. "What say you, Hugh?"

The door to the antechamber that connected to my wardrobe

groaned weakly. Hugh moved from behind it, through the shadows and into the light without a sound.

His arms were crossed, his countenance composed, but something in his words conveyed an underlying disquiet. "I say there is much more to the woman than you or I have ever estimated. She lies. She plots. She has patience enough to work her desires through intricate detail. She is enmity. Spite. And I like none of it."

"Nor I, dear Hugh. But what have you learned today that could put her in shackles? I need weapons, Hugh. An arsenal. What did you learn of this lieutenant that disappeared? What was his name?"

"D'Alspaye. Gerard d'Alspaye. A ferryman, who needed a small measure of convincing, revealed that he took two men across the Thames on the night of the first of August—one fitting the description of d'Alspaye and the other, if not Mortimer, then his twin."

"And from there? Were you able to track them further?"

"Only a little, sire. The ferryman noted that there were half a dozen or so men awaiting d'Alspaye and Mortimer. The stew was well cooked. There was mention of riding swiftly to Hampshire, a boat there . . . no more details than that. In Hampshire, we put spies in all the ports. There were many possible leads. None of them reliable, I daresay. He could be in Wales or Scotland by now. Ireland. The continent. No way of knowing."

"This d'Alspaye—was he a sympathizer of Mortimer's? In his pay, perhaps?"

"He saw Mortimer almost daily, so who is to say what poison the dark lord poured in the lieutenant's ears. D'Alspaye has been on staff here for nearly fifteen years. His station was one of responsibility and relative comfort—a decent life for a baseborn man. Why risk that for nothing? There are holes in this affair that can be filled only with answers. What would Mortimer, outlawed and penniless, have to offer even a common soldier?"

"Mortimer—nothing." I stood, moved to the hearth and stoked the dying logs. "But a queen . . . a queen could offer much."

<u>Tower of London, 1324-5</u>

I KEPT A KEEN watch on Isabella in the following months. Two of her letters to her brother were intercepted. They were replete with the usual whining about rustic English court life and interspersed with yawning anecdotes about her children. She extolled every virtue and accomplishment of young Edward, hoping, I suspected, of building him up in her brother's disparaging eyes.

On several occasions, Isabella took the liberty to tell me how anxious Charles was to meet his nephew. Her incessant begging grated deeply on me and so I at last consented for her to visit the French court and finalize the peace treaty that several of my ambassadors there had been haggling over indefinitely. My heir, however, would remain behind for now. Homage due or not, he would not go until Isabella had achieved her purpose.

"You invite your own undoing," Hugh had protested with a snarl, "by letting her from your sight. Worse yet to let her nestle beneath the wing of her overprotective brother."

"I would say you are right, Hugh, but the cockscomb has me by the bollocks. If I refuse Charles, he'll wage war—and just where would I get the means to field an army? Parliament won't even permit me sufficient funds to run my household. They're still blaming me for Scotland. No, I'll let her go. I regret that I must. But on my terms. Besides, if she can't take her children with her, she'll have every reason to come home. And she'll do exactly as I say."

"And Young Edward? Will you send him in your stead?"

I laughed. "You don't expect me to go there myself, do you?" Sobering, I grabbed him by the arm and yanked him to my chest, my body rigid with pent-up rage. I put my lips to his ear. "She has said things about you, Hugh—about us. That you are the cause for discord between her and me. Demanded I send you away. I won't do that. *Ever*. I'll shove that filthy harlot into the flames of hell's own bowels before I'll give you up."

He pressed his cheek to mine, wove his fingers in the hair at the nape of my neck. His kiss on my temple was light, tender, soothing. "She feels threatened, Edward. As if she has already lost you—and in a way, she has. You see, long ago, I knew that you would be mine. I never dreamed how much so, how completely our souls would intertwine. She knows. She lashes out like a lioness defending her cubs. Just remember: you are king. You have the power. And . . . you have me."

As easily as that, with a touch, a word, he assuaged my anger. He was much more to me than I could ever express or even comprehend. As exhilarating as it is to love someone so completely, it is also terrifying. Without him, I would be incomplete, empty. I might as well be dead.

IN MARCH, ISABELLA SAILED for France with wardrobe enough to fill half a hull. I sent Bishop Stapledon to keep watch over her. Not only would he keep me well informed, he would remind her daily of her duty to me.

The first piece of news that returned to me had nothing to do with Isabella's delight at rejoining civilization, as she had so often proclaimed the French court. The first thing I heard were the complaints that she publicly shared about how wretched my treatment of her was and what a farce our married life had become. She made no secret that she was utterly miserable with me and with life in England.

And then word: the peace treaty had been finalized. The woman, it seemed, had a penchant for mollifying tempers and eliciting compromise. She had been in France the better part of a year now. Her mission complete, I sent word to Bishop Stapledon, summoning her home. She refused outright, stating that I had not fulfilled my promise to send our son to pay homage. Her brother buttressed her demands by stating that if I did not, my lands in France would be forfeit.

For weeks, I agonized. If I went and left Hugh behind, his life would be in jeopardy. Yet Hugh would not be safe in France, either. I could not leave him here. I could not take him with me. I hardly even thought it safe for me to go. Yet if this matter of homage was not settled, I stood to lose immense sums of income and thus power.

I called my son to me. "Your mother has been too long gone."

Young Edward's footsteps slowed until he stopped halfway across the tiled floor of the throne room in St. Thomas' Tower. A light summer breeze tossed locks of his fair hair across innocent eyes. The sounds of busy London drifted in from open windows, accentuating the silence between us.

I tapped my rings on the arm of my chair, then curled a finger at him. "Come closer. How am I to speak with you at this distance?"

He looked down, then shuffled the remaining steps to me. "Yes, my lord."

"How old are you now?"

"Almost thirteen, my lord."

"Old enough, then. To be oblique about any of this would be an insult to you. So I'll say it without adornment. Your mother's business in France is done. She has refused to return until homage is paid to King Charles for Gascony, Aquitaine, Ponthieu and the Agenais. I cannot leave my kingdom, therefore, you must take my place in this. If it is not done . . ." I narrowed my eyes at him, but he was still looking down, studying the cracks in the tiles. I slammed my palms on the sides of the chair. "Look at me! When you go to France—and I sorely regret that you must—you will look that bastard uncle of yours in the eye and hold your chin high. You are the firstborn son of the King of England. You are *not* his inferior, do you understand?"

His lip twitched, or perhaps it quivered? I could not tell.

"I will greet him as my equal, Father." He raised his shoulders, suddenly appearing older, more sure of himself. His voice, though, still had the girlish squeak of an adolescent. "I will do as he asks, offer no offense, perhaps I will even win his favor. And when it is done—"

"When it is done, you will return to England *with* your mother. Accept no excuses. Remind her of her promises to me. Make her swear to uphold them. Tarry there not a day longer than needed. Understand?"

He nodded. "I do. And the sooner I go, the sooner I can return, yes? I mean, as you said, she has been too long gone."

In that moment, the boy's insight pleased me greatly.

"Yes, yes. You may go. Your ship awaits. When you return, we can discuss the matter of your future marriage prospects. You're of an age now when it is time to consider the options, forge alliances where they may best serve England."

"Marriage, my lord? I-I-I am but thirteen and—"

"You are yet twelve. But do you not think your mother has some ulterior motive in luring you to Charles' court while she is yet in attendance? Likely, she will try to influence you, introduce you to some young maiden of noble French blood, convince you of the benefits of committing to such a union . . . Do not even pretend to agree. These matters are not hers to decide. She has always had France's interests at heart, never England's. Remember that. So go there. Utter your tenuous oath of fealty. And hurry home. But do not, do *not* come back without her."

I was never so unsure of my decisions. But what other choice did I have? War with France? It had gone badly enough with Scotland. France, if it came to it, would be a far more formidable foe and I could not afford the trouble. Not for pride. Not for the pretenses of preserving a sham marriage. Not for my crown.

ROGER MORTIMER WAS IN Paris. Not only had he had been living quite comfortably there, often a welcome guest at Charles' court, but he and

Isabella were seen together . . . in one another's arms.

I had been right all along. When Mortimer was being held in the Tower, she must have visited him out of pity; somehow he had enchanted and seduced her. Woven his black spell and stirred her carnal desires. Servants were probably bribed to turn a blind eye and none of them had possessed enough loyalty to me to confess their part. Gerard d'Alspaye among them. Whether by witchcraft or choice, my wife had lain with another man. I imagined the two of them, panting and sweating, entangled in silken sheets. Beyond sinful, it was unforgiveable. Revenge consumed me.

Driven by lust, Mortimer had abandoned his wife and children. Obviously, he would gamble their safety to rut with a king's consort. A blessing on my behalf. As a reminder to Isabella that her other three children were yet in my keeping, I snatched up Mortimer's wife and children and locked them away.

The pen is a powerful weapon and I wielded it freely. Charles would learn of my power. The pope would learn of her indiscretions. *She* would learn that I held the upper hand in this game.

Laugh as you bed the devil, my consort. Take your pleasures to your grave. You'll not make a cuckold of me and live to tell of it.

23

<u>Robert the Bruce – Cardross, 1326</u>

BARELY MORE THAN A year passed after Margaret's birth before our Mathilda came into our lives. Ah, Mathilda, Mathilda. As soon as her feet hit the ground she was running. Her nurses could not keep up with her. She had Marjorie's spirit: independent, talkative, ever curious. Meanwhile, her older sister would sit hour upon hour at her mother's knee, absorbing every sacred word that came from her mother's mouth, as if Elizabeth were God Almighty delivering the Ten Commandments.

Robbie was as stout and strong as a young oak. The crook in his spine was not as evident as first feared. His active nature had sufficiently strengthened his muscles to compensate for the impediment. By eight, he could ride as well as any lad and run nearly as fast. He had promise and courage and so I kept him at my side whenever I could, hoping to instill in him some morsel of wisdom garnered from my years of trial and misfortune, just as my own grandfather had done for me. Walter wrote often from Berwick the first few years to inquire of his son's welfare. But as each year passed, the letters became less, the visits fewer, the reunions less exuberant.

Robbie was my shadow, my echo and my reflection. He followed me always—whether hunting with James, for whom he had a special affinity, or hawking with Elizabeth, or even as I ambled about the grounds of Holyrood. He begged for my stories, then told them to the other children, embellishing them with god-like feats and golden dragons that breathed fire. Most haunting of all, I saw in him that stubborn, unbreakable spirit that was my own. Already I felt blessed by my daughters and grandson and if God had given me yet another daughter, Robbie would have been more than fit to follow in my steps.

Then, gloriously . . . David came into the world. My son. My own. And I fifty years of age. Elizabeth near forty—a time by which many women were looking after grandchildren, not giving birth to bairns of their own.

For Elizabeth, it was as if a great trouble had been banished from her soul in the event of his birth. David was a quiet babe: content at his mother's breast, often falling asleep there, and when he awoke he would hold his own fingers in front of his face and contemplate them peacefully for incredible lengths of time. He was long of limb, delicate of feature and born with a full head of russet, silken hair that curled around the rims of his ears, making him appear more angel than little boy.

Elizabeth coddled him overly much, so I often told her. But mother and son were like two lost halves that had finally joined and could not be cast asunder. If she had openly conceded to taking second in my life to the affairs of the kingdom, then I myself had silently stepped to the side in hers in favor of our children.

In order to spend time with my growing family, I had a house built overlooking the mouth of the Clyde near a tiny village called Cardross, just beyond Dumbarton. I deigned not to raise my children within a ring of stones, but rather within the comforting warmth of timber-framed walls, where they could listen to the rain drumming on the thatch or run barefoot and wild in the hills beyond. Cardross was such a place: always smelling of salt air, the seabirds gliding overhead on fairer days from shoreline to hilltop, the wind as constant as my own breath. I would teach Robbie to sail on the open water, and one day David, as well.

It was in 1325, that another son was born to us. Unlike his brother, John cried from daybreak to evening and on through the night. Never willing to pass the care of her children entirely to nursemaids, Elizabeth suffered for loss of sleep, trying to soothe young John.

The following summer I remained in Cardross, rather than return to Edinburgh, leaving the business of the kingdom in the competent hands of Thomas Randolph. When he could, he came to me at Cardross to seek my guidance.

So he did that summer. Being too good a day to waste, my nephew and I strolled from the house down the path that led to the shore, where the three oldest children were playing. Elizabeth, holding Mathilda in her arms even as the lass kicked and cried to be let down, waved to us from the crest of a dune and came to join us.

I had never seen my Elizabeth so content as that summer at Cardross. Bathed in the golden rays of summer, she would stroll along the Clyde every day, hand-in-hand with the girls, watching keenly over Robbie and David as they played in the water. The two lads would splash each other, laughing raucously as they wiled away the days, no cares to the future, no pasts yet to trouble them. Too aching and weary, I could but watch from the shore, sometimes with Margaret and Mathilda clambering on the rocks around me, but more often alone.

Elizabeth smiled broadly as Randolph kissed her on the cheek.

"You look well, Thomas."

"And you never better. Truly. Why, if you were not my uncle's wife . . ." he teased.

"Ah, but you have a wife of your own, I recall. How would we ever do away with them both?" As Mathilda began to fuss, she bounced her on her hip.

"That *is* a problem." Then Randolph bestowed a little kiss on Mathilda's rosy cheek. "My wee cousin is in a fit of unhappiness, I see. Wanting to run and play, are you?"

"Aye, but last I set her down near the water she was up to her chin in it before I could blink. Not again. I try to amuse her with searching for shells, but it never lasts long enough."

"And how is the newest prince?" he asked. "Asleep in his cradle as we speak?"

At that, Elizabeth's smile faded to a frown. The sun beating down on her face clearly showed the deep lines that fanned out from the corners of her eyes. "Cried all night, he did. They say it is the colic and he'll outgrow it in time. I only hope they're right. The other children were so different. I don't know at all what to do with him. It tears at my heart and when I hold him he only cries that much more." She sighed. "Sometimes I think that if he had been born my first, he would also have been my last."

"Last what, mama?" Margaret had scrambled over a small hill of sand behind us and stood with a treasure of shells collected in the apron of her skirt.

Elizabeth looked down, then quickly gathered her composure. "Never mind. Up to the house with you. Mathilda here is past due for her supper. And put those mussels back where you found them. You smell of seaweed, Margaret. Go on, then. Don't stand there staring at me as if you don't understand. Off with you."

Margaret frowned. "Can I sing to wee Johnny, mama? He likes it when I sing to him."

"Of course you may. Now go on." She set Mathilda down and shooed them away. Margaret took her little sister by the hand and they went along the path that wandered past the sand dunes, up the rocky hillside and on toward the house. Before setting off after them, Elizabeth said, "Will you gather up the lads when you're done?"

I laid my hands upon the gentle curve of her shoulders and gave her a kiss. "It won't be long. Let Margaret sing her brother a lullaby."

She waved good-bye and left. At water's edge, Robbie teased David with a crab, its pincers snapping furiously. David squealed and flailed at the crab, knocking it into the water, at which Robbie only laughed. Ten now, Robbie was eight years the senior of his own uncle, little David, and he accepted the duty of looking after him with a mixture of begrudging disdain and simple amusement. David, the timid follower, was half-enamored of Robbie and half-terrified. An interesting relationship. I often wondered how it would develop in years to come. It was imperative that I set things aright for my son and allow him a secure kingdom to inherit—especially if it happened before he was ready for the duty.

I thank My Lord that I have James and Randolph to oversee things, to do what I can no longer do for myself. Without them . . . without them I would have no peace.

"A fine pair of lads," Randolph said.

"The best. David will do well with Robbie to lead the way for him."

"Do you think it goes that way—Robbie as the leader?"

"I think, nephew, it's too early to tell or ponder on. But my family has grown a lot in a little while, hasn't it? There were so many times when I thought I would never see this day, and now that I have it . . . Ah, when I asked God for all this all those years ago, I bloody forgot to tell him to hurry up." I stopped myself before I could go on anymore. Age had made a cynic of me. "So, you've been to see the pope, have you? What says our venerable pontiff? Have I his blessing to go to the Holy Land? Although I don't see where I should have to ask him first before I do God's work, but that, I suppose, is how it's done."

Randolph shook his flaxen head subtly. "He'll call you 'king' and welcomes your aid against the infidels, but with one stipulation."

"Ah . . . Berwick."

"Aye, Berwick. He wants you to give it back to the English. King Edward harps on it incessantly."

"Hah! England's king has good cause to be in a whining mood. His queen will have none of him. But what a bloody bunch of rubbish . . . If we returned Berwick, next they would be asking for Stirling and Edinburgh. After that Perth and Dunbar. No, you know as well as I—and the pope knows it, too—we keep Berwick. It's ours. Always has been. The excommunication?"

"Still on you. He would not lift it."

"Then if the price for Berwick is my soul, so be it." We had walked along the shore a ways, enough to tire me, and so I sat down on top of a small overturned rowing boat and stretched my legs. "And France? Do they agree to renewing the alliance with us?"

"For the time it seems so and aye, they do agree. But not publicly. Queen Isabella has overseen the signing of a peace treaty between France and England, I understand."

I mopped at the sweat on my brow and pushed up my sleeves. "Wickedly warm for September, don't you think?"

But Randolph didn't answer the question. He stared at my forearms, then suddenly poked a finger at my left arm.

"What are these bruises?" His brow furrowed intensely. "So many. Heaven, it looks as though you've been given regular beatings."

"A rash, 'tis all. Rambling through the nettles. I should keep closer to home in my old age."

He towered before me like some elder scolding a stripling. "That's no rash, Uncle."

"Whatever it is," I said, rising to my feet so I could look down on him, being taller yet in stature than he, "it's nothing to be concerned over. You'll see for yourself soon enough. Seems like you are young and strong forever and then one day, you're just more tired than you used to be, your bones ache when it rains, your cuts don't heal as fast. You don't believe me now, but you'll see, Thomas. You'll see."

But what I said to him I meant more than I could say. I no longer sailed or hunted away the days. I couldn't. Every joint ached—more than I would ever reveal to Elizabeth or anyone. Lying down at night was a welcome event. Rising in the morning a toil. Always, I hid the discomforts, not wishing to burden anyone. First came the small pains: in the knees while climbing the stairs or mounting my horse, in the hands when I reached for a quill or grasped a spoon, in my shoulders and elbows when I tried to lift my own children. Then the bruises with every bump—deep purple turning green, then yellow—and the tiny speckles of red on my arms and back. I learned to keep my marks well hidden, but as time progressed, even that became impossible.

More than my attempts to deny my own gradual decay, I was struck hard by the irony that my father had suffered a like affliction. How little I had understood of him then, seeing nothing but my own life awaiting me, possessed even then by the ambition that had defined me to this very day. But as my father shrank from the world in grim solitude, I desperately tried to cling to it and deny what was happening to me, praying it would pass of its own or at the least get no worse. Inside, though, I knew there was something wrong, something that would gradually eat away at me and steal the life from me.

As I called to Robbie to bring David along and follow us home, the effort snatched the breath from me. Climbing back up the hill toward the house was a task and if not for the wind at our backs I might not have made it without pausing to rest.

My God . . . I would rather have died looking into the eyes of my foe as he thrust a blade into my gut, than slowly decaying like this.

As much as I made light of it, the pope's blessing was more important than ever. Something was happening to me, some slowly growing sickness nibbling away at me from within. Time was like sand sifting through my fingers, and more than grain by grain.

ONCE I SAT DOWN in my chair to wait for supper in the great hall of Cardross, I did not move for hours. My knees throbbed as if they had been hammered and my feet were on fire from the pounding of the short walk.

Randolph appeared never in better health. At Elizabeth's polite prodding, he spoke of his wife and children with rare pride, for Randolph, always humble and pious, never boasted.

Elizabeth idled over her meal of fresh venison. John's colic, which had begun rather abruptly four months past, had robbed her of having her usual patience with the children. That Margaret was old enough to hold her little brother in her lap and sing to him was the only reprieve from his constant caterwauling that Elizabeth had.

She sipped at her wine, a gift from the French king. "What of James? Does he ever leave the forest anymore?"

Randolph leaned back in his chair, his overstuffed belly giving him an ache that revealed itself in the grimace on his face. "Only when he needs to chase the English away, which lately is not often. No, he is content there in Lintalee with his woman."

Elizabeth perked. The tenderness she'd always had for James was evident in the intense narrowing of her eyebrows. "The same one? The English woman?"

"The same: Lady Rosalind de Fiennes. A fine woman, but she has no wish to go back to England and he has none to send her away."

"And has he spoken of marriage to her?"

"To my knowledge, no. But you know James—he'd sooner cut off his own hand to give you than share a private thought."

She fell silent a moment, contemplating. A servant reached over her shoulder and took away her trencher. "A pity, then. If a man and a woman truly love one another, they *should* be married . . . and have children. A house full of them."

We shared a smile across the table and I laid my hand over hers to give it a squeeze. The love we once shared had returned to us in a different form: that of the love for our children. A bittersweet exchange, but I regretted it not. All things change. All things pass.

"There is something . . ." Randolph began, his eyes suddenly dropping to inspect his fingernails. Then he curled his fingers over the table's edge and went on, his words tinged with sorrow. "Something I must tell you. I wanted to wait until the children were asleep, to let you both know first."

"What is it, Thomas?" Elizabeth slid her hand from mine.

"Walter died just over a week past. Spoiled meat, they say. One night he sat down to dinner, ate heartily, went to bed with a stomach-ache, began vomiting in the night . . . gone by sunset the next day. Several others took ill from the meal as well, none with such grave results as Walter." Finally, he met my gaze. "I'm sorry. I didn't want to say anything with Robbie present. If you want me to, I can tell him tomorrow."

I pushed away the goblet of wine in front of me, absorbing the news. Robbie was fully an orphan now, although Elizabeth and I had filled the role of his parents essentially from birth. Despite his tendency to doubt any outcome, Walter had served well as governor—a position few men would have imperiled themselves in. To hold Berwick against the whole of the English army had been no small feat.

Elizabeth rose then. Her mouth was drawn down sadly. She kissed me along my graying temple. "I'm going to see the children to bed. We can tell Robbie in the morning together."

After she went from the hall, Randolph and I sat silently for several minutes—me staring at my half-empty goblet of wine and him running his fingertips along the edge of the table.

"We'll talk, tomorrow," I said, "about who to set in his place. It's a precarious post. I trust you've given it some thought already?"

He shook his head. "Actually, no. I was too—"

A curdling scream ripped from someone's throat upstairs. In a second, I was on my feet and sprinting up the stairs three at a time, my heart ten steps ahead of me, my breath ten behind.

As I entered the room the two girls shared with John, I saw Elizabeth standing with her back to me, crushing her infant son in her arms as she cried out again. It was a sound I had heard before—of mothers and wives who have searched the battlefields and come upon the mangled, lifeless bodies of their fallen menfolk. The keening of the aggrieved. The cry of death.

I reached for her, but she ripped herself away, clutching at her child as she collapsed to the floor in a quaking heap. I moved around her, knelt down, looked upon John's small body—blue as an icy loch in wintertime. He was not breathing.

"No, no," she repeated lowly. Trembling, Elizabeth peeled away the blanket that partially covered his head. "No, it cannot be. It *cannot* be."

Then she raised her face to heaven and opened her mouth in a silent plea as tears cascaded down her cheeks. I wrapped my arms around her, John's small, cold body cradled between us.

Mathilda raised her head sheepishly from her pillow, then tunneled beneath her blankets, terrified by her mother's grief. Margaret slipped from the bed and stood before us.

Her tiny red lips quivered. "I sang to him. He went to sleep and I covered him up. What's wrong with Johnny, mama? Mama? Did I do something wrong? Mama!" She burst forth in tears, her fists mopping at her eyes.

I placed a hand on her shoulder. "You did nothing wrong, dear heart. Nothing. 'Tis not your doing."

Robbie appeared behind her. Gently, he guided her away. Then he coaxed Mathilda from the bed and took both girls by the hand.

"Come along," he said, as they went out the door. "David and I have a big bed. You can stay with us tonight. I'll protect you, Margaret. Mathilda, don't be afraid. Come on, now. Come with me."

How to tell him of his father after this? How? The lad is growing up before his time. He will bear an even greater weight all too soon, I fear.

I looked down at John's face—so peaceful—and held Elizabeth tight.

DAYS SHORT OF HIS first birthday, my son John was buried on a hill overlooking the sea near Cardross. I could have carried his coffin under one arm, so small it was. The greatest grief of all is that of a parent for his child, the hollow pain for a life not yet lived in full.

Summer fled away in the blast of winter's first winds, as if there were to be no subtle change of autumn that year to ease us into winter's icy hold. Elizabeth's grief devoured her. The day John died, she withdrew not only from those around her, but from the world entirely. She left the children in the care of nurses, no longer personally attending to their studies with rigorous diligence as she once had, or reading to them or teaching them any of life's many small secrets.

Robbie took the news of his father's passing stoically. He was more despondent over John's death than his father's, not having known or seen much of Walter in the last few years.

James arrived at Cardross with Gilbert de la Haye straight from Berwick, where they had attended Walter's wake. I received them that evening in my private quarters, alone. Elizabeth, since the day of John's death, had moved to her own chamber, leaving me copious time to wallow in my own sorrow. Other times I would have been glad to see the two men. Now their presence was an intrusion upon my self-induced solitude. A man needed time to reflect when his life was slipping thread by thread from his grasp.

"How are you faring these days?" James gave a slight bow, then pulled up a stool and sat on it before me. Gil hovered at his shoulder, perusing me keenly in that ever-observant way of his.

At my foot slept a hound, a descendent of my loyal Coll. I nudged the dog with my toe and he opened one eye, rolled over and went back to sleep. I gazed forlornly into the cracking embers of my hearth, flopped to one side of my chair and propped my jaw wearily on my fist. "How do I look, my good James? Quite a mess, I imagine."

"My condolences on both John and Walter. Walter will be missed as both cousin and compatriot to me. And John—he was far too young." He grabbed the poker from beside the hearth, nudged the logs about, and then added another. "How is the queen?"

"Gone, here." I thumped the thumb-side of my fist against my chest, then tapped at my head with a fingertip. "And losing it here, too, I fear. She goes to Johnny's cradle every night to look for him, certain it was all a nightmare. She is angry, bitter, deeply in woe one moment, then the next chatting as if nothing were wrong and talking of how John had slept without a sound the night before. So odd. When I talk to her, it's as if I can see right through her. Like there's no one there." The new log began to burn, casting a stronger light, drawing me in with its amber glow. "We spoke over the summer, did you know, about a betrothal between David and King Edward's daughter, Joanna of the Tower. Elizabeth won't hear of it now, of course. Won't let her children leave this place, even though she'll have little to do with them. But I *have* to move things along quickly. More than you or anyone knows. It is more important than ever that I secure peace between Scotland and England. There is no other way. And if England will not give David a bride—France will."

Gil stepped forward, took my chin in his hand and tilted my head to peer into my eyes. "So bloodshot, my lord. Have you slept? And these blotches upon your flesh—have they been long?"

"I am an aging man, Gil. Aye, I am weary and my skin has not the rosy blush of youth to it any longer, but spots and veins and scars too many to remember."

"Hmm, no. I don't like the looks of it." He crossed his arms like a mother hen. "I've seen the likes of it before—in the sailors that come to Leith after long journeys. Too much salted meat and stale bread in their diets, it is said. Let me go and have a stew made up for you."

He left with a purpose, but I could see that James shared his concern. In minutes, Gil returned and placed a bowl of watery stew on the table before me. "Leeks and cabbage. I've instructed the cook to make you something similar twice a day and to restrict the amount of meat, bread and ale available to you."

The smell alone was enough to make me retch. "And how long must I endure this unpalatable remedy? You know me, Gil. I'll eat venison fresh off the carcass before I'll stuff myself with turnips and the like."

"Give it a month, sire. If that does not improve your state, then tell me I was wrong to suggest this. Until then, your health is worth displeasing your tongue, is it not?"

I grumbled at him, cupped the bowl between my aching hands and sipped from it. "Well, James, if the English are amassing a force you should go back home. Watch over things."

James turned a critical eye on me. "The border will be quiet through winter. That much I can assure you. England has too many problems of its own to pester us."

"Go back home, James. You're more needed there. There's nothing you can do here. You too, Gil."

When they left, I let the stew go cold and placed it on the floor. Even the dog refused it.

AYE, ENGLAND HAD ITS own problems. Many. But my own sorrows were not over with. They were to come in threes, always it seemed. Once it was the loss of my brothers Thomas, Alexander and then Nigel. Now this. John and Walter. What else, I wondered.

Elizabeth began to miss meals. I sent them to her room. She refused them. By Christmas she had taken terribly ill. By spring she was recovering. Then the sickness came again and would not go away. Had she kept up her strength, she might have fought it. I sent the children to her often to try to lift her spirits, give her reason for hope, but in my heart I knew what the end would be.

On the 26th day of October, in the year 1327, Elizabeth went from me . . . forever. It did not seem right that I, so much older than her, should be left to go on without her. It seemed even less right that she had left three young children behind.

When we are young, we live for all our tomorrows: hopeful, vigorous, tireless. As we grow old, we yearn for the past: regretful, dispassionate, weary.

Many were the regrets in my life, but loving her was never one. Alas, our time with those we love is never long enough.

God in Heaven knew that our love was not perfect. I had done so much to ruin it. Yet time and time again, she had forgiven me, stood by me, given so much of herself. What would I have ever been without her? I dared not think.

Like the grief that pervaded my soul, my affliction was worsening. There were not enough bolts of cloth in all the kingdom to hide the red bumps and purple bruises on my skin. My gums bled, my teeth loosened and my eyes were a bloody sight to behold. I had the mirrors removed from my chambers at Cardross. I kept to myself there when it was at its worst and made myself public at Edinburgh on my best days, but those were becoming ever fewer and the rides far too painful to endure much longer.

Often, I wandered the gardens that Elizabeth had laboriously planned. Although the trees were yet small, the orchards were bearing their first fruits upon willowy branches bent low by the weight. Since I could not manage the riggings myself, I lounged in my boat, giving direction, while Robbie took in the tack of the sails or put the full force of his chest and arms into the rudder.

My days were thus slowly spent, like the hound that no longer hunts or the plow horse that is no longer fitted to the harness.

24

<u>Edward II – London, 1326</u>

AYMER DE VALENCE, EARL of Pembroke, had the slightest rasp in his throat and a runny nose when he sailed for France. He had been charged to retrieve my consort and heir from King Charles' court. The voyage was rough, the weather beyond miserable. Waves spilled over the deck and a cold, stinging sleet assailed them all the way. By the time his feet touched shore, Pembroke was possessed by fever. One day's journey from Paris, he died.

My noblest of nobles, smote down by Providence. Even the Creator saw fit to contravene the simplest of my designs.

England lay in peril. My heir was being played as a pawn by his own mother. I had no time to mourn for Pembroke. I had to act. But how to do so was not so easily arrived at.

Hugh and his father were persistent in telling me to raise an army and punish those who did not comply. But everything I said or did or ordered others to do was completely ignored. Even my closest advisors yawned and nodded at my commands, then turned away and did nothing.

Parliament conspired to uproot and topple me by doing nothing, leaving me completely ineffectual. Crowned, throned and sceptered, but as impotent as a halfwit on a milking stool brandishing a willow wand. A cuckold for a king.

My court is overrun with rats and they will gnaw away at the very foundation of my house. I must be the cat—stealthy, silent. I need not sink my teeth and taste of blood to be rid of them. A flick of the tail, a hiss, and they will retreat into their holes.

When Bishop Walter Stapledon of Exeter returned from France and stood before me in the Tower, it did not bode well for the success of his assignment.

Stapledon had not quite recovered from his channel crossing when he stooped, green-faced and wobbly, before me in my great chamber in the Tower of London. He had come straight from the French court, he muttered, and I could read the ill news in his sagging countenance.

"News from France, your grace?" I pressed my ink-smeared finger-tips upon a page of my book to keep the hot breeze that was blowing in from the open window from flipping the pages over.

Stapledon glanced uneasily over his shoulder at the sound of foot-steps. Hugh Despenser hovered in the doorway. I gestured for him to enter. He closed the door softly behind him, but respectfully stayed his distance. There if I needed him.

The bishop drew a breath, closed his eyes and pressed two fingers to his right temple. "You must understand . . . how hard it is that I tried. Counseled her. Quoted scripture. Begged of all near to her. Yet my words fell on deaf ears. I bring you not news from Paris, sire, but . . . Hainault."

I chased away a fly with the tail of the ribbon that marked my place in the book, then laid it thoughtlessly between the pages and snapped the book shut. "Enlighten me, if you will. Was the queen not in Paris when you were with her? Your duty was to speak convincingly with her. She was to come home, leave her brother's court. The pope wrote back to me that he was demanding Charles send her away."

"Even kings bow to popes, my lord. He did as told, asked her to leave. And she went. To Count William of Hainault's court in Valenciennes."

"Hainault?" Hugh echoed, stepping forward.

"By invitation of Sir John of Hainault," Stapledon clarified, nodding his head. He pulled his hands within his long sleeves, shoulders hunched. "It would seem that Sir John is deeply enamored of the queen. I begged with her to forsake Mortimer, my lord. To return with your son to England. But she declined . . . nay, ordered me away."

"Why so?" I slid the book away from me, pushed back my chair to stand, but my knees were weak, knowing part of what was to come. "I swear, had Pembroke not stumbled into his grave it would be the queen now groveling before me and not you and your pathetic tongue devising excuses."

I had dispatched him in Isabella's company because he was one man I could trust to watch her every move. He had been my spy all along. I imagine she knew of it, but never cared, flaunting her lover Mortimer ever more openly as the days and weeks went by.

"An answer, Bishop Stapledon. *Why* did she refuse?"

His left eye twitched. He swallowed hard. "Because you would not banish Lord Despenser."

A sharp, white pain cleaved my skull. "That she would so persist . . . Should I cower at the haranguing of a woman whose jealousy rules her every action? Lord Despenser has been naught but loyal. She has been anything but. And my brother Edmund—did he return with you?"

"He, too, is in Hainault."

"I . . . don't understand. Is he spying then? Ah, yes. How clever of Edmund. Brilliant, brilliant. Has he returned reports of her activities? Come, your grace, what does Edmund say?"

"He sends no word, sire. Nothing at all."

Edmund in Hainault? Trailing after her with his nose aquiver as if she were a bitch in heat. Ah, Edmund, Edmund. Are you, as well, under the spell of her witchcraft? Did she bestow on you one of those shy, seductive glances that she now uses so freely, touch you in an alluring way, confide in you?

Hugh came to my side. "Then why is the queen in Hainault, your grace?"

"To find her son a wife."

"What?" I threw my chair back as I leapt to my feet. Gripped the table so hard that a splinter pricked beneath my fingernail. "She can't possibly . . . I have already entered into negotiations with the King of Aragon for his daughter. No, it is not her place to decide such a thing. Impudence! Flagrant impudence! The disobedient bitch. Had I no care for her children, I would slit her open from her belly to her lying mouth and let the buzzards have at her liver. Oh, her heart is the wellspring of corruption. I should have seen the evil in her there at Boulogne, disguised as an innocent, and left her weltering at the altar in the cathedral as they doused her with holy water and burned the flesh from her bones. That deceitful, devil-whoring bitch!"

My entire body jerked with an uncontrollable spasm. Hugh kneaded at my shoulder to soothe me. I cursed and ranted for minutes before his gentle touch had chiseled away at my granite wall of anger. Ever calm, his voice carried no murderous edge to it, no intimation that he had lost any control. "Count William has three . . . four daughters, does he not?" Hugh explored. "None yet betrothed?"

"Yes," Stapledon said.

"And an army, well equipped."

Stapledon shook his head.

Hugh took my arm and eased me back into my chair before my knees completely failed me. He sank to his haunches beside me. "This is more grave, my lord, than a disagreement over mates for your heir. This is about your very life. Your crown is in jeopardy. You must—"

"In jeopardy," Stapledon broke in, "because my lord has succumbed to ill influences and committed iniquities so—"

"Get out of here!" I bellowed, hammering my fist on the table. The heel of my hand cut into the table's edge. I winced. Tears sprang to my eyes, not from the pain of my flesh, but for the roiling troubles of my realm sucking me downward like a whirlpool while the heavens rained down on my head. A farce of a marriage. A son who would betray me.

"But sire," Stapledon objected, stiffening his jaw, "I implore you, heed me in—"

"Out! Out!" I pulled a throbbing hand to my chest. "Every blessed day of my existence, badgering clerics and overweening advisors have scraped out my ears with their pointed tongues. In the course of my life, I can count on one hand the number of men who granted me the respect and honor due a king." I spread out my quivering fingers before me, then tucked my thumb against my palm. "You are *no longer* one of them. Away with you! You have more than failed in your task. You have made a laughingstock of me."

He took one step back, faltered, then blurted out, "Sire, I—"

"Away! Out of my sight. Do not show yourself to me or speak to me again, you sanctimonious shit-mouth. Go back to godforsaken France. Out!"

Step by step, Stapledon retreated, until he reached the door and tugged slowly on the latch. "Even the word of Our Savior Jesus Christ could not be heard by those who covered their ears and would not listen."

I lurched across the table, grabbed a spiked candlestick empty of its candle and flailed it after him. The door banged shut just as the candlestick smacked against the iron hinge of the door.

Hugh's hand slid gently from my shoulder to my forearm. "Shall I have a guard sent after him, sire? He should be made to pay for those words. A few weeks in the dungeon? A hefty fine?"

I slumped in my chair, my head filled with a fog of rage. Slowly, the blood returned to numb limbs. My thoughts gathered clarity. "Bring me ink and parchment, dear Hugh. I must write a letter."

"You have written dozens upon dozens of letters, Edward. What good is one more? What good were any of them?"

"The pope is on my side, Hugh. He is. He knows . . . about Isabella and Mortimer. About their adultery and treason. And Charles fears for his own soul so much that he threw her out. The letters—they did *some* good, did they not?"

"But not enough. Not nearly enough." He knelt beside me and drew my head against his shoulder, letting me give way to the tears I could not keep in. How long I wept, I have no recollection. I felt as though I were beginning to drown beneath a sheet of ice and could not break through to fight for breath.

"Oh, Hugh. I told that she-wolf I would take her back. That she had only to abandon that troublemaking Marcher Lord and desist in her demands to rid you of me. So simple. And yet, Lord God, I never envisioned this—that she would take my son away and put him before an army against me. What do I do? I don't know anymore. Tell me what to do."

"Gather your own army. Issue a summons."

"No. No more fighting, Hugh." I tried to take heart in his counsel, to place faith in his eternal loyalty, to believe that somehow I would overcome those who rose against me. "She will not do it, Hugh. She will lose heart. She'll come home with my son. Come crawling to me. Begging forgiveness. She will. And all will be right. You'll see. There won't be any war. I won't fight my own son. I can't. Won't."

"Then present your belly, Edward. Give your queen the power she craves."

I pulled away. "No, not that. I—"

"If you make it so easy, one day soon it will be Roger Mortimer commanding the kingdom. And as he beds your willing wife, he'll whisper his wish into her ear: that he wants you . . . *dead.*"

Forest of Dean, Wales, 1326

BERRIES WERE DOTTING THE buckthorns when they landed on the Suffolk coast in late September. Queen Isabella and the fawning Sir John of Hainault rode with my son at the head of a band of mercenaries onto English soil—hired killers from Brabant to as far as Bohemia—and yet no one barred their way.

Mortimer rode well back in the ranks. He was, to his credit, sly enough to give ground when so much depended on the queen being able to garner sympathy for her cause. One would have thought the English people would be smart enough to see both Isabella and Mortimer for what they truly were: adulterous traitors.

My summonses went unanswered. A plague of apathy had infected the land. They all sat on their hands while foreigners pilfered from them and marched their merry way to London. If I met with Isabella without an army at my back, larger and better equipped than hers, I was as dead as a duckling in a fox den.

I had to go. Find refuge until allies could be mustered. It would only be a matter of time before England would sour on the queen and her bedfellow.

Needing to move swiftly, I fled from London. I left my son John with Hugh's wife, Eleanor, in the Tower. The girls I sent with all haste to Bristol in the guardianship of Hugh's father—the elder Hugh Despenser.

Fields of ripened grain embraced the hills of England and spilled into the dales. Our company was small, numbering only a dozen in whole: a handful of guards, a few of my household staff including Jankin, and my two last loyal supporters, Hugh and Chancellor Baldock. We followed the narrowing Thames westward and then swung sharply north.

The road to Wales had no end. To guard the secret of our passing, we kept to the countryside and forests. At Bristol, Hugh took as much coin as he could carry and so we feared thievery. Whenever we passed by a small village, Jankin or a couple of my guards would go into the nearest village to buy meat, bread and ale. I cursed the bitterly cold October nights and dreaded each dawn for the toil it held as we were forced to flee further and further west into the wilderness.

In Gloucester, again, I found nothing but a brotherhood of indifference and disdain. And then, a few leagues beyond the city, we came across a Benedictine monk passing from Glastonbury on his way to Leominster. I took him aside and shared some bread with him as we chatted idly at first about the bounty of the year's harvest. Unaware of my identity, he delivered to me a stream of terrible news. I gave the holy man a shilling and asked him to say a Mass for my mother's soul.

Aimless, we continued vaguely westward, until we came to the Forest of Dean. We claimed a little embowered place cut into a hillside among the beeches and threw down our blankets with weary relief. As the rest of my party settled for the evening, I climbed a slope a hundred feet away and sat down on a large rock beneath a yellowing larch to ponder on my shrinking kingdom.

The sun sank behind the furthest hill. I pulled my face down within the tattered pile of fur bordering the neckline of my soiled cloak, shivering so violently my teeth clacked like a stick slapping over the spokes of a turning wheel. Hugh approached. His head was covered with a liripipe, its long tail arranged meticulously in a swoop from one shoulder to the other. As he neared me, I could discern the distinct, damp, wooly smell of his serge cloth cloak.

"Jankin stole three fat hens this morning," he said. "The men have struck up a fire. Come. Eat. Warm yourself. No need to catch cold or starve."

"I told you: no fires. They'll find us."

"Eventually, yes," Hugh conceded blandly, "they will. But fowl served up raw would give us all aching bellies and I, for one, am starved." He crumpled down beside me and sighed. "You're troubled. What did that monk have to say? You've confided in no one. I take offense."

Starlight filtered down through barely leafed branches. What I knew . . . how could I say it?

I scraped my dry, cracked fingers over the roughness of the rock on which we huddled. "A fitting throne, is it not? A prickly crown of hollies and what a king I would be." I gave a raspy laugh, my throat raw from thirst. "Look at us, Hugh. What a pitiful lot we are. Loathsome, starving. How pathetic. They'll beat us for stealing. Perhaps we should turn to begging. More pride in that."

"What were you told, Edward? You've dismissed hope altogether since we left Gloucester. Why?"

"Must you know everything?" I laid my forehead on my knees. Finally, I looked up at him, his sleeves torn from the thorns, a smudge of road grime on his chin. "All right, then. I'll tell you. When they land-ed, my half-brother Thomas threw his arms around her and welcomed the queen and her foreign slaves. Leicester joined her immediately. The bastard's no better than his dead brother. He must have known long ago when and where she would arrive. Knew all along. They were conspiring from the moment she left London. And London? London threw open its gates for her. Your own wife gave up the Tower *and* my son John to that French harlot. And do you know what else they did? Can you even imagine? They cut off Bishop Stapledon's head and buried his body in a rubbish heap."

He turned his head away. "I'm sorry . . . about your son. My wife— I thought that . . . She must have had no choice."

"Isabella and Mortimer—they're in Bristol already."

I saw a cloud of shock pass over his face just then. No use in hoarding the ill tidings, I gave them up. "As Isabella took my daughters to a window overlooking the courtyard, they took your father, your namesake Hugh . . . and hung him. Lynched like a common thief. How horrid that must have been, dangling there, kicking his feet, praying for the rope to break."

Hugh's eyes glassed over as if the sentence of death has just been passed on him. His father had been his constant mentor, a friend even. He slid from the rock, went and leaned against the trunk of the larch, clenching his fists. There was a glint of hatred in his glance. Blame.

"You can't possibly know how it was for him," he murmured.

A rift of silence grew between us until it was like some bottomless chasm that could not be overcome. Once, a lack of words had been a comfortable thing. Many were the times I had fallen asleep with my head propped against Hugh's square shoulder as we took respite during a ride through the forest. Hugh had been there when we sailed from Scotland's shore with only the clothes on our backs. There to give comfort when Lancaster met his fate. There to offer support when Isabella clawed at my last nerve and left me for that villainous traitor. There in all things. Never the shining champion of the joust or merry drinking mate that Brother Perrot had been, but a solid voice of reason when all others sought to leave me shaken and shredded. Solace and support. Pillow and pier.

At times he was a reticent man, but I had learned to read Hugh through the tilt of his head, the position of his jaw, the way he folded his arms across his chest or clasped his hands behind his back. But now, the silence hovered over us—something unfamiliar, something completely wrong, something . . . unraveled.

"Baldock insists you meet with the queen," Hugh said in a voice so low and measured that it came as a growl.

"And let you join your father at the end of a tattered rope? No." I laughed inwardly. Isabella, that meek waif that I had taken as wife all those years ago and frightened her by my touch, was now so wholly wicked that by her nearness she could tempt married men and with a fleeting glance command them to execute her crimes. I saw Jankin's red tuft of wild hair bobbing as he trotted through the trees. "Ah, Jankin calls us to yet another bucolic meal. I can hardly wait to dine on stale bread and watered ale again. And once more we will bed down under a canopy of trees. As much as I enjoy communing with nature, I desire a mattress and roof just as any man. Where do we go tomorrow then, Hugh?"

Hugh began down the small hill toward Jankin and said with his back to me, "To the abbey in Neath. From there—Lundy Island."

"And from Lundy?" I asked. "They'll go there eventually, you know, looking for us."

He froze, paused before speaking. "If you will not barter for your kingdom, I would rather drown in the sea, swimming for my life."

"Sire! Sire!" Jankin cried as he scrambled up the leaf-littered slope. "They are on the road behind us, not a mile away. Baldock recognized Lord Wake's standard." Leicester's crony. Jankin halted and braced his hands on his knees as he gulped for air. "Two hundred men, more maybe, in his company. Knights and archers. Coming fast, my lord."

"Are the horses ready?" Hugh asked.

Jankin nodded. "But our supplies—"

"Leave them." Hugh turned to me. "Hurry."

He sped down the hill, his form blurring in the patchy shadows of forest dusk as Jankin stumbled after him.

"Stapledon was right," I called after Hugh.

He caught himself on a sapling and swung around to face me. "About Queen Isabella. Yes, he was. And you should have heeded me when I warned you about her. Now hurry and to your horse."

"No, not the queen. He was right about you. You were supposed to oversee the treasury. There should have been money there to raise troops, to defend me from attacks like this. But the lords and knights would not come when I called because they knew. Knew there was no money. Knew that you had robbed me."

I wish I could have seen his face better then, but we were too far apart, the light too dim.

"I haven't time to quibble with you," he spat. "And I won't offer myself up to be your scapegoat—ever. Stay or come. It's your choice."

Having offered that ultimatum, he sprinted away and tossed out orders to my men as they came up leading our horses. We left the road and plunged through a maze of bracken, fallen branches and beech trees, darkness cloaking our escape.

Several miles later, at the crest of a steep hill, we paused and strained our eyes to survey the valley by the silver light of a half moon. Beside me, Jankin's hand shook as he gripped the short sword I had given him when we left London.

Twigs cracked. His head jerked to the right. Then, closer, a piercing sound. A whistle, like a bird. The shout of orders from across the valley. More cries. Hooves drumming on dry earth.

Jankin groaned softly and brought his hand up to touch the feathered shaft protruding from his eye socket. He slumped in his saddle, swayed to one side and fell to the ground, dead.

I barely saw the enemy archer who had loosed the arrow until Hugh rode him down and swiped his blade through the man's bare neck. The bloodied head rolled across the roadway and bounced down the hillside, its eyes open wide, tongue hanging out, changing directions as it slammed against the staggered trunks of trees. I fought a wave of nausea, unable to act or move. In moments, Hugh was at my side. He shoved his bloodied sword into its scabbard and grabbed the reins of my horse.

For the third time in my kingship, I raced for my life. This time, it was not Scots trying to run me down, but Englishmen—pack-mates of the She-Wolf.

Can a man be king and yet not be so? What am I? A man, called king, and yet hunted, spurned as less than a man, scorned and spit upon. I, who have done nothing wrong but be something less than my sire. I would be better off running straight to the court of the Bruce and giving myself up. He would treat me more kindly than my own.

TWO DAYS LATER, HAVING stopped but once for a few hours to sleep, we reached the abbey in Neath, where the abbot there, a friend of Hugh's family since before he was born, offered us a safe haven in our time of greatest need.

Half-fed and barely warmed, we sped to the coast and hired a ship to Lundy. But the weather had finally failed us. Three times we were forced back to shore by storms packed with strong winds. Our lines of retreat were closing up on us at every turn. Lord Wake's soldiers were combing every port from Brighton to Bangor. Isabella's spies lay coiled like a pit of vipers in every inn.

By cover of night, we escaped on horse—again without food or money—hastening back toward Neath.

We never made it.

On a road somewhere in Wales, far from any town or manor or castle, when the leaves had fallen from the trees to blanket the forest floor, the queen's soldiers found us, took our weapons and shoved us into a pile while they kicked and cursed us. Baldock, Hugh and I were mounted on old nags, our hands bound behind our backs, and roughly escorted to Llantrissant. The remainder of my guard was forced to walk on foot, prodded along by the tips of spears, and spat upon.

Above a floating mist that crept beside the River Usk, the Raven Tower of Llantrissant rose before us. The sun had not yet risen high enough to burn away the fog. A damp chill gnawed at my numb fingers. Despite my requests and demands to loosen the bindings about my wrists, my captors had not once lifted a finger or acknowledged me except to keep my mount in line. Baldock whimpered constantly, but Hugh . . . Hugh did not utter a word—neither protest, nor plea. He had not even so much as looked at me.

The gate on the north end of the bailey opened before us. We were barely inside the outer wall when more soldiers rushed at us, as if we were charging them with lances, and dragged Hugh and Baldock from their horses. Baldock squirmed and wailed on the ground.

Hugh went down upon his knees, refusing to look at them. A broad-shouldered soldier smacked him in the back of the skull with the pommel of his sword. His face slammed onto the cobbles. A trickle of blood sprang from the back of his head and flowed down his neck onto the ground.

"No!" I shouted, trying desperately to rip my hands from their ropes. I nearly fell from my horse. "Leave him! You will not harm him!"

"But who is there to save him?" came a gloating voice from nowhere.

I strained my eyes through the vapor of fog to see Henry, Earl of Leicester, gloating at me.

"Mercy, Lord Henry," I pled, my voice so strained with terror that it cracked. "I beg mercy of you. We were on our way back to Gloucester to entreat for a peace with the queen and—"

But the earl paid me no heed. With a flip of his hand, the soldiers flanking Hugh hoisted him to his feet. Barely able to stand, still stunned, Hugh blinked away the pain as Lord Wake's men knotted a rope about his waist and tied the other end to the tail of a horse.

Spitting the blood from his mouth, Hugh raised his sorrowful eyes to meet mine. "You are my ruin, Edward . . . Your own, as well. We always knew this day would come, did we not? Fate is such a satirical bastard."

I yearned to reach out, hold him one more time, take his face in my hands and tell him I would love him forever. My horse whinnied and stamped a foot. I smiled sadly—for I felt both overwhelming love for him and insufferable regret for never having been able to show that love for him fully and unashamedly.

"'Tis not the curse of this day I will cling to, Hugh," I said, "but the blessing of every day I have known you."

Lord Wake signaled the party forward. The rope around Hugh's waist tautened, then yanked him forward.

"Hugh!" I cried.

He stumbled, fell to the ground—hips, shoulder, jaw grinding against rough stones. The horse dragged him several feet over the cobbles before the man guiding it looked back and eased up. The soldier riding next to Hugh butted him in the ribs with his spear, then prodded him back to his knees. Head down, Hugh stood, staggered forward, but did not look back.

I twisted as far in my saddle as I could to watch, saying Hugh's name over and over until my voice went hoarse and it was but a croaking whisper on my parched lips.

Take from me my kingdom, for it has been nothing but cruel to me. But do not take away the one I love most in this world. More than my own worthless life. Do not take Hugh from me . . .

When they lifted me from the saddle and set me upon the ground, I had ceased to beg for mercy. Hugh, I knew, would go down staunchly fighting, never giving in.

I, however, had no fight left in me. No will.

Without Hugh, I had nothing. *Nothing.*

25

Edward II - Kenilworth Castle, 1327

F OR WEEKS, I WAS shut away—first in Llantrissant, then finally I was shuffled at night and under heavy guard to Kenilworth—a more stalwart prison. There, Henry, Earl of Leicester, served as my keeper.

My quarters were spacious enough for two men, the linens changed out often, the food, while not of a diverse menu, was palatable. My possessions were meant for practical use only—a table barely big enough to hold a plate, a lopsided stool, a pair of candles and a small cross studded with pearls. I was given quill and parchment with which I wrote copious letters to Isabella, begging her forgiveness, and in turn to young Edward, swearing my support of him if he could but convince his mother to grant me my freedom. I gave these letters to Henry, but no reply ever came. I doubt they were ever delivered.

Still, I wrote. Every day, I wrote. What else was I to do? My sleeves were black to the elbow. I scrubbed at the ink on my hands until they were raw, but the stain would not be banished.

They gave me one change of clothing, both shirts of stiff, black serge that scratched at my skin, a servant with the brains of an ox, and an ever-changing army of guards. From my window looking out on the courtyard, I watched as soldiers paced back and forth across the icy cobbles, guarding me from no one. Who would come to aid me? I was forgotten. The people of England had cast aside their king—tossed me into the river like a runt piglet to be drowned without a thought.

Winter wore dully on. Drafts hissed through the cracks in the walls and around the windows. For a short while I clung to a wild hope that Leicester would awaken to Isabella's wickedness and aid me. But I had confused complacency with pity, apparently.

The heavy groan of door hinges woke me. The faint, muted light of dawn spilled pink across the room. I turned my face from the glare. I tried to look, but it pained my head. Parchment crinkled beneath my forearms as I raised blackened hands to cover my eyes.

"Visitors, sire."

Leicester held an oil lamp at arm's length, its smoke twisting from its top like a black serpent. Two grim-faced guards flanked him.

Shivering from the winter chill, I looked about for a cloak, then remembered I had none. They had taken even that from me. So I pulled my tattered blanket up around my neck. A bolt of hope shot through me. "Has my son Edward come?"

Leicester's features were slack, his mouth expressionless. "No, not him, my lord."

My heart plunged downward.

It is her. Her . . .

He opened the door leading to the antechamber beyond my private quarters. I followed, bleak of heart and hope. Before me stood a dozen men: lesser nobles I vaguely recognized, justiciars garbed in their robes of office, and two bishops. How sober they all appeared. Was it such a miserable task for them to call upon their king?

A man of snow-white hair and wearing a bishop's ostentatious robes shuffled forward from the brooding huddle: Adam of Orleton, the Bishop of Hereford. How often had I seen him standing behind that witch Isabella? It made all too much sense now. This day had been long in planning. The players were many.

The moment his thin lips parted, every word came as if drifting through a haze of smoke. "Sire, I am elected apropos by just authority to put forth the charges against you. First, you are informed that in direct relation to said following charges, that Sir Hugh Despenser the Younger has been summarily tried for his crimes against the kingdom and found guilty. He was hung from the gallows in Hereford and beheaded. The four quarters of his body have been sent to the furthest part of the land to serve as warning to all who might give false counsel to their sovereign and—"

Hugh!

In the core of my soul, I was as hollow as a coffin without its corpse. My arms and chest went numb. I stopped breathing, swooned. The blanket dropped from my slumping shoulders. My knees buckled. The floor vanished from beneath me.

I felt myself falling . . . But hands were holding me up. I looked up and to my left and saw the sympathetic face of the Bishop of Winchester, with his muted brown eyes and weathered face. He pulled me gently to my feet.

"Take strength in Our Lord, sire," he said.

"When?" I clung to his sleeve. "When did they do this?"

"Some time ago. If it heartens my lord—he would take nothing but bread and water since he was parted from you."

Oh, Hugh. You did indeed suffer to be without me. And I you, Hugh. A hundredfold so, now that you are gone. But no, no, it cannot be. If they have already killed you Hugh, what is to be of me?

So, this is to be the day. God, hear me, I am not ready. What have I, your devoted servant, your worldly implement, done wrong but love those who gave me loyalty?

Adam of Orleton's bland voice went on: "Sir Edward of Caernarvon, son of Edward Plantagenet, King of England, you are hereby charged with—"

Why, why did they not address me properly? I was crowned in West-minster, anointed with holy water, have wielded the Royal Seal . . . I am more than a mere knight. I am king!

I looked around the room at the rigid faces of these men who had come to denigrate my name. Some averted their eyes from my gaze. Others leered at me haughtily.

"—devoid of honor and wisdom, have unjustly administered to your kingdom and—"

Although I heard the words, their sound, their meaning, they all passed over me as if in some fading dream. Not until Adam of Orleton's venomous censure ceased did I notice that Sir Thomas Blount, my royal steward, stood before me, awaiting my attention. He held the white staff that symbolized his office in my household. Stiffly, he held it out before him and then with one swift jerk brought it down across his upraised knee. It splintered lengthwise. He struck it again three times on the floor. Finally, it broke in two and clattered to the ground.

"Thus are you, Edward of Caernarvon," Blount said, "removed from the throne of our kingdom, in light of your incapacity to rule wise-ly. From this day forward, those who have heretofore sworn an oath of fealty or allegiance to you are no longer held in accord of such oaths, for you are king no more."

I stood dumbfounded. What way was there out of this? My army would not come when I called for them. The people of England wel-comed traitors to their breasts and turned me out without succor. My own servants had turned on me. Even the clerics had fallen victim to Isabella's lies.

Tell them what they want to hear. Get it over with. There's no other way, for now.

"My lords,"—I folded my hands together and sank to the floor, willing the false words to march across my tongue to their wicked pleasure—"compassion, I beg. I have sinned, yes. What man has not?

In this, I have invited your wrath upon me. But how, *how* can I possibly amend this?"

The Bishop of Winchester stooped forward and clasped his chilled hands over mine. "Make a public confession of your wrongs. Yield to your son, my lord. End this strife. Step aside in his favor. Do that and you shall return peace to the land."

Was a king ever more alone, ever more hated than I? Even doe-eyed Winchester is a wolf in sheep's clothing. I am surrounded by devils and so is my son. That is the only certainty in my wretched life.

I shook violently, as one with the falling sickness would. "Your grace, I accept my punishment, and give up my crown. Tell my son . . . tell him I am glad for him. Tell him that."

Silent, they stepped aside. On the table lay a parchment, its ends weighted down by river-smoothed stones, a stream of words already written there. What it said I neither knew nor cared. Bishop Orleton dipped a quill into the inkhorn, blotted its tip on a scrap of cloth and extended it toward me.

Shall we meet in heaven soon then, my false friends? Oh, I think not. I will be there on the other side, as all of you beg and argue with Saint Peter himself over your admittance. May grace visit upon you all, that you may come to embrace your sins before your own deaths.

What rare days that are left to me, I shall live in peace. God alone will have my trust and confidence. I have had enough of this world . . . and the likes of all of you.

26

James Douglas – Berwick, 1328

W HEN WORD CAME NORTH that King Edward II of England had been removed from the throne, it was no awful shock to anyone. It was, in fact, a small cause for celebration, as none in Scotland had any pity for him. Within the year, he was dead.

Even as England crowned a new king in young Edward III, Queen Isabella and her undisguised lover, Sir Roger Mortimer, ruled absolutely. For now though, Isabella was eager for peace. She had much to atone for, it seemed.

They agreed to Robert's terms: that Scotland remain free without homage to England, that the new king, Edward III, would employ his best persuasion upon the pope to have the interdict lifted from Robert and the Scottish Church, and that Robert's son David was to wed the King of England's own sister, Joanna of the Tower.

The betrotheds were both children, unaware of their significance in the matter of international relations. But Robert was impatient and Edward III . . . who is to say how he felt on the matter? He had already been married to the Count of Hainault's daughter in order to secure an alliance that was to the distinct advantage of his own mother's agenda. Edward III sent word that various matters prevented his attendance, but his mother, the queen dowager, would escort her daughter north. Robert claimed illness and retired to Cardross. I was sent in his stead, to attend and guide the young heir of Scotland on his wedding day.

The boy had no idea what was going on. David did as told and acted predictably like a lad who would rather have been elsewhere. He fidgeted. He squirmed. Pulled up the bottom hem of his gold-embroidered tunic and tugged at the seat of his leggings.

In the front row of the grandest church in Berwick, Sir Roger Mortimer gazed on haughtily. I knew him the moment I saw him. Women swooned when he glanced their way. Men seethed with abhorrence. He possessed a cool, commanding confidence, which wisely used might have served him well, but behind his dark eyes was also the hint of smoldering anger that warned of resolute danger.

Young Robert Stewart slumped with drooping eyelids against the arm of Gil de la Haye. Gil poked him sharply in the ribs and Robbie awakened with a jolt. Beside me, David wriggled. A tiny squeak escaped his throat. I touched him lightly on the shoulder, leaned over and whispered to him, "My lord, you must be still until the end."

"I can't." His tiny mouth twisted. "I have to . . . have to . . . ." His eyes began to water.

The Bishop of Berwick, sensing an urgency in David's chagrined countenance, began to speed through the ceremony, the Latin words blending unintelligibly, his gestures blurring.

To his right, little golden-haired Joanna pouted at her husband-to-be. David shuddered and pulled his hands up inside his sleeves. At the back of his throat, he made the faintest grunt.

This time I pinched his shoulder, "David, listen . . . it's nearly over. I beg you—wait. Your father will be proud of what a big man you are."

He stiffened his back, clenched his teeth, but the strain made tears spring forth. He whimpered and clutched at my hand. Next to Joanna, Isabella of France scowled.

David pulled at my little finger. "Please?"

"Your grace?" I interrupted the bishop, seeing no need to cause David this humiliation. He was but a boy of four. Asking him to stand like a statue for a ceremony several hours long was preposterous. "The important part, if you will. My young lord is not feeling well."

The bishop curled an offended eyebrow at me and sniffed. I looked down at David, whose face was momentarily frozen. He bent his knees ever so slightly. Then the odor drifted my way. I rolled my eyes and bit my lip.

Ah, dear heaven. The lad had soiled his pants on his wedding day.

THE MOMENT THE BISHOP uttered the closing words, I snatched David up and exited through a side door. His nurse was standing close by and as fast as could be done, he was stripped of his fine wedding clothes, wiped clean and redressed. I ushered him back out the door and into the nave to rejoin his bride. The English sneered at him, turned their faces away, and shook their heads. The Scots frowned forlornly at their future king.

Beyond Berwick's gate, Queen Isabella clutched tearfully at her daughter. Little Joanna clung to her mother's neck and had to be pried away. I pitied the children most of all. Why this rush to carve their future in stone and yoke Scotland to England? Robert was well intentioned, but his thoughts were more on Scotland and less so on his own son.

In the past two years, I had not seen Robert more than twice: once after Walter had died and the next time following Elizabeth's death. Each time Robert's head had been grayer, his eyes more deeply sunken, his skin sallower, his shoulders more stooped. The once stubbornly brave dreamer had given way to a prematurely old man, frequently ill and quietly resigned to his own death. To see him lately, slouching in his chair, each line in his face dark and exaggerated . . . it dulled hope for the future and gave me little to cling to but memories.

At a time in my own life when thoughts of settling down with Rosalind and a family were becoming more and more appealing, it looked as though my duties would only grow bigger. If Robert . . . I could not bear to think on it. In truth, I had never thought much beyond the next battle. Life, for me, was lived in each moment. Whatever transpired, Randolph would be there to oversee the statecraft of the kingdom and I alongside him to keep it from harm. It seemed I would never escape that fate. But I preferred being the perennial soldier to playing nursemaid.

David began to whine over an ache in his belly, the result of too little food. My temper dangerously short, I left him in the care of others and rode on ahead.

We were halfway to Edinburgh and just west of Dunbar when I realized that Robbie was riding beside me. I ignored him for well into an hour, certain that he, too, only wished to part himself from the two younger children in the party. At twelve years of age, he was on that awkward cusp between boy and man. I felt his curious stare boring into me and shot him a look of perturbation, at which he merely blinked unfazed and looked back ahead. A minute later, he was staring again.

I said, "I amuse you?"

"Hmm, no . . ." He thought it over and shrugged. "Well, aye, in a way. My grandfather has told me stories about you, Sir James. I want to be just like you someday."

"In the name of heaven—why?"

"I don't know, really. Maybe because you always win."

"Do I? The truth is I win at some things, I lose at others. I'm simply more persistent than most—or as Lady Rosalind would say: stubborn."

"I want to be a soldier, like you. Didn't you ever want to be like someone?"

I nodded. "Aye, my father." I remembered how he had defied Longshanks there in the hall at Berwick, his chin upraised, his voice clear and strong, even with his wrists bound behind his back and Longshanks himself holding a blade to his throat.

Robbie fell silent, taking in the sights around us. The road ahead wound and dipped about the outlying Lammermuir Hills. The wind blew gentle from the south, carrying on it the smell of promised rain.

"I once mentioned to my father," he said, "that Grandfather had told me the story about how you took Berwick from the English. Father became suddenly very angry with me. Nearly struck me. He said Berwick was mostly his doing—said that he saved you when he took an arrow for you."

"He did now?" I could not help but raise an eyebrow at that. The arrow had been intended for Walter and it was his own thoughtlessness that had put him in its path. But who was I to tamper with the embellishments of a father's stories to his son? "Aye, he did. Your father was a good man, Robbie. Brave and kind. And he loved your mother dearly. Remember that . . . always."

Robbie grew pensive for a while. He had spent so much time with Robert that he acted more like an old man sometimes, than a lad of twelve.

"You'll come with us to Cardross," he asked, his chin held aloft as if he were Alexander the Great leading his troops across Persia, "to see my grandfather?"

"Alas, I can only go as far as Edinburgh for now. I must go home first." Perhaps in time, I could train him to take my place, to be a soldier, to look his foe in the eyes and cheat death. If I could not publicly admit to him as my own, at least I could be his mentor, teach him something useful. Aye, I would write to Robert about it. First though, I would need to speak to Rosalind. Tell her the truth. It was much to bear alone and I had never told anyone, not in all this time.

Robbie blew a burst of air from his nostrils, as if disappointed. "You're going back to Lintalee for good reason, I assume?"

Again, such old words from such a fresh mouth. He was old

enough to know. "Good reason, aye. My lady is with child. If I'm not home before the blessed event, Rosalind will give me a tongue-lashing that will send me to my grave."

His lips tilted in a smirk of amusement. He giggled. Ah, there was the boy again.

The rain began suddenly, cool and fresh. The riders around us pulled their cloaks over their heads, but Robbie and I raised our faces to the rain and laughed.

Lintalee, 1328

"YOU CAN'T FORCE A woman to marry you against her will, Sir James," Father Simon said.

"It's done all the time, Father." I led him along the path toward the stream that ran in the valley below Lintalee. My steward had directed me there, saying Rosalind often walked the footpath to sit by the cool water. It was high summer and as grand a day as I had ever seen, although blisteringly warm. "Nonetheless, who said I was going to force anything upon her? A little gentle persuasion should do the trick."

Father Simon, his head barely at the height of my shoulder, was usually a gay character, but on this occasion he was peevish. "All the same, my good lord, she will not look kindly upon the surprise of this all."

"'Tis no surprise, I assure you. I simply haven't been insistent enough. Now, if you don't mind waiting here a bit, I see her there. Her favorite place, down by the water. Ah, she shouldn't be alone so far from the house, not so late into her . . . A moment, please."

I treaded softly down the narrowing path as it dipped toward the stream. Rosalind, her feet dangling over the bank, twisted to look over her shoulder. Her face lit.

"James? You're home!" She struggled to stand, thrusting her

overripe belly out before her and arching her back as she pushed at the earth behind her with her hands.

"Stay, stay." I slid down the last of the hill, plopping down beside her on the bank before she could get up. "I wish to talk with you."

Relieved, she eased herself all the way back to lie flat upon the bank. Her feet were bare, washed clean by the water. She smiled tiredly at me. "Thank you, James. It was so dreadfully hot today, I had to come here. Do you see how my feet have swollen about the ankles? I don't remember being this miserable when I was carrying Alice . . . but I was younger then." She turned her face to me, her dark eyes glistening. "And more beautiful."

Lying beside her on the damp grass, I propped myself up on one elbow. I kissed her on her full lips, moist as morning dew. "I did not know you then, Rosalind, love, but to me you have never looked more beautiful than now. I have the envy of all the men in Scotland, did you know, for keeping you captive all these years?"

She blushed profusely. "Eloquent words from such a reticent man as you. What do you want, James Douglas?"

"One thing. Promise me you'll agree. Have I ever asked anything of you?"

"I'm afraid you'll have to tell me what it is first. The last time I agreed to do someone else's bidding . . . let us just say I've learned better. Go on."

I sat up, gazed into the silvery rippling water. "At Berwick, I watched two children stand at a ceremony and speak vows for which they had no understanding. There was no love or affection there, not even familiarity. And I thought how very fortunate I was not to have been born a prince. It made me understand why it is that some noblemen so often stray from their marriage beds to find someone who . . . who makes them feel what love truly is. I could never stray from you, Rosalind. Not in deed or even in thought."

I glanced at her, but she was studying the sky where a pair of sparrowhawks glided, looking down on us.

"I loved a woman once," I said, "deeply."

Curious, she looked at me. "I never presumed that there had not been others before me. Why do you tell me this now?"

"Because it's important. The woman that I loved . . . she was the daughter of a dear friend of mine. It was . . . complicated. You see, she was betrothed to another man—a friend. But I didn't care . . . I mean, I did, but . . . In the end, I gave her up, because I felt that being with her would hurt more people than just the two of us, and *that* I could not bear. Sadly, though, it was not meant to be. She died.

"For a long time, I grieved inwardly. I swore off women. Became something of a monk. Then I met you. And that, can we say, was more than complicated? But my days grew brighter and the future closer and I found myself hurrying home to see you and be with you. Through all that time, we kept coming back together, you and I, drawn to each other somehow and yet both of us keeping our distance. So it is that I ask myself—why? What have we been waiting for? What are we unsure of? Rosalind, I'll not commit the same mistake again—giving up the woman I love."

Her lips parted, wordless. I waited, but Rosalind only stared up at the sky, biting her lip as if to keep from crying.

"I want you to be my wife, Rosalind. And I'll not take 'no' for an answer this time."

I put out my hand for her to take. She closed her eyes, clenched her teeth. A tear escaped her eyelids.

"It would be good, for the child to—" She drew in a sharp breath and arched her spine upward. "It will have to wait, though."

"But why? After so long, how can you—"

"Have you never seen a woman in labor, James Douglas?"

I began to panic then, afraid for her and the child since we were so far from the house. "Should I fetch the midwife here? Or carry you back to the house?"

"I can walk. It's not so far." She laughed at me, her pain seeming to ebb away. "Don't worry, we have hours yet. It has only just begun. That was the first. I think the baby was waiting for you. Then again, this might not even be the day. Sometimes small pains come like that before it is time. And yes, James, I do think it's time we married, you and I. I wouldn't want our child to be ashamed of his mother or robbed of his inheritance."

"*Now* then?"

"Yes, we can go back to the house now. You don't think I want to deliver your child in the river, do you? I'll have my handmaiden make me a tea of chamomile and she can rub my back while it's brewing. I can hardly tell you how much it aches right now."

"That's not what I meant, Rosalind. I've a priest, Father Simon, waiting on the near side of the hill to marry us. You'll have to assure him this is your wish, as well as mine."

She rolled her eyes at me, and then nodded as I helped her up. I fetched her shoes from the top of a sun-drenched rock and helped her put them on. As we walked slowly up the hill, me supporting her weight as much as I could, she stepped carefully over every twig and stone.

"Will you ever tell me," she asked, "who she was?"

"You never knew her."

"Would I, perhaps, have known *of* her?"

"Perhaps. I don't know." I plucked a bloom from a tall, spindly flower stalk and handed it to her. Even though I had intended to tell her Marjorie's name, I couldn't. That was all in the past and didn't seem pertinent right now. "Ah, there's Father Simon—looking rather dubious, isn't he? Are you glad this is to be your wedding day?"

"Happy as any blushing bride." She stopped, kissed me on the cheek, and brushed the bits of weeds and grass from my shirt and hair. "All those years ago, in Lancashire, when you asked for my hand . . . I'm so sorry. I should have either said 'yes' right there or left then. But I couldn't do either. I was still hurting, even though I never said so.

I needed time—to heal. Yet in that process, your patience has only made me love you more. If I have hesitated, held back . . . it's only because I know that to love . . . is to risk losing that love."

"But Rosalind, we have loved each other longer than either of us ever admitted, aye? Why not, then, love completely? I love you, and you me. Simple? Must we complicate it further?"

She shook her head and embraced me. We went to where Father Simon waited. I placed a garland of daisies upon her head, plucked fresh from the field.

Before Father Simon and God, we stood side by side, holding hands, as nervous as if we were sixteen-year olds.

"It's a wee bit urgent, Father Simon. Can you make quick of it?"

He glanced at Rosalind's round stomach, one thin eyebrow arching in judgment. "Ah, I see. I didn't realize . . . No matter. We'll save confessions for later, my children."

"I'll double my tithe to your parish this harvest. Now please . . ."

"I have not seen you at Mass for . . . years perhaps?"

"Very well. I'll attend this Sunday if it will make you hurry."

"It would seem to me that you had a great deal of time before today to arrange this ceremony, had you wanted. And if you wish a christening for the child, I had best see you at the kirk for more than one Mass. I believe this favor should keep you coming until Christmas. Now let's begin then. Have you a ring, Sir James?"

ROSALIND GAVE BIRTH TO a boy just before midnight. He entered the world wailing lustily. The strength of his cries reminded me of my youngest brother and so we named him Archibald. It seemed fitting.

I had a son and a wife. A new purpose. Something besides serving my liege. But while my joy was never greater, all was not well for my good King Robert.

27

Robert the Bruce – Cardross, 1329

"Edward of Caernarvon was not much loved." Tenderly, Aithne dabbed at my face with a soft cloth, blotting away the cold beads of sweat. She sat me up in my bed and helped me change my shirt. "Unlike you."

"That would depend on who you ask," I jested, but the words stole my breath and I sank back.

She readjusted my pillows, piled five high, then picked up a silver comb. Strand by strand, she combed my hair. At first I had found her attentions humiliating, insisting on taking care of myself, but the efforts were always so draining, my pain so intense, that I could not accomplish them on my own. Humility is a heavy stone to swallow.

When Elizabeth died, Aithne came to me. I would have thought she would leave soon afterward, given the feeble and often cantankerous state I was in, but she never went back to Carrick. She stayed. She knew I needed her. Once I had thought us nothing more than lovers. How wrong I had been—about more things than I cared to ever admit.

In the spring, I had made what was for me an arduous pilgrimage to St. Ninian's shrine in Galloway. Aithne accompanied me. Progress was dreadfully slow, but the journey through the land of my boyhood brought back dear memories of riding with my grandfather there. At St. Ninian's I offered my peace with God and what a litany of crimes I confessed to. I had not gone to the trouble, until then, to reflect on them. My voice must have been heard above. England consented to the Treaty of Norham, agreeing to our terms of peace. Then . . . word from the Holy See: my excommunication had at last been removed.

For all that has ever been taken from me, much more has been given unto me.

"And the new King Edward?" I asked her. "How goes it for him?"

Her weight on the edge of the bed was light. She stroked the inside of my arm, her fingers never pausing at the little bumps there. "He's a boy. In above his head. Been across the border already and chased back by our good Sir James."

"Ah, James . . . is he here yet? I've been waiting."

"Not last I looked, but I'll send him in as soon as he arrives from Lintalee. For now, rest, dear Robert. I've kept you awake far too long."

"You used to keep me awake all night and I never tired of you then."

"That was a long time ago." She leaned over and gave me a kiss, then went.

King Edward II: dead. A wasted life. They had moved him from Llantrissant to Kenilworth and finally to Berkley. Within the course of a year he was dead. 'Natural causes', they said. 'Doubtful', said I. He had many enemies—all very close to him. His queen had abandoned him for an underhanded lover, run him from London, forced his hand and put her son on the throne. A convenience that Edward of Caernarvon could no longer throw a shadow of suspicion on his short-grieved widow, but the man was dead.

No man lives forever. Not even a king.

Bishop Lamberton of St. Andrews, too, gave up the ghost in 1328. What an enormous debt I owed to men like him, now gone—those who embraced my dream as their own: the bishops Lamberton and Wishart, one wise, one comforting; my brother-in-law Christopher Seton who was taken at Methven; my squire Gerald, who fled from certain death with me from Longshanks' court at Windsor and then later gave his life for me; Torquil who knew the waters about the Isles better than any man . . . and those I loved and caused to suffer: most of all Elizabeth, my beloved wife; sweet, beautiful Marjorie who never held her own child; and my brothers Nigel, Thomas, Alexander, Edward . . . all dead now. All dead.

A man lives his whole life fearing death. But if he has lived a good life, a full life, and if he has done the work he was set upon the earth to do, then death is a part of that life. And it is welcome. It is peace. The life hereafter: God's reward.

I glanced about the room, grayed by the half-shadows of a long evening. Familiar objects around me dimmed, blurred and began to fade from my weakening sight.

Beyond my chamber, my wardrobe contained leather shoes from Portugal and shirts of the finest cloth from Rheims. During the course of Scotland's growing trade these last few years, I had amassed a wealth of worldly objects. Such things had pleased me once, pleased Elizabeth even more. But now all those things were merely trinkets: belongings that meant nothing to me now.

I was almost eager to let go. To lay my head down one last time, close my eyes and greet Our Savior. I wanted to. I was tired . . . and I could feel the pull. Strong, heavy. Like the weight of my own body, coaxing me downward as I swung from a thread by a single finger. And beneath, the fall would be soft, comforting, warm and cool, bright and dark all at once. Only . . . I did not want to leave them. Aithne. James. Thomas. The children. Would that I could take them with me. But it was not their time. Not yet.

It was mine. Time to join Marjorie. Little John. Alexander. Nigel. Thomas. My squire Gerald. My brother Edward, even. And . . . my dear Elizabeth.

I drifted off to sleep, my life flowing past me in memories both sharp and blurred. Memories of times good and bad, often hard and seldom easy. Times of much love and great loss. Of suffering and dreams realized. Memories of a life lived fully.

WHEN I AWOKE THE next morning, it was to the vision of Aithne, older and yet still breathtakingly beautiful. She held out a cup of water. "James and Randolph are here."

As I drank from the cup, trying hard not to let it slip from my feeble grasp or the water dribble down my chin, Aithne left the room. Yielding to weariness, I let my eyelids close, the cup still resting on my chest.

I was vaguely aware of the rumble of my own snoring. The low muffle of voices. The brush of footfalls. Someone's hand on my shoulder—slight at first, then grasping more strongly as it shook me into arousal.

"I got the message from Thomas." James took the cup from me and placed it on the table beside my bed. "I came right away. How *are* you, Robert?"

"I've had better days." I held out my hand and he squeezed it gently before letting go, as if afraid he might break my fingers. Randolph stood just behind him, ever watchful, always with that proud, nearly arrogant bearing of his. "Enough of me. How are David and Joanna getting along?"

Randolph moved to the foot of the bed. "Mostly they play with their own friends. The princess came with her own entourage of playmates. She very much misses her home. I think David in particular is a bit young to grasp the arrangement. He sometimes talks of his new 'sister' Joanna."

"So very young, they are. You'll help David understand, Thomas, how important this marriage is? He must treat her with kindness, see that she is happy, aye?"

"I'll try."

"And you'll succeed. By God, you always did." How faint my voice was, even in my own ears. I rested several breaths, my heart glad to see them and yet sad that I might not again. "How far we've come. Do you remember, James, my good man . . . Thomas"—I tried to grin, but the effort sapped me—"remember running free in the hills, plucking berries from the brambles, drinking from the rivers . . . sleeping beneath the stars, game so fresh it squirmed on your knife?"

"I remember being cold and wet and starving near to death," Randolph said. "The toil of battle. The thrill of victory. The peace in between."

"I remember standing frozen to a tree trunk," James reflected, inspecting his hands as if he held a weapon there and was pondering its power, "my heart banging in my ears, my breath held, while an English soldier scoured the thicket a few feet away in the darkness. The game of waiting, moving without making a sound, judging fear in a man's eyes. I remember being able to guess the number of dead by the strength of the smell of blood. The pain of metal biting into my flesh. Hunting for good arrows in a pile of corpses. Reuniting with a friend after battle, only to learn of those who had not lived. I remember it all."

"How is it," I asked, "that we all remember so differently? Were we not in the same places together at the same time?"

James' voice bore the strain of burgeoning grief. "This is not how it is supposed to be, Robert. Not like this."

"How should it be? Should we have died fighting at Methven, Dalry, Bannockburn, Byland Moor? That would have been too soon. We are older now. Our work is done. What better way to die than with my friends beside me?"

"You're not going to die."

"We all die, eventually. Only our deeds live on."

"We'll go to the Holy Land: Randolph, you and me. We are going to fight the Infidels."

"Aye, that was my dream once, too." I closed my eyes and lay there so long and with breath so shallow I could sense them pressing closer to see if I was still breathing. "I . . . I don't want to die in battle anymore. Or in some other land. Here is where I will rest. My home. My land. *Scotland.* This is where they shall inter my bones. This is where I choose to die."

James' eyes were pressed tightly shut, his head tilted back, his mouth open. Weeping, he sank to his knees as he held my hand. So stoic to the world, yet underneath was a soul as deep as the Forth itself.

"You have many years ahead. A son to watch grow. More to come, maybe?" There I paused. "You'll both look after my David and young Robbie, won't you? Thomas—how to conduct one's self in the company of popes and kings and how to compose a proper letter. You are good at those things. James, teach them to pull a bowstring well, wield a sword and ride a horse lightly. It is time you gave such pursuits up to those younger than you and settled down—stayed in one place awhile. Time for gentler things. Will you?"

Still kneeling at my bedside, he bunched a handful of my blankets in his fists and nodded.

"Thomas, will you leave us?"

With true dignity and never a flicker of jealousy, Randolph bowed and departed. I could not turn my head to see, but I heard the curious onlookers dangling at the doorway as they moved aside to let Randolph pass. The door closed and it was just James and me. I put out my other hand for him to hold. Whether his grip was heavy or light, cool or warm, I could not tell.

"At first, I regarded you like a father does his son, did you know? There you were, alone on the road, seemingly ignorant of highwaymen, oblivious that English soldiers might run you down. So eager to throw your lot in with a rebel. You needed guidance and I, in my arrogance, thought to give it to you. But then you became my teacher. A knight among knights." I paused, not for thought, but to let pain pass. It stayed and so I swallowed, fought for breath. "Has any king . . . any man ever known such loyalty? Such . . . friendship?"

His fingers tightened even more around mine, willing me to stay.

"Yet, I denied you what mattered most, even when I knew . . ."

Again, the pain. Rolling like thunder. White as lightning.

"—that you loved each other. How could I have done that to you?"

He lifted his head. "Done? What, Robert? I don't—"

"No more pretending. I knew, all along, and closed my eyes to it, just as you both tried to hide it. You loved Marjorie, dearly, deeply. And yet, I think, you would not ask to have her because, could it be, that you loved me more? Fool that I am, I forced you to choose. I also thought I knew my daughter. I doubted what she felt was the same as it was for you. Whether right or wrong, I should never have questioned either of you."

The tears were drying on his cheeks. This unspoken truth that had wrecked the past decade between us was out. What could not be said then had now tumbled from my clumsy tongue as easily as a lullaby. How I had wronged him. In no way could I put it right, except to say I regretted it.

"But you have Lady Rosalind now and a son of your own. I do hope you have found your happiness, James. I am never quite sure I had it myself."

He drew breath, preparing to speak. But speeches were hard for James. Words were never his weapons or tools, only actions.

"What, James? We've nothing anymore to keep from one another, have we?"

His grip loosened. His chin sank to his chest, so that the words, when they came, were a muffled whisper. "It is I who has wronged you."

"Well, then," I reassured, "if you have done me any wrong, don't speak it. I will forgive you, if you do but one deed. Aye, James? When I die, carry my heart to Jerusalem. Will you? Pay me that honor. I had

Thomas ask the men whom they would choose. You, they said. It is all I ask. The one thing that I pray will get me into Heaven, *if* there's a place for me there. But I shall not worry on it. I've done as well as I could and if that's not good enough . . . well then, I've no time left to put it right. So I'm depending on you—for this. When you come back, look after the lads. Be here for Randolph. I have such boundless faith in the two of you. How would I ever have done so much without you both beside me?"

He nodded. "I would do anything for you, Robert."

"I have never doubted that. Ever." I tried to lift my arm, to point, but I could barely summon the strength for even that. I was cold in my core, numb in the extremities. "There, James. Do you see it against the wall? I had it made for you."

His steps dragging, he retrieved the shield from where it was propped in a corner. He studied it a moment before picking it up and testing its weight by slipping his forearm inside the straps. At the top were three stars on a band of blue and below them a field of white.

"The stars—those are for you, me and Randolph. Just don't ask me which is which. I couldn't decide what to put in the middle, though. Thought I'd leave that up to you."

"Thank you, I . . ."

But if he said anything more, I did not hear it. A tide of pain swept over me again—every joint wrenched with it. A hand, strong as iron, gripped my heart, challenging it to go on beating. I fought, for I was not yet ready to go.

James put the shield down so abruptly it thudded against the wall. In three strides, he was back at my side.

"Call them back," I said.

Through tears, James found his way to the door and opened it wide. They came in then: Gilbert de la Haye, who had been with me from the very start; Robert Keith, so brave at Bannockburn; Cuthbert, the stuttering spy; Neil Campbell, husband to my sister Mary; William

Bunnock, who took Stirling by a simple ruse; Robert Boyd, whose blood ran with ale until a young wife sobered him up and fattened him; and more, their faces blending together as the pain behind my eyes pulsed wickedly. Behind them all, Aithne shepherded the children in. Our son Niall was there, grown strong as an ox and more handsome than myself, I admit. Robbie held his chin high, but David, Margaret and Mathilda all trembled with tears as they held hands.

"James shall carry my heart to the Holy Land." My voice was so weak that I wondered if any of them heard. "I thank you, my friends . . . your courage . . . loyalty. Thank you, all."

Friends they were, above all. Not servants. Not soldiers. Not subjects. But friends that I loved and to whom I owed everything. I had been blessed to know them. Honored that I was struck with a dream I could not part from. A simple dream.

Freedom.

All men are born free. We Scots have merely fought for what God intended us to have.

I have done all that I can do. All I was meant to do. In that, I am at last content.

28

<u>James Douglas – Lintalee, 1330</u>

F OR TWO DAYS MORE, Robert clung to life, half-sleeping peacefully, half-awake in terrible misery. I slept beside him in a hard-backed chair, rousing at every moan or rustle, determined to be there with him to the very last.

Aithne of Carrick saw to his needs with a tender hand, but never a tearful eye. In her strength, she reminded me much of Rosalind. Whenever I left the room to relieve myself or partake of a meal in the hall, I would return to find her sitting on the edge of his bed, delicately cleansing the perspiration from his brow with a cool cloth and speaking as if she were carrying on a casual conversation with him. But Robert spoke very little in those waning days. He never cried out in pain, even though we could all see every wave of it crashing through his enfeebled body.

For two years, I had known Robert was ill—that he would in time die. But no matter how long the knowledge had preceded the fact, I was not ready for it. Every moment that I remained beside him those last days, I could but wish for one more year, a month, a day even. I listened to his breath fading, watched his eyes go grayer, saw him growing weaker, paler. Yet with all my will and all my love, I could not bring him back from that brink of nothingness.

The saddest of all the days in all the ages for Scotland came at last: the 7th of June in the year 1329. Robert the Bruce, King of Scotland, Champion of Freedom and Independence, died. His body was laid beside Queen Elizabeth's in Dumfermline Abbey. His heart was embalmed and placed in a casket of silver and given unto my care. I traveled many miles in a dazed, empty fog with the weight of that casket slung about my neck, as heavy as ten stones, before I arrived home.

Around me, it was summer, yet I felt nothing but winter, cold and dark, in my heart.

IN THE MONTHS FOLLOWING, my duties as co-regent for David took me frequently to Edinburgh and elsewhere, but I returned to Lintalee as quickly and as often as I could.

During those brief times we had together, I said nothing to Rosalind about my final promise to Robert. I lived foremost as husband and father. My son, Archibald, I carried on my shoulders and spoke to him of things he could not even begin to understand. I did not know how to speak to him as a child should be spoken to and for that Rosalind often chided me.

"James, he is an infant—not a forty-year old soldier! If you want to put him to sleep, though, you're quite effective. Now bounce him on your knee or sing him a song. *That* is what he likes."

I could only laugh at her. Little Archibald, it seemed, found me quite amusing no matter what I said to him, fingering my lips as I chatted to him in a hushed tone, or gazing into my eyes and breaking out in a spontaneous smile whenever I posed a question to him. I showed him my horses and explained to him how to shoot a bow and arrow and wield a sword. The bright flash of metal intrigued him. The arrows were not so interesting. The horses he was afraid of. A bittersweet time it was, both happy and sad. But I was there, his chubby hands clenching the ends of my fingers, when he let go and took his first step, wobbling like a drunken sailor. I was there when he said his first word: "Da-da." *Father.*

Every night, I held Rosalind against me as we lay in our bed. She understood, I think, the grief and hollowness I felt over Robert's loss. Her presence was a comfort. But her nearness was a source of pain, as well, for I knew I would have to leave her once more for too long a time, and so I said nothing, until my last visit to Edinburgh and there the subject came up among several young knights, eager to serve their lost king's cause. Many of them had been too young to take part at Bannockburn and so they craved a part in Robert's legacy. As fast as it was said, arrangements for passage were made. A date was set. Letters were received and others dispatched.

I had to tell her. I *had* to. If I did not, soon enough she would learn it from someone else: that Sir James Douglas was scheduled to sail for the Holy Land on a mission honoring his deceased king. And in her head, she would hear that I was leaving her alone with a son not yet weaned off her breast.

She had just finished nursing the bairn when I entered our room. Archibald, his stomach full, was fast asleep, but smiling still. Rosalind laid him in his cradle, halfway between our bed and the hearth. I tended to the fire, then knelt by Archibald's cradle and gazed at him long.

"Your brother came to see his namesake while you were gone," she said, parting the covers and sliding into bed. "He and Beatrice just had their fourth child. It was a girl or else he said he would have named the child 'James'." She drew the pins from her long black hair so that it tumbled about her shoulders like a cascade of midnight. Then she curled her finger at me. "Come, James. We've much catching up to do."

I stripped down to my tunic and braes and joined her. She rolled onto her side and tugged lightly at the sleeve of my shirt. "Do you need this?"

"It's October, Rosalind." I stared into the dancing yellow of the fire. "I'm cold."

Her hand wandered down my ribcage, traced the curve of my still slim waist, and stopped at the point of my hip. "I know that faraway look. I don't like to see you so sad, but, James . . . you must stop grieving like this. Please. He's gone."

"I know that." I glanced at her, wanting to make love to her before I broke the news, but just then Archibald fussed.

Rosalind rose up on her elbows, looked her child's way and, content that he was fine, settled back down beside me snugly, her hand upon my chest. "Then what has you in such a state of melancholy? Are you weary? Ill? Can I do anything for you?"

I laid my hand over hers. "Know that I love you."

At that she sat up, staring at me hard.

I told her, "I have been given the honor of carrying King Robert's heart to Jerusalem."

"What? *When?*"

"After Christmas. As soon as the weather allows."

"This is decided then?"

I nodded. "It is. I was chosen by those closest to the king."

"I see." She threw back the covers and snatched a shawl from the bedpost. "Then you would choose a dead man over your wife? Would you?"

"It is not a matter of choosing you or him, Rosalind. He was more than king to me. He was my friend. This is the one last thing I can do in remembrance of him."

Never had I seen such fury in her. The veins in her neck stood out tautly. Her jaws were clamped together. Her indrawn breath hissed between her teeth. "Would you?!"

Even though I had rehearsed this a thousand times in my mind while traveling home, still, it tore at me to have her question where my heart lay. I got up from the bed and marched around to face her. I tried to restrain myself, to understand her disappointment, to not give in to anger myself, clenching my fists next to my thighs.

"*Would you?*" she repeated.

I exploded. "You don't ask a man that, Rosalind! You don't!"

"Don't ask a man what? To stay home with his wife and his . . . his . . ."

Roused by our heated argument, Archibald began to sputter.

"What? His child?" I kept my feet planted firmly where they were, struggling for control, searching for reasons that would make her understand and yield to my purpose. "Archibald is barely old enough to discern one face from another, let alone be aware of whenever I have left here. The sooner I go, the sooner I can return. I'll be back long before he can carry on a conversation."

She wrapped her arms about her middle and turned her back to me. "Then you'll not stay for the birth of your next child?"

My breath was the sail in the full gale of anger that had suddenly gone windless. My stomach flipped. "Next? Is this true?"

"Do you think it's but a clever ploy to keep you at home? Yes, it's true, James."

"Let me ask then—*when?*"

Slowly, she turned sideways, smoothing her gown against her belly. "You did not notice I was growing plumper? Then you, my good Sir James, are either foolishly blind with love or just plain oblivious. Less than five months from now we will have another. But you'll be gone, again. This time fighting men who have something greater to defend than their possessions: their faith. Do you truly believe you'll be able to fight those foreigners, heathens you would call them, with the same tactics? Ah, James, I fear it will not be the same as you have known. If there was anything I could say or do to keep you here forever, God knows I would. But I also *know* you. And I know what this means to you. I would rather you were not chosen, but I also know there could not have been any other worthy in Robert's eyes to do this. As true as that is, I still hate it. I don't want to bear a child that will be fatherless before he is born."

I gave her my hand and pulled her gently to me. "I'll send word that the expedition is to be delayed." Then I picked her up in my arms and laid her down in bed again. Stretching out beside her, I ran my hand over the slight bulge in her belly. "I'll stay awhile, Rosalind. Long enough to see our child born. And the day I'm done I'll come swiftly home. I'll never leave you again, then. Never."

Tearful, she smiled. "You're a bloody liar, James Douglas . . . and deaf. Did I not just say I *know* you?"

Aye, you do, Rosalind. Better than I know myself.

THE LAST SCREAM SHE let out was loud enough to lift the roof off the rafters. I heard it from outside the house, standing there in my wet boots in a puddle of melted snow and looking up at the window of our room.

For a very long time I stared at the window, but no one opened it to beckon me up. I looked at the door to the hall and it too stood motionless and silent. I walked in a circle, toward the byre, then back toward the house where I stopped and gazed up at the night sky. The light of a full moon shone argent upon still bare branches.

Damp and chilled, I finally went back into the house and as I made for my favorite chair closest to the hearth in the main hall, a voice from the stairs called softly to me.

"My lord?" said the white-haired midwife, Edna. "You may come up now."

"How is she?"

"Tired, but she and the bairn will be fine."

When I reached the room, warmed by a roaring fire, I saw the new arrival in the arms of a young woman, whose name I knew not, only that she was the midwife's daughter and had an older babe of her own and often served as wet nurse locally when an infant's mother died or could not produce enough milk. She rocked the swaddled babe in her arms and smiled at me as he turned his tiny, seeking mouth toward her ample breast.

"A boy," she said, sure that I was proud of the fact.

"He is well?"

"Aye, and strong."

I knelt beside Rosalind. Her hair lay in matted clumps upon her pillow, with rebellious strands stuck here and there to her forehead and flushed cheeks. Gently, I swept them away with a fingertip and kissed her on the head. Her eyelids fluttered open long enough to see me. Then she closed her eyes to save her strength.

"William," she whispered.

"Aye, we'll call him William—after your first husband and my father both. 'Tis a fine name." I held her hand and squeezed it softly, but she did not squeeze back. She was finding it hard not to drift off. I cast a glance at the midwife. "The birth—it was more difficult than it was for Archibald?"

Edna nodded. "He wanted to come out the wrong way. Sideways, I think. Or upside down. Wrong anyways. I had to turn him. It was not easy."

I stayed beside Rosalind for many minutes, arranging the covers around her, wiping the sweat from her brow, but she was fast asleep and unaware of even her newborn's cries. The young woman settled down on a stool close to the fire and began nursing the bairn. He was greedy and not at all aware that the woman caring for him was not his own mother.

I asked Edna, "Will she be all right?"

"In time. But it will take a while. Likely she'll sleep hard for the next few days. In a week, we will know better how she is doing."

Despite the midwife's encouraging words, I was not so easily heartened. I delayed my departure from Leith two more weeks as I remained at Rosalind's side. Slowly, she regained strength and began to nurse little William on her own. Even when I was in the room with both of them, she kept her attention on the child. We did not speak of my mission—only William and her health. Over and over she assured me that she was well.

"Must you hover over me like that, James?" she protested from her bed, surrounded by mountains of pillows. In the crook of her arm, little William slumbered, his small pink thumb shoved into his mouth. Rosalind took the corner of a blanket and wiped the spittle from his chin. "We'll be fine, really. Now off with you."

I stood above them, running my fingers along the hem of my cloak. The first bold light of spring spilled in from the window, promising a fair day for riding. Outside, the birds sang in a chorus of joy, heralding the season.

I took her hand, kissed it and then brushed the top of William's fuzzy head with my fingertips. "Going away has never been so hard. I don't want to . . . but I . . . I . . ."

"Yes, James, I know you have to do this. But you're not making it any easier by standing there longer, you know." She bit her lip and gazed out the window through bleary eyes.

I would tell her of Robbie when I returned, ask that he come live with us. Until then, I could not tell her about him. Certainly not now. But perhaps I could broach the subject gently?

"I was thinking," I began, a knot constricting my throat and making it hard to speak, "that when I return, I will have to go to Edinburgh a lot, or wherever the young king might be holding court, at least until he grows up a bit. I have considered resigning as co-regent, but I promised Robert I would look after him. And Robbie . . . it is time he learned to be a soldier. I could teach him how to fight with a sword, how to—"

"Of course."

"He could stay here, at times. That would make it easier."

"Of course."

"Well, then . . ." I shook my cloak for no good reason, slung it over my shoulders and fastened it with the silver clasp Rosalind had given me that Christmas. It would be warm enough by noon to do without it though and there was not a cloud in the sky. "There's a ship awaiting me in Leith. I've half a dozen men outside ready to go."

Finally, she looked at me. "God be with you, James Douglas."

I bent to her and kissed her full on the lips. "Know that I love you . . . and that I did from the very first day I saw you."

"You're a terrible liar. We hated each other then. Go, now. *Go*."

In all the years I had ridden off to battle or on state business for the king, I had never taken a step with hesitation or regret. Not until that day. I cannot even count the number of times I stopped on the road, looked back toward Lintalee and nearly told them all to go on without me.

When I saw the great black rock of Edinburgh rise gradually on the road before us, the young Sir William Sinclair eased his horse abreast of mine. "Shall I send word on to the Earl of Moray that we will be calling upon him before we set sail?"

The smell of the sea drifted faintly on the wind. My stomach lurched. "No, no, we'll go straight on to the ship. Send word to Randolph to meet us there."

Somewhere in the distance, from years ago, I heard Robert's voice again:

"This life we've chosen, aye? Is it all truly peril and sacrifice, though? No, we've something to show for it. Something they all doubted possible when you were but a wet-eared squire startled by the sound of your own voice and I a free and easy blade with a flaming temper. We're hard in the head and mayhap it's that they said we couldn't, that we had to prove we could."

Aye, Robert. We proved ourselves well.

EPILOGUE

James Douglas – Spain, 1330

I BLINK AT THE sweat that stings my eyes. Scotland is many months and miles behind me now. Indeed it is a world away from this dusty realm. Even in the shade of the poplars, the air is on fire. I can barely breathe. Sinclair edges his mount closer and hands me a cloth. I mop my forehead dry. The horses, too, hang their heads, beaten down by the rising heat of afternoon.

From horseback, King Alfonso surveys the plain below, where fields of parched grain stand brittle and golden beneath an azure sky. Further off, along another line of hills, a stark sun-bleached fortress overlooks the same plain. In his lap rests his crowned helmet. He leans on it as he gazes intensely into the distance, waiting for the enemy to emerge.

We are arrayed at the foothills of the sierra: a collection of Scots, English, Flemish and other knights from across the continent, including a number of the mysterious Templars. After a brief respite in Seville, word came that the Moors were preparing to march on the city. Very quickly, Alfonso had organized his troops and was leading his army out from Seville to arrest their threat here at the Castle of the Star near Teba before they could advance.

The king shifts in his saddle and shades his brow with his hand. His eyes are keen for his age. I know not his number of years, but he must be close to the same age Robert would have been. Across the way, from between two jutting sand-white mountains toward the plain, rides an army of Moors.

"He comes to take Seville," King Alfonso says, referring to his adversary, King Osmyn of Granada, as he strokes his silvering black beard with a gloved hand, "but we will stop him here, yes?"

I nod.

"I give you the vanguard, Sir James: your Scots, the English, and Flemish knights. Ride along the hills, there. Take their left wing—from behind if you can."

"And you, sire?" I ask him. Whatever the tactics of Moors, I know only that they do not follow the same rules as English armies.

"We take the rest." He smiles broadly, eager to get on with the battle. He lifts his helmet up so that it reflects the sun and places it over his mail coif. Then with a noble tilt of his head, he orders me on.

I touch the breast of my blue and white surcoat, beneath which lies the casket containing Robert's heart.

I give Sinclair the order to ready the knights, expecting protests from the English among them. But when I don my own helmet and turn to look back at them, every man is fully prepared for the charge, their eyes set resolutely on the stampeding foes swallowing up the distant plain below. Argent lance tips glint in the sunlight. Horses snort and stomp their feet. Fingers grip sword hilts and reins.

My squire hands me my shield—the one Robert gave me before he died. Its surface is without dent or scratch, the colors yet vibrant. This will be its first battle and, I pray, not its last. I wedge my arm inside the straps, raise my other hand and lead the charge.

We cut across the slope of the hill. As we come nearer, a group of Moors separates from the main body to meet us. I urge the men to continue along the slope and then, when we are to the rear of the main force, which King Alfonso himself is close to engaging, I jab my lance to the left and we veer sharply toward our attackers. We bear down on them hard, riding in a tight line. Before we reach the foot of the hill, their leader pulls up, gives a cry of retreat and begins to speed back toward the gap through which they had come.

I can hear the first crash as King Alfonso's column meets the front-line of the Moors. I am too intent on my quarry to check back. Sinclair is beside me, riding fast, fearless.

We are far out ahead of the rest of my division now. The Moors are slowing, turning back at us. This is not right. I cast a glance at Sinclair.

"Hold, hold!" I say.

Baffled, Sinclair shakes his head at me. Then he sees them. There are more, riding out from the gap. Others, spilling out from behind an outcropping. Cutting us off.

I look back. My vanguard is still riding furiously, hoping to save us.

But it is too late. We are being encircled.

I make the sign of the cross. Then I lift the casket from my neck and throw it on the dusty ground before me. Sinclair and I drop our lances as they begin to come at us from all sides. We draw our swords.

"In the name of God and King Robert!" I cry.

As I raise my sword and ready for the first blow, I am thinking of Rosalind. Of the boys. Of Robbie. And how I must survive this one more battle, one more day . . .

When I am home again, I will hold them in my arms. And I will not let go. When I am home . . . in Lintalee. Where the pines sway and whisper in the summer breeze and the deer roam unafraid. Where Rosalind waits for me and my sons thrive and grow.

Home . . . home. Where I long to be.

Afterword

While trying to save the young knight Sinclair, as they were surrounded by the Moors of Granada, James Douglas was killed at the Battle of Teba. The Scottish and Spanish forces did, however, win the battle that day.

Douglas' body and the heart of Robert the Bruce were recovered and returned to Scotland. James Douglas was buried at St. Bride's Church in Douglasdale. He had two sons, Archibald and William. The name of 'Douglas' has since appeared time and again throughout Scottish history.

Multiple times during the English occupation, James Douglas captured and razed Douglas Castle. It became a known curse to accept the governorship of that fortress, but a few Englishmen did so out of either denial or daring and paid with their lives at the hands of James Douglas. Douglas was known both as James 'the Good' Douglas and also the Black Douglas. The former was most likely assigned to him by his Scottish admirers, for he was reputed to be a soft-spoken, well-mannered and devoted adherent to King Robert. The latter designation was given to him for both his dark looks and his furtive and merciless actions toward his foes.

One of the many folklores surrounding this period in time is that of James Douglas happening upon a young mother singing the frightful lullaby of the 'Black Douglas' to her crying infant during a Scottish attack on an English-held castle. It was for convenience that I introduced the character of Lady Rosalind de Fiennes in connection with this tale. It is recorded that James Douglas did have at least two illegitimate sons who later inherited the Douglas estates. Who their mother is, is not known.

Both Robert and Edward Bruce had numerous affairs and illegitimate children. A woman named Christian of Carrick was undoubtedly an early part of Robert's life and did inform him of the capture of his wife and daughter. In this trilogy, she is named Aithne of Carrick to avoid confusion, as there were also Robert's sister Christina and the lady Christiana of the Isles, another of Robert's love interests.

Whether loathed or pitied, Edward of Caernarvon is worthy of his own story. Few historians are gracious enough to lend him credit of any sort. His lack of successes on the battlefield were in marked contrast to his ruthless father, Longshanks, known for his subjugation of Wales and Scotland, and the militant son that followed him, Edward III. The depth of Edward II's affection for two particular men, Piers de Gaveston and Hugh Despenser, was perhaps his fatal flaw. So devoted he was to these two, that he was ignorant to their ambitions and greed. Deprived of his mother at a young age, publicly belittled by his father, and undermined by his cousin, the Earl of Lancaster, Edward II's circumstances were further exacerbated by the betrayal of his consort, Queen Isabella. Her openly flaunted affair with Sir Roger Mortimer and subsequent rebellion would have been spectacular fodder for our contemporary tabloids. As much a victim of the intentions of those surrounding him as he was a cause for his own misery, Edward II's life was indeed a tragedy, punctuated by his defeat at Bannockburn and further born out in the clandestine manner of his death.

The Scottish people were then and still are fiercely proud and, as evidenced by his fellow compatriots, Robert the Bruce was not wholly unique in either his courage or his tenacity. He certainly could not have accomplished what he did in his lifetime if it were not for the likes of James Douglas, Thomas Randolph, Gilbert de la Haye, Robert Boyd, Robert Keith, Angus Og, Neil Campbell and the thousands of brave men who fought at Bannockburn and elsewhere. And yet most undoubtedly, Scotland could not have rested on the laurels of victory if it had not had Robert the Bruce to lead the way. He understood that to strengthen Scotland, he first had to do so from within. Separation from England, international recognition and acceptance by the Church were all needed to complete his complex plan.

The casket containing King Robert's heart was buried at Melrose Abbey and over the years its whereabouts were forgotten. In 1921, it was discovered during an archeological excavation and then later in 1998 was reburied in a private ceremony beneath the floor of the Charter House at Melrose. Many historians proclaim that Robert the Bruce died of leprosy; others say it was scurvy. But whatever afflicted him in those final years and caused his death matters not.

What matters is how he lived and what he lived to fight for:

Freedom.

<u>Author's Note</u>

Many thanks are owed to the scholars of history who have investigated the past with painstaking detail. While researching the Scottish War for Independence, Robert the Bruce, James Douglas and King Edward II of England, I found the following works of non-fiction to be invaluable:

Brown, Chris. *Robert the Bruce, A Life Chronicled.* Stroud, Gloucestershire, U.K.: Tempus Publishing Limited, 2004.

Duffey, Sean. *Robert the Bruce's Irish Wars: The Invasions of Ireland 1306-1329.* Stroud, Gloucestershire, U.K.: Tempus Publishing Limited, 2002.

Fawcett, Richard and Oram, Richard. *Melrose Abbey.* Stroud, Gloucestershire, U.K.: Tempus Publishing Limited, 2004.

Haines, Roy Martin. *King Edward II: His Life, His Reign and Its Aftermath, 1284-1330.* Montreal: McGill-Queen's University Press, 2003.

Ross, David R. *James the Good: The Black Douglas.* Edinburgh: Luath Press Ltd., 2008.

Scott, Ronald McNair. *Robert the Bruce: King of Scots.* Edinburgh: Canongate Books Ltd., 1996.

Acknowledgments

In this final stretch of what has been a decade-long journey, two people were instrumental in giving my vision even more polish and clarity: Sarah Woodbury, who reminded me to keep the big picture in mind, so that I didn't get lost simply stringing words together, and Rebecca Lochlann, who so often understood what I actually *meant* to say and is responsible for helping me make sense out of the details.

Above all, I owe an eternal debt to the noble and kind-hearted Jacques de Spoelberch, who once snatched a shy novice writer (who didn't know the difference between 'Foreword' and 'Forward') from the obscurity of the slush pile and instilled her with just enough confidence for her to believe that maybe, just maybe, she *really was* a storyteller, after all.

I count you as one of the angels in my life, Jacques.

And to all the readers who have written to me and patiently waited for this final installment in the trilogy, I am more grateful than I can ever express. Your letters not only break up an otherwise tedious and reclusive day of writing, but more importantly they also make all the years of hard work worthwhile.

About the Author

N. Gemini Sasson holds a M.S. in Biology from Wright State University where she ran cross country on athletic scholarship. She has worked as an aquatic toxicologist, an environmental engineer, a teacher and a cross country coach. A longtime breeder of Australian Shepherds, her articles on bobtail genetics have been translated into seven languages. She lives in rural Ohio with her husband, two nearly grown children and an ever-changing number of sheep and dogs.

www.ngeminisasson.com

www.facebook.com/ngeminisasson

Made in the USA
San Bernardino, CA
28 February 2017